PRIVATE WOODS

PRIVATE WOODS

A N O V E L

Sandra Crockett Moore

HARCOURT BRACE JOVANOVICH, Publishers

San Diego New York London

Library of Congress Cataloging-in-Publication Data
Moore, Sandra Crockett.
Private woods.
I. Title.
PS3563.065P75 1988 813′.54 87-25115
ISBN 0-15-174710-5

Printed in the United States of America
First edition
A B C D E

To Larry, Susan, and Summer

PRIVATE WOODS IS DEDICATED

TO EVERY MAN AND WOMAN

WHOSE LIFE WAS TOUCHED BY

THE VIETNAM WAR:

TO THOSE WHO WENT AND

NEVER CAME BACK;

TO THOSE WHO CAME BACK

FOREVER CHANGED;

AND TO ALL OF US AT HOME

WHO WAITED.

PRIVATE WOODS

1

"You've got to get close enough without him smelling you—and he's got a sense of smell that is out of this world. And he's got eyesight that's good, and he can hear, hell, a deer can hear lots better than you or I can. I'm half deaf anyway."

Dinner was over, and Trudie and I were cleaning up the kitchen. Braxton Vaughn, Trudie's husband, and my husband Dick were sitting at our dining room table, talking. Dick was saying that he had been practicing in the backyard since the last part of August, aiming at a target he'd nailed to the fence.

"That's what it takes," Braxton said. "If you're going to be serious about it. A good bow hunter starts shooting at least a couple of months before the season opens. Because you consider pulling sixty pounds—these big boys that like to talk, they'll have it seventy to seventy-five pounds."

"Wait a minute," Dick said. "We're still talking about a compound?"

"Compound, yes." Braxton pushed his chair away from the table. "But even with fifty percent strikeover, you're still pulling thirty to thirty-five pounds, and some bows aren't true fifty percent. You're crouching there, and you're waiting on a deer that's standing behind a tree, and it's all you can do to get the thing pulled out there, anyway. So your arms get to quivering. That's why I like to bow hunt. You feel like you've done something when you get a deer with a bow."

We'd been home for about a year; at least, Nashville was home for *me*. Dick was born and raised in southern California, but the way things were getting out there, he had been ready to come back, too.

Trudie hadn't changed much. After more than fifteen years, she and I picked up where we'd left off. There aren't many people you can do that with. The first time she'd walked into my kitchen, she knew where everything would be, the dishes, the pots, the spices.

"Sarah," Braxton said to me. "Hon, would you mind fixing me a spittoon?"

Braxton is several years older than Trudie. He is a big man, over six feet tall and barrel-chested. His forearms and chest and the backs of his hands and fingers are covered in a pelt of dark hair. He was growing a beard for the hunt. He and Dick get along well, which is not always the case; just because two women are friends doesn't mean their husbands will be.

I dug an empty tomato sauce can out of the trash, rinsed it out, and put a couple of folded paper towels in the bottom.

"Bow hunting, now, your range . . ." Braxton paused to spit. "Your maximum range is thirty to forty yards. You can shoot farther, of course, and some people do, but very few can shoot beyond forty or forty-five yards and hit what they're aiming at. A good hunter won't shoot at a deer if he isn't reasonably sure he can hit it."

"What about this little dab of salad?" Trudie said.

I told her to put it in a smaller bowl, and I'd have it for lunch the next day.

Dick had never killed a deer before. This would be his first bow hunt, and he was nervous about it.

Dick is blond and blue-eyed and handsome to the point that it is almost a handicap; he looks like what a California ad agency might have put together to sell Porsches. He is often embarrassed by the way heads turn (and not only women's).

"What have they got for stands?" Braxton said.

Dick's company, Precision Computers, bought the lodge last year from a rod and gun club that was going broke trying to keep it up. Trudie's father is chairman of the board, but she and Braxton hadn't been up there yet. Technically, the lodge is for company employees only.

It's a four-bedroom log house on twelve hundred acres in the Appalachian Mountains. It's bordered on two sides by federal game reserves, the Little Pidgeon River on a third side, and small farms on the other. The acreage is mostly forested, and from what we could see last summer when Dick and I were there fishing, it has been a long time since the lumber was harvested. Although it's posted against hunting except by company employees, Dick feels sure the local people take what game they want.

"Tell you the truth," Dick said, "I don't know much more about the stands than what Clifford's told me. And take that for what it's worth." He smiled at me as I picked up the last couple of plates.

"You're in for a real treat," he told Braxton. "Getting to spend four days with Clifford Hurley."

Braxton teaches computer courses at Middle Tennessee State University. In the early 70s, when he and Trudie married, he was teaching at Vanderbilt. They're good together; I never would have pictured her with a man like Braxton after some of the jerks she dated. She used to have a real thing for lowlife.

She was pouring the coffee, and then he pulled her onto his lap. "The experienced buck, if he suspects the least thing is wrong, he'll send the squaws on ahead."

"Pretty smart," Dick said.

Trudie stretched to the buffet behind her for the cream. "Yeah? Well, there are some pretty smart does, too, you know."

"The *old* does might be," Braxton said and waited till he got her reaction. "They're probably *as* smart, or smarter, than the bucks. But they're not as used to being shot at, so they may be a little less cautious."

I had finished in the kitchen. I let the door between the kitchen and dining room swing shut and sat down next to Dick to drink my coffee.

"A deer can hear things you don't hear, that *you* did," Braxton said. "If your arrow barely taps the rest—any little thing—he's going to hear it. And more than likely, if he hasn't already smelled you, it's because you're wearing something to mask your smell."

" 'Doe in Heat,' " Trudie said.

"Yeah, or 'Buck in Rut.' I don't know much about this now . . ."

She laughed at him.

"You hear all kinds of tales about scents. But the buck scents, the theory behind that is if one buck smells another buck in his territory, he'll go find him to run him off."

"What about 'Doe in Heat,' sweetheart?" She cupped her chin in one hand and batted her lashes.

Dick laughed and put his arm around my shoulder.

In truth, I was apprehensive about the whole business. A broadhead arrow is an extremely ugly thing.

While Braxton droned on about deer and their habits, I started to think about how much I had to pack the next morning, all the things we would need on the trip. Braxton had arranged for someone to cover his classes, and Dick had scheduled three vacation days. The lodge is so far away from a decent grocery, Trudie and I had divvied up the huge food list.

"I wear an acorn scent," Braxton was saying. "Because most of where I've hunted around here is hardwood country. And if you've ever been around where horses or cows or deer have been eating acorns, you can *smell* acorns. If they've been mashed or crushed, they've got a definite smell."

"I knew I'd forget something," Dick said. "Maybe I'll have time to pick some up in the morning." He looked at me, meaning maybe *I* would have time in the morning.

"Naw," Braxton said. "I got plenty, you can use mine. I've got some skunk scent, too, but my wife won't let me use that."

Trudie looped a strand of shoulder-length black hair behind her ear, exposing one of the gold hoop earrings she usually wears. She's gained a little weight since we were younger, but it looks good on her, it's softened some of the angles.

"You've smelled skunk, right?" she said. "Get a whiff on the highway? Well, that just *smells*. This goop he was putting on his clothes last year was *sickening*."

"I'll admit it's hard to use," Braxton said. "People get a little bottle with an eyedropper, so they can reach over, put a drop or two on the stand, then seal it back up.

"If you got hit with a full load of real skunk, it wouldn't be the smell you'd be worried about. You'd run for your life. It burns your eyes, it burns your mouth and skin. You'd be gagging and rolling over things. You wouldn't be able to breathe. I believe if you couldn't get away from it, it'd kill you. It'd make you run blind in the woods, and *that* can kill you."

He paused to spit in his can. "But any of it—acorn scent, skunk, fox urine—you can't do away with your human smell. You're just covering it up."

I swallowed a yawn.

"Now a *serious* deer hunter, if he's really serious, he'll wash his clothes two or three times, or get his *wife* to. Then he airs them out, hangs them outside in the fresh air and all that kind of stuff."

"Wash them in what?" I said.

"Just keep washing them," Braxton said. "To get any human odor out of them, rinse them two or three times . . ."

"Looks like the soap . . ."

". . . to get the soap out of them."

"Oh," I said.

"Then he hangs them and lets them air out so they don't have *any* smell. That's a *serious* bow hunter."

"And puts them on just before he leaves," Dick said.

"And you don't smoke," Braxton said, "and you don't chew. Hell, you don't *eat*, and you get up in the morning an hour or two early and drink coffee so you can go to the bathroom."

Trudie and I exchanged looks.

"I'm talking about number two. Then you make sure the last thing before you start for the stand, you do number one."

"So you don't make wee-wee in your pants," she said.

Braxton ignored her. "I carry a jug with me, a plastic milk jug. If you have to go, you're not going to do it off your stand, if you're a serious deer hunter, because think of the stain you're going to leave. And you're not going to get down and run half a mile either."

"This deer hunting is some serious shit, folks," Trudie said.

"I carry a jug and tie it up there in the stand with me, especially on cold mornings. On cold mornings you have to go more often, I don't know why." He leaned over and spat.

"Do you spit in that same jug?" she said.

"Naw, I don't."

Dick was having trouble keeping a straight face.

"You mean you chew?" I said.

Braxton grinned around the wad in his cheek. "Yeah, I do! I didn't for a while and I watched the cows . . . you know what cows will do underneath a stand where you've been chewing? They'll eat the grass, they'll eat the dead oak leaves."

"What happens if you fart?" Dick said.

Trudie clutched her throat and fell over, feigning death.

"Oh, I see," Braxton said. "Well, I'm telling you some things that maybe you ought to think about. People that bow hunt take all that stuff seriously."

Dick tried to stop smiling. "There's this guy who's going to be there. To hear Clifford talk, *he's* a serious hunter." Dick finished his coffee, and I got up for the pot.

"You know how wild Clifford gets. Well, you don't, but Sarah does. Anyway, this friend of Clifford's is some kind of hunting guide. His name even sounds right. It's Woods. *Something* Woods. I can't remember, but like a kid's name."

My stomach lurched. I turned and looked at Trudie, but her face didn't register anything.

"What could I do?" Dick was saying. "The place has four bedrooms."

Not long after we'd moved home, I had taken Dad aside and asked him what had become of the Woodses. I knew Sonny's parents no longer lived where they used to, and that was all I knew, and I told myself I hadn't made any real effort to discover that information, just happened to notice the house was empty and falling down, as I was driving by one day. Dad didn't know what had become of them; it seemed maybe he'd heard they moved.

I'd asked him if he knew where Sonny was now, but he's gotten vague on so many things, since my brother Joe died. "No," he'd said, shaking his head. He had no idea where Sonny was. Sonny Woods had been Joe's best friend. And he was the boy I was once supposed to marry.

It could be someone else, I thought, as I watched Dick's animated imitation of Clifford. *Woods is a common enough name*.

"So what we'll do," Braxton said, "is we'll use a little acorn scent on our boots . . ."

But I knew it would be Sonny.

2

Dick went in to work the next morning, but he was home from the plant by ten o'clock. I had everything packed and ready, except for his hunting clothes and the arrows and bow, hatchet, skinning knife—all the sharp and deadly instruments that go with blood sports. He would want to pack all that himself.

It made an impressive heap in the middle of the floor when we were finished, and I could see from his expression that he was wondering if all this stuff was necessary for a four-day trip. I have a tendency to take everything I *might* need, and I had included some art supplies. *I* wasn't going to be hunting.

"You sure you didn't forget something?"

"I could leave part of this food, let the mighty hunters feed us," I said.

He picked up the bow. "I hope I don't do anything stupid, especially in front of Clifford Hurley. I tried to think of some reason why he couldn't come, short of just telling him we didn't want him. And then he tells me he's bringing this other guy and his wife. 'The more the merrier,' he says."

I hadn't thought about Sonny married. *You don't know for sure it's Sonny,* I reminded myself.

"You could have given him extra work," I said. Clifford's in charge of shipping at the plant.

"Right."

"Don't worry about it," I said. "It'll be okay."

"I guess." He drew back on the new compound bow, and sighted down an imaginary arrow.

I ducked underneath it and locked my arms around his waist.

He put the bow down. "Braxton told me one time about this hunter who shot himself in the foot."

"How could that happen?" I said.

"I don't know." He laughed and held me close. "I don't want to find out either."

We loaded Dick's Skylark to drive the twenty-five miles to Braxton and Trudie's place, where all our gear would have to be unloaded again. Their house is on the way to the lodge, and the four of us were going in their new van.

They couldn't afford the luxury van, or the house they live in, on Braxton's salary as an associate professor, but Trudie's family has money, old money, and lots of it. She has a substantial amount in trust, and sees no sense in not spending the income, which alone is close to double what Braxton makes in two semesters, teaching a full load. She's asked me about it, did I think they ought to try and live on his salary? And if so, what in hell were they supposed to do with hers? Her reasoning is that they ought to enjoy the income from the trust, at least, while their children are growing up. She's an only child, and someday will be one of the wealthiest women in Tennessee.

I tell her there's nothing particularly moral about being poor. I think having money bothers her more than Braxton. He certainly enjoys teaching—nobody's in *that* for the money—and they discuss how to spend, what to buy. Neither of them wants their two boys spoiled by money.

Their house is comfortable, but not ostentatious. They have a pool and the paraphernalia that go with children, but the boys have chores they're responsible for, and the oldest one, David, who is fourteen, has a paper route.

When I got out of the car, the four-year-old, Rusty, ran down the front steps and hugged me around the legs. They are beautiful children, both of them.

In their driveway there was a huge pile of stuff that Braxton was growling over. I wondered how everything was going to fit after we added ours to the pile, even in the large van. Trudie came out in jeans and a sweatshirt.

—

"Will you *please* finish your lunch," she said to Rusty.

I gave him a squeeze, and let go.

"He eats about like you do," she said.

His cutoffs rode just below his navel, barely hanging on his hipbones as he ran across the yard.

"And let those frogs go!" she yelled after him.

I thought about the leftover salad that I had meant to eat for lunch, but hadn't gotten around to. I'd made Dick a sandwich, and he'd eaten it while looking for the felt liners to go in his boots.

Trudie was standing with her back to the porch. "Get a load of our babysitter," she said. There was a pretty dark-haired girl beside one of the porch columns—she smiled and said something to Rusty on his way in. "That's an A student, according to Braxton. All *I've* seen her do since she got here this morning is bat her lashes and moisten her lips. David, naturally, has been drooling from his fangs."

Trudie can't seem to believe that David is old enough to be going through puberty. She says all he does these days is lurk in the bathroom with the door locked, and that his total vocabulary has shrunk to fifty words, punctuated by grunts.

"There *is* a telephone at this place," she said.

"All the comforts of home."

She went inside to give the girl last-minute instructions, while I watched Braxton and Dick try to load the van.

So what if it *is* Sonny?

Trudie had fallen asleep in the seat next to me. She knew there was something on my mind, and she knew I would tell her when I was ready. She doesn't pry, and she gives advice sparingly. She'll tell you if she thinks you're getting ready to do something stupid, but she doesn't say 'I told you so' afterward. After the last time I saw him, she helped put me back together.

It's old news, I reminded myself. *It all happened a long time ago*. I'd never told Dick about Sonny. He knew there had been *someone,* and Trudie had told him a few things once. But in all the growing-up stories involving my older brother Joe and me, I'd always left Sonny out, even though he was usually there.

Joe and I, and Sonny, grew up in Cedar Point, a town of about twelve thousand located northwest of Nashville between the Cumberland and Harpeth rivers. My parents still live there. Growing up in Cedar Point, we had the advantages a small town offers, only forty minutes from the city.

Sonny was Joe's age, two years older than me. He was named Walter after his father, but no one ever called him that. His family lived just outside the city limits in a small frame house set up on concrete blocks. It didn't have any underpinning and on hot summer days, his dog and his mother's chickens shared the dusty shade underneath. His mother sold eggs.

I hadn't really known Sonny's parents when we were kids. I saw his father only a few times—usually, he was leaning over the insides of his truck, his shirt off and his big arms greasy to the elbows. He had a beer belly and his skin was white as a cave cricket. He always had his shirt off but he never seemed to tan.

The time I remember especially, Joe and I had ridden out there on our bikes to see if Sonny could go swimming with us. We should have realized the only reason he wasn't at our house already was because his father was home. Most of the time Sonny's father was away on cross-country hauls. But when he was home, he wouldn't let Sonny go anywhere.

That day it was awfully hot, and his father was working on the truck. Sonny asked if he could go swimming with us. Joe and I stood out of the way beside our bikes, but close enough that I could see sweat and the red patches on his father's face as he turned around. He yelled and raised his hand with the wrench in it. It scared me and it scared Joe, too; we both flinched and stepped back. Sonny didn't move a muscle.

Even though Sonny's father wouldn't let him go anywhere, he never seemed to want Sonny around.

His mother was a slim, pretty woman with large gray eyes and curly dark hair that she wore short, framing her face. Sonny got his coloring from her. The times Joe and I went to buy eggs, she would invite us in if she could, if her husband wasn't home. Her house was immaculate.

In the summer, Sonny slept at one end of a screened-in back porch. I remember thinking how great that was, almost like sleeping outdoors. In the winter, I suppose he slept in the living room or a corner of the kitchen. It's funny that I knew so few of the details of his home life. I knew it wasn't like ours. When his father was gone on a trip, Sonny was mostly at our house anyway.

A few times he came to school with a busted lip or black eye. On those afternoons, he and Joe wouldn't let me be with them. They'd lock themselves in Joe's room or run away and hide.

In the front seats, Braxton and Dick were still talking deer hunting. Trudie slept on. She can go without sleep for days if she has to, but she's a marathon sleeper when she gets the chance. She had one foot tucked under her and her hands curled in her lap.

"More than likely," Braxton said, "there'll be ladder stands—that's just a ladder with a platform made out of rough sawmill lumber or something. They might be scattered around several different places where there's cover or a ridge, or where they think deer might feed, or overlooking a trail crossing . . . in other words, there are a lot of possibilities. How well do they know the area?"

"It's hard telling what Clifford knows," Dick said. "This guy he's bringing is a guide."

Maybe it would be Sonny. He and Joe had hunted in these mountains on land belonging to some of Dad's relatives.

We had grown up. I had long since stopped following them around; they were upperclassmen, hot jocks on campus, and all the girls were after them. And I had had interests of my own.

Then Joe started college, and Sonny tried working with his father. When he was drafted, he said it was just as well. I still thought of him as Joe's friend, someone who was around a lot. It didn't enter my mind that he might think of me as anything more than Joe's kid sister.

Braxton lifted his cap and wiped his forehead. He glanced over his shoulder at us. "You warm enough?" he whispered. I nodded that I was. He turned the heater down, and resumed speaking in his normal voice. "People will tell you that deer don't look up, but that doesn't apply to the ones that have been hunted a lot. They'll look everything over at ground level, and then throw their heads straight back and look in the treetops."

My junior year in high school, Sonny was traveling much of the time, picking up and delivering freight. My senior year, he was in the army, and my folks and I were conducting a running battle over what I was going to do when I graduated. They wanted me at Vanderbilt with Joe, but I knew Joe was the brilliant one—I wasn't. I wanted me in art school, or studying with an artist whose work I admired. In the end, we compromised. I took art courses at Peabody, and rented studio space from Joshua Barnes.

"Cows can smell you, too, but they can't look straight up like a deer can," Braxton said. "They've got to turn their heads like this."

But before that happened, before I left for school in Nashville, and Sonny left for Vietnam, something else happened.

Joe was home from school that weekend, and Sonny had a weekend pass from Ft. Campbell. I knew they were going out; it was Saturday night and Joe had gotten them dates with a couple of Vanderbilt coeds. I said hello to Sonny when he came in and went back to my homework.

Joe was worse than any girl about his wavy blond hair, and Sonny was waiting for him to finish his primping in the bathroom. I was sprawled in the recliner in the living room, chewing on my eraser and staring at the trig textbook in my lap.

—

And then my chair was falling backwards, and I screamed. Sonny had come up behind me and tipped it over. He was laughing. He set it upright again, and leaned over the chair back, so that our faces were very close. I could smell his after-shave, feel the shoulder of his jacket pressing against my hair. And I was sure, I was suddenly positive that if I turned my head just a fraction, he would kiss me.

"I had one, last year, a buck, here he comes down the trail. I could hear him, clop, clop, clop, he came almost within range."

Trudie moaned and shifted her position, and Braxton lowered his voice.

"There was a dogwood bush, all the leaves on it, and here I am drawn back and waiting on him. All he's got to do is step out. He's just behind that dogwood bush. You know what he did?"

"What?" Dick said.

Sonny had called the next day—Sunday afternoon—and asked to speak to me. Could I ride around for a while? He had a couple of hours before he had to start back to base.

"He stuck that nose out and looked up at me, at that stand. Maybe he'd seen somebody in it before. He may have come up on me before, and I hadn't even known it. He stuck his nose out from underneath that bush and looked up at that stand, and he pulled his head right back in, he turned around and just, he clipped away just . . . so pretty . . . it made me sick."

"No chance for a shot?"

Braxton shook his head. "Not a clear shot, no."

"I'm afraid if I don't have a broadside shot, I won't know where to aim."

"You'll have to think on it longer, all right. I shot one straight up its butthole one time, hit the spine. I tell you about that?"

Dick nodded.

"Now if these stands have been used a lot . . ."

Trudie introduced Dick and me. She rescued him one evening from her father's club and brought him with her to the

Catacombs where I occasionally filled in as hostess, and where I had a more or less continuous showing of my work. The bartender there, Jake, was Trudie's current love-interest, but they'd had a fight. Maybe Dick was supposed to make him jealous. He certainly was good-looking enough.

I was working that night. Trudie introduced us when they came in, then she and Dick took seats at the bar. Later he told me that she and Jake, once they'd made up, passed the time planning exactly how they were going to spend the shank of the evening, once Jake got off work.

Dick caught me staring. It was hard to believe anyone could be that handsome. I wondered if an artist could draw features that classic and not end up with a cliché.

After the dinner rush was over and I'd put the menus down, he asked me to dance. He was a good dancer, and a good listener. He asked questions about my paintings, many of them the right kind of questions. I didn't notice when Trudie and Jake left.

He asked if he could take me home. I said no. He asked if he could see me again and I told him I was around the Catacombs pretty often. He didn't push.

A few days later, the regular hostess told me that the best-looking man she'd ever seen in her life had bought one of my paintings and wanted to know how to take proper care of it. She'd given him my address and phone number. That was all right, wasn't it?

3

The lodge is isolated, at the peak of a twisting mountain road. As we wound our way toward it, the van laboring in low gear, I thought it must have been quite an undertaking to get the materials and labor on site to build it. Dick and I had been there just once before, last summer. We'd had the place to ourselves then, and I had loved the quiet, and felt intimidated by it, too.

Only enough trees had been cut and enough ground bulldozed to make room for the lodge and a small oval clearing around it. Everything else had been left alone. Whoever designed it did a good job; the log house blended well with its surroundings.

It was almost five o'clock that Thursday afternoon in October when Braxton pulled into the driveway and parked beside Clifford's Jeep.

Clifford must have been watching for us. He's a short man with a ruddy complexion and a stocky build. He has a nervous habit of hitching at his pants and clearing his throat when he's getting ready to speak, and what he says is often profane. His eyes are small and direct—a muddy brown—and he stands too close when he's talking to you. I didn't like him much. Dick says he's a whiz on the job; nothing in shipping gets past him.

He was down the front steps and pumping Braxton's hand almost before he could get out of the van. "I'm Clifford Hurley."

Braxton introduced himself and Trudie.

Clifford ducked his head inside the door. "I was starting to think maybe you-all weren't coming."

"You know how it is," Dick said. "You bring women, you spend half the day packing." He took my hand as I got out. "No, actually, I had a couple of things to take care of at the plant."

Clifford was watching Trudie. She wasn't all the way awake yet, rubbing her eyes and stretching. "Thought I'd come on early," he said. "You know, get the place aired out some." He was having a hard time keeping his eyes off her chest. The caption on his tee shirt read "Compound Users Have Deeper Penetration."

"Good idea," Dick said. Braxton had the back of the van open and had begun unloading.

"Hope we won't be crowding you any," Clifford said. He was standing in Dick's way. "We've taken the bedrooms on the east end, if that's all right."

"No problem," Dick said. "Whatever. Excuse me, I ought to . . ."

"Oh hell, yes. Here, let me help you with some of this stuff." Clifford picked up the largest piece of luggage and my makeup case and followed me up the steps. "Janice didn't come this time," he said.

I glanced back at him.

"She wasn't feeling good."

"I'm sorry," I said. I had Dick's bag and our down jackets, more bulky than heavy. I opened the door and tried to decide which direction was east. "I hope it's nothing serious." I crossed the living room, passing the huge fireplace that took up most of one wall.

Clifford opened the bedroom door for me and set the luggage at the foot of the bed. "It's her monthlies. She gets the cramps real bad."

"Oh," I said. "I'm sorry."

He looked around the room. "This is sure a nice place."

"Yes, it is." I laid the jackets on the bed.

"Aren't we glad the old fart bought it."

"The 'old fart' is Trudie's father, by the way," I said.

"No shit!"

Dick came in with an armload and raised his eyebrows at me before he went out again.

"I thought you were bringing some people, too," I said.

Clifford tugged at his pants. "Lou's unpacking. Sonny'll be here later."

When I heard the name, I had to turn away from Clifford

for a minute and pretend to look for something in my purse, even though I'd been thinking about Sonny the whole drive.

Clifford followed me outside and insisted on carrying in the cooler.

While I was transferring our steaks and other cold foods to the refrigerator, he pointed out a box of filets in the freezer compartment. "Sonny brought these," he said. "This ain't your supermarket range beef either."

I wondered if he meant the steaks we'd brought.

"This steer was stalled and grain-fed, butchered and aged just right. You have to know somebody to get beef like this."

"I guess so."

"This guy Buster has a cold locker. He's gonna hang our deer for us."

"Great." I put in the cans of orange juice.

"Him and Sonny are pretty tight."

I was down on one knee, moving things around to find a spot for four cartons of eggs. Every time Clifford said Sonny's name, I felt funny. "There's a lot of food here," I said.

"I hope it's all right, me inviting them. I didn't know Fed Cavanaugh's daughter and son-in-law was gonna be here."

"It doesn't make any difference, Clifford. Really." I closed the lid to the cooler and stood up. "That does it."

"Lou and Sonny're real nice." His short thick body blocked the passage between the counters and the refrigerator. He was still holding the door to the freezer section open. "Sonny's the best damn guide in the southeastern United States."

"Is he?" I said. I hoped my face wasn't showing anything.

He gave the steaks another poke and closed the freezer door. "Lou's people live down on the river, run a bait shop and sporting goods place."

"Is that right," I said.

"I wouldn't want, you know, I wouldn't want them to feel out of place."

Clifford and I are about the same height; he was looking me right in the eye.

"Pretend I didn't tell you who Trudie's father is," I said. "You'd never know it, believe me."

Walking down the hallway to the bedroom, I heard Dick and Braxton come into the kitchen, and I heard Clifford follow them outside to the woodpile, talking about how he was just fixing to get a fire going when we drove up. I heard Trudie say something.

In a minute I would go back to the kitchen and help her. In just a minute. I closed the bedroom door behind me and braced myself against it.

We'd had so little time together before Sonny left for Vietnam. In one sense, we'd been together nearly all our lives. But not like this.

That Sunday afternoon, after he'd called, we drove around town, aimlessly cruising the square and the quiet residential streets. He was wearing his uniform, dressed to leave for the base. As he drove, he told me about jungle school and the training he'd just completed, how he and the other rangers had had to fend for themselves deep in the Georgia swamps.

At the football stadium, behind the bleachers, he pulled over and cut the engine. He laid his arm along the seat back. "I don't know how soon it will be," he said, "but as soon as I can swing another pass, will you go out with me?"

The night before, after he and Joe left, I'd decided it was my imagination that there'd been anything unusual in his manner. He'd always done things like tipping my chair over, to tease me. Then this morning Joe had mentioned that Sonny was against the idea of his joining the Air Force. I'd thought maybe that was what Sonny wanted to talk about.

"You mean on a date?" I said.

He smiled. "You're not going steady, I hope."

His fingertips brushed my shoulder. Then he leaned over and softly kissed me, not trying to part my lips.

There was a car coming, and he sat back, looking out across

the hood, until it had passed. Only now was I beginning to register the sensation of his mouth on mine, and the way his hand had felt on my waist.

He leaned toward me again. From nervousness, shock, maybe even a little from fear, I pressed my palms against his chest.

He touched my face, drawing his thumb along the curve of my jaw. This time my lips opened under his.

I heard another car approach, and go by, and didn't care. His mouth and tongue traced the arc of my neck to the base of my throat. I felt his breath through the fabric of my blouse. Then he held me hard against him, and held me away. "If I'm late, they'll never give me another pass."

"When will they?"

"I don't know. Not soon enough."

They gave us just two more weekends before they sent him to Vietnam.

A year later, in August, 1968, Sonny was back from Vietnam, and Joe was getting ready to go. Sonny was stationed at Ft. Campbell with the 101st Airborne, and Joe was at Sewart Air Force Base outside of Nashville. Joe was a flyer; Sonny, a ranger. At the time, I thought it was all pretty glamorous.

Joe had called me before he brought Sonny that weekend. He'd called specifically to tell me that Sonny might seem changed, that he'd had a pretty bad time of it over there. I told him I knew that, of course; I understood that.

But he's back now, I'd thought, *he's home*. All I could really think about was seeing him.

Joe hadn't been able to get over it when we'd first told him about us. His best friend and his kid sister. He said it took some getting used to. Sonny left for Vietnam before any of us had time to get used to it—we were still a threesome, and I was still a virgin.

I wrote him every day. I wrote about what was going on at home and with people we both knew. I told him about my classes at Peabody, what a fine teacher Joshua was and how my work was progressing. I told him over and over how much I loved him.

His letters were sometimes stained and wrinkled as if he'd carried them around a long time. As the months went by, they contained less and less information; there was never anything about the fighting. Toward the end, they were just notes, sometimes weeks apart, telling me he loved me and asking me please not to stop writing, even when he didn't, or couldn't, write back.

I tried to imagine what his life was like. The evening news terrified me, but I watched it anyway. I had to know where the fighting had been each day. I prayed each night for his safety. I invented elaborate fantasies about how it was going to be when he finally got home.

And then he was.

I had fixed Joe up with the hostess at the Catacombs. She was a part-time art student at Peabody, too. Her name was Janet. I'd wanted Trudie to be Joe's date, but she was involved with Jake at the time.

I'd been waiting a year for that moment. When I opened the door that night, Sonny was wearing his uniform, the trousers bloused in spit-shined jump boots. He was deeper through the chest than I'd remembered, taller, leaner. Veins stood out on the backs of his hands, and he was tanned bronze. I thought he looked wonderful.

I stepped aside to let Joe and Janet come in, and then Sonny, his overseas cap held in both hands in front of him. He didn't put his arms around me, or kiss me. I might have been a total stranger to him. For several awkward seconds, I simply stood there, unable to think what to do.

Joe took charge, pointing the way to the living room. "You two have a seat. I'll help Sarah with the drinks." In the kitchen he hugged me. "Give him time," he whispered.

I'll never forget the strain, the incredible awkwardness as we sat around the coffee table. Joe and Janet made a brave attempt to keep a conversation going, and they'd just barely met. Sonny volunteered nothing, and answered my questions in monosyllables.

"How was Ft. Campbell?" I asked him.

It was okay.

Would he be there till his time was up, did he think?

He wasn't sure.

He seemed way down inside himself somewhere.

At dinner he ate little, drank little. He seemed so tense, constantly scanning the room. I gave up trying to draw him out, and the long excruciating silences between us didn't seem to bother him at all. It was like he was there, but not there.

When the band started playing, Joe and Janet spent most of the time on the dance floor. I think they were trying to leave us alone, thinking that might help. Besides, they were having a great time. I watched them dance, slow and close, Joe looking so handsome in his dress blues.

Sonny didn't talk, he didn't ask me to dance. We sat at the table and played with our drinks. I remember my palms starting to sweat.

Then we were in Joe's car, Janet snuggling under his arm in the front seat. He leaned down and whispered something, and she giggled. Sonny was on his side of the back seat, staring out the window, and I was on mine. When Joe stopped in the parking lot outside my apartment, Sonny at least came around to open the door for me.

Then Joe got out, too. He unlocked the trunk and dropped a flight bag at Sonny's feet. "Pick you up at ten hundred hours," he said. He was grinning. Then he got back in the car and slammed the door. Janet waved as they pulled out of the parking lot and left us standing there.

My apartment was on the second floor. On the first landing I started digging in my purse for the key. At the door, I handed it to him. Neither of us said anything. I felt panicky. He opened the door, and I turned on the lights.

The bedroom was straight ahead, the bath to the right of the tiny foyer, efficiency kitchen to the left, and living room in front of that. As I laid my purse and sweater on the kitchen table, I began to hope that it might be all right. Now that we were truly alone.

He stopped in front of one of my paintings and pretended to look at it. I watched him, and I waited. Finally, he took his jacket off. I folded it across his bag in the foyer.

"What would you like?" I said. "A drink? Coffee?"

He had his hands in his pockets, jingling coins together. "Nothing, thanks."

"Let's sit down then," I said. I walked past him into the living room and closed the drapes on the window that overlooked the parking lot and a Shell station on Franklin Road. I turned on one soft light and sat on the couch. He hesitated at the armchair before he sat down beside me. I gave him time to say something.

"Sonny."

He was sitting with his hands between his knees.

"What is it?" I said.

He shook his head and laughed. He held his palms together, lacing and unlacing his fingers.

"Talk to me."

The light from the window fell across his back, outlining individual muscles beneath the shirt.

"I love you," I said.

He made a sound. It was like he was trying not to cry.

Touch him, I thought. *Hold him.* And I did, or I tried.

It might have been a wasp instead of my hand on his back, or fire, the way he moved away from me. All of a sudden, he was standing over me while my hand hung in midair. I didn't know what I was seeing in his face, whether it was rage, or terror, or disgust. He started to say something, and then turned away.

I was speechless, stunned by his reaction.

Then he'd crossed the living room and gone out the door.

Hours later, lying stiff and straight in bed, I heard him come in. I heard water running, and the commode flush in the bathroom. I lay there waiting, thinking he'd come to the door next, and through it, the way I'd imagined it happening. He didn't, and I almost went to him. I lay awake the rest of the night. *What was happening? What had I done?*

At dawn I got up and showered, brushed my teeth, put on makeup. All the routine things.

In the kitchen, I started taking things out of the refrigerator: bacon, eggs, milk. I'd take something out and set it on the counter and then stand there for a long time thinking, *Okay, what else?*

I heard the sofa creak in the living room. I remember the cool feel of the counter under my hands. I could sense when he'd reached the door to the kitchen.

He was barefoot with his shirt open on his chest. He took a cigarette from the corner of his mouth and ground it out in the ashtray he was carrying.

"How do you want your eggs?" I said.

He set the ashtray on the kitchen table. "I'm not really hungry."

My face was hot with the memory of last night, how he'd jerked away from my touch.

I scrambled some eggs anyway, hoping he would do something, say something. Anything. He sat at the table with his head in his hands.

I put the plate in front of him and went into the bedroom and closed the door. I stood at the window watching for Joe. When he came, I asked him to please wait in the car. He took one look at me and did what I asked.

And then we were walking to the door. I was aware of the smell of his shaving lotion. I could hear the fabric of his uniform rubbing against itself. I couldn't believe it was going to end like this.

I reached for the doorknob, and he pulled me around to face him. And he could have taken me there, right there on the floor, with Joe waiting in the car. I loved him so much, wanted him so much. He said, "Next time, don't invite your brother."

And I hit him. I slapped him as hard as I could, hard enough to bring tears to his eyes.

"Get out," I said.

"Sarah . . ."

I leaned all my weight against the door, and shoved, and closed it in his face, and the last thing I remember seeing was the imprint of my fingers where I'd slapped him—greenish-white against his tan.

I leaned against the door, crying, and listening to his footsteps fading on the stairs.

I decided that Joe probably engineered the whole thing, knowing how much I wanted it. My own brother acting as procurer. I wondered what they were saying to each other on the drive back to base.

I opened a bottle of gin and poured a water glass full. I threw up a couple of times before I could finally keep the raw liquor down on an empty stomach. By taking small sips, and lying down, I was able to bring on sleep.

4

That was the last time I'd seen him. Even at a distance of seventeen years, the memory was vivid. And he was here, or would be soon.

I jumped at a knock on the door, and then Trudie opened it and looked in at me. I was sitting on the bed beside my open suitcase with our stuff in a jumble around me.

"Are you all right?" she said.

She had come to see about me late that Sunday night, seventeen years ago, when I hadn't answered the phone. She knew both Sonny and Joe had to be back on base by early afternoon. When I hadn't answered the door, she'd let herself in with her key.

She'd held a cold compress to my forehead while I threw up alcohol fumes and what was left of the bottom layer of my stomach. She'd rocked me in her arms, combing tangles from my hair with her fingers. She'd let me cry, and listened while I tried to tell her. The humiliation. The despair.

"I was just about to make the bed," I lied now. I gave her a smile, which she wasn't buying.

Trudie opened the door wider, then all the way, and I could see someone in the hall behind her. "Sarah, this is Louellen Woods." She stepped aside so I could see the woman clearly. And for a crazy, spinning moment, I thought I knew her, too.

"Are you sure you're all right?" Trudie asked again.

"A little dizzy," I said. "What I get for skipping lunch."

"There's a tray of cheese and crackers in the kitchen," Louellen said.

"I'm glad to meet you." I had to swallow a rash of hysterical giggles. Trudie was watching me, her eyes narrowed; I could almost hear the wheels turning in her head.

Sonny's wife was lovely. Her hair was shoulder-length, a

profusion of auburn curls. She had good skin, and a good figure displayed in a plaid flannel shirt and Levi's. But it was her eyes that made her so stunning; they were the color of jade, or a certain type of emerald. A deep and swirling green, and slanted slightly at the corners, like a cat's.

I stood up. "Here," I said. "Let me show you where the sheets and towels are." I led the way down the hall and opened the door to the linen closet. "Here you are."

She smiled at me before she leaned into the shelving and sniffed the air. Up close, her eyes were the exact color of fine jade. "I just love the way cedar smells," she said.

Again I had the feeling I knew her from somewhere. Her accent was wrong for the west coast. It had a pleasant, but definite, mountain twang. And then I thought, *It's just because she's Sonny's wife*.

"Whoever built this place didn't cut corners," Trudie said. "This is my idea of camping out."

"Clifford was telling me that you live near here," I said.

"Not far." Louellen Woods picked up another set of linens. "I might as well make Clifford's bed for him. Do you know Janice?" She glanced at both Trudie and me.

"I do," I said. "A little. I've met her a few times."

"She's such a lady. Sonny thinks Janice is the grandest thing."

"You have to wonder, don't you?" I said.

She laughed. "I have."

"What?" Trudie said.

"Janice and Clifford are so, shall we say, different," I said.

"What's wrong with him?" Trudie asked.

"She hasn't really met him yet," I said.

Louellen shifted her armload of sheets and towels. "You know, sometimes I don't think he realizes how . . ." She searched for a word.

"Offensive," I said.

"Yes." She shrugged. "But Sonny likes him."

When she'd gone to make their beds, Trudie turned to me. "Something's wrong."

She hadn't recognized the name. There was no reason she should, really. Trudie had never met Sonny, just heard me talk about him a long time ago.

There was finally nothing else I could find to do. I had made the bed, unpacked and hung our clothes, and put our toiletries in the bathroom that divided our bedroom from Trudie and Braxton's. I freshened my face and went out to the living room. I was relieved, and somehow disappointed at the same time, to find that Sonny still wasn't there. Louellen wasn't in the room either.

Braxton was starting a fire, building a methodical structure across the huge andirons on the hearth. He'd begun with a base of dry leaves and bark, then added twigs and kindling.

Clifford chafed his hands and pretended he was freezing. "Any time this winter'll be fine," he said, and winked at Trudie.

Dick came from behind, wrapping his arms around me and resting his chin on my shoulder. "Should have brought something to keep you warm."

"Shee-it," Clifford said. He was crowding Braxton at the hearth, standing too close. "Reckon you'll have the heart to set fire to that?"

Braxton balanced a forearm-sized stick on top of the pile and rocked back on his heels. He looked at Clifford, appraisingly, I thought. "You want it to burn right, you got to lay it right." He stood, pushing up on knees that crackled from old football injuries.

He looked like a bear towering over Clifford. "Now you watch," he said, and selected a fireplace match off the mantel. We were all watching the wood burst into flame when Louellen appeared.

A woman who is entering a room where there are people knows she will be seen. By the way she carries herself, by the tilt of her chin or the cant of her pelvis, you can often determine her sense of herself. A plain or timid woman may hunch her shoulders, trying for invisibility. A woman confident in her looks will move with confidence, head up, shoulders back. With either kind—plain or beautiful—there is some degree of self-consciousness. As Louellen Woods crossed the living room and cupped her hands to the fire, I was aware of a little hitch in Dick's breathing.

I introduced her to him, and to Braxton.

"This ole boy's a regular pyromaniac," Clifford said. "He built him up a little house of Lincoln Logs and then set fire to it."

Braxton smiled. It was clear that he was still trying to decide how he ought to take Clifford.

"What would everybody like to drink?" Dick said. "Clifford and I'll go fix it."

"I'll get the cheese and crackers," Trudie said. "If Sarah doesn't eat something soon, she'll pass out."

"What do you want, Lou, a Seven and Seven?" Clifford said.

She was looking at Dick. "That'll be fine."

"Bourbon and water for me," Braxton said.

"Just Coke," I said.

Dick was on his way out. I didn't think he'd heard me.

Braxton brushed his hands on his trousers, and the three of us listened to the fire crackle.

"So," he said to Louellen. "Your old man must be getting a head start on us."

"I'm sorry?" She gave him those green eyes, a direct, level gaze.

"I was inquiring if your husband was out hunting," Braxton said.

"No, he had some business to finish up."

He picked the poker out of the fireplace rack and nudged the burning logs into a neater pile. "What business is he in?"

"Sonny's a guide."

"Oh, really? A professional hunting guide?"

I supposed he was just trying to make conversation, since he already knew this.

"Yes," she said.

"Is he any good?" He was smiling now, trying to make a joke.

I started to say that I knew he was, and besides that . . . guess what? But I didn't get the chance.

"He's a fucking genius," Clifford said, coming in from the kitchen. He was balancing his drink and Lou's in the palm of one hand and carrying a brown stone jug in the other. "He could show you fourteen ways to make a fire *without* no matches."

"Is that right," Braxton said.

Clifford set the drinks on the hearth and uncorked the jug. He laid it across his shoulder and drank. "Whew, this'll put hair on your chest." He looked at Braxton. "Not that you need it."

Trudie passed between them, offering the tray of cheese and crackers to Braxton. He picked up a wedge of cheddar, and bit down on it.

Dick set his tray of drinks on an end table.

Lou got up from the hearth and took the jug from Clifford. She raised it and drank. "My brother made this. It's an old family recipe." Ceremoniously, she offered it to Braxton.

Then Dick and Trudie took their turns and passed it on to me. They laughed while Dick slapped me on the back.

"Where's Sonny?" Clifford said.

Lou set the jug on the hearth. "He wouldn't want us to wait supper on him."

"Hey," Dick said, "we're in no hurry."

"I'm getting hungry though, aren't you?" she said.

"I'm so hungry my stomach's digesting my spine," Clifford said.

"I'll get the steaks." I set my drink down. "Lay them here on the hearth, they'll thaw quicker."

Lou got up to help. I told Trudie to stay put, there wasn't

enough to do for three. I wanted to talk to Lou Woods alone anyway. I wanted to tell her I knew Sonny, and I still had a nagging feeling I knew her from somewhere, too.

"These are thick, but they're small." She had the box of filets open on the counter. "I think the men will eat two, don't you?"

"We brought some steaks," I said.

She waved that away. "Sonny got these for everybody. When they start bringing in fresh deer liver, we'll have yours to fall back on." She wrinkled her nose. "You like deer liver?"

"I don't know. I've never had any." I opened the stove drawer and got her a cookie sheet to lay the steaks on.

"Sonny *says* he likes it, so I cook it for him." She looked up and smiled. "I think he just hates to waste anything."

I was taking potatoes from a grocery sack and putting them in one side of the sink. "If it tastes like calves' liver, Dick would probably like it."

"A lot depends on how it's killed and dressed out." She rummaged through the utensil drawer and found a vegetable brush. "Let me do those," she said.

I stood beside her washing lettuce for the salad.

She pushed an eye off a potato with her thumbnail. "I hate liver anyway, but Sonny says there's a big difference in the taste of a deer that's dropped instantly and one that's had time to get scared."

She loves him, I thought. You couldn't miss it in the way she talked about him.

"If it runs far after it's shot, then it's got adrenaline and sex hormones and what-all through its system." She brushed the hair off her forehead with the back of one hand. "He says that's what makes it taste wild."

"That's interesting. I'll have to tell Dick about that."

"I hope you don't mind my saying this, but your husband is about the best-looking man I've ever seen. He could be a movie star."

I was nodding, knowing what she would say even as she said it. "I keep having the feeling I *know* you from somewhere. Did you ever live in Nashville?"

"No," she said. "I've lived here all my life. Do you know where the foil is?"

I showed her which drawer. "What was your maiden name?"

"Tolliver."

"That's it!" I said. "I knew it!"

She stopped, her hand hovering over the foil; she picked it up and turned to look at me.

"We're cousins!" And now I remembered where I'd seen her. "Your mother and my grandmother were sisters. Roy Wheatley is my father."

She stared at me, then laid the foil on the counter. "When have we seen each other before?"

"A family reunion, I think. We weren't very old."

Her smile was strained. "This is something, isn't it? Cousins. My daddy was always telling us how you people had made something of yourselves." She kept smiling in that strained way and picked up the steaks. "I better get these out by the fire."

She didn't come back, and in a minute, I heard a door close down the hall.

The day I had remembered, we were maybe twelve or thirteen. I remember her mother pushing her forward, telling her to play with me. And I remember she'd had those striking eyes. Not kittenish even then. Big-cat eyes.

Obviously, something about our being related had upset her. My mother didn't think much of this branch of Dad's family, maybe that was it. And what she'd said about us "making something of ourselves."

I wrapped the potatoes and put them in to bake, and finished making the salad. I tried to think what else it could possibly be. Whatever it was, I was sorry; and I'd wanted to tell her I knew Sonny.

5

It had taken me weeks to accept that Sonny didn't love me; it was a nightmare I kept trying to awake from.

Trudie came by or called almost every night to see how I was.

"I'm fine," I'd tell her. "Yes, I've eaten something."

Joe was about to leave for Vietnam. He would be based at Pleiku. The guys in his barracks had already hung a black wreath on his door, their macabre ritualistic send-off that was supposed to protect him from harm, like telling a performer to break a leg. It didn't work.

Sewart was close to Nashville, so I was able to see Joe several times before he left. Only once did he mention Sonny directly, and then it was really a reference to the war. Sonny had told him this: *Carry a pistol, and if you go down, don't let the fuckers take you alive*.

I hated the whole idea of Vietnam by then, and Joe's attitude wasn't what it had been when he enlisted. You had to wonder what we were doing there and, after Tet, how long it would last. My Lai had already happened, though we didn't know it. Graphic color photographs of women and children, showing the horrible effects of chemical burns, were starting to circulate on college campuses; at the same time more and more American soldiers were dying. I hated to think about Joe dropping napalm and white phosphorus; and I hated to think of the guns that would be aimed at his plane.

There were times I thought Joe wanted to ask what had happened between Sonny and me, or to say something himself, but he didn't. And I was glad. What was there to say anyway? We didn't talk about war, and we didn't talk above love. We looked for distraction and entertainment. We watched Vanderbilt play basketball and the Dixie Flyers play hockey. We went to movies and a Dave Brubeck concert. And then he went to Vietnam.

After Joe was gone, I submerged myself in my art. I funneled everything onto canvas. I'd work at the studio until Joshua put me out in the evenings and made me go home—I had long since stopped attending my classes. At home I'd paint until I could hardly lift the brush. The canvas Dick bought was done during this time. My "blue period," so to speak. I can almost laugh about it now.

After weeks went by and not a word from Sonny, I told Joshua one evening what I wanted. I wanted him to take me to bed. Tonight. Right now.

His other students had left; we were the only ones there. "That's not very funny," he said.

I agreed that it wasn't.

He'd looked at me over the rims of his glasses, wiping his hands on a turpentine rag. "I make it a rule not to sleep with my students. It raises bloody hell with the work."

"I need you to break it."

He sighed. "Look, Sarah, I'm flattered, but I won't do this. And I'm old enough to be your father."

"Then you should know what you're doing."

"That's right." He tossed the rag aside. There were knots of muscles in his shoulders and arms from working in clay and metal sculpture. He wore a beard then, neatly trimmed. "This may be the sexual revolution for you kids . . ."

"I'm a virgin." I said it again. I told him if he wouldn't do it, I would go into every bar up and down the street until I found a taker. Because by the end of the night, I didn't intend to be a virgin anymore.

"That's blackmail."

"I guess it is," I said.

He called it a gift. I considered it a burden. He was a fine lover, gentle and considerate, even funny. He made me feel wanted and special. And our friendship survived.

This is where I was in my life the night Trudie brought Dick to the Catacombs. The next week he called about the painting he'd bought, and we had lunch. The next week, dinner. Before long, we were spending most of our free time together.

We didn't get dressed up and go out much. We'd go to Percy Warner Park, and he'd lean against a tree and watch me draw. And sometimes, in the apartment, when I was cleaning my brushes and he'd fallen asleep on the couch with a book open on his chest, I'd watch him, and wonder what he was doing with me when he could have had any woman he wanted. When he'd hold me or rub the stiffness from my shoulders, when he kissed me, I could tell when he made himself stop, that he was holding back. I wondered about it, but not much. I think I took it for granted that he was infatuated with what I did, rather than with me—with some mythical idea of the artist.

The afternoon he asked me to marry him, I was working on a portrait, trying to soften the mouth, and I was having trouble getting it right. I was using a resin gel glaze, which meant I couldn't just white out the mistakes. I was standing in front of the easel in a dirty smock, the paint brush clamped between my teeth, trying to smudge and blend the colors with my fingertips.

Dick had sailed his jacket toward a chair. "You shouldn't leave your door unlocked, it's not safe."

"Nashville's a small town. It's not L.A."

We looked at the painting together, and then he took the brush out of my mouth and laid it across the palette. "Paint has lead in it," he said.

"Right," I said. "That's why I'm not eating it."

"Let's get married."

"Right," I said. There was something proportionally off about the features, if I could just figure out what it was.

He took my shoulders and turned me around. "Look at me when I'm asking you to marry me."

He leaned down and kissed me and held me to him. "I

know what you've been going through," he said. "I'll make it up to you."

Suddenly, his arms tight around me, I could hardly breathe. I hadn't told him about Sonny.

"I'll make you forget him. God, I've wanted you so much."

I hadn't told him anything. I struggled against him, and he let me go. "What do you know?"

He had this funny look on his face. "Maybe it was none of my business."

"*What* was none of your business?"

He looked away for a second. "All right. Trudie told me."

"Trudie told you," I said. I felt hot and cold in waves.

"Calm down. It doesn't matter."

I could see them, their heads together at a corner table at the Catacombs. *What* didn't matter? "What did she say?"

"You want her exact words?"

"Exactly. Let's have the exact words."

He threw up his hands. "She said you'd been badly hurt. She said some guy had really messed you over."

I laughed. The blood was pounding in my ears.

"I'm being transferred to California," he said. "I want you to go with me."

I jerked away when he tried to touch me.

"I love you," he said.

"Did she tell you he wouldn't even screw me? Isn't that what she told you?"

I picked up the brush, dragged it across the palette, and smeared paint over the face on the canvas. "Go away," I said. I felt sick. "I don't need your pity."

I think I stood there for a long time after he'd left before I actually saw what I'd done to the painting.

I was furious with Trudie. I asked her who the hell she thought she was. *I'm your friend,* she said; *I'm his friend, too.*

The next few days, I began to realize how much time we'd spent together during the past weeks. I began to miss him, badly.

I'd start thinking about Sonny, and end up thinking about Dick. I felt lost; I was lonely in a way I'd never been lonely before. When he hadn't called by the end of the week, I asked Trudie if she'd seen him. She was noncommittal. *Why?* she said. *What's wrong?*

I went to the Catacombs every night whether I was working or not, hoping he might come in.

Finally, one Friday afternoon, I asked Trudie if she knew when he was leaving, if maybe her father had mentioned a date. It had been almost three weeks.

She watched me without saying anything, rubbing the sweat off her Heineken bottle.

"Great," I said. "Forget it."

"When are you going to call Sonny? Get that out of your system?"

"All I asked you was do you know when Dick's leaving."

"Call Sonny first."

"I don't have a number."

"Call the fort, they'll give you a number."

"He could have called me, couldn't he?"

Trudie shook her head. She pushed her chair back, and picked up her beer. "You want some advice?"

"No."

I went home, made a pot of coffee, and tried to paint. I couldn't even do that anymore. I hadn't been to the studio in days; I'd told Joshua I was sick. I tried to read, I paced and stared at the phone. *This is ridiculous,* I told myself.

I picked up the phone and called Dick's office. His secretary told me he was gone.

I could hear the muted clicking of IBMs in the background.

"Hello?" she said. "Are you there?"

"I'm sorry. Would you happen to have his other number?"

"I'm not authorized to give out Mr. Lannom's home number."

"No, I mean his California *office,*" I said.

"He's not in California! I mean he's left *here* for the day." I could hear exasperation in her tone. "May I take a message?"

I pushed the button down, weak with relief. Then I dialed his apartment. I let it ring twelve, thirteen times, and was about to hang up when he answered. "Hello?" He sounded out of breath.

"Dick?"

He didn't say anything. It sounded like he put his hand over the receiver.

"I'm back," he said.

"Are you busy right now?"

"So how've you been?"

"Fine," I lied. "Working hard. I sold two more paintings last week."

"Did you? That's great. Really, that's wonderful." Someone was laughing in the background.

"The same couple bought both of them, didn't even try to get the price down."

"Maybe you should ask more."

I waited, trying to get my voice under control. "You haven't called."

"I thought we left it pretty much settled." It sounded like he put his hand over the receiver again.

"I don't want it to end like this," I said. "Dick? Maybe you could come over?"

"I don't think so."

"Please."

"I've got company."

I was curled into a corner of the couch when I heard him pounding on the door, calling my name. Before I could get the chain off, he'd put his shoulder to it, breaking the chain like a piece of string and throwing me against the wall.

"Some great lock," he said, and slammed the door. "What

do you want?" His voice sounded flat, like whatever it was, he didn't care.

"I'm sorry if I interrupted something," I said.

"Goddamn it, what do you want?"

"When are you leaving?"

He put his hand on the doorknob.

"All right, all right!" I was crying.

He closed the door again and turned around.

"I want to go with you."

I thought he would leave anyway. He looked at me with no change of expression. "Don't play games with me," he said.

"I love you. Take me with you."

I went to him and laid my face against his shirt, put my arms around his waist. I could feel the tremor in his thighs. "Please don't make me beg."

6

We were waiting for the potatoes to bake. Lou sat on the hearth and stared into the fire. All of us were nursing our second drinks, except Clifford. He had the jug. He leaned down and offered it to Lou.

"I don't want any more," she said.

He straightened, a little unsteady on his feet, and planted them wider apart. Dick and Braxton glanced at each other.

"What we need here's a microwave," Clifford said. "Dick could get us one. *You* could get us one, couldn't you?" he said to Trudie. He hoisted the jug, then pushed it at Lou.

"I don't want it," Lou said again.

"Aw, come on, it's a party. Let's have a little fun around here." He was trying to make her take it when Dick took it out of his hand. Clifford blinked, and looked surprised.

"I've got an idea," Trudie said. "Let's cook the steaks." She smiled at Clifford. "Unless you'd like yours raw."

By the time we sat down to dinner, it was after eight o'clock. The men ate like wolves; Lou had been right about allotting them two filets each. She was seated across the table from me and beside Trudie. Dick was on my left, and Clifford at the end of the table to my right. Braxton sat at the other end. I wondered how we'd shuffle the chairs to make a seventh place for Sonny.

Lou kept her eyes on her plate, using her knife and fork to cut small bites of meat. I ate my steak without tasting it and wondered if I should say something first, or wait for her to mention our kinship. I was thinking about Sonny walking through the door any minute. What would we say to each other? And what was she going to think when she found out we grew up together and I hadn't told her? And I hadn't told Dick. I thought about standing on my chair and making an announcement.

"Sarah?"

"What?"

Trudie was watching me. "Pass the salt?"

Clifford and Braxton monopolized the conversation, talking about deer hunting. That held Dick's attention; he didn't want to miss anything that might be helpful in the morning. Without really thinking about it, I was listening for a car door to slam.

Clifford tilted his chair to get at the lighter in his pants pocket. He lit his cigarette and blew out a cloud of smoke. "Let me tell you a little story. It's what these old boys that live around here do."

He wiped a hand over his face as if he were rubbing the grin off. "Lou's only heard this a few hundred times. You don't mind if I tell it again, do you?"

She folded her napkin and laid it beside her plate.

"This same thing happened to Sonny when he first lived here. See, when a hunter gets the first buck of the season, he cuts off the genitals and gives them to the man he most wants to rub it in on. One-upmanship. You follow me?"

Trudie stared as if she couldn't believe she'd heard him right. I couldn't either. Dick and Braxton looked fascinated.

" 'Course, your man's not going to stand there with his hand out while you lay some cock and balls on him." Clifford laughed.

Braxton's well-laid fire hissed in the background, casting drunken shadows on the walls.

"On opening day last year, Sonny went out and got his buck. Took him about an hour. He field-dressed it—laying those goodies aside—tagged it, and drove it in to Buster's. Twelve-pointer, wasn't it, Lou?"

She didn't answer him. She appeared not to be listening, her eyes focused on something outside the room.

He scratched his ear. "Anyway. He had a fair idea where Boyd Holland would be hunting, and sure enough, Sonny finds his pickup pretty close to where he expected, parked in a dry streambed."

He paused to drag on his cigarette. "So he leaves udderboy and his jewels in the middle of Boyd's front seat. Laid it on some plastic to protect the velour—Boyd sets a store by that truck. And one of his arrows so Boyd can't miss who's been there.

"So Boyd pretends it never happened, right? But he knows who did it, and Sonny *knows* he knows and gets a kick out of it every time he sees him.

"In a few weeks then, when it's all blown over, Lou picks up the mail and brings it to the house and asks Sonny what he's ordered from Montgomery Ward. 'Nothing,' he says. 'It's addressed to you,' she says.

"So all curious and unsuspecting, Sonny opens the package that Boyd has dummied up to look real, except for hand-canceling the stamps, which you wouldn't notice unless you looked close."

Clifford had us. He arched back in his chair, making it groan under his weight, and stretched his legs under the table. He waited, smoking, and grinning at the fire.

Trudie finally asked, "Well? What was it?"

He rocked back to the table to stub out his cigarette and leaned directly into her face. "You know, Sonny said he smelled it before he got the paper off." He looked at each of us before coming back to Trudie. "About the time he got the wax paper *all* the way off, he remembered doe season opened the day before."

The men laughed. Trudie shot Braxton a look.

"Boyd Holland's dead," Lou said.

Clifford stopped, the lighter halfway to another cigarette.

"Didn't you know that?" she said.

"You're not kidding, are you?" A look of disbelief was on Clifford's face now.

Her voice was low. "Somebody shot him."

"Holy shit. No, I didn't know."

"The arrow had a pod of that paralyzing drug." She glanced at Braxton. "You probably know what it's called."

"Jesus!" Clifford said.

"It's too dangerous for the average hunter to use," Braxton said. "It shouldn't be legal."

"It's not," Clifford said.

"Sonny says it would be better for the deer if it were, if people could be trusted to use it." She pushed back her chair.

"Do they know who did it?" Dick said.

"No." She stood and placed the chair under the table.

"When did this happen?" Clifford said.

"Opening day. I think I'll get a little air." She took a red windbreaker off the coat rack by the door and went outside.

Clifford cleared his throat. "I wouldn't have told that story if I'd known. Boyd Holland was a real good friend of theirs."

Trudie and I cleared the table. When we'd carried the last load to the kitchen, she set her plates by the sink and turned around. "Are you going to tell me what's going on, or not?"

"Lou Woods is my cousin."

She pushed a strand of hair behind her ear. "Oh. That's nice. Isn't it?"

"She doesn't seem to think so."

Trudie washed her hands at the sink and dried them on a dish towel. "How'd she know you were cousins?"

"I recognized her. What she *doesn't* know yet, is I used to know her husband. You know him, too."

Trudie frowned.

"You've never met him, but you'll remember if you think back."

"Why not just tell me?" But I could see she was trying to get it. "Sonny Woods," she said.

I watched her face. It started in her eyes.

"Right," I said. "That's her husband."

She stared at me. "Does Dick know about this?"

"I haven't even had a chance to tell *her*."

"You knew before we came, didn't you? Does he know *you're* here?" she said.

"Why would he?"

She thought for a minute. "Look, I'll load the dishwasher. You go talk to her, I guess, would be the first thing."

"It's not that big a deal."

"Of course it's not." She didn't sound convinced.

"I mean it was *ages* ago. Don't say anything to Dick yet, okay?"

She just looked at me.

Dick was sprawled in a chair, his feet to the fire. He smiled when I leaned over and kissed him. I took his jacket from the coat rack and went outside.

A damp wind was blowing, its gusts sending maple leaves scuttling across the yard; there was no moon or stars. I could barely make Lou out at the far end of the porch. I shivered and turned up my jacket collar.

As I walked the length of the porch, she kept her back to me, the wind playing with her hair.

When I stopped, she turned around. "It's getting colder," she said. She had her hands tucked into the front pocket of the windbreaker. "This wind will probably blow the clouds past, leave it clear and cold in the morning."

"Will that be good for hunting?" *What are we doing,* I was thinking, *talking about the weather?*

"You'll have to forgive me for acting the way I did. It took me by surprise."

"There's something I meant to tell you," I said.

"Joe and Sonny. Sarah and Joe. Joe and Sarah and Sonny." She looked away into the dark. "Is that what you wanted to tell me?"

I didn't know what to say.

"They used to hunt on us, Sonny and your brother, did you know that?"

"I knew they hunted up here." I hadn't known it was her family's land.

"Listen," she said.

Between the gusts of wind I could hear the distant sound of an engine.

"I don't remember meeting either of them back then," she said. "Carlton does. That's my brother."

Inside, someone switched on a lamp, and the light streamed through the window and across her face. And now car lights flashed through the trees.

"They were best friends," I said.

"Yes, I know." She moved a step closer. "He's told me all about it."

I looked straight into her eyes.

"He's going to be so glad to see you."

The car turned into the drive. We heard the engine shut off and the door close. In the seconds it took him to reach the porch, I had time to remember a thousand things.

He was wearing jeans and a blue chambray shirt, open at the throat, the sleeves rolled up on his forearms. His hair was longer, not the harsh military cut I remembered. A touch of gray at the temples. I held out my hand. "Hello, Sonny."

Recognition flooded his face, and then pleasure. Genuine pleasure, I decided. He covered my hand with both of his. A few seconds passed while we stared at each other. "Lou, this is Sarah Wheatley! You look wonderful," he said to me.

I had tears in my eyes. "So do you."

"My God, this is a nice surprise." He let go of my hand. "Your husband must be . . . is he Clifford's boss?"

"Yes," I said. "Dick Lannom."

"How long has it been, sixteen, seventeen years?"

"A long time," I said.

We were still looking at each other. There was a pause.

"You must be starving," Lou said.

"The steaks were excellent," I said. "We should have waited for you."

"Clifford would have been stone-blind drunk by now," Lou said. "Somebody would've had to shoot him."

Sonny laughed. "Then I'm surprised you didn't wait."

"I'll put your steak on." She glanced at me, then walked to the door, opened it, and went inside.

My heart was suddenly thudding inside my chest. I put my hands in the pockets of Dick's jacket.

"Getting cold," he said.

"Yes, it is."

He waited until I looked at him. "It's good to see you, Sarah. You look just the same as the last time."

7

"Here she is," Dick said. "I was about to come see if something got you."

They were in a circle around the fire—all but Lou. Dick was still in the easy chair, and Braxton and Trudie shared a love seat next to him. Clifford slouched splay-legged on the hearth with his back against the stone, and Sonny was in a straight-back chair pulled close to the fire.

I hung Dick's jacket on the coat rack, then crossed to his side. I felt self-conscious and out of breath. I had intentionally remained out on the porch long enough for him and Sonny to be introduced and have a few minutes to talk.

"Hey!" Clifford said. "Why didn't you and Lou tell us you were kin?"

"We just found out ourselves." I sat on the arm of Dick's chair.

Sonny's legs were crossed on the hearth. "Would it be third or fourth cousins?"

"Third," I said. "I think that's right."

Dick reached around and laid his hand on my hip. "I didn't even know you had relatives up here."

Across from me, Trudie kept her head bent over her needlepoint. "Lou and I only met one time before that I can remember," I said.

I could recall parts of that day like photographs in an album. Certain scenes came back to me in great detail, but they had no continuity. The most vivid image was of Lou in a print dress and bare feet. "I remember my grandfather standing over a black wash kettle of boiling grease, frying fish."

Sonny lifted his boots off the hearth and hitched the chair forward. He reached across and picked up the jug.

"And you remembered Lou after seeing her just that one time?" Clifford said.

"Sarah's an artist," Braxton said.

Sonny took a drink, then offered the jug to Dick.

"I believe I will." He took a drink and balanced the jug on his knee. As far as I knew, this was his first experience with moonshine. "It's amazing how often these things happen."

Sonny nodded, attentive to what Dick was saying. The gray at his temples, a few squint lines around his eyes—other than that, he looked the same, too.

A log burned in half and fell off the andirons. Braxton put his spit-can down and got up, taking the poker from the rack.

"For instance, something that happened when we first moved back to Nashville. Sarah, you remember me telling you about that guy?" Dick set the jug on the floor. His face looked flushed.

"The one at the handball courts," I said.

"I *knew* I'd seen him somewhere, but I couldn't figure out where. And I could tell he was trying to place me, too," Dick said.

Trudie looked at me, then back to her needlepoint.

"So finally, I went over and asked him. Come to find out, we were in the guard together out in Long Beach where I'm from, and then Sarah and I moved back to Nashville where this guy's from. What would be the odds on that?"

"Pretty slim," Clifford said, and yawned.

"Then here we are, we've never met, and it happens our wives are cousins."

I expected him to go on and say, *Not only that, but you and Sarah grew up together*. He didn't.

I looked at Trudie. She shook her head slightly.

The door to the kitchen opened, and Lou backed through it, carrying a tray. There was a potato she'd kept warm in the oven, the steaks, a bowl of salad, bread, and a steaming mug of coffee. Sonny set the coffee on an end table and the tray across his knees. "This looks great," he said. He unsnapped the scabbard on his belt and slipped the knife out. Lou sat on the floor beside his chair, crossing her legs Indian-style.

Why hadn't one of them told him?

"Whee," Clifford sighed. "I'm tighter'n a tick."

Trudie laid the needlepoint down, a square of white daisies on a field of blue and green. She had completed a few of the flowers and about half the background. "We ought to thank you for the steaks," she said.

"You're welcome." Sonny glanced at her, then cut another bite of meat. It looked very rare.

"Yes," Braxton said. "They were good."

"That's pretty," Lou said. "May I see it a minute?"

Trudie handed her the needlepoint.

Lou examined it, touching the raised stitches, and turning it over to look at the back.

"It's simple to do, and it's relaxing," Trudie said.

Clifford leaned against the fireplace, shoes off and legs stretched in front of him. I was suddenly aware of how tense I was, my hands locked together in my lap. Clifford cocked an ear and closed his eyes. "Hear that?"

Braxton quit popping his knuckles.

"Do you hear it?" Clifford said again.

We listened. Sonny held his knife poised over the second filet. "I don't hear anything," Braxton said.

"That's right, I don't either. Not a goddamned thing! No cars rip-shitting by, no TV blaring." Clifford turned to Trudie. "You-all have kids?"

"Two boys," she said. "David's fourteen, Rusty's four."

"They watch much TV?"

"Not a lot," she said. "They're allowed to watch some."

"How do you handle it? You have cable?"

Trudie and Braxton looked at each other. Sonny was eating, and Dick was half-asleep.

"Seriously," Clifford said, scratching the inside of his elbow.

"I'd be interested to know. Seems like we argue all the time at our house."

"We negotiate which shows they can watch, of course," Braxton said. He laughed. "But the other night we came home early from a meeting, and caught them watching *Tattoo*."

"Yeah, I saw that," Clifford said. "That scene where Bruce Dern's about to shoot his wad and she stabs him in the back with the needle."

"If people aren't watching television, they're talking about watching it," Sonny said.

Braxton looked a little nonplussed.

Clifford snickered. "Maybe if I had *that* at home, I wouldn't watch TV either."

Lou was bending over to take the tray. She ignored him.

"I'd like more coffee," Sonny said. When she'd gone, he turned the knife in his hand, looking at it. "Someday, Clifford, you're going to run across somebody who doesn't understand you're harmless."

"Shit, man! Just like on TV!"

Sonny shook his head. He cleaned the knife on his napkin and put it back in the scabbard.

When Lou came back with the coffeepot and extra mugs, I got up to help her. She filled the cups and I passed them around.

Braxton took the mug I handed him and leaned forward, speaking to Sonny. "You don't watch television at all, I take it?"

Sonny blew steam across the top of his cup. "How long has our set been broken, Lou?"

She smiled and shook her head. She was sitting by his chair.

"We haven't missed it much," he said.

"It sounded like you disapproved of it altogether," Braxton said.

"I wouldn't go quite that far."

Lou leaned her head against his knee.

"We have a television hookup with colleges and universities

throughout this whole region, for instance," Braxton said. "You can get college credits via television."

"Is that right?"

"Yes, that's right."

I felt Dick's hand tighten on my thigh; it was Braxton's tone.

"There's some excellent programming on public television."

"Braxton," Trudie said.

"Don't you like any sports? Or watch the news?"

"Why don't we change the subject," Dick said.

Clifford reached for the jug. "Sorry I brought it up."

Braxton refused to let it go. "Clifford mentioned a while ago—I forget exactly how he put it—but that you're opposed to technology."

"Did he really?" Sonny's eyes had changed.

"Now just a fucking minute," Clifford said.

I was amazed at Braxton, and embarrassed for him. Trudie's cheeks were red.

Lou had her hand on Sonny's leg, looking up at him. He took a strand of her hair and coiled it around his finger. Then he smiled at Trudie. "Take those cop shows," he said. "Somebody gets shot with a forty-five-caliber handgun. There's no point of entry, no blood. Your boys watch this, and they think that's how it is, cops and robbers, just like they go out and play it, and with no more damage." He turned to Braxton, still smiling. "Have you ever seen a man shot?"

"No, I haven't, but this doesn't address my point."

"A forty-five slug will carry even a man your size and slam him against the wall. The heart is a pump; until it stops, it'll put out a spurt of blood each time it beats. A man's body holds a lot of blood. The exit wound is huge, and it may be spilling entrails. There are smells, too, quite definite smells. You don't get that on TV."

"Even my four-year-old understands that a TV show is not the real thing," Braxton said.

"Then he can watch the news and see a busload of Jewish

schoolchildren blown up by a bomb. Of course, the footage is sanitized to look just like the cop show. What's the difference?"

"Take the old war movies," Clifford said.

Braxton reached around Trudie and set his cup down. "What about them?"

"I guess you weren't in Nam, were you?" Clifford said, sarcastic.

"What kind of courses do you teach on television?" Sonny said.

"I don't teach any myself. But there's practically no limit to what you *could* teach."

"Could you teach a man how to hunt?" Sonny laughed. "Because I had a college kid today who could have used some instruction."

"What happened?" Dick said.

"The boy's father hired me to help him get his first buck. This morning early, I was taking him in . . ."

"You going to show *us* where you took him?" Clifford said.

"I pushed one down a gulch right at you the last time, and you let him go by."

"That was a doe," Clifford said. "I don't shoot does."

"There were two does, and a buck."

"So what happened?" Lou said.

"It's hard to shoot an *imaginary* buck," Clifford said.

"Will you let him tell this," she said.

"Take it easy." Sonny touched her shoulder. "I was walking in front of him, it was just before daylight, and when I turned around to motion him to move up, he has an arrow notched and about half drawn. He said he thought he ought to be ready."

"Probably somebody just like that shot Boyd," Clifford said. "Hell of a thing."

"I told them," Lou said.

"They got no idea who did it?" Clifford said.

Sonny finished his coffee and set the mug on the hearth. "It was opening day. There were hunters all over the place."

"Surely not many of them would be using a drug like that," Dick said.

"Slow-motion potion," Clifford said.

"It's hard to say; more than you'd like to think, probably. And by the time Boyd was discovered, well, it was the end of the day."

"Who found him?" Clifford said.

"His boy."

"Jesus."

"It gets worse. The choline didn't kill him."

"Succinyl choline chloride," Braxton said.

We ignored Braxton, waiting for Sonny to go on. His eyes met mine and held for an instant before he spoke to Clifford. "The arrow caught him high, in the groin. Severed the femoral artery. The coroner said it looked to him like Boyd tried to brace himself against a tree and apply pressure to staunch the bleeding."

"Hell," Clifford said. "He couldn't . . ."

"Right. He passed out from blood loss. Died in under five minutes." Sonny sat up straighter. "The choline would have killed him, but it takes a little longer."

No one said anything for several moments. Then Clifford said, "Lou, I'm sorry about supper tonight, telling that story."

"Anyway," Sonny said, "that's how his twelve-year-old found him, on his own land, less than five hundred yards from the house."

"What's to keep people from hunting on this land?" Braxton said.

Sonny looked at him. "It's posted."

"Say you decided to bring one of your clients on company land," Braxton continued. "Who's to stop you?"

Dick shifted in the chair. He looked uncomfortable. "Did you know any of the former members here?"

Sonny looked at Braxton a moment longer before he turned

to Dick. "Most of them live around Knoxville. I put up a few stands for them."

"They didn't sell because there was a shortage of game, then?"

Sonny shook his head. "They found it too expensive to maintain. And like Braxton was saying, hard to manage at a distance."

"Are you going hunting in the morning?" Braxton said. "If you located the stands, I guess you know the best spots."

Trudie stood up. She was pale with vivid spots of color in her cheeks, the way she looks when she's angry. "I'm going to call and check on the boys."

Dick stood, too, and took my hand. "We do have to be up early in the morning."

Braxton started to say something else, but Dick cut him off. "Neither one of *us* knows where the stands are, or how to get there."

Clifford was smiling, his arms crossed on his chest. Sonny waited, not saying anything.

"Tell you the truth," Dick said, "this is my first deer hunt."

The tension and strain of the entire day hit me like a fist. *You sweet, brave man,* I thought.

"We'll have to make sure it's a good one then," Sonny said. He stood up and they shook hands, and then Sonny and Braxton shook hands. And then he reached down to Lou and pulled her to her feet beside him.

Clifford stretched, and picked up his shoes. "Say we leave about four o'clock?"

When I came out of the bathroom, Dick was putting his hunting clothes on a chair, with the bow and its quiver of six broadhead arrows propped against it. When he was satisfied he had everything ready, he pulled his shirttail out and sat on the bed.

"You'll do fine," I said. The soft bedside light cast mauve

shadows across his face. "It could be you won't even see a deer."

"Could be."

"You be careful."

"I'm going to get a shot, Sarah. I can feel it."

"Pretend it's a target and shoot the bull's-eye."

He caught my wrists and pulled me down beside him. "Why haven't you ever told me about your cousin?"

"She's kind of beautiful, isn't she?"

"I don't believe I noticed."

"Sure," I said.

"He seems all right, too." Dick was undoing the buttons of my blouse.

Tell him, I thought.

He lowered his voice. "What's with Braxton?"

"I don't know, but I hope Trudie straightens him out."

"You said it." He opened my blouse. "I think he's afraid Sonny may be as good as Clifford says."

Tell him.

"What if I do something dumb, like that kid today?"

"Stop worrying," I said.

"I thought he might as well know I'm a greenhorn."

"A very smart greenhorn, who's been practicing."

"A deer is a *moving* target."

"Stop it," I said. "Stop the worrying."

He reached to unhook my bra. "How would you like to try and make me?"

I decided, after we'd made love, and he was asleep, that it was better I hadn't told him. I'd tell him about Sonny tomorrow. He didn't need anything else on his mind in the morning.

But I wondered why Sonny hadn't said something. Maybe he'd thought I would want to tell Dick myself.

I lay in the dark, thinking, for a long time.

8

Trudie hadn't exactly rejoiced when I told her Dick and I were getting married. I'm sure she felt partially responsible—she had introduced us. She was probably worried for him as well. Their families were friends; their fathers owned stock in the same corporation. It *was* sudden; we had known each other, all told, less than four months.

"Aren't you moving a little fast?" she'd said. "What about Sonny?"

"What about him?" I had made up my mind and nothing was going to change it.

"Don't you think you ought to talk to him, at least? Give him a chance to explain?"

"There's nothing to explain," I said. "He made it perfectly clear. That's over; I'm over him."

"You can love Dick, baby, and still not be over Sonny. If you don't talk to him, you're always going to wonder."

"No," I'd said.

No way.

I didn't know whether she'd told Dick her concerns or not, but I doubted it. She knew how I'd felt the other time, after she'd talked to Dick about Sonny; it had almost cost our friendship. And even if she'd tried, he wouldn't have listened. He was confident I loved him, and so was I.

I didn't want any of the trappings, no showers or teas. My old friends in Cedar Point didn't know Dick, and I didn't want to have to answer any questions about what had happened to Sonny. Dick's job in California started in a matter of days. We decided to get married immediately.

Trudie threw us an engagement party at the Catacombs. Joshua was there, and several people from Dick's office. Trudie and Jake weren't getting along too well by then, but they made an effort for the sake of the occasion.

Joe called me on a MARS line after he'd gotten my letter, and wished us the best of luck. He didn't mention Sonny. "You love this guy?" he'd said.

I told him I did. It was hard to hear him, and I kept forgetting to say "Over."

"You haven't known him long," he said.

"I love him," I said. "I think I've learned what love isn't. Over."

"I want you to be happy, Sis. I wish I could be there. Over."

I mustn't cry, I told myself; there wasn't time on an overseas hookup for tears. "I wish you could, too. I miss you so much. Are you all right? Over."

He'd assured me he was fine.

"You be careful," I told him. "And don't worry about me. You'll like him, Joe, I know you will. Over."

We were married at city hall by a justice of the peace, with Trudie as our witness.

After the ceremony, we drove to Cedar Point and told my parents; it was the first time they'd met Dick. As far as they had known, I still had a "crush" on Sonny. Under the circumstances, they took it pretty well. Mother got out the silver tray and the best china and served coffee in the living room. She kept refilling his cup and crumpling paper napkins in her hands.

He and my father discussed how long it would take us to drive to California and the advantages of taking I-40 over the northern route. I was afraid Dad was going to break down; he kept clearing his throat and blinking. He was losing two children in a matter of weeks, both of them to faraway places.

That evening I dropped by the studio and said good-by to Joshua, maybe the hardest parting of all.

Dick's parents were as surprised as mine, but they seemed pleased and happy for us. They were glad to have their son back in Long Beach.

We'd been married a few weeks when we agreed that neither of us was satisfied using prophylactics. I asked his mother to recommend a gynecologist so I could get a prescription for the Pill. She gave me the name of her own doctor, and during the examination, he discovered that one of my ovaries was enlarged; he ordered a series of X rays.

Dr. Medgers was a thin jovial man with a slight lisp. "I'm almost positive it's a benign tumor," he said. "It's called a *teratoma*. It contains various kinds of embryonic tissue, such as hair and teeth, which is why it shows up on an X ray, don't you see." He waited, rocking from his heels to the balls of his feet, giving me time to absorb all this before he went on.

"Had your body developed differently as an embryo, those cells might have matured into an identical twin. At any rate, I'm afraid it'll have to come out; it's destroyed your entire left ovary."

I had been too stunned to ask any questions of him then, but later, I looked up *teratoma* in a medical dictionary. The base word is *terato*, from the Greek. It means *monster*.

Poor Dick, who was trying to get the hang of a new job, would fight his way each evening through the traffic to my hospital room. I'd look at myself when it was time for him to come, comb my hair, put blush on my pale cheeks. I'd place the mirror back in the drawer and lie there, waiting for him and thinking about the thing they'd taken out of me.

"Nature gives us two of most things, Sarah, in case we should lose one," Dr. Medgers told me. "You'll be able to have a dozen children, if you want them."

But he was wrong. When I stopped taking the Pill, we tried to have children. We tried for years. I kept charts, I took my temperature morning and night for months. I lay perfectly still after lovemaking, cradling Dick's sperm inside me. Dick suggested we have fertility tests, but I knew it was pointless—*he* hadn't seen the horror they'd taken out of me: a ball of bone and hair and teeth, one fully formed finger, and a tiny sightless eye.

I had to face it: I would never bear him a child. I would never bear anything other than that twisted clot of flesh I had carried from my own mother's womb.

9

Dick shut off the alarm before it rang and eased out from under the covers, careful not to wake me. I had been awake for some time, but I let him think I was asleep. Even to wish him luck might seem to indicate that I thought he was going to need it. I let him dress and think his early-morning thoughts alone, while silently I hoped he would get his deer, that it would be a respectable buck, and that he would kill it well.

After I heard Clifford's Jeep start up and drive away, I showered and dressed. Moving quietly in the kitchen, I made a fresh pot of coffee and filled a thermos. I was glad that Trudie and Lou were still sleeping; I didn't feel like talking yet.

I wanted to get away by myself for a while. I put the thermos and a couple of apples into the canvas tote that held my drawing supplies and was standing on the front porch at sunrise. The men should already be in the stands by now.

As I leaned against the pillar where Lou had stood last night, and breathed in the sharp mountain air, I thought it was going to be one of those fall days of cobalt blue sky and intensely clear light that is such a beautiful light for drawing.

About three-quarters of a mile from the lodge, I remembered, through woods reasonably free of underbrush, there was a small clearing near the top of a hill. Below was a swift mountain creek cutting at the hill's base. It was a spot Dick and I had discovered last summer when he was trout fishing, and I'd thought of it again this morning. I had my folding camp stool and my canvas tote. I was dressed in jeans and a sweater with insulated socks inside my hiking boots. I wore a down jacket to protect me from the morning chill.

I crossed a meadow to reach the hill I had to climb. It felt good to be out early, the clean, cold air scouring my lungs.

In California, after I was finally resigned that there would be no children, I'd decided I wanted to live near the ocean, and though it meant Dick had to drive farther to work, he said he didn't mind. We sold the tri-level with the playroom and the nursery and moved to a beachfront cottage. There in the early mornings, I'd carry my blank white canvases to the shore of the Pacific, and sit at my easel, staring at the sea. I loved the sounds and smells of the ocean, the colors. I wanted to get them down, faithfully.

In the evenings, I'd scrape the paint off the canvases with a palette knife, destroying painting after painting, and little pieces of myself. I knew it hurt Dick, seeing me do this, and sometimes I meant to hurt him. If I could tell from his expression that he particularly liked something, I'd watch his face as the knife came down, taking off a wave or a patch of gray sky. On some of the canvases, under layers of gesso, there were as many as fifteen aborted paintings. When, at last, I stopped trying to paint it, the Pacific did give me peace.

Many evenings, I'd walk down to the docks to see the boats bring in the day's catch. There was a retired fisherman who'd often watch, too, leaning against the rail. His hair was thick and white under his seaman's cap; his skin was the color of chamois. He'd tell me the names of the fish and how they were caught, and when he'd point something out to me, I could see exactly what he'd have looked like young. He reminded me of Joe. Joe might have looked like this if he'd had the chance to grow old.

We'd watch the unloading together, the sun going down in the ocean, and he'd tell me stories. While he talked, I'd open my book and sketch portrait after portrait in that extraordinary evening light. These I didn't destroy.

I looked around for the best place to set the camp stool, settling on a spot that overlooked a still pocket of water. I balanced the sketchbook on my knees with the morning sun at my back and the Prismacolor pencils within reach at my feet. A haze swirled on the top of the stream. It was remarkably quiet.

After about an hour, I rested a while. I stood and stretched, then opened the thermos and poured the top full of coffee. I warmed my hands around it as the rising sun warmed my back.

I shook the last drops of coffee from my cup and recapped the thermos. I began drawing in finer details, blending and softening with a kneaded eraser. I tried to work patiently, but it wasn't taking shape as I wanted it to, and I had to resist the impulse to snatch the page from the book and wad it into a ball. I couldn't seem to concentrate. Then I heard something behind me, twigs snapping and leaves being scuffled.

I saw who it was, and knew he'd meant for me to hear him, or I wouldn't have; he stopped at the edge of the clearing and leaned his bow against a tree. I turned back to my paper, holding the pencil too tight.

For a minute or so, he stood behind me, watching over my shoulder. Then he sat on his heels beside me and pointed to the lower left quadrant of the page. I looked from the drawing to the streambed where the water ran quickest over the rocks. Instantly, I could see what had been bothering me about the drawing; the water was wrong, too static. I shut the book so fast I almost caught his fingers.

"It's not *that* bad," he said, laughing.

I leaned over and started picking up the pencils, trying to fit them into the box. "It's just a rough sketch." I dropped a pencil; there seemed to be too many all of a sudden. "Aren't you deer hunting?" I said.

"Have you seen any?" He was picking up the rest of the pencils.

"Deer? No, I haven't."

"Here, let me."

He took the box and neatly fitted the pencils in it. He was wearing the blue chambray shirt from last night, a pair of torn and stained hunting pants, and a bright orange vest. I wondered that he wasn't cold. Even with the sun on my back, my jacket felt good.

"Is that coffee in there?"

—

While I was pouring it, he stretched out beside the camp stool, resting his weight on an elbow, one leg straight in front of him, the other cocked at the knee. "I crossed your trail and thought I'd better see who it was. It's getting dangerous not to."

I gave him the cup.

"Then I watched you frowning over that picture. Looked like you were mad at it."

I had picked up the box of pencils and was turning them over and over in my hands. I made myself put them down. "I'm sorry about your friend." I wondered how long he had been there without my knowing it.

"Yeah. It was too bad about Boyd."

Then neither of us said anything for a while. He sprawled there, drinking the coffee and staring off into the trees. I took a No. 2 pencil out of the tote and opened the book to a blank page, my hands needing something to do. He reached for the thermos to refill his cup. "Do you mind?" I said, when he saw what I was doing. "You can talk, but turn your head back the way it was."

I think he realized it was easier for me like this, something like having him on a leash. He talked a lot about deer hunting; maybe he was a little nervous, too. He said he had found a couple of scrapes that had probably been made by larger bucks, because of the size of the spots, and the distance between them—I didn't know what he was talking about. He hoped his moving through the woods might have turned some deer toward the stands.

I had started with his right eye. Every artist has his own starting point with a portrait, and that is mine. I construct the rest of the face from there, working outward. While he talked and leaned on an elbow with his hands folded at his waist, my pencil reproduced his features, tracing along the line of his jaw and throat and into the contour of his shoulders. His olive skin lay taut across his cheekbones. There was a scar disappearing into his hairline that had not been there before, but his eyes were the same clear gray, capable of becoming lighter or darker, depending on his mood.

"Deer will drink just about anywhere there's water, at creeks and springs. Livestock ponds."

"Really?" I said.

"Walking a creekbed like this, I was nearly shot once, mistaken for a deer." He picked up a twig and started breaking it into small pieces. "That's probably what happened to Boyd."

"Someone thought he was a deer?"

"Someone took a sound shot."

"Turn your head back." I was excited by how well the sketch was going.

"It wasn't quite daylight, and I had on camouflage. I was walking down in the creekbed, pretty high banks on either side. I wasn't making much noise, but not *trying* to be quiet, and I hear this little metal click. Once you've heard that sound, you never forget it. I hit the ground with my nose in the dirt."

I used the pencil tip to check distances—the distance between his eyes, between temple and hairline, between nostril and the curve of his upper lip.

"I hugged the ground, keeping my head down, and I yelled, 'Hey! Hey!' Nothing. No answer. And I know somebody's out there, and I *know* he can hear me—hold it a minute." He sat up and scratched between his shoulder blades, then lay back again.

"What did you do?"

"At first I thought I'd stumbled across somebody's still. I crawled as close to the bank as I could get, trying to fix in my mind where the sound of that rifle bolt had come from. I sure didn't like it that he wouldn't answer me. 'All right,' I said. 'Either you talk, or I start shooting at where I *think* you are, and we'll see how close I can come.'

"All I had was a bow. Finally, he spoke up and said he thought I was the game warden and he'd lost his tag. He was hoping I'd go on past. We talked a little more. He said he was hunting alone, wanted to know if I was. By then it was starting to get light, and I was worrying about getting out of there before it was light enough for him to see that I wasn't carrying a rifle."

"You can move now." I was almost finished; I couldn't believe how good it was. "I don't understand," I said.

He sat up.

I was adding a line here, darkening one there. I had gotten it all, even the scabbard and knife, and the suggestion of his bow against the sycamore in the background. "Why would it matter?"

"When he chambered the shell, he was going to shoot."

"I know, but . . ."

"At a sound, *assuming* it was a deer. If I hadn't yelled, he would have shot me."

"Yes, but . . ."

"It embarrassed him."

"Well, it should have."

"Maybe enough to go ahead and shoot me."

"Oh, come on," I said.

"No, he was thinking about it. You can tell what people are thinking sometimes."

I met his gaze for an instant, then looked back to the drawing.

"So I thought I'd see who you were." He paused. "We wouldn't want any poachers on company land."

"Braxton's not usually like that."

He didn't say anything.

I didn't know if I should but I went ahead and said it anyway. "I think he feels intimidated."

"I showed your husband the best stand. Maybe he'll have some luck."

"I hope so. Thank you. It is competitive, isn't it?"

He glanced at me.

"I mean who gets the first deer, the best deer."

"Sometimes." He picked up another stick, breaking it into pieces and throwing them away.

"Why *aren't* you hunting? Not because of what Braxton said? Dick would feel awful."

He shook his head. "I didn't come to hunt. When I take a deer now, it's for food or advertisement." He tossed the last piece away. "If I get a good rack, a friend of mine mounts it and hangs it at his hunting camp. It's good business for both of us."

"I see," I said.

"Lou needed a break from her mother."

I was thinking about that, and he was quiet, staring at the stream. "So where's Joe now?"

When I didn't answer, he turned, his eyes questioning.

"Oh, God," I said. "You don't know? Sonny, Joe's dead. He died in Vietnam."

10

Dick and I had been married about seven months when Dad called to tell us Joe was missing. He'd been flying what was supposed to have been a routine bombing mission to soften up a landing zone. The area was hot, the way the officer who came to tell them explained it, much hotter than anticipated; the planes had taken heavy fire, and Joe's was hit. There were preliminary reports from another pilot that one or more parachutes might have been sighted.

They landed a helicopter at the crash site the next morning but couldn't determine whether Joe and his copilot had died in the wreckage or not. Pieces of his OV-10 Bronco were scattered over half a mountainside overlooking the valley. His body might have been incinerated, or spread over half a mountainside as well. They didn't find any parachutes.

Joe was officially listed as Missing in Action. Eventually, of course, that was amended to Presumed Dead. Even then, my parents were haunted by hope. *Presumed* dead is not final enough.

After the first four or five years, I stopped hoping he was alive. If he had to be dead, I preferred to think of him vaporized when his plane exploded, in an instant of painless light. My beautiful blond American brother in a North Vietnamese prison, or worse—I couldn't "hope" for that any longer. So in my mind, I killed him. After they'd brought the others home and he wasn't among them, I prayed he was dead. It's a terrible thing—not to know.

But now, for Sonny, it was as if Joe had just died. And having to tell him the details was bringing it all back to me.

"They told us he radioed when he was hit," I said. "And somebody in another plane thought he saw a parachute, maybe two. They wouldn't tell us who the somebody was. I never have understood that."

Sonny was standing with his back to me, his fists jammed in his pockets.

"That's all we ever knew. A couple of months, and his tour would have been over."

"I was in Washington when they dedicated the monument," he said. "Have you seen it?"

"No. I don't think I want to."

"So many slabs of black stone . . ."

I stared at his back and waited.

"I couldn't get over how many it took just to hold all the names. I was going to look for a few myself—guys in my squad—find out if they made it home." He laughed. "This is crazy, but standing there, I was thinking maybe if I didn't see their names, they wouldn't be dead. It never crossed my mind to look for Joe's."

He turned his head in profile. "How many times over the years I've thought about him, and I could *see* him, behind a desk, or arguing a case. I kept expecting to hear his name in the state legislature." He turned and faced me. "That was it? There wasn't anything more about the parachutes?"

"He told me you advised him to carry a pistol, and use it if it came to that. I used to wonder if he'd have been able to. I used to wonder whether he'd think about it too long. I'd read these awful stories about prison camps . . ."

"I guess I thought your mother had told you." I wiped at my eyes. "How *are* your folks?"

"Mom lives in Florida with her sister now. They've got a little house on Ft. Walton Beach. He's dead."

He instead of *father*.

"Yours?"

"They're fine," I said. "Still in Cedar Point, same house."

"I ought to go see them."

"They'd love to see you." My throat ached. "But they'd

make you go through it all again, asking you questions. What it was like over there, everything about Vietnam. When you and Joe were kids—they'd want to relive all that." I was too warm. I stood and took off my jacket. "They dwell on the past too much," I said.

He took the jacket and laid it carefully on the ground. The movement of his body through the still morning air brought me his scent, and the faint gamey scent of his hunting pants. He and Joe never allowed their hunting clothes to be washed; they'd wear them stained with the blood of birds and animals until thorns and briars had torn them past wearing.

He was looking at something over my shoulder. "You remember that fox horn of Joe's?"

It had belonged to my grandfather, and to his father before him—a beautiful thing, gracefully curved, almost translucent, and the mouthpiece exquisitely scrimshawed.

"That's the one thing I ever envied him." He glanced at me. "Well, *that's* not true."

"Dad gave it to Dick. *His* way of giving up hope."

He nodded. "Pass it down to your children."

"I can't have children."

He nodded again. Something sparkled in his lashes.

"You?" I said. "Any kids?"

He shook his head. He took a deep breath and rested his hands on his hips. We stood in a small clearing in the Appalachian Mountains, both of us needing very much to cry. Trapped in our separate and common pasts, and hemmed in by questions neither of us would bring up.

He was still looking away into the trees behind me. "They fox hunt quite a bit up here, you know. Lou's brother has some hounds." He coughed. "Anyway, he had a horn that reminded me of Joe's, when I first came up here, after they let me out of the hospital."

"I didn't know your wound wasn't healed." I was stunned, thinking back to that night in my apartment.

"I wasn't wounded. It wasn't a wound, I mean." There was an odd expression on his face. "Come on, Sarah. Joe told you why I was in the hospital."

"Joe didn't tell me anything," I said.

We stared at each other. Somewhere overhead, a squirrel was barking.

"That's where I spent my last four months in the army. You mean Joe didn't tell you?"

He could see the answer in my face.

"I checked myself into the psycho ward." He lifted his hand as if to touch me. "I was scared you'd wake me during the night and I wouldn't remember in time who you were."

"No," I said.

"When I wasn't doped up too much I kind of wondered why you didn't come to see me. After I kicked the Thorazine, I called you. Your phone had been disconnected.

"I caught a bus to Nashville. You remember my old man had sold my car. I had one hell of a time finding Trudie's apartment."

No. I was shaking my head.

"She wasn't home, so I waited on her front steps. I don't remember for how long. It didn't matter, they trained us to wait, too. I knew when Trudie got back, she could tell me where to find you."

I sank to the ground, my legs wouldn't hold me. Trudie knew about this, had known all these years?

He knelt on one knee in front of me. "She told me you'd just gotten married."

Then he stood, and crossed the clearing and picked up the bow. And walked off through the trees.

I kept starting at the beginning and going through it again and again, always arriving at the same wall and no way around it: I hadn't known because Joe hadn't told me.

Losing a brother was supposed to have been enough. Was I to lose the memory I had of him, too? If Sonny was telling the truth, and I knew he was—there was no doubt in my mind—then Joe had withheld information that belonged to me, that might have changed my entire life.

Sitting there thinking about it, the best I could come up with was that if he hadn't told me, then he must have thought he had a good reason. And what about Trudie? What were her reasons?

The thought of trying to explain this to Dick made me feel weak; it had gone past simple explanations. If it was possible, I would get through the remainder of the weekend without him having to know anything about it.

And there was Sonny, and what he had to have believed all these years. And there was this: he *had* loved me.

What in God's name was I supposed to do with that now? What can you do about things that happened seventeen years ago?

It was past nine o'clock; I had to go back to the lodge eventually.

11

I suppose my plan, if I had one, was to avoid Sonny as much as possible. I expected the men to be hunting most of the day, and at night, they would be tired. I could plead a headache and go to bed early myself.

I went in through the back door, into the kitchen. Trudie and Lou were sitting at the counter drinking coffee, their breakfast plates in front of them. The lingering smell of sausage made me realize I hadn't eaten. They turned their heads when the door opened, and my face must have passed inspection.

"Aren't you the early bird. Where've you been?" Trudie said.

"Just some sketching." I laid the canvas tote down and stood in front of the glowing coils of the wall heater. After where I'd been, and what I'd just learned, the ordinary warmth of the kitchen brought tears to my eyes. I turned my back and held my hands to the heat. "That sausage smells good," I said.

"I'll fix you some," Lou said, and started to get up.

"No, I'll do it," I said. "I just want to thaw out first and go to the bathroom."

Trudie laughed. "That reminds me. I wonder if Braxton remembered his jug—not the one he drinks out of!" She and Lou seemed comfortable with each other, breakfasting, and lingering over coffee. There was Trudie's needlepoint from last night and another piece on the counter between them. I guessed Trudie had been showing Lou how to do the stitches. "What's a *woman* supposed to do?" Trudie said. She pushed her hair behind her ear. "I hadn't actually thought about this before, but Braxton's been after me to sit in the stand with him. What if *I* had to go?"

Lou picked up her cup. "You take along a mason jar. A wide-mouth mason jar."

"You're kidding," Trudie said. "I mean, when you hunt with Sonny?"

Lou laughed. She was wearing a creamy cable-knit sweater, which looked wonderful with her hair and skin. And with those green eyes. "I used to go with him more than I do now. He *used* to have more patience." She took a sip of coffee and smiled at me. "You know how it is when you're courting. Anything you do is all right, they think it's cute. He'd help me climb down out of the stand so I could go behind a bush. Now I just try and hold it."

"There's no way I could hold it," Trudie said.

"Well, you have to be so still," Lou said. "And not make any noise. Sonny can sit for hours without batting an eyelash." She shook her head, smiling. "He told me one time if there'd been any deer in the county, they were gone by the time I got through."

"Biology is destiny," Trudie said.

Lou turned to me. "You want a cup of coffee?"

"I'll be right back," I said. "I *do* have to go to the bathroom now."

I left them talking and laughing, and walked down the hallway. I would take it one minute at a time. Trudie and Lou were getting along fine. We'd talk girl-talk and have huge meals ready for our husbands when they came in.

When I got back to the kitchen, they had their heads together, looking at something on the counter.

It was my sketchbook, open to Sonny's portrait.

I'm not secretive about my work, certainly not anything in my sketchbook. Occasionally I'll drape a canvas I'm working on, particularly at the critical point when someone's inadvertent comments might ruin my perspective of it.

Once, Joshua was working on a painting of the dark side of childhood, when a dear sweet lady from the Arts Council stumbled into the studio, lost. She had looked at the child on the canvas, with its face like an angel out of hell, and said, "Oh, isn't she just adorable!" Joshua had quietly cut the painting to ribbons.

There are times when a work-in-progress ought not to be shown. But generally the sketchbook contains my exercises. Trudie knows this; she's always been free to thumb through it, which is what she must have been doing this morning, in all innocence, and showing it to Lou.

I had forgotten about the sketch of Sonny being in there. I'd had more pressing things on my mind.

Trudie turned around first.

I smiled; it was probably a grimace, but I was trying. "Do you like it?" I said. "I did it this morning."

"I didn't think you'd mind if I showed Lou some of your sketches," Trudie said. She looked stunned.

"Of course not. Do you like it?" I said.

I crossed to the counter and poured myself a cup of coffee. My hand was steady. "Sonny almost scared me to death this morning."

Lou had been looking at the drawing; now she looked at me.

You can focus on the middle of someone's forehead and give the impression of looking them straight in the eyes. I did that now; I could no more have met her direct gaze than I could have flown. "He said he was hoping to move some deer toward the stands."

Lou touched the page, careful not to smudge the drawing. "You're very good," she said.

Sonny's eyes looked back at us. The drawing was good, maybe one of the ten best I have ever done. It was not overworked, the strokes were bold. And it was more than representational; it almost breathed. "I want you to have it," I said to Lou. "I have some fixative in the bedroom."

"Had he . . . seen any deer?" Trudie said. Lou was still staring at the drawing.

"He said he'd seen some scrapes, or pawings. Whatever those things are," I said. I sipped my coffee.

—

"How long did it take you to do this?" Lou said.

"Oh, I don't know. Not long. He told me hunting stories while I drew. He told me someone almost shot him once."

"That's comforting," Trudie said.

"Yes, isn't it? That's why he came to see who I was when he crossed my trail." *That's enough,* I thought; *that's enough explanation.* "Here," I said. "Let me spray that with finish."

I carefully tore the page from the book and took it to the bedroom. I dug through my box of supplies, found the spray can and some masking tape, and sprayed the pencil portrait of Sonny. While I waited for it to dry, I admitted to myself how much I would have liked to keep it. In the kitchen, I rolled it in another piece of paper, secured that with a piece of tape, and handed it to Lou.

"Thank you," she said.

I told her she was welcome.

I couldn't imagine what she was thinking. Oh, but I could. She took the drawing and smiled and said she'd be right back. Down the hall, we heard the door to their bedroom close.

I opened the refrigerator and got out the sausage. I unwrapped two of the patties and slapped them in a pan that had already been used. While the sausage cooked, I made myself some toast. I had no idea in the world how I was going to be able to swallow it. Trudie sat and watched me.

"Quit looking at me," I said.

"Do you think she believed you?"

I didn't answer her.

"He told you, didn't he?"

"You're goddamn right he told me. A lot of things somebody else should have told me a long time ago." I got a plate out of the cabinet. I ripped off a paper towel and drained the sausage on it. I sat down at the counter with my breakfast.

Trudie tented her fingers over her mouth. She massaged the bridge of her nose. "Sarah, I couldn't."

"It was mine to know!" I said.

"For what! You'd been married less than a month!"

"Keep your voice down," I said.

She took a breath. "Eat your breakfast."

I stared at the plate in front of me. The food disgusted me. "He didn't know Joe was dead. When I told him, he almost cried."

Trudie swallowed and looked away.

"I want to know everything that *you* know. Every word he said."

She shook her head. "There's no point in it."

When I laughed, I sounded hysterical even to myself. "It's too late for that, believe me."

"What else happened out there this morning?"

"You first," I said.

She glanced behind her. "Eat your breakfast," she said again, softly. "You didn't eat enough supper last night to keep a mouse alive." She caught herself twisting her hands. "Then we'll go somewhere, and talk."

12

Trudie apologized about the sketchbook.

"Forget it," I said. "There was no way you could have known."

Now she was saying, "When we got to that page, both of us gasped like fish. The first thing I thought was, when did you do this? God knows what *she* was thinking."

We were in the bedroom. Trudie sat in the armchair where Dick had laid his clothes last night, and I sat on the side of the bed. Last night seemed light-years ago. I sat with my knees together and my hands clasped in my lap. My breakfast was a stone in my stomach. "I want to know one thing first," I said, "and then I want the rest of it. Did she say anything to you this morning?"

"Like what?" Trudie said.

I waited.

"All right, we did the what-a-surprise, what-a-coincidence business. I did get the feeling she knew there was something between you and Sonny once. But she didn't seem particularly concerned." Trudie thought a minute. "Until I got the bright idea to show her some of your sketches."

"I know," I said. I rubbed my temples; I was getting a headache.

She leaned closer. "It was rather *inspired-looking*, wouldn't you say?"

"Cut it out," I said. Now my forehead felt like it might split down the center.

"What have you told Dick?"

I shook my head. "Not until we get home. Then I'll tell him."

"What if Sonny tells him?"

"He won't."

At least, I didn't think he would. It was a confusing mess, and ought to have been funny, except it wasn't. Joe's death kept it from being funny; and what Sonny had told me wasn't the least bit funny. I'd have a hard time ever laughing about that. "If Sonny was going to say anything to Dick, he would have said it last night. Why do you think I stayed outside so long?"

"All right," Trudie said. "What about *her*?"

"I don't know, I don't know." I got up and went into the bathroom for some aspirin. I took three and drank a glass of water. "I can't think," I said when I came back.

"Other than Braxton's being such a butthole last night," Trudie said, "everything else seemed fine. A little tense, maybe, but not too bad. Whatever happened out there this morning is what's got you so upset, isn't it?"

Trudie leaned back in the chair and crossed her arms and legs. She was wearing a long-sleeved sweatshirt and baggy pants, with argyle socks and flats; she looked both fashionable and comfortable. Her long hair was glossy, her long nails polished; she was well-groomed and composed, while I felt myself coming apart. For an instant, I hated her.

I was hurt and furious—with the situation, with the frustration of not knowing how to handle it, with the feeling of guilt for circumstances which had never been under my control, and yet for which I still, even now, felt responsible. Perhaps just because she was there, the nearest one to take it out on, I was furious with Trudie.

"Sarah, if you won't tell me, how can I help?"

But there *was* her part in it, I thought. She had introduced Dick and me, and she had told him about Sonny, or at least, that there was *someone* I was getting over, which may have been the only reason Dick had the patience to hang around long enough for us to fall in love. What if she hadn't done those things? *What in God's name are you thinking,* I asked myself.

I lay back on the bed, and put an arm across my forehead. "When did we first hear about Vietnam vets having flashbacks?"

I said. "Or about post-traumatic stress disorder? Or Agent Orange?"

"I don't know," she said. "Why?"

"It's only been a few years. The government still won't officially recognize the effects of Agent Orange."

"I'm not following you."

"I don't think we even started calling them 'baby killers' until after My Lai."

Trudie started to say something, and I waved her to silence. "I'm trying to tell you," I said. And I was trying to imagine it for myself, what it must have been like for him, coming home straight from hell.

"I know you've heard this before," I said, "but think about the war movies we grew up on. Gary Cooper gets off the plane in his dress blues and runs straight for June Allyson's arms. Or John Wayne does. Or Tab Hunter does. In the movies, all the ones who came home, came home winners and swept somebody into their arms." I'd known wars weren't like in the movies. All except for that last part.

I waited with my arm across my eyes. I wondered how long it would be before the men got back. Finally, I turned my head to look at her. "Tell me it was seventeen years ago, and it doesn't matter any longer. But this morning, he told me *why* he couldn't . . . love me."

Trudie put her head against the back of the chair and closed her eyes. I remembered how she had begged me to call him.

"Joe was supposed to have told me some things," I said. "He didn't tell me anything." I wasn't crying, actually, but tears ran from the corners of my eyes and into my hair.

Her eyes were open now, staring at the ceiling. "Joe was supposed to have told you some things."

"Yes," I said.

"Sonny shouldn't be telling you now. You do realize that?" she said.

I thought about it. Maybe she was right, but she couldn't

know how it had been. "He didn't even know Joe was dead."

"What happens now?"

"Nothing." I sat up. "It's just sad is all."

She had her feet tucked under her, watching me.

"Joe had been alive, for Sonny, for seventeen years; now he's dead all over again. Does that make any sense?"

She nodded, cautiously, I thought.

It was quiet then for a while, she in the chair, I on the bed, both of us trying to sort through it. I had a constant nagging in the back of my mind that we needed to be in the kitchen preparing a meal for the men. It's funny how nothing takes precedence over the habits of a lifetime.

Finally, I put a pillow between me and the headboard and crossed my arms over my chest. "All right," I said. "You can see now that I have to know all of it."

"I don't like this," she said.

"I don't like it either, but I have to know all of it now. I know you thought you were doing what was best for me. So did Joe, and look what happened. Why not let me decide this time?"

Trudie had been in a business meeting till late afternoon. She'd grabbed a quick supper and shopped until the stores closed at ten. Christmas was just around the corner.

She hadn't turned on her porch light when she'd left that morning, not expecting to be so late getting home. So she was startled, then frightened, when she approached the steps of her townhouse, carrying an armload of packages, and someone reared up in the dark in front of her. She stumbled, backing away, dropping packages in an attempt to get a grip on her car keys, or anything sharp.

In the weak light from the street lamp, about all she could distinguish was that it was a man lurking on her steps. He did not reach out to grab her.

"I'll scream bloody murder," she said. She had found the keys.

"My name is Sonny Woods," he said. "I'm trying to find Sarah."

Instantly, she recognized who he was. Not the name so much, as she had soon forgotten that, but the enormity of what it was he wanted.

"I'm sorry I scared you," he said, and stooped to pick up a package.

She said the first thing that came into her head. "You must be freezing." It was cold; she was shivering inside her fur coat. Together, they picked up the rest of the packages. When he stood with the last one, he was close enough that she could see his face. And for a few seconds, she gripped the keys tight again. "Come inside," she said.

He was dressed in civilian clothes that fit him badly, a sport shirt and chinos. His jacket was too lightweight for the season. When she took it from him to hang in the foyer closet with her coat, she pushed the thermostat beside the door to eighty.

"Make yourself comfortable," she said. "I'll put on a pot of coffee." She had a bottle of Bacardi to lace it with, to take the blue tinge from his lips.

He followed her into the kitchen. "I guess she's moved to another apartment," he said.

She filled the percolator with water and measured the coffee. "How long were you out there waiting?" she said. "How did you get here? I didn't see a car." Please, she thought, let me get some coffee and rum in you first.

She leaned against the counter and smiled. In his eagerness, he stood too close. He was much too thin for his height of six-one or two and there was something manic about his eyes. She would think later that he looked like a prisoner of war, just home. She would think, seventeen years later when she saw him, that he was so changed she wouldn't have recognized him. At the time, he frightened her. And she felt sorrow for what she must tell him.

He had put his hands in his pockets. He watched her face. "I took the bus," he said.

The last bus to her neighborhood ran three hours ago. She made herself meet his gaze without looking away. There was the beginning of understanding in his eyes; he knew it would not be good news. She indicated the breakfast table. "Sit down, the coffee will be ready in a minute."

While she got the cups, the cream and sugar, finally the rum, he watched her. Without asking him, she poured a generous dollop into his cup, and hers, then filled them with coffee. She carried the tray to the table and set it down.

"May I use your bathroom?" he said.

She told him where it was: at the top of the stairs, the door to the right and straight ahead. He was prepared to hear something, she could tell. But not what she had to tell him, not that Sarah was married and living in California. That might be too much to expect in the few months since he'd last seen her.

When he came down the stairs, she waited until he pulled the chair out and sat down. She had started to carry the tray into the living room where the chairs were more comfortable, and the distance between them was greater. But she had thought better of it.

"Where is she?" he said.

"California." She waited until he'd had time to take that much, watching him understand, the disappointment that Sarah wasn't somewhere in Nashville, nearby, and then the relief. That's not so bad, California, he'd be thinking. He could take the next flight out. "Drink some coffee," she said. "You look frozen."

"Where in California?" Obediently, he picked up the cup and drank. She waited until he put it down.

"Long Beach. Sonny, she's married."

He heard, and first, of course, rejected what he'd heard as impossible. And then he understood.

She nodded.

His hand around the cup began to tremble, rattling the

china pieces against each other; he locked both hands between his knees. Once again, he looked to her, in his eyes a prayer that it would be a joke, a lie. Then he began to rock, bent almost double in the chair. Oh sweet Jesus, she thought, why didn't you call her?

She found herself rocking along with him, as he embraced the pain, holding it clenched and hard against him.

She talked to him, gently, quietly, trying to answer what he was unable to ask; trying to cover as best she could the awful sounds of his breathing. She told him Sarah was happy. She told him Dick was a wonderful man who loved her very much, and who would take good care of her. That he must try and understand. That after that weekend . . .

She wasn't sure how long they sat there. She kept hoping he would cry. What he was going through not to was almost more than she could stand.

She got up and refilled their cups. Brought the Bacardi to the table. "Will you eat something?" she asked.

He shook his head, then rubbed his eyes, finally covering his face with his hands. His nails were bitten to the quick.

He'd stood and walked from the room. She heard the front door open before she realized he was leaving.

"Wait!" She ran after him. "You forgot your jacket!"

He waited with the door open while she brought it, the cold blowing in around them. "Stay a while," she said. "Let me fix you something to eat. Then I can take you wherever you're going."

He shook his head and started down the steps.

"There aren't any buses running, it's too late!"

He was already halfway to the street.

At first she thought about getting in her car and going after him, but she knew he wouldn't want that. He didn't want anyone to see him right now. Still, she wondered where he would go, and if he would be all right. And then she'd thought, *That's ridiculous. What could possibly happen to him, any worse than what already has?*

13

I remembered how it was with Dick and me in our first house in Long Beach, putting up our first Christmas tree, meeting Dick's friends, the whirl of parties. Life was close to perfect for us that December. What would it have been if Trudie had called to tell me what I'd just now heard?

She had gone to get the food ready. That morning, Lou had predicted that the men would be in by early afternoon. Whether they went out again would depend on how they'd done.

I lay there and thought about what Trudie had told me. I wanted to go home. I wanted *out* of this mess and away from Sonny. And I had the feeling Lou would be glad to see me go. It was simply a matter of making some believable and graceful excuse for leaving ahead of time. Trudie wanted to tell Braxton the truth, but I was against it; the truth was too preposterous. The mind has its own defenses; lying there thinking about it, I drifted off to sleep.

The next thing I knew, Dick was sitting on the side of the bed, gently shaking me and telling me to wake up. I felt better after the brief escape into sleep. I looked at my watch; it was two o'clock in the afternoon. "Why didn't you wake me sooner?" I said.

"We just got back."

I sat up and yawned, and laid my head on his shoulder. "I'm glad you're back. How'd it go?"

He held me, held me tight. "Not too good," he said.

I opened my eyes, but I stayed where I was.

Dick took a deep breath. "Braxton gutshot a deer."

I helped Trudie and Lou serve huge bowls of chili and sourdough bread. There were also cold cuts and a relish tray. Lots of coffee and milk.

Lunch was grim. For the most part, everyone's attention was directed to his or her food. Dick sat beside me, and when I touched his thigh under the table, he squeezed my hand. But he didn't look at me. Trudie had placed a chair at the corner of the table next to Braxton, and straddled the table leg to be close to him. I had wondered last night where we'd squeeze in the odd chair at a table designed to seat six. Sonny and Lou sat across from Dick and me, with Clifford at the other end of the table to my left. For once, even Clifford was subdued. There was no conversation except the polite requests for things to be passed, and for refills on coffee and chili.

As one consequence of Braxton's bad luck, the pressure on me had lessened. Now there was a tangible problem to be dealt with, and terrible as it was, I was glad. But there was also this: we were not likely to be going home early.

I don't suppose there could be anything worse in the society of deer hunters than what Braxton had done, unless it would be shooting a human or a head of livestock. And for a hunter of Braxton's caliber, those two things would be virtually impossible; he would never release an arrow until he had identified, beyond doubt, his target. So for Braxton, this was the absolute worst. He had made a bad shot; as we were soon to find out, an extremely bad shot.

Sonny spoke to me as we sat down to eat as if nothing had happened; though, of course, he made no reference to this morning. He seemed grave but calm; not overly disturbed or angry. I imagined he had this situation to deal with often, as a professional guide.

Nothing was said during the meal to try and make Braxton feel better. It was understood that words would not help him with this, and could very well make him feel worse. I could sense that Dick was sorry for him, and at the same time, glad that it wasn't *him*. I felt sorry for Trudie. If anyone was taking any pleasure in the situation, it was Clifford. He was trying to look serious and concerned, but the corners of his mouth kept twitching each time he glanced toward the opposite end of the table. Actually, I thought, it would be better if either Dick or Clifford had done this. Either of them could be more easily excused: Dick as a novice, and Clifford as Clifford. We suffered through the meal in silence, until Braxton pushed back his chair from the table. "I feel bad about this," he said.

Still no one said anything. Trudie laid her hand on his arm. Clifford lit a cigarette and blew smoke the length of the table.

"Nothing to be done about it now but find him," Braxton said. He put his hands on the arms of the chair, preparing to stand up. "I'd best get at it."

"Honey, wait!" Trudie said. "Can't you rest just a little while longer before you go out again?"

Braxton did look tired. His normally ruddy complexion looked sallow, with a grayish cast to it.

"I don't imagine that buck's getting any rest, do you?" he said.

"You're being pretty hard on yourself," Dick said.

"Where did it happen?" Sonny said. His voice sounded calm and neutral. "Where did you wound him?"

Braxton seemed to be considering the question. He looked at his plate, then at Sonny. "I appreciate your interest," he said, "but I can handle it. I made this mess, it's mine to clean up."

"Sonny and me can help you track him," Clifford said.

"We'd be glad to help," Sonny said.

"Thanks just the same, but I'd prefer it if you'd go ahead after your own deer, and leave this one to me." Then he spoke to Trudie, having dismissed the offers of help. "I'm going to need some food to carry along. Some sandwiches would be all right."

"How long are you going to be gone?" she said.

Sonny and Dick exchanged looks.

"Till I get back. I'll take the van as far as it'll go. If I haven't found him by nightfall, I'll sleep in the van and head out again in the morning."

Braxton stood up, and without saying anything else, he left the room through the kitchen door.

Trudie glanced at Clifford; she looked at Lou, and then to Sonny. Finally, she turned to Dick. "You don't believe he really wants to do this by himself, I hope."

Dick put his arm around her shoulder. "Make enough sandwiches for two," he said.

"Hell," Clifford said. "Just make a lot."

Trudie got up and followed Braxton; it was quiet for a minute after she left. Then Dick said, "What do you think?" He was talking to Sonny.

Sonny pushed his plate aside and crossed his forearms on the table. "Depends." I thought he wasn't going to say anything else; he was staring out the window overlooking the front porch. Then he seemed to collect himself, and he turned to Dick. "How big was he, do you know?"

"Why don't I tell you *all* I know, and we can go from there," Dick said.

Sonny smiled. "That would be a help."

They had all agreed that morning to break for lunch at noon unless there was something hot going on, and meet back at the cars; Clifford had driven his Jeep, and Sonny his Blazer. Braxton had spotted the deer after he'd left the stand and was headed back to the cars.

The wind was with him, and by some stroke of luck, he had seen the deer before it saw him. It was a big buck, over one hundred and fifty pounds, he estimated, with a beautiful ten-point rack. And there had been cover; Braxton had frozen behind a tangle of honeysuckle and blackberry briars. He'd hardly breathed, he said, guessing the distance at about sixty yards. He'd stood as still as a fence post, hoping for the buck to move closer. He began to think about getting a clear shot.

For what seemed the longest time, the buck tested the air, its magnificent head held high, ears rotating to catch the slightest sound. Braxton began to think about the route they had taken to the stands that morning; he'd been following pretty much the same path back, and if he was right, within the next fifteen to twenty yards, the deer would come across their scent and be gone like a puff of smoke.

Finally, the animal dropped its head and began snorting through the leaves for mast. With infinite care and slowness, Braxton began to notch an arrow.

He lost track of time; all the world constricted to the deer in front of him and the bow in his hand. The buck continued to move slowly forward, grazing for acorns and keeping a watchful eye. Then Braxton started thinking about the others, coming through the woods to the cars.

Thinking about them perhaps coming any minute, and with the buck moving slowly toward the scent trail they'd left that morning, and because the buck was so big, Braxton got in a hurry. When the deer was turned and quartering toward him, with its head down, and while it was still fifty yards away, Braxton picked his spot behind the right shoulder. He bent his knees to keep them from shaking, drew the arrow back and sighted—trying to clear briars and honeysuckle at the same time. And released.

Maybe the arrow jumped the string, or maybe he flinched. Maybe the buck moved before the arrow had time to reach its mark. The results were the same. Instead of hitting the heart-lung area he'd aimed for, the broadhead traveled straight through the animal's lower belly and out the other side. Braxton found it five minutes later, the razor-sharp point buried in the base of a tree. There was gore and fecal matter all down the shaft of the arrow to the fletching. The buck was gone.

He had tracked it for almost an hour, until he admitted to himself that it was going to be a longer job than that. He had gone back to the car to find Dick and Clifford waiting for him. The Blazer was already gone.

Sonny had listened without interruption as Dick told him everything Braxton had said. Dick had paused once and sipped his coffee, when he heard Braxton talking in the kitchen. Then Trudie had come out and sat down at the table. A minute or two later, we heard the door slam on the van. We heard it start and drive away. And then Dick went on talking. "He said he lost any sign of blood within the first thirty minutes."

"Maybe it's not hurt really bad then," Trudie said.

"Shit no," Clifford said. "Just a razor blade through its guts."

"Shut up, Clifford." Dick glanced at Trudie. "Just shut the fuck up."

Clifford started to open his mouth again, but changed his mind. He lit another cigarette.

"I think I remember the place he was talking about," Dick said. "In a little valley, about a half mile from where we parked."

"I think you're right," Sonny said. "Why don't you and Clifford start there. Take whatever direction looks likely that Braxton isn't already following." He spoke to Trudie. "It *is* his deer, and even with all of us looking, I don't think there's much chance we'll find it."

"What happens if you don't?"

Sonny shrugged (to cover another reaction, I thought), something more like a wince. "It'll die, of course. There's no doubt about that. It might die on its own in a day or so, or a coyote might bring it down sooner, weakened like it is."

"I see," Trudie said. "Then actually, you're not going to try, is that it?"

"No," Lou said. "What Sonny means is . . ."

"I'd like to go in ahead of where I think he might be." He put his arm across the back of Lou's chair. "Try and drive him back toward Braxton, at least try and keep him on the move. Maybe with the four of us, somebody'll get lucky."

Dick pushed his chair back and stood up.

"How long will you be?" I said.

"I don't know, Sarah. We'll hunt till dark, I guess." His tone was short.

"Did you bring any firearms?" Sonny asked. "We ought to fire a couple of rounds if we find anything."

“There’ll be a thirty-aught-six in the van if Braxton doesn’t carry it with him.”

“I brought along a couple of rifles,” Clifford said. “You can use one of mine.”

Sonny leaned and kissed Lou at the corner of her mouth. “We’ll be back at dark,” he said. “If not before.”

Clifford and Dick left in the Jeep. Sonny went in the Blazer.

14

Lou and I were going for a walk.

We had left Trudie in the living room, huddled at one end of the couch, stabbing at her needlepoint. I had asked her to come with us; a walk would do her good. "He'll be all right," I'd said.

She laid the needlepoint in her lap and stared at the fire. "I try to understand, but I can't. Why does he have to do this every year? What do they get out of it?"

"I don't know," I said.

"Then this happens. He'll make himself sick looking for an animal he didn't need to kill in the first place."

She was worried. Truthfully, so was I. Braxton was fifty-one his last birthday. His job at the university is sedentary, and he had put on some extra weight in the last year. His color at lunch wasn't good.

"With four of them looking," I said, "it shouldn't take long."

Lou was across the room, waiting by the door.

"We don't even like venison," Trudie said. "From one season to another, I end up throwing most of it away to make room in the freezer for the next batch. Last year I carried it to the animal shelter and they fed it to the dogs."

"It's the thrill, I guess," I said.

"Some thrill. Killing a defenseless animal."

"They're men," Lou said. Trudie and I turned at the tone in her voice. It was the quiet way she'd said it, as if we were foolish, discussing a thing completely beyond question. She opened her hands in front of her. "They're men." Her cheeks were flushed. "Would *you* rather have to do it?"

My cat brought me a bird once. Her meowing had summoned me quickly; it was a disturbingly different sound from the usual. She had a titmouse, minus one leg, one wing broken, bloodied at the shoulder, but very much alive. She deposited this prize at the back door and left it for me to deal with. I'd gotten a meat cleaver from a drawer in the kitchen and hacked its head off. I had to hit it twice to get the head completely off; I was shuddering and cringing the whole time. Dick was not at home. Had he been, that little job definitely would have fallen to him.

Trudie jerked the thread through the needlepoint. "It's not a question of *having* to do it."

"You eat meat, don't you?" Lou said.

"Come on, go with us," I'd said then. "Get some fresh air."

"You go ahead," Trudie said. "I'm going to sit here for a while."

So Lou and I had put on our jackets and left her there by the fire.

"I should have kept my mouth shut," Lou said. "That's a sore spot with me though." We stopped at the edge of the yard, deciding which way to go.

It was the warmest part of the day. The angle of light to the earth made the sky intensely blue.

She said, "Killing is part of a man's nature, any man's."

"Trudie's worried about him," I said. "He looked awfully tired at lunch."

"Why did he refuse Sonny's help then? Let's walk up this way."

Our shoes crunching in the gravel, some birdsong, the wind blowing high in a stand of pines—these were the only sounds. Maybe it was this place, quiet and isolated, and the wall of trees on either side of the narrow road, shutting us in, that made me feel very close to her. "Pride?" I said. "Macho stubbornness. I don't know. I think he's afraid Sonny may be a better hunter."

"There's no question about that."

It was a flat statement of fact. I didn't say anything more.

Back at the lodge, there were electric lights and a telephone. Out here, maybe four hundred yards further on, there was wilderness. The road led down a narrow gulley and disappeared over the next ridge. I wondered if it came out anywhere, or if it dwindled to nothing in the woods.

We walked for some minutes without talking. We were almost the same height; maybe she was an inch or so taller, but our paces were the same length. We were almost the same age. We were kin. We had loved the same man. And we were women. She pointed to the edge of the road, to a place where a few trees had been cut. She sat down on a stump, and I took one opposite her. Neither of us knew the best way to start.

"I've been wondering about you for years," she said. "What you'd look like. I was determined not to like you."

We both laughed.

"Sonny looks good," I said. "He looks happy."

"Do you think so?"

"Yes, I do." I was surprised at the question.

She picked up a fallen leaf and started to strip it, vein by vein. "That business last night. He can't stand to watch television because so much of it is about people killing each other. He says there's more than enough real killing without making any up." She threw the leaf away and looked at me. "The news, it's always full of murder and war, terrorism. It upsets him. The day after all those marines were blown up at the embassy in Beirut, I pulled the TV out from the wall when he was gone. I yanked some wires loose and threw away one of the circuits. That night when he tried to turn it on, I told him what I'd done. I thought he'd be mad, but he wasn't."

She paused, took a deep breath. "He watches baseball some with Carlton."

I listened to the quiet noise around us, waiting for her to go on. "Carlton," I said finally. "That's your brother."

"He and Sonny get along great. You ought to hear him tell about how they first met. Now that's a story."

"How'd you two meet?" I said.

She smiled, kind of sad, I thought. "Well," she said, "it's the same story."

. . .

It had been a late fall day much like this one. The air was crisp and invigorating—not too cold, and permeated with the sharp, clean smell of falling leaves and winter coming on. Carlton Tolliver had left the family business, a small bait shop and grocery store on the Little Pidgeon River, in Lou's care; it felt like the right kind of day for making whiskey.

The recipe was his father's, and his father's before him. The equipment he used was carefully maintained by him and him alone; he wouldn't let his mother or sister near it. Fussy. Carlton was very fussy about his moonshine, though he didn't bother to make it by the light of the moon. There was no need any longer; the Feds would not be interested in the small amount of bootleg he distilled for his family's use. The local law was not interested, either, as long as a half-gallon jar of what looked like water appeared under the front seat of the sheriff's car every so often.

Still, Carlton was careful on general principle. He made it a point to pick a breezy day when the smoke from his fire would dissipate quickly, rather than rise in a thin column to advertise what he was doing. He brought his 16-gauge, more from force of habit than need, and to potshot a squirrel or two if he felt like it. But he always brought it. That day he had the shotgun leaned against a tree, and was concentrating on stirring the mash. It took him much too long to reach the gun. The man who'd walked out of the woods could easily have gotten there first.

It unnerved Carlton to be surprised like that, for anybody to get so close without him hearing. When he jerked the gun up, he couldn't remember whether he'd loaded it or not. He laid the twin barrels across his forearm, pointing off to the side. Though he had been born and raised in a tradition of caution, and instinctively distrusted outsiders, he did not ordinarily jump to conclusions; he was not the excitable type. But this man made his mouth go dry and his heart beat fast.

It was obvious he had been living in the woods, not weekend camping either. He was tall and thin, unshaven, dressed in dirty and ragged camouflage fatigues. He wore a canteen and a big knife clipped to his belt. He had a crossbow strapped on his back, the most evil-looking weapon Carlton had ever seen. And cradled in the man's arms was a creature that once had been a dog.

It took Carlton several seconds to recognize it as the hound he'd lost almost two weeks ago. "Good God," he said.

The dog, a two-year-old pedigreed bitch, was too weak to hold her head up. The man supported it in the crook of his arm. His other arm supported the haunches. Carlton set the shotgun against the tree and took a step forward. The dog was literally a skeleton with hide over it.

"I found her caught in a fence," the man said. "I'd say she's been there a while."

"Two weeks," Carlton said. "Going on two. I looked all over for her, called her. I'd begun to think somebody stole her."

"She could reach the ground to lick rainwater and dew," the man said. "That's how she lasted. She may not last much longer."

Carlton stretched a hand toward the dog's head—he could feel the man's faded gray eyes watching his every move. "You want to come on up to the house?" Carlton said. "I'd carry her, but she looks too hurt to move. That's my momma's dog."

With exaggerated slowness, Carlton picked up the shotgun and pointed it at the ground. "Squirrel gun," he said.

"Maybe you ought to load it then."

Carlton led the way up the hill. What else was he going to do? He said the small of his back itched the whole time.

If Carlton's mother, Hester, was put off by the man's appearance, she didn't show it. Of her son's hounds, Gretel was her favorite. She had searched and yelled herself hoarse when the dog hadn't come home. She told the man to sit down on her front steps, and she would be right back.

While he held Gretel's head in the crook of his arm with her body lying slack across his legs, Hester spooned meat stock—

it was to have been soup base for the noonday meal—between the dog's teeth. Part of it dribbled down the man's arm onto his pants. He didn't seem to care.

"What happened to her?" Hester said.

"She was caught in a fence," Carlton said.

"All this time," Hester said. "It hurts me to think about it." She laid the spoon aside and held the bowl in both hands.

Gretel could lap at it as long as the man supported her head. With his other hand, he gently stroked her flanks.

Hester said, "You're one of them Vietnam vets I've been seeing on the television. Aren't ya?"

The man kept stroking the dog.

"I saw on the news the other night where some of you boys was getting off the plane, and people was lined up at the airport, yelling and spitting on you."

"Momma," Carlton said.

"Are you one of them Vietnam soldiers or not?"

"It's none of our business," Carlton said.

"Sure it is," she said. "I expect it's our business he's been over there fighting about, ain't it? What's your name?"

He told her, looking up from the dog.

"Well, I'm Hester Tolliver, and this is my son Carlton."

"I know," Sonny said. "Joe Wheatley and I have hunted on you before."

"You know Joe?" Carlton said. He was going to say more when his mother interrupted him.

"Carlton," she said, "go down to the smokehouse, and bring me up a ham."

During this time, Lou had been getting restless at the bait shop. It was past noon, and she was hungry and tired of waiting for her brother to come and relieve her. Her father had gone to town, and she didn't know when he'd be back. Finally, she locked the door behind her and walked to the house.

The first thing she saw was Gretel lying on an old quilt on the front porch. The poor dog was nearly starved to death. There was a ring of raw flesh all around her neck. Lou was kneeling to pet her, speaking softly, when her mother opened the door. "Come on in here and meet somebody," she'd said.

"You can't imagine how thin he was," Lou said now. "He and Gretel looked almost like a matched set. And that made him seem taller, and with the clothes he had on, and his hair long, this wild look in his eyes . . ." She paused. "He looked completely dangerous, which at the time, I guess he was. I think all of us were afraid of him except Momma. I know I was. It wasn't anything he said so much, or did. Just the way he looked and carried himself, like he might go off any second."

The sun was behind the trees now, and it was getting cooler.

"Daddy and Carlton stayed around that day until Sonny left before they went down to open the shop. They wanted to be sure he was gone before they left Momma and me alone. He just walked off into the woods. We didn't know where he was going or if he'd be back. I still don't know where he went. He never has told me that."

"You could get lost out there forever," I said, nodding at the trees. My voice sounded natural enough.

"That's right," she said. "People have. Anyway, the next time we saw him, it was several weeks later, and it was terribly cold. He came to the house with two rabbits he'd killed and dressed. Momma and I cooked them, and he stayed to dinner again. He was still thin, but he had shaved and his clothes were clean. He wasn't as scary around the eyes.

"He started coming pretty often after that. Momma made a fuss over him and babied him. She tried to fatten him up. He always seemed calmer, less watchful, when she was in the room. Most of the time he was coiled up tight as a spring. Gradually, he told us a little about Vietnam: that he was a ranger with the 101st Airborne; where he'd been stationed. He told us about the Montagnard who made the crossbow. We realized it was what he *wasn't* telling that was eating at him. But I really had no idea," she said.

"Until later when he told me things you'd never want to hear." She paused again, looking back.

"One day out in the yard, he was playing with Gretel. Down on his knees beside the dog pen, romping with her, rolling her around. This was after they'd both begun to look a whole lot better." She smiled a little, remembering. "I was on the front porch, and I started to call to him, tell him to come on in and wash up. He was eating with us two or three times a week by then, and sometimes sleeping at the shop.

"I'd seen him looking at me a few times. But neither of us had said anything, or done anything." She stopped and stared at her hands in her lap.

I waited for her to go on.

"I don't know when exactly, but I'd begun to . . . think about him. And fret when he'd leave; I couldn't stand for him to walk off into those woods, not knowing where he was going, or when he'd be back. I wasn't the least bit afraid of him anymore. He was the one who seemed afraid, so tense all the time."

She cleared her throat, softly. "I was watching him from the porch. He was playing with Gretel. He looked like a boy, carefree for a change, laughing. He didn't often look like that.

"It broke my heart somehow, watching him, and I didn't want to spoil it, but I wanted to be included in it, too. I wanted him to know, that instant, how I felt about him. Am I making any sense?"

Oh, yes, I thought. I nodded, not trusting myself to speak.

"So I walked down the steps and across the yard. I was planning to put my arms around him, just do it, give him a hug. I hadn't ever, until then, but right then, I *needed* to. My heart was so full, that's all I was thinking about. I came up behind him, and with him talking and Gretel barking, he didn't hear me walk up. He had no idea anyone was there. I just leaned down and put my hand on his shoulder.

"Later, when I thought about it, I realized it was a stupid thing to do, knowing how jumpy he was. To startle him like that. I was bending to kiss his cheek when his arm came around. The next thing I remember was the back of my head hurting really bad where it had struck the ground."

Tears glistened in her lashes. "When I could focus my eyes, I saw him over me. He was saying again and again, 'Please God, no. Oh, please God, no.' "

I thought about that night in my apartment, reaching out my hand, and laying it on his back.

"When I opened my eyes and looked at him, he started to cry. He had broken my jaw. I think it surprised us both he hadn't killed me." She sniffed and searched through her jacket pocket. I found a Kleenex in mine and handed it to her.

"He'd spent several weeks in a VA hospital," she said. "They'd filled him full of drugs. He couldn't eat. He couldn't sleep unless they gave him shots, and they finally stopped that because it was making him an addict. They thought he was lying about the things he told them. Making it up." She laughed. "Then they told him he would have to come to grips with his fantasies himself. That's what they called it—'fantasies.' They'd done all they could for him. So that's what he was trying to do when we met."

I thought she was finished, that she'd said all she was going to, but she went on. "He picked me up and carried me into the house, and told my family what he'd done. Carlton drove the car to the hospital. I was starting to hurt pretty bad. Momma and Daddy sat in the back. Sonny was in the front seat, holding me. The tears kept rolling out of his eyes. I got one of his hands and held on to it. It was so awfully quiet in that car."

She wiped her eyes, and blew her nose. "He'll never be over it completely, Sarah. None of them will. Except the ones like Joe."

I thought she was probably right.

"None of us knew Joe was dead. I was showing him the sketch, and he told me about Joe dying in Vietnam. I'm so sorry."

"Thank you," I said.

"If it hadn't been for Joe, he wouldn't have come here in the first place. I think he was trying to go back to a happy time in his life."

"I'm glad you told me these things," I said.

"You loved him."

"Oh yes, I loved him. And I'm glad for his sake that he found you."

"Thank you," she said. "So am I."

I stretched out my hand to her, and she took it. We laughed, giggled almost, with released tension.

"I owe a lot to you and Joe."

Yes, I thought. I would never tell her how much she owed to Joe.

We stood up. The sun was almost down. We were halfway back to the lodge when we heard the shot, faint and far away, followed closely by another. Someone had found the deer.

15

We took our time walking back to the lodge, neither of us in any hurry to get there. I wasn't completely sure why she was telling me these things, or why I wanted to hear them.

"I tried to locate Sonny when we first got home from California," I said. "I wondered then if he knew about Joe." It wasn't the whole truth, but it was part of it. I doubted that I knew what the whole truth was. "My parents didn't know where he was. His parents were no longer listed in the phone book."

If you come from a small town, it will look even smaller when you go back. Buildings you hadn't realized were important to you will be gone, razed for parking space. Maybe it is the alleyway between them that you actually miss, that you used to ride your bike down. But you will feel sudden and intense loss, and the slow passage of years will hit you all at once.

I had driven past the Capitol movie theater where Joe, Sonny, and I spent many a Saturday morning. It was now a Dollar Store. The high school we attended, built at the turn of the century—with garrets and towers, and mahogany banisters—stood vacant and falling to ruin. Its empty windows, vandalized, now gaped like eyes. When I got to Sonny's house, it had been empty, too.

"Dad thought maybe he remembered Sonny's folks moving," I said. "After Joe was reported missing, those years, they lost track of things."

"Yes," she said. "Who wouldn't?"

"So you and Sonny have lived here since," I said.

"We lived with Momma and Daddy for a few months after we married, but then Carlton got divorced and came home. We were looking for a place when Sonny came across the log house on the back edge of Daddy's land that somebody had built ages ago. I'd almost forgotten about it being there. We used to play in it when we were kids. It had a rock fireplace and a sleeping loft. Sonny fell in love with it.

"Momma and Daddy didn't say a word against the idea when he told them he wanted to fix it up for us to live there. Most people would have told him he was crazy. I wasn't too wild about it myself. There was no electricity. The only water came from a spring. It was miles from the nearest road." She laughed. "Those were the things he *liked*."

We had reached the lodge, and were standing at the edge of the yard. I thought she wanted to talk more, and I wanted her to. But it was nice to be where we could see lights.

"Carlton helped him," she said. "The logs were still solid, and they got it squared up on the foundation, and re-chinked. Daddy's health was too bad for him to help, but he loved hearing about it, how the work was going. I think it kept him alive longer, wanting to see it when it was finished."

I told her that I hadn't known her father was dead. "I'm sorry," I said.

She sighed and put her hand on my arm. "I don't know when I've talked this much. Blah, blah, blah. You must be bored silly."

She knew, of course, that I wasn't. It wasn't just a house she was telling me about.

"Daddy had cancer. By the time he finally went to the doctor, there wasn't anything they could do. Sonny took him to more than one, but they all said the same. They gave him painkillers and sent him home to die. He wouldn't take the medicine, said it made him dopey, and he wanted his last days to be clear. So Momma took it instead." She looked away for a minute.

"Anyway, Sonny and Carlton bulldozed a road to the house. They wired it and installed a generator, and added on the kitchen and bathroom. From reading a book they learned how to cap the spring. I made curtains and got old furniture out of Momma's attic. We moved in ahead of a heavy snowfall, and those first few days, we were snowed in. Sonny tried once to get out in our old truck, but he didn't try very hard.

"He loved it. It kept snowing off and on for a week. I had a few jars of vegetables, some onions and potatoes from the root cellar, just the bare staples. We hadn't had time to get in a lot of groceries. The meat we ate was what he trapped or shot. We could have gotten out if we'd had to, I guess. The point for him was, we didn't have to."

I could imagine it. Barricaded together in a log house against the harsh weather outside, eating venison stew in front of a roaring fire, going to bed early to stay warm under layers of quilts. Making love.

It was fully dark. *We ought to go in,* I thought. Trudie was probably worried.

"Let's go in," I said. "I could use some coffee."

"Where have you two *been*?" Trudie said. I could smell coffee, and bacon. She looked cross, sitting on the hearth with her arms wrapped around her knees, hugging them to her chest.

The smell of food, the warmth, walls to enclose us and keep the outside out—after what Lou had been telling me, I felt a sudden appreciation for these basics. I hung our jackets on the coat rack by the front door.

"The bogeyman about to get you?" I said.

She rested her chin on her knees, not answering.

"We've been right outside." I sat down beside her. "We heard a couple of gunshots a few minutes ago."

"Thank God," she said. "That means somebody found it."

Lou sat on the edge of the chair that was nearest the hearth. She ran her fingers through her hair at the temples, combing and fluffing it around her face. Her cheeks were flushed with color.

"I just hope it was Braxton," Trudie said.

Lou and I glanced at each other. It was quiet for a moment, with only the sound of the fire.

"I'll get us some coffee," I said, and I headed for the kitchen, when we heard a car engine, and lights flashed through the front windows. Lou and Trudie got up, too.

As the three of us stepped onto the small back porch and stood huddled together, shivering in the weak glow from the overhead bulb, Sonny stepped down from the Blazer. He looked exuberant, victorious, and somehow savage as he walked toward us out of the night. He pushed his hunting cap off his forehead and stood there, grinning. Lou ran down the steps, and he picked her up and swung her around. I could see the single hoof of a deer sticking out the tailgate.

Trudie moved to the edge of the porch. "Where's Braxton?" Then as an afterthought, "And Dick?"

He kept his arm around Lou and came nearer, pulling her with him. "Clifford and Dick were going to wait by the van. They fired off a couple more rounds. Braxton'll be in soon."

"But he wasn't there when you left," Trudie said. "I mean, you haven't actually seen him?"

Sonny stopped smiling. "No, but I'm sure he's in by now. They should be here any minute."

She nodded, hugging herself.

"I can go back and see," he said.

"That's all right."

"I don't mind," he said. "I'll go right now."

"No, really." She rubbed her arms against the cold. "Let's see the deer."

I went inside to get our coats; by the time I got back he had the buck out of the Blazer and was holding the rack for us to see. With the light shining on its eyes, the deer looked almost alive, until I saw the wound in its belly and the other one higher up.

"He's a keeper," Sonny said. "Braxton's got himself a real trophy buck."

"*You* killed it," Trudie said.

He laid the head on the ground. "I helped it die a little quicker is all."

"How'd you find it?" I said.

"Luck."

"Did you track it?"

He looked down at the deer. "Couldn't."

"Why not?" I said.

"It didn't bleed. The intestines had blocked the wound."

"How *did* you find it?" Trudie said.

"You really want to know?"

"Of course not. I'm just standing here making conversation."

He laughed, resting his fingers lightly on his hips. "Okay," he said. "What you do, you try and think like he would. What would *you* do, if you'd been shot and somebody was after you?"

He was smiling at her. "You'd be scared, wondering how close he was, your wind rattling in your chest.

"Would you hole up somewhere? Would you pick the easiest escape route you could find that had cover, a creekbed, maybe, or a trail? Because you're hurting—there's no question about that. Or would you climb some steep ridge to higher ground, where you could see everything better?"

There was excitement in Sonny's eyes, a kind of glitter. "You *become* the prey, one part of you does."

He squatted on his heels and laid his hand on the broad smooth neck of the deer. He looked at each of us in turn, three women gathered around him. "Another part of you becomes the hunter, a wolf, let's say."

He unsnapped the scabbard on his belt and drew the knife out. "Let's say the wolf—you—is hungry. You haven't eaten in days. The need for food consumes you, making you the ultimate predator. You turn your face into the wind, your jaws click together with lust. You open your mouth and let your tongue loll to deepen the aural and nasal senses. You can hear the faintest sound a mile away, smell the flight of an owl overhead. Then the night air brings you another scent, the richest one of all. The scent of terror."

Beside me, Trudie shivered.

He tested the knife on the ball of his thumb, then reached

inside the deep pocket along his thigh and brought out a small whetstone. He began to sharpen the blade. "The buck circles into the wind, knowing the wolf is near; the pain in his guts has become a ball of fire. If you were the buck, which way would you go now? Would you take the valley, or climb the ridge?"

Outside the circle of light, I heard the wind chasing leaves through the dark.

"As the wolf, which way would you guess?" He was moving the knife blade up the length of the stone, turning it, and bringing it down. The motion was slow and hypnotic.

"This buck was very brave; if he had chosen the valley, I would have lost him." He slid the whetstone back into his pocket. "Which means I happened to get lucky."

He hadn't field-dressed the deer yet because he wanted one of the men to help him. He said it would be a tricky job to keep the torn intestines from spoiling the meat. We were about to go inside to wait when the van pulled into the drive, followed by Clifford's Jeep.

Braxton got out, and Trudie went to meet him. She started to put her arms around him, but he shrugged her off. He walked steadily toward us, stopping when he got to the deer. He stood over it, clenching and unclenching his hands. Clifford and Dick stopped behind him. Clifford seemed to be trying to catch Sonny's eye.

"I thought I told you to leave this to me," Braxton said. His voice was low, and shaking.

"Honey," Trudie said. "I asked him to help."

He ignored her. "Didn't I say I would take care of it?"

Behind Braxton, Clifford turned his head and spat.

"Hold it a minute," Dick said.

"No, you hold it a minute." He spoke to Dick but kept his eyes on Sonny. "I didn't ask for your help either."

"You're making too much out of this," Clifford said.

For once, I agreed with him.

"You told us you had gutshot a deer," Sonny said. He kept

his voice low, too. "You didn't have to tell us, and I admire you for it. I've guided for men who would have let it go, and not said anything about it. But when you told us, I figured we should help you look."

"I don't care what kind of scum you normally hunt with," Braxton said.

I heard Lou's sharp intake of breath.

"I don't require your *services*. I can find my own deer."

"Man, you are way out of line," Clifford said.

"That's enough." Dick got right in Braxton's face. "Don't you say any more."

For a few seconds, nobody moved. We were like some crazy frieze, and then Braxton's shoulders sagged slightly and he looked extremely tired. He turned and went into the house. Trudie was crying as she followed him.

"Fuck it!" Clifford said. "Jesus H. Christ."

Sonny's face showed no reaction.

"I apologize for him," Dick said. "I've never seen him like this, honestly."

I felt sorry for Dick, and ashamed for both of us; Braxton was our guest. But my heart ached for Sonny.

I saw him swallow. "I could use some help gutting this deer. I imagine it's a mess inside."

"You got 'er," Clifford said.

"Help me drag him around by the woodshed," Sonny said. "There's a couple of gas lanterns back there. And a water spigot. We'll need to hose him out good." He looked down at his hand. He was still holding the knife. He put it back in the scabbard.

"Ain't this a bitch?" Clifford said. "The goddamn prettiest trophy buck I've seen in a long time, and not a damn thing to be happy about."

He and Dick each took a grip on the antlers and front legs and dragged the carcass around the porch and toward the shed in back.

Lou stayed close to Sonny until he looked down at her, and

some message passed between them without either needing to speak. He seemed visibly to relax then, and the tension drained out of him. He opened his arms and she came into them.

As I watched, and realized what it was I was feeling, I turned away and went inside.

16

I finally poured the coffee I'd been wanting for over an hour. My hand shook as I brought the mug to my mouth. I leaned against the counter, trying to calm down.

Trudie opened the door from the hallway into the kitchen and came in when she saw it was me. There were mascara stains under her eyes. "We're going to bed," she said. "Braxton's exhausted."

She stood there chewing her bottom lip. She said, "I'm sorry," and started to cry.

I set my cup down and went around the counter, and we held each other. She was sniffling and hiccuping—that sound we made as children when nothing was really hurt but our feelings, one of the worst hurts of all.

"It'll look better in the morning," I said. "Braxton's partly right, you know. It was his deer; he shot it, and he might have found it."

She shook her head against my shoulder. "He's been a jackass, he admits it. He's so ashamed, Sarah. He's . . . he's . . . I've never seen him so . . . so . . ."

"It's just a deer," I said. "It'll look different in the morning. You wait and see."

I rubbed her back. "Braxton will apologize, Sonny will apologize. Clifford will pick his nose."

She laughed, but not much.

"They're acting like little boys. You know how they get. Tomorrow they'll be grownups again," I said. "Come on, let's fix something to eat."

She lifted her head off my shoulder and wiped her eyes with the heels of both hands. "What about you? How are you doing?"

"Good," I said. "We had a long talk. I like her." I tore a paper towel off the roll behind me and gave it to her.

"I know, so do I." She blew her nose. "I fried a pound of bacon," Trudie said. "It's in the oven. I thought you might like omelets for dinner."

"Sounds good."

"I chopped some peppers and onions. In the green Tupperware bowl in the refrigerator." She opened the cabinet, took out a couple of mugs, and poured them full of coffee. "Braxton and I are having the sandwiches I made earlier. In the bedroom."

"Trudie . . ."

"No," she said. "In the morning, maybe. But not right now." She backed through the door into the hallway, balancing the mugs. I put my jacket on and went outside.

An eerie light flickered from behind the shed. When I got there, the deer was hung by its front legs on a crossbar. Gas lanterns swung from the support poles at either end, supplying a bright harsh light. There was an awful stench in the air, a combined odor of feces and blood.

Sonny had a garden hose, washing the gutted cavity of the carcass while Clifford and Dick stood on either side, each holding open the ribcage and a hind leg. Water and blood poured out and ran along the ground. The viscera lay in a pile, still steaming in the cold air.

"That's got it," Sonny yelled.

The water stopped, and then Lou and a man walked out of the darkness. When they came into the lantern light, I could see the resemblance immediately. "This is Carlton," she said to me. "Carlton, this is our cousin, Sarah Wheatley Lannom." He held out his hand.

"I'm glad to meet you."

He was tall, though not quite as tall as Dick or Sonny; standing among these three, Clifford looked like a gnome. Carlton had the same broad forehead that Lou had, and the fine aquiline nose, but there was a look of dissipation about his face, a slight bloating under the eyes. His hand, when it enveloped mine, felt huge. He was heavily muscled in the shoulders and soft in the belly. He was bald. For such a big man, his voice was surprisingly tenor.

Dick pretended he was going to take my face between his hands; they were red with blood.

I moved my head away.

He seemed very up, and excited.

"Stinks," I said.

Sonny glanced at us. He seemed all right again, though not as he had been earlier. "What you smell," he said. "How would you like to eat venison with that all over it?"

"Sonny!" Lou said.

He laughed. "We got it all without tainting the meat. Thanks for your help," he said to Dick.

"I'll know how to dress one now, assuming I ever need to."

"You'll get one. Maybe tomorrow. There's lots of deer around here; too many." He scrubbed at his hands with a rag. "Not many this size though."

"What're you going to do with him?" Clifford said.

Sonny looked at Carlton. "Do you still have a key to Buster's?"

"Yeah. In the truck."

"Might as well take him in tonight then, maybe after something to eat."

"What are we having?" Clifford said.

"Don't you have to skin it first?" I said.

"You can," Sonny said. "I think they skin out easier after they've aged a couple of days. And you don't get a dry crust over the meat from exposure to air."

"Oh," I said. I could tell from Dick's expression that he had been wondering the same thing.

"Buster'll be glad to skin this one for you," Carlton said. "For the hide alone, much less the rack."

"Maybe," Sonny said. "Unless Braxton changes his mind."

It got quiet except for Clifford mumbling an obscenity under his breath.

Carlton looked at us, obviously wondering what was going on.

"Trudie says he's feeling pretty rotten," I said. "I guess they've eaten a sandwich and gone to bed by now."

"When are *we* eating?" Clifford hitched at his pants.

"When are *you* cooking?" Lou said.

She and I left them to bury the entrails and wash up. I noticed as we were crossing the yard that Carlton was coming with us.

Inside, in the kitchen, she acted as if he weren't there. She was carrying eggs, butter, and milk from the refrigerator to stove. When I saw him look at me and then glance sheepishly away, I understood that he wanted to speak to her alone.

"Excuse me," I said.

"Wait," she said. "You don't need to leave."

Carlton looked embarrassed.

"It's all right." I started to go.

She put her hand on my arm. "Maybe I shouldn't involve you, but I'd really like for you to stay and hear this. How long have I been gone, Carlton?"

"Lou," he said.

"One night, isn't it? One whole night and day."

"She wants you to take her to the doctor in the morning." He held his arms straight at his sides. He was wearing a red flannel shirt and khaki work pants.

"You take her," Lou said.

And then she explained to me what was going on, while Carlton stood there looking extremely uncomfortable.

Hester Tolliver was an addict. She had developed a drug dependency, taking morphine and Percodan when her husband was dying. She had taken the medicine he refused to take, to ease her own pain in watching him die. I remembered Lou telling me this earlier, without realizing what she'd been telling me.

After exhausting the supply of drugs prescribed for her husband, an impressive pharmacopoeia in itself, and the sedatives prescribed for her at his death, she had developed a sudden and imaginary case of arthritis. When her doctor realized what was going on, he'd cut way back on her prescriptions.

"So she changed doctors. And started sacrificing her teeth."

"I don't understand," I said.

"Lou, that's enough," Carlton said.

She ignored him. "She'll claim to have a bad toothache. She'll ask the dentist to pull the tooth, and to get her over the pain, he prescribes five to ten morphine tablets."

"But if it's a healthy tooth," I said. "Can't he see that?"

" 'It hurts!' she'll tell him. 'Oh Lord, it hurts something awful. Pull it, Doctor, please!' He can't prove it doesn't, so he pulls it." She glared at Carlton. "There are *some* doctors around here who would do just about anything."

"It doesn't hurt *you* to look pretty and smile," he said. "She's only got a few teeth left."

"It's gone past smiles, Carlton! Would you like to know what he suggested the last time?"

Lou's brother looked sick. I don't know how I looked.

"Do you have any idea what it would do to Sonny if he found out?" she said.

"What would *what* do to Sonny if he found out?" He was standing in the doorway from the back porch, Dick and Clifford right behind him.

It was a good thing Carlton's back was turned, the way his face looked.

I started cracking eggs into a bowl.

"It's Momma again," she said. "I know how it upsets you. I thought you'd had enough for one day." She paused and then said, "I was wondering why Carlton couldn't handle it."

I asked Dick if he and Clifford would mind checking the fire. He almost pushed Clifford ahead of him into the living room, knowing without having to be told that something else was wrong.

I wondered how much Sonny had heard, and if he believed her. He looked tired and concerned. He rubbed the back of his neck and said, "I take it Sarah's heard about the family skeleton."

I didn't know what to say, so I didn't say anything.

"Momma wants Lou to take her to the doctor in the morning," Carlton said.

"And I was saying that he could take her just as well."

"Carlton can't get the good doctor to write a prescription just by asking, though, can he?"

"No," she answered softly.

"Sarah?"

I gripped the bowl in both hands.

"Would you mind going out there with her in the morning? Meet your Aunt Hester?" Sonny said.

"I'd be glad to," I said.

"It might help shame her out of it this time."

"That's a good idea." Carlton looked like he'd swallowed a bug. "Sarah could tell about her folks, how they're getting along. And Joe. How is Joe?"

17

Carlton insisted he'd already had supper, but we convinced him to eat with us anyway. It was late by the time Lou and I had the meal ready, close to nine o'clock. Everyone was tired and quiet. As we ate—Trudie and Braxton conspicuously absent—I thought about Wednesday night around my dining room table at home, the joking and optimism. It was only Friday night now; the hunting trip was less than half over.

But it could be that Braxton might want to leave first thing in the morning; I didn't know what Dick was thinking. Under different circumstances, I'd have been looking forward to meeting Lou's mother. Now I didn't know how to feel, about anything.

Lou had fried a pound of sausage to go with the bacon, and I had made the omelets large, filled with onions, peppers, tomatoes, and grated cheese. We'd made buttered toast on a big cookie sheet under the broiler, using a whole loaf of thickly sliced bread. It was a simple meal, full of cholesterol and comfort; there wasn't a crumb of it left. I wondered if Trudie and Braxton had caught the rich smell of warm food after eating cold sandwiches in their room.

Clifford and Carlton lit cigarettes to go with their second cups of coffee. "That was good," Sonny said. There was murmured agreement, and then, for a minute or two, we all seemed to be thinking our own thoughts, with the fire hissing and popping in the background.

Sonny pushed his chair back from the table. "Don't wait up," he said, placing his hand on Lou's shoulder. "Go on to bed and get some rest."

Her eyes searched his face. I thought she looked troubled, and was trying not to show it.

"You and Sarah be ready by eight in the morning?"

Carlton was putting out his cigarette, chasing down every spark.

"Is that too early for you?" she said to me.

"Eight's fine." Then I explained to Dick that we were going to see Lou's mother tomorrow while he and Braxton and Clifford were hunting. "If you think you'll be going hunting," I said.

"I sure as hell will." Clifford lit another cigarette from the butt of the first one. "That's what I came up here for."

Dick studied his plate. He hadn't shaved for the past three days. The blond stubble on his face made me wonder how he'd look in a beard, and I thought about asking him to grow one. He picked up his fork and pushed a bit of onion around the plate with it, then laid the fork down. "I'd like to kill a deer." He crossed his arms on the table and leaned into them. "I'd like to just get up in the morning and go back out. And forget this other business ever happened."

Sonny sat down again.

"I'll talk to Braxton. I'm pretty sure that's how he'll feel, too."

Clifford made a sucking noise, and Dick's jaw tightened. "How's that sound to you, Clifford?"

"Sounds all right." With the nail of his little finger, he dug at something between his front teeth. "I didn't see the first sign of a deer today, but that's no guarantee I won't tomorrow, I guess." He sighed and scratched his leg, looking at Sonny. "What're you planning on doing?"

"There's a new bunch at Buster's camp, but they look more like a motorcycle gang than deer hunters." He turned to Dick. "Buster told them where the boundaries are, but I saw a couple of their pickups this morning. They were parked on company land."

Clifford grinned, waiting to see what his boss would do with this information. Carlton looked interested, too.

Leave him alone, I thought. *All of you*.

"That's just what I need to hear." Dick rubbed his temples

with the tips of his fingers. "Now maybe Buster can tell *me* where the boundaries are."

"Let Braxton handle it." Clifford sounded sarcastic.

Sonny stood up again. "Buster says they'll be lucky to find their butts with both hands anyway, and they're talking about organizing a drive. If they do, even if they cross the line, they'll be above you. It's possible they could send something your way." He stretched, reaching to massage the small of his back. "I wouldn't bother about them, if it were me. Maybe by tomorrow afternoon, they'll be looking to hire a guide."

"So you're not coming with us in the morning?" Clifford said.

"Not in the morning." He leaned down and kissed Lou's cheek. "I'll take Sarah and Lou out to her mother's. Trudie, too, if she wants to go."

Dick stood, extending his hand across the table. "I want you to know I appreciate all you've done."

"My pleasure," Sonny said.

Then he and Carlton left to hang the deer in Buster's cold locker.

Lou and I had finished in the kitchen and were sitting on the hearth. The fire was a mass of glowing coals; its heat felt wonderful on my shoulders and back. We'd loaded the dishwasher, packed three lunches, and set out the breakfast things. All the men had to do in the morning was plug in the coffeemaker and pour their cereal. Clifford had gone to his room, and Dick was taking a shower. He'd given me a funny look when I asked him not to shave.

Occasionally a timber in the lodge would creak, or an acorn would hit the roof and roll down. Other than these sounds and the small noises of a dying fire, it was completely quiet.

"I feel like a drink," Lou said.

It sounded like a good idea to me. It had been quite a day, and both of us were stretched pretty thin.

She found the jug behind the love seat where Clifford had probably set it. She used both hands to tilt it to her mouth, then passed it to me.

I sat beside her on the hearth and held the jug balanced on my knees. It was heavy, but some of the weight was the container itself. I shook it, listening to the liquor slosh around inside. It was clumsy to drink from, with a wide stone rim. I tried not to taste the liquor going down so I wouldn't cough. I swallowed two mouthfuls and felt them reach my stomach in an explosion of spreading heat. "What proof is this stuff anyway?"

"Something's going to happen," she said.

"What?" I think I meant *what did you say* instead of *what's going to happen*. I was very tired, and Carlton's white lightning was having an amazingly immediate effect.

"I don't know, but something."

"You don't mean something *more*?"

She smiled, but it didn't get past her mouth. We passed the jug back and forth again.

"Poor Sonny," I said, "having to sit on that temper of his." I had to suppress a yawn. "I'm surprised he didn't deck Braxton."

Then I did yawn, I couldn't help it. "Joe was blond with blue eyes. When he got mad, his eyes would get darker, like stormy weather. Sonny's get lighter, like ice cubes."

"Yes," she said. "They do."

"One time, I thought they were going to kill each other. I really did. I don't remember what they were mad about, if I ever knew, but they scared me. Joe's nose was bloody and Sonny was bleeding, too. And they just kept hitting each other, rolling in the tall grass in the field beside our house."

The scene was clear in my memory, the brown hedge like walls surrounding them, blocking off the view from the house, the awful sound of fists hitting flesh and the different sound against bone. The way they were grunting, like animals. I was screaming at them to stop; I don't think they even heard me. The worst sin in their ledger was tattling, but I did it anyway that day.

It had cost me; they wouldn't speak to me for days, weeks. Long after they'd forgiven each other, they dragged my punishment on and on.

"What happened?" she said, and I realized I'd been woolgathering.

"It was a good thing it was Saturday and Dad was home," I said. "When he separated them, I think it scared him, too. One of Sonny's eyes was already swollen shut, and his lips were cut and bleeding. Joe had a gash on his forehead that needed stitches, and a broken nose. They were twelve or thirteen, but big enough to really hurt each other."

"What were they fighting about?"

"I don't know, but Dad made a rule, and made them swear to abide by it. That in the future when they had a disagreement serious enough to come to blows about, that they would each have a shot at the other's bicep. One punch, as hard as they could throw it."

"Did it work?" she said.

"I think what worked was—that they scared *each other* that day."

She drank and passed the jug to me.

"Is it something to do with this doctor?" I said. "Is that what's bothering you?"

"I don't think so."

She was worrying her wedding band, twisting it round and round. "I was surprised he wanted to come here this weekend. That was the first thing."

"Why?" I said.

"He doesn't hunt for sport. When he kills, it's to put meat on the table. Or clean up after somebody, like today. I think he *asked* Clifford to invite us."

"He told me this morning that you needed a break from your mother."

"I think he knew you were going to be here," she said.

I took another drink. It occurred to me that I was drinking

almost pure grain alcohol. I knew what she wanted to know, and I would have told her if I'd known how. She wanted me to tell her what had happened between Sonny and me—and I'd just found out myself this morning.

"I'm glad to meet you, after all this time. I wish I could remember back when we met before," she said.

"Your mother will probably remember."

"Probably."

"He was like a member of our family," I said. "He and Joe were like brothers."

She stood up, abruptly.

I set the jug on the floor and she offered me her hands and helped pull me to my feet. I found myself looking for a moment into those incredible green eyes before she leaned in to kiss my cheek. "Good night," she said.

I closed the door to the bedroom just as Dick was coming out of the bathroom. He came out toweling his hair. "I talked to Braxton," he said. He was wearing blue pajama bottoms, and he hadn't shaved. I knew how he would smell, how his skin would taste, how his arms would fit around me. All I had to do was go over there.

"I've got to tell you something," I said, leaning against the door. "Sonny Woods was Joe's best friend. I've known him all my life. We grew up together."

"I know," he said. "He told me." He was smiling, looking puzzled.

He came across the room and led me to the bed. "Sit down before you fall down." He leaned over me for a second. "You've been drinking."

"Lou and I had a couple of drinks."

"Are you all right?" He held my shoulders and looked into my eyes.

"You didn't shave," I said.

He laughed. He seemed in great spirits. He sat down beside me, put his arms around me. "I think you're a little drunk."

"Maybe I am," I said. I laid my head on his chest, just under his chin. I could hear his heart beating.

"A couple of drinks?" he said.

"Sips. From the jug."

"Oh boy."

"What did he say?"

"Well, just about what you did. That he and Joe were best friends, growing up together. What a little pest you were, always in the way."

"I was not."

"Sonny said he was waiting to see what you'd say about *him*, especially after me and my coincidence story—he said he thought you'd be all set to top it. And then, well, he didn't say it, but that's when Braxton started in." Dick was rubbing my back. "He told me this morning, driving to the stands. He asked me to ride with him."

Why is it men never tell you the exact words? I needed to know exactly what Sonny had said, the look in his eye when he'd said it. I sat up. "Is that all? He didn't say anything else?"

He held my face between his hands and kissed my forehead. I could tell he was humoring me; he really thought I was drunk.

"Why didn't you tell him about Joe being killed?" I said.

His smile went away.

"He didn't know about it. I was drawing—I was in that little clearing where we were fishing, remember?—and Sonny walked out through the trees, and we were talking and he said, just like that, 'Where's Joe now?' When I told him, it was like Joe died all over again. You should have seen his face." I could feel my own face screwing up like a child's. "I loved him," I said. "Dick, I loved him."

"I know you did." He held me, rocking me in his arms. "I know you loved him."

I put my head on his chest and cried. It wasn't so bad. Why hadn't I told him last night?

"It's hard for me," he said. "With just the pictures, and

what you and people like Sonny have said about him. I wish I could have known him, too."

"No," I said. "You don't understand."

"Hush," he said. "Just be quiet now. You're exhausted, and a little bit bombed."

I let him hold me. In the morning, I would tell him. Daylight would put the right perspective on it. *You're a coward,* I thought; *you're a fool. It doesn't matter, it was a long time ago.* He helped me undress, and held me until I slept. "I love you," I said, just before I went to sleep. I don't think he heard me.

And when I woke up the next morning, he was already gone.

18

I reached out to strangle the alarm Dick had reset for me. When I got the thing shut off, I lay back for a minute to assess the damage. My head throbbed and my mouth tasted about like the floor of a bird cage, but considering I'm not used to drinking, and certainly not that mule-kick brew of Carlton's, I didn't feel too bad. Then I thought back to last night and groaned.

I'd been ready to confess a seventeen-year-old love affair that hadn't even been consummated. How stupid the idea seemed, now, in the daylight. I'd been maudlin, and emotional. I remembered crying all over Dick's chest, and his having to help me undress.

I threw the covers back and thanked God that Carlton's white lightning knocked me out before I'd made a bigger fool of myself. I got up and went to the bathroom for some aspirin, thinking how things get blown out of proportion by fatigue and alcohol. I looked in at Trudie still asleep before I stepped into the shower. Braxton's side of the bed was empty. I vaguely remembered Dick last night saying he'd talked to him.

I decided that rather than wake her, I'd leave her a note on the counter in the kitchen, telling her where Lou and I would be, that we'd probably be back by early afternoon at the latest. I didn't think she needed to come along; it might not be too pleasant even for "family." I was thinking of myself that way, as family, all caught up on past events, and ready to be mature and sensible. And no more moonshine.

Dick had set the alarm for six-thirty, which gave me time to wash and dry my hair, and take some care with my makeup. After feeling unraveled all day yesterday, I wanted to look nice. I put on new jeans and a powder-blue V-neck sweater, dark blue socks, and loafers. I gave my hair a final touch-up with the brush and walked down the hall to the kitchen.

Lou was sitting on one of the counter stools, staring into a cup of coffee. It was twenty of eight.

"Morning," I said.

Her eyes looked tender at the corners, like they'd been rubbed too much; she was wearing an emerald turtleneck that brought out the color of her eyes against that explosion of auburn hair. Her skin looked translucent, with a cold bluish undertint. She didn't look as if she'd slept well.

"Sonny's in the shower," she said. "I've called Momma to tell her we'll be a little late. She's been ready since five."

"Five?"

"She never can get it through her head that doctors don't start work till ten."

"I'll fix some toast," I said. "You need to eat something." I sounded like Trudie. "How about an egg to go with it?"

She set the coffee cup down and touched her face with her fingertips. "You go ahead."

"How 'bout a couple of aspirin?" I was standing with the refrigerator door open, a pitcher of orange juice in my hands. I heard footsteps and turned, and Sonny walked into the kitchen.

He was wearing a burgundy wool shirt and hunting pants bloused in the tops of his boots. His dark hair was wet, and brushed off his face, accentuating the scar on his forehead. He was clean-shaven. "I sure could use a glass of that," he said, indicating the pitcher I was holding.

I poured three glasses of orange juice, and coffee for me and him. I topped off her cup.

"I told you I'd be late," he said, swinging a leg over one of the counter stools.

There was a strained smile on her face. "I know you did."

He crossed his arms on the countertop. "Buster had to hear all about the buck, you know how that goes." He glanced up when I set the cream and sugar in front of him. "There must have been ten new guys there, and they wanted to know where I'd shot it, like deer come in coveys. What kind of bow I'd used, what kind of broadheads, all that."

"I know," she said. "It's all right. I got some sleep after you came in."

I was putting bread into the toaster and buttering it as it shot out.

Sonny stirred sugar into his coffee. "Did you call Mom?"

"Yes," she said.

"How'd she sound?" He picked up the cup and sipped.

I set the plate of toast and a pot of blueberry jam on the counter and sat down across from them.

Lou touched her cheekbones with her fingertips again, gently. "Not good," she said, and let her breath out.

He kept drinking his coffee.

I spread jam on a piece of toast, trying to look like I wasn't listening. I laid the knife across the plate and picked up the toast; I was bringing it to my mouth when he took it out of my hand.

She stared at him before she glanced at me, spots of color blooming on her cheeks.

He chewed and swallowed and took another bite, talking around it. "I thought while you're at the doctor's, Sarah might like to see the Indian mounds at Medicine Springs. If you have to take Mom to the doctor. What do you think?"

I was spreading jam on another piece of bread, keeping my eyes on what I was doing.

"You might want to do some sketches," he said to me. "Looks like it'll be a pretty day."

I looked at her.

"Sure," she said, after a moment's hesitation. "That's a good idea."

I laid the knife down and he reached across and picked up the toast.

"Sonny!" she said.

We laughed so hard, tears came to our eyes. We'd almost get control, then one of us would see her puzzled expression, and it would set us off again.

Finally, I dabbed at my wet mascara while he told her what we were laughing about. "It used to make Sarah so mad," he said.

"You were beasts," I said. "You and Joe both."

"If you'd ever offered to fix *us* some breakfast."

"They'd eat the most disgusting things," I said. "Peanut butter and bologna, with mayonnaise. That was one of their favorite concoctions."

"Saturday mornings, we'd wait for her to wake up."

"Do you think I might have a piece of toast now?" I said.

Lou looked better. The whole atmosphere in the kitchen was better.

"She'd make French toast for herself with the crusts trimmed off, cut into little triangles. Maybe powdered sugar and a cherry on top."

"Oh, shut up," I said.

"Joe and I would wait until she had it all ready and was just sitting down."

"That's terrible," Lou said.

"They *were* terrible," I said.

"What's so funny?"

Trudie was standing in the doorway, her eyes about half open. She had on Braxton's robe which completely engulfed her, dragging on the floor like a train, with the cuffs hanging empty near her knees. She yawned and couldn't find her hand to cover it; that set us off again. This time, the three of us.

"Does this mean I don't have to stay in my room all day?" she said.

I patted the stool beside me and went around to pour her some coffee.

Trudie said she needed to do something domestic, maybe bake bread, or a cake. Lou volunteered to pick up another gallon or two of milk and a couple dozen eggs while she was in town. And whatever else we might need to finish out the weekend.

Trudie made us promise we'd be back before dark, in case

Dick and Braxton and Clifford went out again after lunch. She didn't like being alone after dark. We promised her we would. As we sat around the counter drinking coffee, it seemed as if everything would be all right.

It was nine o'clock before Sonny and Lou and I got into the Blazer for the trip to her mother's, which would take us the better part of an hour. Lou apologized for its condition, mud-splattered on the outside, and muddy inside. There was a lot of stuff in the back, and I could smell a faint coppery odor. Probably blood, I decided, from the deer last night.

Lou was still trying to remember when we'd met as children.

"I wasn't all that memorable," I said.

Sonny glanced away from the road, and slowed down a little, after he hit another pothole.

"I should remember something about it," she said. She was in the middle of the front seat, between us. "I don't."

"It was a fish fry," I said. "I'm sure of that much." Again, I could picture my grandfather with his sleeves rolled up, standing over the black washkettle of bubbling grease. "It must have been around here somewhere, because I remember Mother and Dad talking about us going to the mountains."

We drove in silence for a while then, Sonny watching the road, and Lou looking straight ahead, probably thinking about her mother. It was a cold and clear day, and the Blazer's heater felt good on my feet. The blue sky and sunshine gave only the illusion of warmth. I leaned back and watched the scenery go by, huge oaks and hickorys, evergreens and mountain laurel, growing right up to the edge of the twisting mountain road, every now and then a clearing or valley.

I sifted through the past for any memory of my Aunt Hester, and the only one I could come up with was of a pair of hands pushing a little girl in a flour-sack dress toward me.

I remembered a long picnic table draped with white muslin cloths on which my mother and other women were arranging bowls of slaw and white beans, shallow dishes of sliced tomatoes and Vidalia onions, and the platters of fish and hush puppies as they were fried and ready. Joe was off somewhere with a pack of boys; my father stood by the cars with the other men, looking over a couple of foxhounds.

Lou and I were given church fans with mortuary advertising on one side and Jesus on the other, and told to keep the flies away from the food. Nearby there was a pallet on the ground where three or four babies were sleeping.

Mostly, it was the memory of gestures I had preserved from that afternoon, not the faces; it was the movement of hands: Lou's and mine fanning the insects away from the food; my grandmother's scraping the sides of a bowl of slaw with a spoon and smoothing it into a mound; some man's large, gnarled fingers slowly opening a Case knife and carving a plug of tobacco. Sensuous fluid motions of a gentler time. It seemed odd, but the only *face* I remembered was Lou's. I couldn't picture her mother at all.

"Wait a minute," I said. "There was a well, they called it a well, but it was just a hole in the ground, lined with rocks. The water smelled awful."

"What?" Lou said. I'd brought her out of her own reverie.

"Sulphur water," Sonny said, leaning forward to see around her. "Medicine Springs."

"Isn't that where we're going?"

He had one arm across the back of the seat, and one hand on the wheel.

And then Lou screamed his name and threw her hands up and what happened next was a blur.

Sonny hit the brakes. The Blazer skewed sideways, the tires spinning up a cloud of gravel as we skidded onto the shoulder. My hands slammed against the dash, and I banged my knee against the glove compartment. A deer had crossed the road in front of us, bounded across, inches from the front bumper.

And then two men in a four-wheeler burst out of the woods

to our left and crossed the road after it, bouncing over the ditch and into the field on our right. I don't think they even saw us. *Thank God,* I'd thought, *that this didn't happen on a section of road with steep inclines on either side.*

The whole thing took less than five seconds.

"Are you all right?" Sonny said. He looked angry, and scared.

"Yes," Lou said.

I was rubbing my knee. "I'm okay."

"Are you sure you're both all right?" he said again.

Then he straightened the Blazer and pulled forward a few yards. He got out and walked around the front, stopping at the edge of the field where the four-wheeler and the deer had gone.

Lou was trying to see around me, out the side window. "Open the door," she said.

Outside, I could see movement in the trees at the far end of a clearing—like a pasture—and hear the high-pitched whine of engines. I could hear men yelling.

"What's going on?" I said.

Sonny turned to me, briefly, and then a man riding a trail bike came out of the tree line on the left and crossed right in front of us. Then the four-wheeler and another bike broke out of the woods at the other end of the clearing, driving the deer ahead of them. Each time it changed direction, one of them would head it off.

It was a small spiked buck. The men circled it with their bikes, tightening the circle. The deer lunged first one way, then another, its nostrils flaring in terror. The four-wheeler slowed, and the man next to the driver stood up. He sighted down a barrel and fired.

The buck's hind legs gave way. The man holding the gun yelled—an ugly, gleeful sound. Then the other men were yelling over the idling motors of their bikes.

The deer was trying to get up. With its back legs crippled, it pawed the ground with its front legs, its head thrown back and its neck swollen with effort. The man with the gun laughed, and fired again.

The little buck fell on its side. I could see blood now—the second shot had hit it in the belly, and still it was struggling to get up. The men were laughing and yelling. The deer dragged itself forward a few feet, digging at the ground with its front hoofs.

I turned to Sonny. I expected him to do something. What, I didn't know. He simply stood there, watching.

I heard the third shot as I was walking to the car. *Please let it be dead,* I thought. Without looking back, I opened the door and got in.

"Move over," Lou said. She looked sick to her stomach, too.

Sonny slid under the wheel and shut the door. We sat there, none of us saying anything.

The men were tying the buck on the back of the four-wheeler. One of them raised his hand and waved.

"Let's go," Lou said. "We're late as it is."

"That's part of the crew from Buster's," he said.

"Sonny, please," she said. "We have to go."

He leaned around me to look at her, then rolled the window down as the man who'd shot the deer walked to the Blazer.

He was young, about twenty-five. His hunting clothes looked brand-new. He was flushed, his eyes bright. "Did you see?" he said.

Sonny's voice sounded neutral. "Congratulations."

"That's the first one I ever killed." He peeked in at Lou and me. "Hi."

I said hello. Lou said nothing.

" 'Course, it's not anything next to that monster you got," he said.

Sonny draped his wrist over the steering wheel. "The young ones are better eating."

"I only had venison once before," the man said.

"Get Buster to help you dress it. You could grill the tenderloin tonight, just like you would a filet."

"Gee, thanks! I'll ask him. I brought my bow," he said, as Sonny was rolling up the window. "I'm going to try for a bow kill this afternoon."

Sonny waved with one hand and turned the ignition key with the other. As we pulled onto the roadway, I looked back at the little buck, slung across the seat of the four-wheeler, its eyes glazed and dusty, its tongue protruding from its mouth.

Sonny glanced at me. "Get your day off to a good start?"

"I think that's one of the most disgusting things I've ever seen," Lou said.

"The progressive way to hunt. And this is just the beginning." He was rough changing the gears.

Lou was staring out the window.

I remembered how the little buck had wheeled and lunged, trapped by the men and the noise.

"Why didn't you tell him?" I said. I thought about the look in the young man's eyes when he was talking to Sonny. It had been almost worshipful.

"Tell him what?" The corners of his mouth were white. "What would you have me tell him, Sarah?"

"That what he did was wrong."

"You mean illegal?"

"That too," I said. "Isn't it?"

"Technically. It's illegal to shoot them from the road, from your car. These guys have tags for three, two bucks and a doe. He may go out and kill two more today."

I'd never seen a deer killed before. If this was the way it was, I didn't like it. "I don't see any sport in killing something like that," I said. "It didn't have a chance."

"Shall I tell her what I found last week?" He leaned forward again, talking to Lou.

"You're going to anyway. Why ask?"

It was the first angry thing I'd heard her say to him. Her

mouth was set and she kept staring out the window on her side of the car. "He found a fawn, trying to suck its dead mother's teat."

"Great big eyes shining out of the dark when I turned my light on them," he said. "Big eyes that should have run away, but didn't."

"The doe's belly was all swollen, she'd died from infection. This little guy was tucked up next to her, trying to get his dinner.

"Real tearjerker, but legally, whoever shot her was within the law.

"A lot of things that are *legal* are wrong." He looked down at me, then back to the road. "I don't make the rules."

19

We were standing beside the Blazer watching Sonny take the steps down the hill to tell Carlton we were here.

About two hundred yards below us lay the Little Pidgeon River and the bait and tackle shop floating on pontoons and Styrofoam blocks in a quiet bay. It was a small building with a slanted tin roof, painted white with green trim, with a boardwalk and dock area all the way around. There were gas pumps and a Coke machine on the side nearest us. The boardwalks rode high and level in the water, the boat ramp was wide and gently sloping—it all looked well-maintained and cared for.

The frame house farther up the bluff behind us was starting to sag on its foundations. But it too was painted, and the yard had recently been raked. There were flame-shaped evergreens on either side of the concrete steps leading up to the front porch, and a pot of dead foliage hanging from the eaves—a plant that hadn't made it in for the winter. I could hear dogs baying somewhere in the back.

Lou seemed in no hurry to go in. She was staring down the hill after Sonny, watching him take the long tier of steps that had been chiseled into the hillside. He had his head down, his hands in his pockets. Nothing else had been said about the deer; I wished I hadn't said anything at all. I'd made it sound as if he could have done something to stop it, when really, he couldn't.

Lou had her arms crossed and her lips pressed together. "He tries not to let it show," she said, "but things like that tear him up."

How could it not upset him? It had disgusted all of us.

"Every year, before the season opens, I beg him not to guide, so he won't have to be around people like that."

He had reached the dock now and was walking out onto it, adjusting his steps to the roll of the walkway.

"Buster runs what amounts to a dude ranch for hunters. Caters to these men, a lot of them who hardly know which is the business end of their gun. So he recommends Sonny to guide for them. Wet-nursing is more like it. One of these days, one of them's going to kill him."

She'd been pushing gravel into a little pile with the toe of her shoe. She kicked at it. "There's more work right down there than both Sonny and Carlton can handle. People wanting to buy tackle or rent boats, or boat motors to work on, or being a fishing guide. He doesn't have to work for people like that."

I took my gloves off and stuffed them into my pockets, and unsnapped my down jacket. The sun was beginning to heat up.

"That bunch down at Buster's," she said. "Opening day . . ." She looked at me, her mouth thin and tight. "That afternoon, I went with Sonny down there. Buster had called, said he had a client for him." Her eyes snapped with anger, just remembering.

"There was a flatbed truckload of deer, Sarah, most of them small bucks like the one today, some that had barely lost their spots. They were heaped together in a big pile, just this tangle of legs and—and *eyes*."

She paused and leaned against the Blazer. "Some had been field-dressed, or an attempt had been made at it anyway, and their carcasses gaped open, gathering dirt. A good many had been dragged through mud, in the wrong direction, and their coats were ruined. A lot of the meat wouldn't be fit to eat, the way it had been killed and handled."

She turned to look at me, her eyes full of pain at the memory. "Such a waste. It reminded me of those pictures you see of the Holocaust, the stacked-up bodies. Sonny stood looking at that truckbed, I could see how it hurt him. 'I wonder how many they hit but *didn't* kill,' he said. That's one reason he does it, to clean up other people's messes.

"Then later that afternoon, we found out about Boyd."

Down below us, Sonny came out of the bait and tackle shop

with Carlton behind him. Carlton shut the door with one hand and waved at us with the other. We waved back.

"And then, of course, he's good at it." She sighed. "I'm sorry about that business with Braxton yesterday."

"No," I said. "Braxton's the one who should apologize. I have an idea he will tonight."

"I really do like Trudie," she said.

I looked at her and smiled. We stood leaning against the Blazer, watching Carlton and Sonny climb the hill. Then I heard a screen door slam behind us. "That'll be Momma," she said.

"Lou? Girl, is that you?" The voice was quavery, with a nasal mountain twang.

She seemed to hold her breath for a moment before she answered. "Yes, Momma. I'm coming."

Then she turned to me and her eyes were bright with tears she was struggling to hold back. She squeezed my arm, trying to smile.

I'm sure I saw her square her shoulders as we started across the yard. "Look who we've brought to see you! You remember Kate's son, Roy? This is his daughter."

Growing up as I did and when I did, I've come to expect almost anything but growing old. I can't picture myself reaching the age of the woman who was waiting for us at the top of the front steps. She was my now-dead grandmother's younger sister, but I wasn't sure how many years younger she was.

"Hello, Aunt Hester." I took one of her frail cool hands, all bones and tendons, and stooped to kiss her cheek. She smelled of snuff and face powder, and clothes stored in old trunks. The bodice of her navy dress was spotted with grease. Her hair, completely white, was twisted in a knot on the nape of her neck. Her eyes were nearsighted but clear, and there didn't seem to be anything wrong with the workings behind them.

" 'Course I remember you," she said, a firm grip on my elbow, staring into my eyes. Hers were hazel. "You're Roy and What's-her-name's girl."

"Marjorie," I said.

"That's right, *Mar*jorie." She snorted, then looked straight at me again, direct and candid as only the very young and the very old are allowed to be. "Too uppity for the likes of us, warn't she?"

"Now, Momma," Lou said. She was standing to one side.

"You look like her."

"Thank you," I said.

Sonny and Carlton had reached the steps. Aunt Hester held my arm and turned around to face them. "You're late," she said to Sonny.

"I'm sorry, Mom," he said. "We had a little trouble."

"What kind of trouble?" She was looking at me.

Carlton came up the steps and took hold of her other arm. "Let's go in. We shouldn't keep Sarah standing out here on the porch."

She made a move to shrug away from him, but his huge hand held her gently.

"I'm done ready to go," she said. "Been ready for hours."

Lou said, "Let's go change your dress first. Then we'll go."

"What trouble?" Aunt Hester spoke to Sonny, ignoring her children. Then she slapped at Carlton's hand. "Turn me a-loose!"

Sonny was watching at the bottom of the steps.

She grinned down at him, her few remaining teeth stained, her eyes bright. "Get on up here," she said. "Help me back inside. A body could fall and break their neck."

"I've got you," Carlton said, pulling her gently in the direction of the front door. Lou held it open.

"You go on back to the shop," she said. There was a mean edge to her voice.

Carlton's face was red, but he didn't let go of his mother's arm. His tone was respectful. "There's nobody down there right now."

"How would you know?" she said. In trying to pull away from him, she leaned heavily against me, and I automatically put my arm around her.

Sonny climbed the steps. "I'll take her," he said quietly to Carlton, their eyes meeting above her head.

I think I could have carried her myself, she was so tiny and frail, but she was interested in getting her way. Sonny humored her. He took her elbow and locked hands with me behind her. "All right, Mom," he said. "We've got you."

Lou went in ahead of us, holding the door, and Carlton followed. "You just wait," Aunt Hester was saying. "You'll be old some day."

The dark interior of her house struck me with an almost physical force. What little light came through the two corner windows of the living room couldn't soften the effect of the heavy oak furniture. Even the mirror of her massive highboy seemed to swallow light. The couch and chairs were heavy and masculine, upholstered in brown leather. A large wood furnace squatted in one corner of the room. It partially blocked a double doorway that led into what appeared to be the dining area.

The doors, hinged double panels, were folded back into the dining room, but I could see that the panes were beautifully beveled and set in a scrollwork of lead. These doors and a few bright sofa pillows were the only delicate touches in the room.

Sonny and I supported Aunt Hester as she slowly shuffled toward a high-backed recliner directly in front of a large cabinet TV. It was obvious that she was exaggerating her discomfort, punctuating each step with a groan. "My arthritis is so bad this morning," she said. "I didn't sleep none last night." She was such a tiny woman, even more so now that she was shriveled and bent. I had to wonder how she'd ever produced a child who'd turned out to be the size of Carlton. I had no idea what her husband had looked like.

"Lord, I hurt!" she said. "You can't know." She looked sideways at Sonny, then spoke to me, stopping in front of her chair. "I'm sorry if I interrupted your-all's fun, but I have to have some relief." She squinted at Lou standing behind the recliner. "She likes to see me suffer."

Lou didn't respond, and I didn't look at her.

Sonny lifted the old woman in his arms, and was bending to lay her in the chair. For a moment she rested her head against his shoulder, as a child would, or a lover. Then she clung to him and started to cry.

I saw the pain in his eyes as he gently set her down and knelt on the floor beside her.

"Make her get me my medicine, Sonny."

Carlton, Lou, and I stood in a semicircle around the two of them. "Mom," he said gently.

"Please," she said. She rocked her head from side to side against the back of the chair.

"You're taking too much." He took her hand and held it. "Why not try the APF tablets Lou bought for you? Try those, and have some wine with your meals."

Aunt Hester kept shaking her head no, tears running from the corners of her eyes and streaking the powder on her wrinkled cheeks.

Sonny glanced at Lou. Carlton shuffled his feet and wrung his hands. I felt intrusive; it was a painful scene. If it wouldn't have called more attention to my presence, I'd have eased outside. It wasn't Lou that Carlton had needed to find last night, obviously, but Sonny.

As I watched him, on one knee beside his mother-in-law's chair, I remembered what Lou had said about Aunt Hester and how she had been the only one able to soothe him.

She clutched his hand in both of hers now, pulling against it to raise herself. "Please, Sonny." She was begging. "You don't know how I hurt."

I felt so sorry for him, for all of them.

"Yes, I do know," he said.

"Then make her get it for me. She can get it."

"Try the aspirin first, and a little wine. That's what the doctor recommended."

The old woman's eyes became slits. "Doctor. Ha!" She

pushed his hand away. "He don't care nothing about *me*. Hardly looks at me." She pushed against the arms of her chair and leaned into his face. "I'll tell you who he *does* care about."

I could see the pulse beating in his temple.

"He'll say anything *she* wants to hear."

Lou's cheeks were flaming. "Hush!" she said. "You don't know what you're talking about."

"He knows already, anyway. Look at him!"

It was deathly quiet in that dark room for a few seconds. Then Aunt Hester let her head drop back on the recliner. "I need my medicine."

Sonny's voice was still gentle, but rigidly controlled. "Try the aspirin first. Give it two weeks, and if it doesn't help, I'll see you get the other."

She turned her face away. "Got nothing to live for. Just pain and misery. Got no grandchildren."

"Momma, don't start," Lou said.

"That doctor'd make me some grandchildren. He'd sure enough like to try!"

Sonny stood up.

"I need my pills!" She yelled at his back, as he was walking away.

He stopped with his hand on the doorknob. Then he opened the door, and shut it softly behind him.

Aunt Hester lay back and closed her eyes.

Lou came from behind the chair and stood looking down at her mother. "Aren't you ashamed?" She was trembling. "Even if you don't care anything about me, how could you say that to him?"

"Call the dentist, Carlton," the old woman said, without opening her eyes. "I got me five teeth left."

I didn't know what to do, what to say. I wished I wasn't seeing this.

"I'll be back in a minute," Lou said, finally. "I'll help you change into a clean dress. I'm going to say good-by to Sarah." It was costing her a great deal to hold herself together.

Carlton followed us outside. He was careful not to meet her eye as he closed the door and went down the steps. I didn't see Sonny anywhere.

"Get the damn pills," I said to Lou. "The same strength dosage at first. Then have him taper her off. And tell him you'll slap him with a malpractice suit so fast it'll make his nose run if he so much as thinks about anything else. He prescribed the stuff that made her dependent, let him help get her off it."

She searched through her pockets for a tissue and wiped her eyes.

"Do you want me to go with you?"

She was shaking her head. "I shouldn't have put you through this."

"You know he didn't take her seriously."

"Didn't he?" She hugged herself.

"I'll take Carlton's truck back to the lodge, or he can drive me, whichever. You need Sonny with you." Carlton was standing at the edge of the bluff with his back to us, looking off down the river.

"No," she said, her voice hard. "I don't want him there. Maybe she can't help it, but sometimes, I could almost strangle her." She looked away to gain control, and I thought about my own mother, how I take her health and my father's for granted. "He's been so good to her," she said. "Then she does something like this."

I wanted to help her, but I didn't know how. "You know he understands," I said.

"I have to go back in."

"Let me stay," I said.

"I'll tell her you said good-by." She turned to me. "Try and get him to relax for a while, talk over old times. Make him laugh."

I wondered what we would talk about. Outside, it had turned into a glorious day; still, and bright. I could hear a cardinal singing close by.

"Tell me something," she said. "Did he always used to laugh like that?"

I looked at her.

"This morning at breakfast. In the years we've been married, I've never seen him laugh quite like that before."

I thought of all the times I remembered Sonny laughing, though I didn't suppose I could say he had a happy childhood.

"I'll see you tonight," she said.

I started down the steps, and pictured her going back into that dark room. "I brought my book, I'll sketch you something pretty," I said. "Tonight we'll have Trudie's fresh bread and deer liver. Dick's going to get one today, I can feel it."

"Don't keep him waiting," she said.

I was reluctant to go. There was something left unsaid, but I couldn't put my finger on it.

Through the closed door, I heard her mother's querulous voice, calling for her.

20

I waited in the Blazer as Carlton paced the bluff in front of me. Once or twice I thought he was going to approach the car—he kept glancing toward me—but he continued to walk back and forth along the brow of the hill, stopping occasionally to stare downriver. It was a truly spectacular day, with the sky that shade of blue you get only in October and November, and the temperature was rising. It was a day to be happy in, to enjoy being alive; it was not a day to waste. And then I'd think of Lou in that dark house with her mother and feel a rush of frustration and guilt.

Sonny's head and shoulders topped the hill, and then I could see he was carrying a small red-and-white cooler. He set it down and spoke to Carlton, who nodded once and, later, again. Carlton looked at the ground mostly, and downriver; he seemed to be listening without comment as Sonny talked at some length. Finally, Carlton nodded the second time, and Sonny picked up the cooler and started toward the car. He saw me watching and smiled through the windshield as he came around to put the cooler in the back. He set it alongside my canvas bag and the hiking boots he'd suggested I bring.

"Be back around dark," he shouted to Carlton as he opened the door and got in. He started the engine and turned the Blazer in a tight circle. I waved to Carlton as we rounded the first curve and disappeared from sight. The trees and steep rocky bluffs immediately closed in around us, and I felt light in the chest, as if I were breathing very thin air. I checked my watch; it was ten minutes before twelve, with the whole afternoon stretching ahead.

At the first fork in the road—we'd probably gone less than a mile—he pulled off onto the shoulder, letting the motor idle in neutral, and setting the hand brake. Neither of us had spoken;

I sensed that we'd been discarding some of the same topics. He turned on the seat to face me, his arm along the back. "Are you really interested in seeing a puddle of water that smells like rotten eggs?"

He nodded to the split in the road ahead of us, one way going down and the other twisting back up the mountain. "How bad do you want to see Medicine Springs?"

"I don't know," I said. "I just thought . . ."

"I'd rather show you something else."

Sunlight flickered through the canopy of branches and dry leaves overhead, casting patterns on the hood. It was so quiet. "What?" I said, a little breathless.

"It's a surprise. There'll be some walking. And a canoe ride."

"A canoe ride?"

"Trust me," he said. "You won't even get your feet wet." He opened the door. "Be right back."

I watched him disappear into the trees at the right of the Blazer. I didn't know what to think of the change in plans.

In about five minutes he reappeared, dragging an aluminum canoe.

I rolled the window down. "Need some help?"

He smiled to show he'd heard me, and I got out of the car. I tried to help him by pulling one end of the canoe up the incline and onto the shoulder. I think I got in the way more than anything. He hoisted it onto the luggage rack, and opened the back of the Blazer, moving things around until he found some short lengths of rope to tie it down.

"It's not heavy," he said. "A little clumsy to handle."

I wondered where he'd gotten a canoe in the woods, and before I could ask, he told me it was one of theirs that they rented out. I realized then that the river was through the trees, just below us.

As we got back in the car, I asked him where we were going.

"Up there." He pointed straight up the mountain.

"Are you sure we have time for this?" I said.

"It doesn't take long."

"And we end up back here?"

He didn't reply. He seemed a little annoyed by the questions.

"It sounds like fun." I remembered what Lou had said: *Help him relax, make him laugh.*

He looked at me, I guess to see if I meant it, then put the Blazer in gear and released the brake. He took the left turn, heading up the mountain.

I started to shrug out of my jacket, and he took a hand off the wheel to help me. He tossed the jacket in the back with the rest of our stuff. Besides the walking boots, I had brought the tote containing my art materials, a purse, a couple of candy bars and the apples I hadn't eaten yesterday, and a thermos of coffee. There was a jumble that belonged to him, which included his compound bow, a gun case, and a fly-rod case. I assumed the cooler held our lunch, and I wondered what was in it.

This morning when Lou and I had started to discuss the sandwich possibilities in the refrigerator, and what food she would pick up in town, he had told us not to worry about packing a lunch. He said he'd asked Buster's wife, Joanne, to put up a lunch last night. Lou had taken this information in stride, but I thought she'd looked surprised.

I watched the scenery out my window, taking special note of the deep ravines and sheer drop-offs on either side of the narrow winding road. I had my seat belt fastened and the door locked. Our near-miss with the deer this morning had shaken me more than I'd realized. I touched my knee where it had hit the glove compartment; there would be a bruise even now darkening under the cloth of my jeans.

I glanced at him; he was watching the road, a slight frown drawing his brows together. I supposed he was thinking about Lou and her mother.

I was nervous. We had a lot of catching up to do, and

inevitably, some probing of past wounds. I wanted us to be friends again. I remembered a time when, other than my brother, Sonny was the closest friend I had. Maybe by tonight, when we'd be back at the lodge, we'd be more comfortable with each other.

He waited until the road leveled out and he didn't have to raise his voice to be heard above the engine. He said, "Now tell me about yourself. Tell me everything you've been doing."

I started with California. He already knew how I'd gotten there. I couldn't help recalling the story Trudie had told me, how he came to her apartment looking for me. Talking was like picking my way through a mine field, trying not to hit any explosive topics. I talked some more about Joe, explaining that Dick had never gotten to meet him. I told him about Dick's job with Precision Computers, about being transferred home. But mostly I talked about my own work, and what I was trying to do, without getting too technical, and about the satisfaction it brought me.

"So you're back with your old teacher," Sonny said. "The guy you wrote me about?"

I felt uneasy at the mention of the letters I'd written him when he was in Vietnam, but he didn't dwell on it. The road kept getting steeper, and he was busy with the driving and changing gears. We hadn't met any cars coming down, and I was glad; it seemed too narrow a road for two cars to pass safely.

"Joshua Barnes. We're having a joint show this spring, in New York."

"In New York?" he said, appreciation showing in his expression.

"Well, it's not at the Metropolitan, or anything," I said. "But it's a nice Manhattan gallery."

"New York, though," he said.

"How high are we going?"

It felt to me as if we were already climbing at a forty-five-degree angle, almost as if we could fall off the face of the mountain. We'd run out of blacktop into gravel, and precious little of that. The roadbed was mostly hard-packed earth, rutted and washed out in places, making for a very bumpy ride.

I was getting anxious. Heights give me vertigo. I fear that somehow in a moment of madness, I might take it into my head to jump.

"Not much farther," he said. "Pretty soon we turn again, and it's not far after that. Still afraid of heights?"

I laughed, surprised that he'd read my thoughts. "How did you know?"

"Remember the tree house? Joe and I finally let you climb up there so you'd stop crying."

"I don't remember," I said.

"And then you wouldn't come down. Your father had to get a ladder and *carry* you down."

"You're making it up," I said, laughing with him. I suddenly remembered it perfectly. Some time later, Joe had fallen out and broken his collarbone.

I'd whined and pleaded at the base of the enormous white oak, threatening to tell on them, until Joe had thrown the rope down for me to shinny up. Once I'd reached the rickety platform they'd laid between the crotches of tree limbs, and they'd caught me under the arms and pulled me up, I thought I'd won. Until I'd looked down.

"You were always getting us in hot water."

"Most of the time you deserved it," I said.

"Joe used to get so mad at you he'd sputter, the only times I ever saw him speechless. You know how he could talk—I swear, I've pictured him all these years in a three-piece suit, in front of a courtroom, arguing some big case."

"I know," I said.

"He used to say, 'Sonny, you lucky stiff, you're an only child.'

"You know what I used to imagine?" He glanced at me, then back to the road.

"Nights when my old man had worked me over, I'd lie in bed pretending your folks were going to adopt me."

Everybody in the community must have known what was happening, but nobody ever said anything. My parents had to have known, and Sonny's teachers as well. He didn't get black eyes and busted lips from falling over his own feet. But as far as I remembered, everyone, including his mother, had pretended it wasn't happening. Everyone except Joe.

"Sometimes in the bush, when I thought I wasn't going to make it, I'd remember him hitting me, and me thinking, *You'll have to kill me, you son of a bitch, because you're not going to make me cry*. Who knows, maybe he's one reason I got back alive.

"I got home, and the first thing, he wanted to see my medals. He was sitting in his chair in front of the TV, drinking a beer, just the way I'd left him. I went and got them, and he picked them up one at a time and looked at them. 'What'd you get this one for?' he'd say. 'And this one, what'd you do for it?' "

"He must have been proud," I said. "Maybe he was trying to tell you."

"I doubt it," he said. "But who knows?"

The Blazer's engine was laboring, and we were only going ten miles per hour. I twisted around to see where we'd been, and turned back again quickly. The view made my head swim.

"Who knows why things turn out the way they do." He turned off the roadbed into a shallow ditch. For a minute the wheels spun in the fallen leaves, and I thought we were stuck. I couldn't see any evidence of a path or trail, any reason why he had picked this spot to turn.

He rocked the Blazer backwards and forwards, rapidly changing gears, talking to it under his breath. We started to inch forward, almost straight up, it seemed to me. My heart was stuck in my throat; I kept expecting us to pitch over backwards. When we'd gained the top of the incline, he stopped and looked back, and I found I was clinging to the dash with both hands.

"How do you like it so far?" he said.

"Let me ask you something," I said. "We're going down this mountain in a canoe?"

He laughed and traced a spiral in the air.

And then we were driving down the hill we'd just climbed, except the downward slope was more gradual. I still couldn't see any sign of a path or trail, but he seemed to know exactly where he was going, threading us through enormous hardwood trees and evergreens, tangles of Japanese honeysuckle, driving over the smaller fallen tree limbs and the season's new blanket of leaves. It was exciting; I'd never experienced anything like it. *This is wilderness,* I was thinking, *this is the real thing*.

I'd catch him watching me and smiling; I guess my eyes were round, and I was breathing through my mouth.

He stopped the Blazer between two large evergreens. "We walk from here."

When I got out, I couldn't see water, but I could hear it. He unloaded our things while I changed my shoes, trading the loafers for hiking boots. He stood with his hands on his hips looking at the cooler, his bow, gun, fishing rod, my canvas tote, and an army-green rucksack. And the canoe lashed to the top of the car. "I'll need to make two trips," he said.

"I can carry part of it."

"Maybe we could load it all into the canoe, try it that way." He pointed ahead of us. "It's not far but some of the footing's tricky."

"How far is 'not far'?" I said.

"I'll make two trips."

"Put it in the canoe."

"I don't want you hurting yourself," he said.

I insisted that I could carry my end of the canoe, recalling the days when I had to keep up and pull my own weight if I wanted to tag along with him and Joe.

Though the place we descended was less steep than the rocky incline directly in front of the Blazer, it was still pretty steep. Sonny went first; he had overloaded the front end of the canoe and was bearing most of the weight on his shoulder.

About all I had to do was keep the other end off the ground. That still took both hands and made it difficult to see where I was putting my feet. When I got to the bottom of the hill and looked up at where we'd been, I felt proud of myself for having made it.

"I can drag it from here," he said. The sound of rushing water was much louder now.

"I'm okay," I said. I was breathing a little heavily.

Sonny took my elbow, and turned me toward the gentle rise ahead. "Walk on up there, see what you think."

I didn't argue with him. I walked up the slope, scuffing through dry leaves, eager to see the water I was hearing.

I stood looking down at what he'd brought me to see. The words came to mind: *Utopia, paradise, Eden!* I turned to look back at him—dragging the canoe and grinning—then back to the scene in front of me.

There was a pool of clear water maybe twenty yards across; I would see speckled trout swimming at the near edge when I moved closer. The far side of the pool was enclosed by a limestone wall, the top of which I could barely see from where I was standing. On our side was a low mossy bank from which I could have dangled my feet in the water, had I wanted to, and had it been summer. Trees overhung the pool, shading it all around except for one spot of sunlight near the center, which created a shimmer of gold on the still, green surface. The river fed into the pool over a rocky terrace on the right and out another at the end.

I was standing at the base of a fir tree, on a carpet of needles and cones. If I tried to sketch this, I was probably going to end up with something hopelessly romantic and sentimental. I thought about the little hole of foul-smelling water I'd wanted to see.

As I stood there, staring around me, he took an army blanket out of the canoe and spread it down; he set my bag on it, and the cooler.

"This is beautiful," I said. "Sonny, this is simply beautiful."

He pulled the canoe nearer the water and out of our way. I could see he was pleased by my reaction. "Hungry?" he said.

21

It was almost two o'clock by the time we finished eating. Lunch was fried chicken and potato salad, marinated asparagus and broccoli, a chunk of sourdough bread and a bottle of dry white wine. It was delicious. I had eaten my share of everything, amazed at how hungry I was.

I was lying on my side, resting my head in one hand and feeling warm and drowsy from the wine. I was halfheartedly dragging a charcoal pencil over a sheet of paper and watching Sonny snap a dry fly across the pool. He'd caught two trout already, and let them go. He took the fly rod apart and put it in its case, and came and stood beside the blanket. "We'll have to be going soon," he said.

He knelt suddenly and took the charcoal out of my hand and flipped the sketchbook closed, laying both out of my reach. "Sometimes you have to be still," he said. "Say you're in a stand watching for deer, like your husband's doing right now."

He pushed at the sketchbook again and laid the pencil back on top. "Only your eyes move, straining to see through the tree branches, the thickets. And while one part of your mind watches, another part must find something else to do. And sometimes you begin to think about who you are, who you've become."

I thought he sounded overly dramatic, but his tone and the way his face looked kept me from smiling. He was gazing over my head into the distance. "For most people, that's the hardest part of hunting."

He had removed his jacket, and his burgundy shirt was open at the throat. I noted all the color—his shirt, my blue sweater, the army-green blanket on a floor of brown needles, the clear green water. I could smell the fir boughs above our heads, and I heard the sounds of the river rushing over the rocks.

He sat down, facing me. "I want to tell you what I asked Joe to tell you."

Don't, I thought immediately. *Don't tell me anything.*

"I'd like you to understand . . ."

"*I'd* rather we didn't talk about it," I said.

He watched me, his eyes gray and calm.

There had been only the two weekends, sad sweet dates, when Sonny managed to get passes from Ft. Campbell and drive home to take me out. The first one we were both so nervous and awkward in our new relationship that I'm sure neither of us saw the movie we sat through. I'd spent hours getting ready, washing and fussing with my hair, trying on and discarding one outfit after another. I can still remember the sundress I finally wore, and all for the boy I'd grown up with, who had seen me, at one time or another, in every conceivable state of disarray. I was still upstairs in my room when the doorbell rang.

I ran down the steps and kissed Dad's cheek before he had time to ask Sonny to sit down. "Have a nice time," my father said. "Don't be out too late." It was all changed: Sonny wasn't Joe's friend now, he was the potential deflowerer of a daughter.

After the movie, we went to Shoney's where my friends would see us together, all the recently graduated boys and girls of my class. Sonny looked smashing in his ranger uniform; he was so tall and looked so brave, with the lightning bolt on his sleeve, the spit-shined jump boots with his trousers bloused into them. He was Airborne, he was elite. He was mine.

It was 1967. He was not yet twenty, and I was going on eighteen. I was completely naive politically, but I knew I was proud of him and all that I imagined he stood for. I almost burst with the glory of it.

By the time of his second leave, he'd received orders for Vietnam. At first, what that meant to me was that we would be separated; the realization that he could die came later. After he'd told me, we drove around, trying to make conversation. We ended up in the country, parked on a wagon path between two pastures, with the moon shining on a pond in the distance, frogs croaking, cicadas singing, the July night heavy and moist as a sponge.

His arm lay across the back of the seat, his hand cupped my shoulder. Neither of us could think what to say, and wordlessly I turned to him, smelling the summer night as he tilted his head to meet me, at the last instant looking into my eyes, before his mouth covered mine.

He kissed my eyes, my temples. I felt his mouth hot and moist against the pulse in my throat, moving again to my lips. I had never been kissed like this; not by boys who'd hastily pressed their lips to mine, clumsy, bruising, too quick. His kisses were knowing and wise. He held my head against his arm while he slowly and completely set me on fire.

His hand moved across the front of my dress, and I felt my nipples stiffen, and I could feel him trembling. I had never wanted anything in my life so much as I wanted him. I ran my nails from his knee the length of his thigh, caressing him, and then he moaned and took my hand away.

He held my wrist, pressing my open hand against his chest, his head on the back of the seat, his eyes closed tight, pressing my palm hard to his chest, and his heart thudding beneath it. He caught my other hand and held my wrists together. "God," he said. "Don't do that."

"You want to," I said.

"Of course I want you."

I tried to lean around the barrier my arms made between us. I felt beautiful, white-hot and incandescent.

His fingers around my wrists started to hurt. "Don't be a pricktease," he said.

He might as well have struck me. I knew, even by moonlight, that his eyes had gone pale.

He lifted his head from the seat back while I twisted under his grip, trying to pull free. He finally let me go, and I moved away from him, to the other side of the car. My face was burning.

We sat there, not talking, until the insect noises began to sound like screams.

"I'm sorry."

I didn't answer him.

"I shouldn't have said that. I'm sorry."

I stared out the window.

He reached across the space between us and touched my shoulder. I shrugged away from him.

"All right." He sounded tired. "Come on. Let's do it, here in the car with your dress around your neck. I'll hurry, and keep an eye out for someone coming, some farmer with his shotgun. I'll hump you quick, with no protection, and pray I don't get you pregnant."

I put my hands over my ears. He made it so ugly.

He dragged me across the seat. "Is that what you want to remember?" I put my arms around him and hid my face in the curve of his neck and shoulder, crying, and breathing his clean hot scent.

"I love you," he'd said. "Don't you understand, I *love* you."

He'd held me on his lap and kissed me until it was late, and we had to go home. His will was the only thing keeping us apart. It was torture for me; I don't know what it was for him, knowing he could have taken me, knowing I wanted him to.

Later I would realize what he gave me by waiting: something clean to look back on, and everything to look forward to.

After watching his plane leave the airstrip at Ft. Campbell, I'd gone straight home and written a letter, hoping it would reach An Khe before he did. I tried to make myself believe that as long as I didn't miss a day writing, he would be safe; it was a bargain I'd struck with God, or the Devil, whoever was in charge of the war.

"It's all in the past," I said now.

"That's true," he said. "But I'd like you to understand, whether it makes much difference . . ."

"I understand. Let's leave it at that."

He was looking at his hands; when he looked up, his eyes were cold and nearly colorless. "Right. The war's over. Let's fucking forget it ever happened."

"That's not what I meant," I said. He might have been carved of stone. I lay back and stared at tree branches. We were quiet for a long time.

"Joe probably thought I belonged in a psycho ward," he said. "He didn't know, he hadn't been there. He knows now," he said. "I'm not blaming Joe, Sarah."

"What happened to you?" *To us* is what I meant. "I want to know, too." He didn't answer; I began to think he wasn't going to. He'd brought me out here to explain, and I'd told him I wasn't interested. When he did speak, I didn't interrupt. I listened.

"I landed at An Khe, cherry and scared out of my mind. You were cherry until you'd been in the country a while and managed to stay alive. I thought I knew a lot. I didn't know anything.

" 'It's usually you virgins that get it,' they told us—the ones who'd been there longer. They told us to tape our dog tags together, or, better yet, tie one on each shoelace so they didn't clink. 'Then if your leg gets blown off, you'll still have a tag on the other leg. You get both blown off, fuck it, you're dead anyway. Don't wear your canteen or rifle clips so they rattle.' I remember one kid slapping on aftershave. 'Charlie can smell, too, numbnuts,' they told him. Some guys wouldn't eat meat for a couple of days before going on patrol. You didn't shower before patrol; Charlie could smell the soap.

"They weren't telling me these things because they cared about *me,* particularly. Cherry boys could get the whole squad killed. Later, I treated new troops the same. I didn't want to be their friend—their chances of getting killed were too high—but if I told them some things they needed to know, and they died anyway, at least I'd done what I could.

"You had to learn, and you'd better learn fast. You didn't necessarily listen to your officers, either; you listened to the guys who'd been alive the longest. I listened to a little Israelite named Isaac who was doing his second tour.

"Officers would rotate in who didn't know the first thing about the country or guerrilla warfare, but they'd be too proud to ask their men. You'd see them leading platoons into the jungle, chatting and talking, yelling back and forth to each other. Where did they think they were going? I wonder how many died simply because they didn't know to be quiet.

"I killed my first gook before I'd been in the country three weeks; it was ridiculously easy. That's the first thought I had afterward, how easy it was. I was walking point and caught a flash of sun off a piece of metal. It was probably his AK 47, or his cartridge belt; the important thing was, I saw him before he saw me. I had to swallow my heart back down where it belonged. Till then I'd never seen a VC. Normally, all you saw was jungle.

"I motioned to alert the men behind me. The VC was a little skinny guy, he looked old to me, maybe he was forty. I waited to see if anyone was with him, and held up five fingers. Then I had him in my sights, and before I had time to think about it, I squeezed the trigger.

"His chest exploded. Just like that. I must have stood there with my mouth hanging open, while the squad blew the others away, full automatic, killing them before they could kill us.

"I'd gotten there mid-September. By the first week in October, I'd killed somebody. 'Not *somebody*, asshole,' Isaac said. 'A fuckin' gook.' I couldn't eat that night, didn't even open my rations, and the guys razzed me. 'What's the matter, Woods? Got the whoopsies?'

"By the time all hell broke loose with Tet, I had learned to joke about killing, too. There were seven in the squad now; another guy who'd come in when I did was already dead. The rest of us worked well as a unit and we asked our CO not to make our squad any bigger; we didn't want an eighth man.

"There was Isaac Levine; he said seven was the perfect number anyway; it was in the Bible. He'd been there the longest. There was a big Pole named Bannowski, and Jesus Ortez, a Puerto Rican we called 'Jess' because he said 'jes, jou are right' to just about everything. Bannowski would say, 'Who are jou calling a Jew, jou fuckin' Spick?' There were two black guys, Huel Batts and Dumas Hastings; we called them Huel and Duel. Batts carried the radio, and Hastings carried the M-60. And there was Billy Riley, a Georgia cracker, and me.

"Bannowski called us the United Nations. He said, 'We got us a Jew and a Spick, a fuckin' Polack, two Africans and a Irishman. And Woods. What the hell kind of a name is Woods, anyway?'

"Isaac said, 'That's a purely American name.'

" 'Hell, shoot the motherfuck!' Bannowski said. 'He's the one got us into this war.'

"We trusted each other, and we could depend on each other. Eventually, there got to be a sort of mystique about us. We were considered lucky. And for a while, we were.

"But no matter how long we'd been there, or how tough we acted, we never got over being scared. We developed little habits, little rituals we thought would keep us alive. One of mine was carrying your letters. I kept them wrapped in plastic, in my chest pocket. Or somewhere in my gear, but preferably on my person, next to me. I'd memorize them, knowing if I was a good boy and didn't get myself killed, I'd have another batch waiting for me back at base camp.

"I got more and more edgy. After a while, I got so I couldn't stand for anyone to touch me. I didn't want anyone throwing an arm around my shoulder or slapping me on the back.

"At first I counted the months, the weeks until my time would be up. Then that became something else to avoid; I'd see short-timers lose their nerve and die a month, two weeks, two days before they were due to go home. So I quit counting. I was in the field the day I was supposed to leave for Nha Trang.

"There was so much I wanted Joe to know about. I wanted him to know there was nothing over there worth dying for. I wanted him to know what death looked like. There was nothing imaginable that these people hadn't already done to each other decades before we came. And then we came and killed the land along with the people. The bomb craters, the defoliants, the napalm—what we did will take generations to heal. I wanted him to know what a total fuck-up it was.

"They'd take us out in a Slick and set us down in the boonies, and leave us. Sometimes we'd be out a day, sometimes several days, depending on the mission. We might be supposed to locate a suspected NVA stronghold and call in the coordinates so flyboys like Joe could do their job.

"We might be looking for our own, a helicopter down, or a squad they couldn't raise on the radio. Sometimes we were supposed to bring Charlie back alive for interrogation. Most of the time, at least at first, we did what we were told. A few times we didn't. We developed our seventh sense, we called it; if something wasn't right, if it didn't feel right or smell right, we might just pass. We'd set up our perimeter and wait it out. Call in a day or so later, 'Nope, nothing out here. Come get us.' We were the experts; we'd had the training and experience and we weren't about to get ourselves dead on some stupid mission for an officer who'd never been *in* the bush. But most of the time, out of a sense of pride or patriotism, I still don't know what, exactly—conditioning, I guess—we did what they sent us to do.

"We'd been taught to think of them as gooks, the enemy, dinks, slopes. We weren't supposed to think of them as human beings. We'd walk up to a body and say, 'Yep, a head shot—ten-pointer. Went in through the eye, and took out the back of its skull.' At nineteen, with death all around, you begin to realize you can die, too. You wonder why you ever wanted to be a ranger in the first place. You make jokes to keep from crying.

"There were times we couldn't afford the noise of a rifle shot. Our lives depended on stealth, getting in and out without being discovered. So we used knives, pinching off the nose and mouth like we'd been taught, severing the vocal cords so they couldn't scream, then the jugular. And I had a crossbow that a Montagnard had given me.

"One morning, just at dawn, we found a camp of eight VC, still asleep. We killed them silently, one apiece, while the eighth slept. We thought about waking him up, but we didn't.

"Isaac was our spiritual as well as our physical leader. He knew the Torah, and he'd talk about the wars the Israelites had waged against the Babylonians, the Assyrians, the Philistines. He said it wasn't wrong to kill in war, it was our duty, with God's blessing. He could quote chapter and verse, so that we might be surveying the carnage we'd just wreaked, and still feel righteous. But we weren't to do atrocities. He told us about some Korean soldiers who disemboweled pregnant women, and said that was wrong.

"We didn't rape, we didn't mutilate. We weren't doing anything bad, we were doing our jobs. He could pray when the rest of us wouldn't, so he prayed for all of us, out loud sometimes, and it didn't sound ridiculous when he did it. It made us feel good.

"He was a wiry little guy. They'd wanted to make him a tunnel rat, like Clifford was, but he was too claustrophobic for that, he couldn't take being closed in. So that they wouldn't think he was chicken, he volunteered for the rangers. With Isaac for our rabbi, we could justify the killing. Until we lost him.

"We'd been out for five or six days in a VC valley when we were almost overrun by a large group of North Vietnamese regulars. We'd heard them coming; it had sounded like a whole division. There were way too many of them to engage, so we split up and tried to disappear. I climbed a tree, and all a gook would have had to do was look up. I sat up there and shook for I don't know how long.

"We had a system for getting back together, and when we finally regrouped, Isaac wasn't there. We waited that night and part of the next day, then went looking for him.

"We found him late that afternoon by the sound of his voice. He wasn't calling to us—he didn't want to give us away. He was singing, talking to himself, just sort of making noise so that if we weren't dead, maybe we'd hear him. He was in a clearing, sitting on a tree stump, naked.

"I started crawling to him with the others hanging back in the trees, covering me. I couldn't believe Isaac had gone off his rocker. He was the strongest mentally, too.

"He didn't see me coming. He was swaying on the stump, talking Yiddish or Hebrew, something I couldn't understand. Another odd thing—he was holding his knife. Then as I got closer, I could really begin to see the shape he was in. They'd had him, all right, and it looked like they wanted us to find him. He was a mess.

"Normally, if the NVA caught you, they tortured you to death, killed you outright, or took you prisoner. They'd knocked Isaac's teeth out, probably with a rifle butt. One cheekbone and his nose were smashed; that eye was closed. His entire upper body was a mass of bruises and open sores, cigarette burns. It looked like they'd started to skin him; there was a large flap of loose skin on his chest. They must have thought they'd done enough damage that he wouldn't live long, or they wouldn't have left him.

"He must have been hallucinating from all the pain, slipping in and out, but he hadn't given up, and he hadn't given us away. You sorry bastards didn't know Isaac, is what I was thinking.

"I'd crawled within five yards and he still hadn't seen me. He was swaying on the stump. He'd almost fall, and then he'd catch himself.

" 'Isaac!' I said. 'Hey, man, you booby-trapped?'

"It took him a minute to come to enough to locate me. I was on my stomach, keeping my head down.

" 'Sonny,' he said. 'Is that you?' And he started to cry.

"I wanted to get up right then and go get him, but I couldn't risk it. I asked him again if he was booby-trapped, and he shook his head no. I asked him where the NVA were, and he says they're gone, maybe back to Hanoi, he doesn't know. But he's sure they're gone.

" 'Can you walk?' I ask him, and he starts crying again, shaking his head no.

"While I waited for the others to check the area and get back to me, I lay there, watching Isaac fade in and out.

"When we were reasonably sure they were gone, I got up and took the knife out of his hand, and had him under the arms, trying to pick him up. He was screaming for me to stop. I didn't get it. And then he showed me.

"The bastards had nailed his scrotum to the stump. They had used a piece of rusty barbed wire, and nailed his testicles to the stump. And left him his knife, so he could either sit there and die, or geld himself.

"He'd been working at trying to pry the wire loose, but they'd nailed it all the way across and down both sides. Hammered it down solid.

"We called in the chopper, told them to bring wire cutters, told them to bring a fucking chainsaw, for Christ's sake. Don't ask questions, just bring it!

"We gave him water and morphine and stood around feeling helpless, swearing and cursing about what we would do to the next filthy scum we got our hands on. Isaac had been there for the better part of two days, in that humidity and heat. We were thinking we'd found him too late."

For the first time since he'd begun, Sonny paused.

"So one day, they come to the bush and get me: 'Woods, you stupid jerk, your time's up, you're going home.' A few days later, I'm sitting on the couch in your apartment."

He waited, but I couldn't think what to say. I was sitting up now.

"I tried to make the adjustment. Believe me. But it was like I'd had to learn to breathe water, and done that for a year, and then I was being jerked up and thrown out on the bank again. I kept hearing things, and reaching for my weapon and it wouldn't be there. For a year I hadn't slept without my rifle beside me. When they wouldn't let me have it on the plane . . . I thought I'd go crazy. I almost didn't get on.

"And then, so quick, back in the states, and it's like there isn't any war. Not in polite company, certainly, nobody wanted to talk about it. Even the uniform was an embarrassment; I'd catch civilians in the airport looking at me like I was an animal. Don't remind us, the looks said.

"Back on post, they wanted me to keep my socks lined up straight, my bunk made just right, all that regimental spit and polish. I couldn't believe it. I couldn't believe they expected me to take that crap seriously any more. I almost got busted my first day back.

"And then you opened the door, and there you were." He laughed. "I'd *heard* about miniskirts. And you'd let your hair grow longer, you looked beautiful, simply wonderful. And I was scared to death of you. I felt all twisted up inside.

"I didn't know how to tell you, so driving back to post that Sunday, I told Joe. He was going, he *needed* to know. I asked him to tell you a little of it, whatever he thought right, enough so you'd understand that I needed to get myself straightened out.

"I was lucky to have a CO who'd been over there; he fixed it so I wouldn't get bad paper for spending the rest of my hitch in the hospital. So that's what I did. I felt guilty, being in a hospital, being safe, sleeping between clean sheets while my squad was still over there. I'd dream they'd all been killed, blood everywhere. I dreamed about Isaac. I'd wake up, the whole bed drenched in sweat, screaming for my rifle. They started to give me a lot of medication."

He got up and stood with his back to me, looking across the pool.

It was quiet except for the sound of rushing water.

I thought of how he must have wondered when I didn't

call, or come. What he must have thought, how it must have hurt him.

Why hadn't Joe told me these things? What had he thought, after listening to Sonny that Sunday afternoon? What had he imagined happened between us, that neither of us would talk about it? Something awful? Something worse? Joe must have believed he had a good reason not to tell me. Hadn't he?

All these years, Sonny believing I knew, believing Joe was alive. Believing his two best friends in all the world had turned their backs on him.

I longed to tell him how sorry I was, but it was a little late for that. By about seventeen years.

22

He turned his head, speaking over his shoulder. "So now you know."

"When you saw the monument," I said. "The names you didn't look for—they were the men in your squad?"

"Yes." He turned away from the pool. "We all said when we left there that we'd look each other up back in the world. Knowing we probably wouldn't."

"Maybe it *is* better not to know some things." Then I realized what I'd said. "I didn't mean . . ."

"I know you didn't." He came and sat on the blanket again. "I knew you were home when Clifford dropped his new boss's name." He glanced at me when he said this. "I knew you were going to be here."

I didn't say anything. Lou had been right then.

"Clifford thought it was strange when I asked him if we could come along. Like taking a busman's holiday. I wanted to see if you'd gotten old and fat."

"Dick couldn't remember your first name, but he told us what Clifford said. How you leaped tall buildings in a single bound, walked on water."

Sonny grinned. "Clifford's a little much sometimes."

"Sometimes?"

"Lou has trouble deciding how to take him."

"I can appreciate that."

"He's all right, though."

"If you like trolls," I said.

He was laughing. I was glad we were laughing.

"Okay," I said. "I admit I did like him better the other night. But I kept expecting Braxton to squash him like a bug."

"Braxton might have tried," Sonny said. "Size can be misleading."

"How do you know Clifford anyway?"

"Met him at Buster's."

"Lou doesn't like *him* much either," I said, and wished I hadn't. I remembered the scene from this morning, the men from Buster's chasing the deer, and thought I'd reminded him of it, too.

He was frowning. "Buster is just trying to make a living like the rest of us. He doesn't approve of some of his guests. But you're right, Lou doesn't like him."

I was starting to compliment Joanne's lunch again to change the subject, but he interrupted.

"Hold on a minute, let me tell you something about Clifford and Buster." He paused and rubbed the back of his neck. "The Viet Cong had tunnels that ran all the way from Saigon to Cambodia, over two hundred miles of tunnels. Some of them were four stories deep. They had hospitals underground, factories, theaters. Westmoreland called the VC 'human moles'; Clifford would leave off the 'human.'

"Because he's small, like they are, his job was to go down after them. There were trapdoors to the different tunnel sections so that they could be shut off if one was damaged, or to trap some guy like Clifford. There were side passages leading to booby-traps: mines, say, or things like a panel with spikes in it, rigged to slam in your face. And it was dark down there, Sarah, and tight, maybe not enough room to turn around in, even on your hands and knees, even a little guy like Clifford."

"All right," I said.

"It was hand-to-hand combat with pistols and knives.

"Buster was in the Navy. He thought he had it made. He thought he'd spend his time on a nice clean ship, offshore somewhere. They made him a medic for the Marines."

"All right, I see your point."

"What is it, what's my point?"

"Well . . ."

"At breakfast yesterday, Braxton told me he spent the war

helping as many boys as he could evade the draft. I can respect that, and we hold many of the same opinions about Vietnam." He was leaning toward me, very intense. "But we reached our conclusions by different roads. We don't have the things in common that I have with Buster and Clifford. People who were there share a common memory. Maybe it shouldn't, but it makes a difference."

He leaned back. He seemed embarrassed at how he'd been right in my face. "We have to go, it's getting late."

I looked at my watch. We'd been talking for an hour. "I have to pay the Indians a visit first," I said.

It was a euphemism from Sonny's and my childhood, when we were in the fields playing, and it was too far, or too late, to go inside to the bathroom. I thought of all the "common memories" *we* shared.

When I came back, I folded the blanket, and he stowed it in the canoe. He handed me my life vest, and put his on. "How long will this take?" I said.

"Forty-five minutes to an hour."

"And then what?"

He adjusted the strap on his vest. "Then we walk."

"Walk where?"

Again, as he had earlier, he looked annoyed with the questions. "There's an old man runs a gas station. One of his sons can give us a lift back to the lodge."

He pushed the canoe into the water and held it against the bank. "Ready?"

"What do I do?" I said.

"Get in." He was holding a hand out to me.

"I *know* that," I said. I laughed, sounding nervous, as he helped me step down into the canoe and held it steady against the bank. "What do I *do?*"

"Stay on that seat, hold to the sides. If you get scared, slide off the seat to your knees. Don't stand up, whatever you do."

"Am I going to get scared?" I said.

He was kneeling on the bank, holding the canoe, and taking one last look around. When he turned, leaning over, I could see the flecks of color in his eyes. "What's to be scared of?"

"Are there rapids?"

"Not any bad ones."

"I don't paddle or anything?"

"Better let me do that." Then his eyes were grave. "I thought you might enjoy this." He made a sweep of the clearing, the pool.

"Sonny, I have. Really, I have. Thank you for bringing me." I sounded so formal, I laughed.

"I love it up here," he said.

"It's beautiful. Where are we anyway?"

He was still holding the canoe against the bank. It rocked side to side as he stepped in.

"I hold on is all I do, right?"

"Not that tight." He looked at my hands on the sides of the canoe. He was seated facing me, facing downriver. "This is supposed to be fun." He picked up the paddle.

"I know. It is."

We hit the first fast water leaving the pool, and my stomach knotted up.

"You can turn around if you want to," he said.

"Isn't this all right?"

"You're fine." He was lazily dipping the paddle. "I just thought you might like to see where you're going."

The current, I noticed, was carrying us right along. I glanced over my shoulder, and turned back around. I had seen real white water coming up.

I gripped the sides of the canoe, my knuckles white, and waited for us to hit a rock and drown. It seemed to me he ought to be in the front where I was. I watched him switch sides with the paddle, then back again. He was concentrating on what he was doing, somehow making adjustments in our approach, and I watched his face for any sign of worry or dread. "Relax," he said. "Let yourself go with it."

Suddenly I felt us sucked forward and down, sliding and plunging; like being on a roller coaster or in a fast car topping a hill. And then we were through it, smoothing out, and I felt exhilarated, and only a *little* terrified.

"That's as bad as it gets," he said.

"I liked it. I think." I risked another glance behind me, and let go of the sides, flexing my fingers. I turned on the seat to look ahead of us. The river was wider here, a flat green surface extending a hundred yards or more into a curve, with sloping rocky banks on either side.

When I turned back around again, Sonny had been watching me. He looked away, dipping the paddle in smooth, long strokes. He started to say something, then changed his mind. He let his gaze follow the bank as he pulled us along.

"It's not that I'm really scared," I said. "I've just never done this before."

He didn't say anything. He continued to paddle, a couple of strokes on one side, then a few on the other.

"Dick and I talked about floating the Buffalo one time."

He nodded and glanced my way, indicating he'd heard, then went back to watching the banks.

"We never did, though." I trailed my fingers in the water; it was cold. "How deep is this river?"

We were rounding the bend, and he eased the paddle up and held it out of the water. "Be still," he said. "Turn your head real slow."

I did what he said, looking where he was looking.

At first I didn't see anything; then I did. It was a bear, two bears actually, standing in the shallows of the river ahead of us: a large one and a small one, a mother and her cub, I realized, when I got over the initial shock and my mind began to function.

"Those are bears," I said as we drifted past. The mother heard me and herded her cub into the trees.

"Those were bears," I said again.

"I believe you're right." The corner of his mouth was twitching.

"I didn't know there'd be bears." Now that I'd thought about it, I was delighted.

"Why wouldn't there be?" he said, smiling now. He was paddling again, and the river was getting narrower, and swifter.

"I don't know," I said. "I just didn't know there were." I'd always connected bears with the Smoky Mountains, and mostly in those sad tourist exhibits. I wondered if there were any bears around the lodge.

"The cougars may be coming back, too, maybe even a few wolves."

"Come on," I said.

"Buster swears he's seen a red wolf."

I felt a thrill, a brief shiver of danger. This wasn't Centennial Park we were in.

"They follow the food chain. With wildlife conservation, there are more deer. And most predators are protected. Except coyotes. They're doing so well, there's a bounty on them again."

"They're not dangerous, though," I said.

"What? Coyotes?" I could see he was laughing at me.

I looked around, *really* looked around me: trees and hillsides, then mountains. I listened; except for the river sounds, there was a vast and terrible silence. "Where are we, really?" I said.

He seemed to be considering his answer; he looked amused. "You mean, if I give you a name, you'll know where you are? We're in the Ochokee Wildlife Management Area."

"All right," I said. "So long as *you* know where we are."

"Hold on."

We went through another stretch of fast water with the rocks around us and beneath us. This time I wasn't afraid.

"I'm sorry we have to hurry," he said.

I thought about Lou with her mother; about Dick, and wondered if he'd shot a deer yet; about Trudie and wondered what she was doing, whether she was baking bread, or, knowing Trudie, sleeping. I was glad she didn't know there were bears, or maybe she did. Maybe that was why she didn't want to be alone after dark.

"There probably won't be real wildlife much longer," he said. "Animals learn to adjust like people do, if they survive. Deer, for instance, you see them grazing alongside the road, like cattle. They've learned to run only if a car stops."

He smiled, but it was a sad smile. "Take a good look," he said. "This won't last much longer."

In the quiet places, I would turn on the seat to see what was ahead of us. Most of the time I was content to see where we had been. I liked watching him handle the paddle, the sure and easy way he used it to move us along, or in swift water, as a rudder.

We didn't see any more animals, and I was a little disappointed about that. I guess I assumed we would, after seeing the bears. He said we were lucky to see those.

We didn't talk much, and I thought it pleased him that I was trying to appreciate the quiet. There were sounds, of course; I could hear what was ahead by listening to the river. There was wind in the treetops; I heard a crow cawing. But behind everything was an enormous stillness. After a time, it had actual presence and texture for me; it was loud in my ears.

From the corners of my eyes I watched Sonny more than I watched the landscape. He looked completely at home and at peace here. Just before he brought the canoe to shore and we got out to walk, he asked, if we had the time, how I'd like to paint a scene like this.

I explained to him why it would be hard for me. I'm not a landscape painter. What I'd like to paint, I thought then, though I didn't tell him, was not the place so much as how he was in it.

23

I watched his boots, stepping where he stepped; that helped me ignore for a while longer how tired I was getting.

He had left the canoe tied to a tree. No one was likely to come along and bother it, he'd said; later he would float it all the way to the bridge. He'd volunteered this information. I'd decided not to ask any more questions if I could keep from it.

We'd left the life jackets and the paddle, of course, and the cooler. Sonny was carrying the rucksack with the army blanket rolled up and tucked under the straps. He'd left the fly-rod case, exchanging it for the rifle which I hadn't noticed him putting into the canoe in the first place. I'd suggested leaving the thermos and getting that later, too, but he said he'd carry it.

He'd pulled the rifle from behind the struts and taken it out of its case. I wondered what was *in* the rucksack that he couldn't leave it, but I hadn't asked. I did ask what we needed a rifle for—the bears? He'd smiled and said it was just part of the dress code.

I had only my canvas tote to carry, and it was getting heavier all the time.

I wondered how far we'd walked already. I hated to admit it, but I wasn't going to be able to maintain this pace much longer. I realized we were running late. He'd told Carlton to expect us around dark, so I was doing my best to keep up. But for every step he took, I was taking at least two.

Only once or twice did he hesitate about which way to go. I couldn't make any sense of where we were going, not even our general direction; I couldn't even remember which side of a tree the moss was supposed to grow on. We'd go up one hill and around the next one, along a ridge, then into a ravine. I was simply following, trying to keep up.

Finally, my lungs felt ready to explode. My throat was dry

and burning; I was hot, and wheezing like a bellows. "Sonny," I said. "Sonny!"

He stopped and came back for me.

"I'm really sorry," I said. "This is embarrassing. I'm going to take up jogging when I get home, I swear to God." I stopped to pant. "Just let me rest one minute."

I couldn't read his expression. "Let me carry that for you," he said.

"Absolutely not. You can carry *me* if you want to."

He did laugh then, a little. "You're doing fine. I've been pushing it." He set the rifle on its stock.

"How much farther? Not much, right? Couldn't be." I was bending over, my hands on my knees, taking deep breaths.

He was looking past me, off to the side somewhere, one knee bent, resting his weight on the other leg. We stood at the base of a large hickory. *There sure are lots of hickory nuts this year,* I noticed, and I remembered Braxton mentioning the acorn crop, one of the largest he'd ever seen. Funny how the mind will wander when it senses trouble. Delaying tactics. A nasty little worm of anxiety was beginning to squirm in my guts, but I stilled it.

"We're not lost or anything, are we?"

"No," he said. "We're not lost."

I didn't feel reassured. There was something about his manner. Earlier he'd seemed to be genuinely enjoying himself. Now he looked tense; I could see a muscle working in his jaw.

"I can make it, don't worry. I didn't realize it was this far is all. How in the world do your clients keep up with you?" I was trying to keep a light tone, but in the vast and empty silence around us, I sounded silly.

Now that we'd stopped moving, the air felt cooler. The light angling through the bare branches held no warmth. In another hour or so it would be dark. "How much farther to our ride?" I said.

He turned toward me, slowly, it seemed. Everything that

happened next happened slowly, like a film grinding down, or movements under water. His eyes at first looked cold, but it was pain I was seeing.

Then I thought how it must hurt him, having to watch me, as fear began to displace my trust. "We *are* lost," I said.

He stood so still. There was no panic in his expression, and I began to take hold. Even lost, he would know what to do. I had no doubt that he would know exactly what to do.

He said, "I'm afraid there isn't a ride."

"There's not?" I said.

"No."

Like some dumb animal, a cow or a mule that has been poleaxed, I stood there, staring at him and trying to comprehend. "Don't kid around," I said. I brushed at the hair falling in my eyes.

"Are you rested now?" He shifted the rifle until it was balanced in his hand and shrugged his shoulders to resettle the weight of the pack.

"What?" I'd forgotten about being tired.

Finally he stopped avoiding my eyes. "We're not going back," he said.

"Not going back?"

"No."

"You mean to Lou's mother's?"

This was Sonny, the boy I'd grown up with and gone to high school with; this was Joe's and my best friend. That's all I could think of, as I stared at him like someone suddenly struck dumb. I tried to laugh. "Where are we going?"

He glanced at the sky, a deepening blue. "It gets cold up here at night."

"I don't understand," I said. My voice sounded thin. We had to get back, they'd be worried. They didn't even know where we were.

He looked at me, as if he were reading my thoughts.

"This isn't funny." I tried to stay calm. "You tell me right now what this is all about."

He stood for what seemed a long time, considering. "We'll talk later."

"We'll talk now."

He took a step toward me then, looked straight into my eyes. "We'll talk later."

"You take me back to the car. This instant." I folded my arms across my chest, and locked my knees to keep them from shaking.

"I couldn't if I wanted to," he said, matter-of-fact. "That's a long way upriver."

I couldn't understand; it didn't make sense. I had an image of Dick, Trudie and Braxton, Clifford, and Lou, all of them back at the lodge, laughing and warm around a roaring fire and wondering what was keeping us.

"Maybe now you realize where you are?" he said.

This had to be a nightmare. *This isn't happening,* I thought.

My nose was running, and I dabbed at it with my sleeve. He reached in his back pocket and offered me a handkerchief which I refused. He held it out to me, his calmness underscoring my womanish hysteria, until I took it and blew my nose. "You're crazy," I said.

Maybe he flinched slightly. "Don't think I haven't wondered."

"You're out of your mind."

"We can discuss that later, too. Right now, we have to go."

The sun was going down. The trees a few yards away were starting to blur. The air was still, but increasingly cold. Night was coming on. "I'm not moving until you promise me we're going back."

Impatient now, he reached down and picked up my canvas bag. "Let's go."

I walked away from him, to the base of the ancient hickory, and sat down. I leaned against it, shaking with a combination of rage and fear.

He watched me, expressionless, as he ducked his head to sling the bag across his chest, the bulk of it resting under his arm and against his left side. He took deerskin gloves from the pockets of his goosedown jacket and put them on. He snapped the top snap—very loud in the quiet—and turned up his collar. "Coming?"

I heard him go. I kept my chin up and my eyes flinty so he'd know I meant it. I gave him plenty of time to come back. I didn't believe for a second he'd leave me.

When I looked for him, expecting him to be in sight, it took me a full minute to accept that he wasn't. I stood up and circled the base of the tree, looking in all directions. "All right," I said, almost to myself. I said it louder. I called his name. Then I realized I was alone.

Don't panic. That's what people always say. *Keep your head; don't panic*. All right, and after you don't panic, then what? I walked around and around the tree, trying to see into the thickening darkness, believing any second he would emerge from it. When he didn't, my heart started to pound and my breath was ragged. I gritted my teeth not to cry.

Soon it was night, black night. He'd left me, he was gone. When I wouldn't go with him, he'd simply left me.

I had my hands in the pockets of my jacket. I was cold. My gloves were in the canvas bag. I had no scarf. I was thankful that my hair was shoulder-length to cover my ears and neck, and that I'd changed my loafers for the hiking boots. But I was wearing only one pair of thin socks, and no long johns—only my jeans between the cold and my skin.

I kept moving to stay warm, stomping my feet, talking to myself, staying close to the tree. I tried not to think; I deliberately resisted thinking. I had no matches or lighter; therefore, no fire or warmth or light. I wasn't hungry, but I was extremely thirsty. He had the thermos filled with hot coffee; he had a canteen clipped to his belt. He had the blanket, and the rifle.

I stopped dead in my tracks.

What's the rifle for?

The cougars are coming back, he'd said, *following the food chain. Buster swears he saw a wolf.* And the domestic hogs now are breeding with wild peccaries, producing a particularly vicious and destructive strain. Maybe, Sonny'd said, Dick would like to hunt one of those sometime?

I knew there were bears; I'd *seen* them. I listened, straining to hear into the night, afraid I *would* hear something. A twig snapping, or a grunt. *Don't be silly,* I told myself. I laid my face against the rough scaly bark of the tree. My throat felt too dry to swallow. *Think about something else.*

What a beautiful afternoon. I'd been so touched by all the trouble he'd gone to. Such a lovely scene, such an enjoyable lunch. He'd been so pleasant, so *normal.*

Yes indeed.

It seemed like hours went by. I was terrified, for as long as I could sustain terror, then my mind brought out its heavy defense: numbness. If something out there was going to get me, it would just have to get me. I was too tired to worry about it. I thought about Dick. He would be crazy with worry by now. And Lou.

I wondered where Sonny had gone. He couldn't just go back without me.

It didn't occur to me to leave the tree and strike out on my own. Where would I go? I had no idea where I *was,* how far from the lodge or in what direction. And it was black, pitch-black night. Somewhere in the back of my mind, I knew I should stay where he'd left me.

I thought about why he was doing this. This afternoon, he'd tried to make me understand what it had been like for him. Did he want me to feel fear as he had? Was that it? He'd tried to make me understand how ordinary death had become, and killing. Easy, he'd said. Ridiculously easy. *No,* I thought. *Somebody will find me.*

I heard a noise that momentarily paralyzed me. *That was an owl. Just an owl, ninny. You've heard owls before.* I started to cry.

How could he hate me this much? It wasn't my fault.

They would find me. Dick would start looking in the morning. He'd already be working on it, right now. Calling the police or the park rangers. They'd start looking at first light. In the wrong places. They thought we'd gone to Medicine Springs.

I sat down at the base of the tree, brushing away the hard sharp nuts. I could barely feel my fingers and toes.

No matter how angry he was at the past, I couldn't understand Sonny's doing this. He and Joe had always looked out for me. I rested my head against the tree trunk and shut my eyes for a minute. I was so tired.

Something was shaking me. My first thought was of a bear, some wild animal, and I opened my mouth to scream.

"Wake up," he said.

My head lolled from side to side, and bumped against the tree trunk. "Stop it," I said. "That hurts."

He shook me again.

I slapped at him, but couldn't feel my hands. They were frozen lumps at the end of my wrists. "Damn you," I said.

"Get up." He helped me to my feet.

The moon had risen, huge and full. I could see by its light.

"Walk around."

"Just leave me alone," I said.

"Move around!"

"Go to hell!"

He shook me until my teeth rattled.

"If I have to drag you by the hair," he said, his voice shaking, "I can do that."

I felt oddly relieved. "That won't be necessary," I said.

He held my arm, his fingers like a vise on my elbow. He walked me around.

I told him I was thirsty, and he opened the thermos and poured coffee into the top. It was still warm. I held it in both hands, concentrating on not spilling it; I was shivering from the cold. If he noticed, or cared, he didn't show it. He waited, silent as a stone, while I drank.

I took the thermos and attempted to screw the top back on, my fingers numb and fumbling. He did it for me, then took his gloves off and thrust them at me.

"Mine are in there," I said.

He handed me the bag, then slipped the rucksack off and laid it on the ground between us. He opened it and took out a flashlight, positioning it to light our things. I found my gloves and put them on. "Aren't you going to say anything?" I said.

"Sit down."

"Why? You just made me stand up."

"*Sit down.*"

I sat down. "Can't you build a fire? I'm cold."

He shook out the blanket and draped it around my shoulders. I put it around my head, burrowing in, covering my ears and cheeks with the scratchy wool. It felt wonderful.

"What are you doing?" I said. He was unlacing my boot. "Why are you doing that?"

He pulled it off my foot and dug through the rucksack and brought out a pair of socks. He straightened the thin one I was wearing, and worked another one over it. He pushed my boot back on and straightened the tongue.

"Why'd you come back?"

The flashlight beam cast eerie shadows that made his eyes look hollow and deepened the cleft in his chin.

"Hey. I'm talking to you," I said.

"I never left." He started lacing at the toe, pulling each lace tight.

I thought about his being out there the whole time, probably enjoying himself, listening to me cry. "Bastard."

He paused, holding the tension on the strings, then went on with the lacing.

He was careful not to leave any wrinkles in the sock, smoothing it as he laced the boot. "How does that feel?" he said.

When I didn't answer, he started on the other foot.

I leaned my head against the tree and pulled the blanket closer. The police would ask for a description of us. Trudie would be the one to remember what I was wearing. Lou or Carlton would say we'd gone to Medicine Springs. I wondered how Dick would handle himself in this crisis; we'd never had one like this before.

"Why are you doing this?" I said.

He finished tying the shoelace. He lifted my foot off his knee and set it on the ground. "Let's go."

I hurt all over. My feet felt like pincushions, the muscles in my legs ached from the walking we'd done earlier, and my knee hurt from this morning when I'd hit it on the dash. "Where?"

"Come on, get up."

"Why can't you build a fire right here and let's talk about this sensibly?" I wanted to stay where I was, with gloves, warm socks, and the blanket around me.

Then he took the blanket, pulling it out of my hands. He folded it, rolled it tight, and tied it to the rucksack.

I hated him, and myself for how my voice sounded. "I don't understand why you're doing this."

"Get up."

"I'm tired!"

"You'll feel better once you start walking." He turned the flashlight off and packed it in the rucksack. He stood up, putting his arms through the straps and settling it on his back.

So we were going to walk again, miles and miles, probably. He took my arm and helped me to my feet. *Who are you?* I thought. *I don't even know you anymore*. "Can't you tell me where we're going, at least?" I said.

"You wouldn't know if I told you."

He carried everything; all I had to do was keep up. The moon was bright, an enormous full moon that somewhere was romantic. I realized that was what he'd been waiting for. He'd sat out there in the dark waiting for the moon to rise so we could see to walk by its light. And maybe he'd thought to himself: If

I let her think she's alone, she'll have time to decide she doesn't really want to be left. He was right.

It was hard to keep up with him. He didn't walk fast, but he walked steadily, like a machine. In rough or steep places, he'd give me his hand and, a few times, he let me stop to rest. He'd wait until I could breathe normally again, or until I asked him a question.

Stumbling through the wilderness by moonlight was surreal enough, like a dream-scape—but not being able to understand why it was happening terrified me.

I thought about Dick, wondered what he was doing, what he was thinking. I wondered how long Trudie would wait before she took him aside:

"Dick, I think you ought to know something . . ."

"What're you talking about? Who he is?"

"Remember in Nashville, before you and Sarah got married, I told you about . . ."

I could see his face. He'd wonder why I hadn't told him. If I had, this might not be happening.

My feet got so heavy I began to stumble more often. I stopped thinking about anything except taking the next step. Then I started to stumble and fall. The first few times, he was patient. He'd stop, come back, and help me up.

I'd say I was sorry.

He'd say, "You're doing fine."

Finally, he slung me across his shoulder, like a side of beef.

It hurt my pride. I insisted, and he put me down. "How much farther?" I asked him. "Can't you just tell me that much?"

The next time I fell, he carried me.

I woke up not knowing where I was, but I remembered how I'd gotten there. I remembered him putting me down, and lighting a lantern. I was watching him build the fire when I must have fallen asleep.

I tried to see if he was in the room before I opened my

eyes all the way. He wasn't. Then when I moved, it seemed every muscle and joint in my body hurt. I sat up and looked around.

There was just the one room, and it was primitive. Log walls and a rough board floor, a small rock fireplace at one end. I could see where both the logs and the fireplace had been re-chinked with cement. *This must be where he came,* I thought, *when he walked off into the woods*. I remembered Lou trying to tell me something was going to happen. I swallowed back tears and looked at my watch. It was two-fifteen. I'd slept what was left of last night and most of today. I had to struggle to come up with Sunday; today was Sunday.

There was a fire burning in the small stone fireplace with a trivet and a kettle hanging under it; the room was comfortably warm. An army blanket was nailed wall to wall, partitioning one corner. There were some clothes, a couple of jackets and shirts hanging from nails. I guessed the room to be about fifteen by twenty. There was one door and one window.

I was on a wooden platform about three-quarters the size of a double bed. There were plastic-covered foam pads and the sleeping bag on top of those. My boots had been set neatly together on the floor, my jacket lay across my feet. I wondered where he was. I dreaded having to see him. I realized it was absurd, but my dominant feeling at the moment was shame.

There were some crude shelves next to the fireplace with an assortment of cans on them—mostly army-green—and plastic jugs, a few dishes. There were two coal-oil lanterns, a camp stove, a kerosene heater, some pots and pans. There was a stool and a trestle table near the center of the room.

I threw the sleeping bag off my legs and put my feet on the floor. I wiggled my toes in the socks, then pulled them off to check the damage. I was surprised to find there were no blisters, just soreness in my heels and arches. I felt used and stiff all over, and thirsty. I very much needed to go to the bathroom.

I was tying the second shoelace when the door opened.

"You're awake." He had something in his hand, something skinned and bloody. It made my stomach roll to look at it.

He held it up. "Dinner," he said.

He crossed to the shelves and put it in a metal pan. He opened one of the plastic jugs and poured what I assumed was water over the carcass. Then he rinsed each hand and recapped the jug, and came and stood in front of me.

"How are you feeling? Hungry?"

All the helplessness I'd felt yesterday came flooding back. Dick would be frantic by now, wild with worry. We'd been gone a whole day and night.

"Don't feel like talking yet?" He turned and went back to the pan. He took his knife out of the scabbard and started cutting the thing up.

"I'd like to wash my face, please, and brush my teeth. I have to use the bathroom." I sounded about ready to cry. I was.

He had on the same clothes he'd been wearing yesterday. There was a smear of fresh blood on the new hunting pants to match the burgundy shirt. There was dark stubble on his face and his eyes looked tired. "I'm sorry," he said. "I wasn't thinking."

The blanket in the corner was the bathroom, probably constructed just for me; he must have tacked it up last night. It sheltered an enamel chamber pot and lid—what my grandmother would have called a slop bucket—and a roll of paper. He set a large aluminum pan on the table and poured water from the kettle into it. He took a bar of soap off one of the shelves, along with a washcloth and a towel. "I'll cut you a toothbrush," he said.

He pointed to my canvas bag next to his rucksack in one corner. He picked up the metal pan with the dead animal in it and went outside.

I bathed as well as I could, emptying the soapy water from the aluminum pan into the slop bucket, and refilling the pan from the kettle hanging over the fire. I used the towel as a pot holder to keep from burning myself. In my totebag I had the usual cosmetics and a comb and brush. There were deodorant and toothpaste on the shelf behind me. I wished I had a change of clothes, but I didn't.

I rinsed out the washcloth and the pan, put the lid on the chamber pot and carried it outside.

There was no problem deciding which way to go. The narrow path led straight down the hill from the front door. The other three walls of the cabin were overgrown with weeds and briars and bushes.

He was waiting at the foot of the hill. He tried to take the chamber pot, but I held it behind me. "Where's your latrine, or whatever?"

He showed me, and showed me where I could rinse the pot downstream from where he'd been cleaning the game.

I walked back to where he was standing and looked around me at the brown hills. I breathed deep; the air felt clean and good in my lungs. I bent to the stream, cupping my hand. I drank a lot of the icy water before I dried my hand on my jeans and stood up. "What was it?" I pointed to the pan.

"It's rabbit." He paused. "Did you find everything you needed?"

"I couldn't find the bubble bath."

"You probably looked in the wrong closet." He reached in his shirt pocket and handed me a stick with the bark peeled off one end. "It's black gum," he said. "You chew . . ."

"I know what to do with it. *I* probably showed *you*."

"Maybe you did."

I put it in my mouth and chewed the end, mashing and separating the fibers with my teeth, making my own toothbrush. I waited for him to say something.

He did look tired. His eyes were red and the lines around them seemed deeper. "I guess you're all wondering why I called this meeting." He laughed. When I didn't, he glanced at me and went back to staring at the hills.

"Why not just go back," I said. "Tell them we got lost."

He didn't say anything.

"They'd believe it. Who wouldn't believe it?" I waved an arm at the wilderness around us. "Even *you* could get lost, couldn't you?"

"I've been lost lots of times. But not out here."

"Then what's wrong with you?" I regretted the tone of my voice. And then I didn't; I was angry. "Look what you've done."

"Let's go inside where it's warm," he said. "You'll catch cold."

"People are looking for us right now. Dick will have people looking for me, they'll find the canoe."

"Probably they will," he said. "I tied it with a slipknot."

I couldn't decide if he was lying or not.

"When they do find it, or pieces of it, what do you suppose they'll think?"

He turned and looked down at me. "You don't have your jacket on. Let's go in."

I paced the room, looking things over and trying to stay calm. Once we got inside, he ignored me. He hung a cast-iron pot on the trivet where the kettle had been. He'd put the rabbit into the pot, with water, salt and pepper, and some pearl onions he took out of an ammunition box. He fed the fire from a stack of wood beside the hearth.

There were more army-surplus things stacked beside the door: some tarps or maybe a tent, an ax, a small chain saw, other tools, and a few more of the ammo boxes. There was a vicious-looking thing hanging on the wall above all this—probably the crossbow the Montagnard had given him. There was another sleeping bag rolled up, and an extra blanket.

He was still on one knee poking at the fire, his back to me. I stopped at the window and looked outside. There was nothing to see but the path and trees and underbrush growing on either side. It was almost as if he'd cultivated the tangle; it was obvious he hadn't done much to cut it back.

I got my sketchbook and a pencil out of the bag and sat down with them on the platform that served for a bed.

He dragged the stool close to the fire and sat staring into it.

It was almost four o'clock. We wouldn't be going back today.

The afternoon light slanting through the window was hardly enough light for drawing, but I had to be doing *something*.

Dick would be doing everything possible, and no matter how worried he was, I was sure he'd be holding up. Braxton and Trudie would stay with him. I tried to imagine what they'd say to him and what they'd be thinking that perhaps they wouldn't say.

Maneuvering in a boardroom or on the L.A. freeways, chairing a conference or making everyone feel welcome at a reception, putting together budgets and negotiating hard contracts—Dick could do all these and more. But I was afraid he wouldn't be able to do *this*; he'd be as lost out here as I was. He'd want to find me, and not be able to. He certainly wasn't going to find me today.

I looked at Sonny and drew the first line on a clean page.

What did he want?

24

I was thinking about the lodge, wishing I could suddenly and miraculously be back there. But thinking about it just made my chest hurt, so I concentrated on drawing; it occupied my hands and made the time pass. I wasn't afraid—I couldn't imagine being afraid of him, but now I was starting to wonder if maybe I should be.

I used the side of the pencil and bold strokes to show the crude stone surfaces of the fireplace, and Sonny hulking on the stool, staring into the flames. It was like a gesture drawing, harsh and brooding. He'd been sitting like that for half an hour or more, not talking, hardly moving.

I was drawing and trying to imagine what he was thinking when I realized he was standing over me.

"I used to wish you'd want to draw me," he said. "At least then I'd have been sure you saw me."

He was holding the stool. He plunked it down in front of me, and sat on it, leaning in.

"Did you?"

"I was about as interesting to you as a history assignment."

I met his gaze for a moment, then looked back to the page.

"One morning I dropped by your house to see Joe, nothing unusual. I started to say, 'Hey, Squirt,' like always, except the words died in my throat. You were about ready to leave for school. You reached for your books and your hair fell across your cheek, one gold barrette holding it back. Suddenly I couldn't get over how brown your eyes were, how high your cheekbones had gotten, the slow way you smiled. You said, 'Have some coffee, Sonny. Joe's upstairs.' And you were out the door, and I was standing there staring after you like I'd been hit between the eyes with a two-by-four.

"After that I'd come back off a haul and hurry over to see

Joe, when it was really you I wanted to see. He didn't even suspect, the dumb jerk."

Sonny laughed. "And neither did you. You'd say hi and then tell me where Joe was. You had your sights on college and all the smart college boys like your brother. You didn't even *see* me. I was just a piece of the furniture.

"I was drafted, and you didn't care about that either. I volunteered for the rangers hoping that might impress you. And when it didn't, I hoped I'd be too busy with all the training to think about you.

"When I got home from jungle school, Joe wanted to talk to me about the service. He was thinking about joining. He knew he wanted to fly, but he was wondering if he should try the Navy or the Air Force. And he told me if I could get a weekend pass, he had some dolls lined up, some real honeys. So I thought, great, that'll show her.

"I got to your house, and you were sprawled in your daddy's television chair, swinging a foot. I'm right there in the room with you, you haven't seen me in months. I'm getting ready to go lay some girl your brother's fixed me up with, and you couldn't care less. 'Oh, hi,' you say over your shoulder, like you're bored to death.

"So I walked over and tipped your chair back. I wanted to pick you up and shake you, anything to make you notice me. You reached for something to hold on to, and your arms came around my neck, just for a second. I could smell your hair, your skin. I wanted you so much, I could have swallowed you whole."

I kept my head down, gripping the pencil.

"How about some coffee?" he said. He lit the camp stove and poured water from one of the jugs into the pot. After he'd measured grounds from a bag of coffee he'd taken out of the rucksack, and searched the shelves for sugar packets and powdered creamer, he came back and sat down. "I've got some crackers, or trail mix . . ."

I shook my head.

"It'll be a while before the rabbit's cooked enough."

"I'm not hungry." I put the sketchbook aside, not knowing whether he expected me to say something, or if I should just listen. I wanted to get up and move around.

"I knew they were going to send me to Vietnam, that's what they were training me for, but I didn't know it would be so soon. I was hoping it would be later, after we'd had some time together. Saying good-by to you was the hardest thing I'd ever had to do. There I was, supposed to be a soldier, and I had to wear sunglasses so you wouldn't see me cry.

"I wasn't afraid of dying so much as I was afraid of never seeing you again."

I let him talk, but why was he doing this to himself, rehashing the war and our past? I pressed my palms together and concentrated on sitting still.

"If it hadn't been for your letters, I wouldn't have made it; it's that simple. I felt for guys who didn't get much mail. I actually lived for mine. I'd think, if I let them kill me today, I won't get to read Sarah's letters."

He got up from the coffee. "Cream and sugar?"

"Just cream," I said.

He added more wood to the fire, though it didn't need it, and checked the rabbit, lifting the lid with the tip of his knife.

I stretched and tucked one foot under the other knee. I rubbed the muscles in the small of my back.

"Sore?" He handed me the cup.

I tasted the coffee. It was good and strong.

"In the hospital I didn't worry too much when you didn't come. I knew you didn't understand, and I expected it would take you some time even after Joe explained it to you. And the first weeks, I didn't want you to see me anyway. The dreams kept getting worse. I'd dream my whole squad was being wiped out. I'd hear them screaming and see it happening, and I could have stopped it if I'd been there. They'd call my name, over and over.

"I dreamed about doing things that I never would have done. In one I was holding this gook down and carving my initials into his chest.

"I'd try to tell the doctors . . . one of my doctors wasn't much older than I was. He was scared when he finished his residency that they'd send him to Vietnam. He didn't want to believe what I was telling him.

"It's almost funny; in Vietnam I hadn't even smoked a joint. But in the hospital, I stayed high all the time. I'd save my medication for a few nights, and take it all at once, and finally get a night's sleep. I could buy practically anything I wanted in the hallways. It got so I was stumbling around zonked to my eyeballs most of the time.

"It helped to be stoned. At least, I'd come back with all my parts, but this corpsman down the hall from me—he'd lost the entire lower half of his face. I'd get really high before visiting him."

He set his coffee on the floor beside him. "I'd look at this poor guy and think, what if that was me? And I'd think, it wouldn't matter, she'd still love me."

I made a move to stand up. His eyes stopped me; they were like chips of glass.

He got up and walked to the table, and leaned on his hands, his back to me. When he turned around, he seemed almost sick, he was perspiring. "Did you love me at all? Did you mean any of the things you said in your letters?"

I felt the blood rise in my neck and face. *Damn you,* I thought. *How dare you ask me that?*

He came and sat down. He rubbed his mouth with the back of his hand. "How can you love someone, and marry someone else just four months later?"

There it was.

He'd said it in a flat, even voice. Now he was trying to appear calm and maybe even bored, but I could sense the emotion he was restraining. Tension hummed in the room like high-voltage wires.

Maybe he was right. How could you love someone and forget him in less than four months?

But I hadn't forgotten him; I hadn't forgotten anything.

"I think I'll have some more coffee," I said.

"Help yourself."

I walked around him and refilled my cup. *I didn't know I was hurting you,* I thought. *It wasn't my fault what happened. Instead of asking Joe to do it, you should have told me yourself.* "Would you like some?"

"No."

What about me? I was thinking. *How do you think I felt?* I came back and sat down.

"I'm not sure I can make you understand," I said.

"Why don't you try."

All right, I thought. *You deserve it.*

"Sonny Woods," I said. "Upperclassman. Football star, track star. Big Man on Campus. Lots of girls had the hots for you. I'd heard the gory details of your conquests. They'd come to *me* about you, cry on *my* shoulder. Because you were practically a member of my family, another big brother. I didn't *see* you, no, not in that way. Why should I? As far as you were concerned, I was just Joe's kid sister.

"The night you pulled my chair over. After you and Joe left, I sat there, kind of stunned. I couldn't believe it. I didn't know how long your leave was, I didn't know if I'd see you before you went back, I didn't know if I'd seen what I thought I'd seen in your eyes."

He looked at me now.

"We were pathetic, Sonny, both of us, trying to learn a whole new way of approaching each other. I was seventeen. You'd been one thing all my life, and suddenly you were something else. Instead of being Joe's friend, you were my lover. I adored you.

"Your uniform, the way you looked in it. The whole concept of fighting for your country. 'Ask not what your country can do for you,' and all that. Spangles and glory. So patriotic, the way

John Kennedy might have wanted it if he hadn't been assassinated.

"I thought it was glamorous that you were going to war; I thought it was exciting. It took a while for me to realize you could be *killed.*

"Our second and last date, do you remember? We drove out to the country. I knew you'd made love to other girls. I wanted you to make love to me. I wanted it to be *me* you thought about while you were gone."

I saw him swallow. I got up and set my cup on the table.

"I didn't want you to forget me while you were over there. That's one reason I wrote you every day.

"I attended my classes, worked in the studio, and came home. I'd watch the news, listening to the daily body count, and how many of our boys had been killed, and where. That's what I did for the year you were gone—that's all I did. Trudie tried to get me to go out with Jake's brother once, just so he wouldn't feel like a drag on her and Jake, and I couldn't. I don't know, I think I felt it would jinx something, jeopardize some delicate balance of *us* that I carried around in my head.

"At first you wrote fairly often. You described your base camp and told me what the climate was like. You said it was a beautiful country, you told me about water buffalo and elephant grass. You told me about this Montagnard family you'd met. But you didn't tell me anything about what was happening to you. I had to bump into your mother at the grocery store to find out you'd been wounded. She told me about your Purple Heart. I pretended I knew already."

Sonny's eyes were fixed on me as I returned to the bed and sat down; I unlaced my boots and took them off. I sat on the sleeping bag, my legs crossed Indian-style. "I planned how it was going to be when you got home. Everything we'd say to each other, and do for each other. Every look, every touch. But it didn't turn out like I'd expected. Of course, I understand now; I didn't understand at all then."

Maybe his eyes were wet. I couldn't be sure, but I hoped so; I wanted him to know how *I'd* felt.

"When you were due home, I couldn't wait to see you. I worried Joe half to death making sure he had the arrangements straight, that he for certain had leave and would pick you up on time. When I opened the door, the first thing that was *supposed* to happen, of course—like in every movie—you were supposed to sweep me into your arms. Simply *crush* me to you. Night after night, I'd imagined how that was going to feel. Then we would kiss . . .

"In the kitchen Joe put his arm around me and said he thought you'd had a pretty bad time, and told me to be patient.

"When they left, and we were finally alone, I thought, *now* it will be all right. For months I'd imagined this beautiful scene, how you'd want me. How you'd make love to me."

He stood up.

"I'm not finished."

He stopped with his back to me, then came and sat down again.

"I lost a lot of weight. My parents thought I was sick; they wanted me to see a doctor. I couldn't tell them what was wrong, I couldn't even talk to Joe. I was so ashamed. To imagine that I'd thought you loved me.

"I pictured you with dozens of Oriental girls.

"You didn't call or write. Trudie kept after me to call you. I couldn't; I cringed every time I remembered the look on your face when I touched you. I relived that night a million times, trying to see what I'd said or done wrong.

"I met Dick at the Catacombs where I showed my paintings. Trudie introduced us. He bought a painting. He was kind; he didn't press. I don't have to explain Dick to you. You've seen the man he is.

"I treated him badly, at best. I didn't tell him about you; I didn't want anyone to know. I was furious when I found out that Trudie had. I was too busy feeling sorry for myself to care about anyone else's feelings."

I stopped; my mouth open as I heard myself. I *heard* what I'd just said. I stared at Sonny, not able to tell anything from his expression.

The night in my apartment, even with Joe's warning—had I really stopped to consider that something might be wrong with Sonny? No, all I cared about was that he seemed to find something wrong with *me*. Trudie had begged me to call him, but I'd protected my damaged pride instead. When I wouldn't be honest with Dick, she had been honest for me, letting him know the chance he was taking.

And Joe. In the back of my mind, I'd immediately rationalized that he hadn't given me Sonny's message because he was protecting me from a returned killer whose hands were still dripping blood. More likely, I realized now, he'd wanted to protect Sonny from me, a selfish child who'd made no attempt to understand what he'd been through, but who'd sent him out the door with her handprint fresh on his face.

"Trudie begged me to call you," I said. "I wouldn't listen."

He was looking at me with something like compassion.

"Whatever Joe's reasons were," I said, "I *know* he loved you; he loved us both."

Maybe for the first time in my life, I couldn't feel sorry for myself. "You've every right to despise me," I said. "Who in the world could blame you."

"Is that what you've been thinking?" he said.

I'd have done anything to get away from his eyes.

"Do you really think that I *hate* you, and that I'd hurt Lou, or a man like your husband because of that? You still don't get it, do you?"

25

He'd stood up and gone outside.

For a while I sat where he'd left me. Then I put my shoes on and walked around the room. I stopped beside the table; he'd left the rucksack on it, open, when he'd made the coffee. I looked through it and took out a packet of dehydrated vegetables.

I poured water from the kettle into the metal basin and rinsed our cups. There was a film of dust on the shelves, so I washed them and the few dishes on them. I carried the pot from the trivet to the table and spooned the pieces of rabbit onto a plate. When it was cool enough to handle, I tore the meat from the bones and put it back into the broth, along with the packet of vegetables.

I tended the fire.

I took the apples from my bag and set them on the table. We'd go back now. Not today, it would be night soon; but we would start back in the morning. I was sure of it. *He had loved me. Did he still?*

I stood at the window, looking out. I paced the small room.

I was replacing the pot on the trivet when he came in. He took his jacket off and laid it at the foot of the bed.

I waited for him to see that I'd opened both sleeping bags and placed them together.

When he turned around, I went to him. He stood with his arms at his sides while I unbuttoned his shirt. I pulled his belt free of the buckle, and opened it. Neither of us had said a word.

Abruptly, he sat down and started unlacing his boots. He yanked one off, then threw the other after it. He took my arm and pulled me down beside him. He threw my boots and socks after his, then stood, stripping off his shirt and tee shirt.

He lifted me to my feet again. "Raise your arms." He pulled

my sweater over my head. I unhooked my bra while he took my jeans and panties down together; holding his shoulder for balance, I lifted each foot while he pulled them off. There was a dimpled scar on the left side of his back that I barely had time to see before he kicked his own pants away and pushed me down, opening my legs with his knee.

I wasn't ready. I tried to help him as he forced his way, hurting me. I couldn't understand his brutal haste.

He was barely inside me when I felt him come.

I could feel our hearts thudding against each other. I lay still, bearing his weight. I didn't say anything. I stroked his back, touching the scar.

In a minute he turned his head and the stubble on his jaw scratched my cheek. I felt his breath warm against my throat, then his mouth on my breast.

Now he gave me his full attention. When, later, he slipped his hands beneath my hips and entered me again, I was brought so sudden and sharp to completion that I cried out.

When I opened my eyes, he was watching me. He kissed my forehead, the corner of my mouth. Still inside me, and keeping me with him, he rolled onto his back.

I watched him sleep. Lying close, my leg over his, my head on his shoulder, I studied each angle and shadow of his face. He looked younger asleep, almost boyish. His lashes were thick, and as long as a girl's.

Outside it was dark. I studied his face by firelight, wanting to memorize it as he looked now. I meant to ask him about the scar on his forehead, how he'd gotten it. And the one on his back, and the one above his knee.

As I watched him sleep, I thought how we'd cheated the fates. We'd gone back and taken what should have been ours. For one chilling instant I considered how much it might cost us. Then I pulled the sleeping bag over us and closed my eyes.

When I awoke, the dull glow of embers was the only light in the room. Careful not to wake him, I got up and pulled on his shirt.

I got the fire burning again and laid on heavier wood. I stood on the hearth in my bare feet, waiting to be warm. I was starving.

I tried to remember where I'd seen the box of Diamond matches. I found them and I took one of the lanterns down and lit the wick. I was replacing the mantle when I saw he was awake.

"Come back to bed."

"I'm famished," I said.

"I know." He lifted the corner of the down bag. "In a minute. But now come back to bed."

We ate, sitting in bed, our knees touching. I couldn't remember ever being this hungry before, or anything tasting so good. A fresh pot of coffee was brewing on the camp stove. He had opened a tin of biscuits, or crackers, Vietnam's answer to hardtack, he said. They were broken inside the can. We picked out the larger pieces, and he dumped the crumbs in the broth.

"The miracle of preservatives," he said. "These things may be ten years old."

"I don't care."

"They could be from World War II."

"Give up," I said. "I intend to eat my share."

We ate all of it.

He hadn't dressed. He sat with his legs crossed and a corner of the sleeping bag covering him. I was still wearing his shirt. He finished the stew and laid the spoon on his plate.

He put his hands on either side of his neck and moved his head around.

"Why not let me do that?" I said.

He pushed the plate aside and turned around. I got on my

knees and kneaded the muscles in his neck and shoulders. *We'd made love; we were lovers.*

"So this is where you stayed," I said. "How'd you get all this stuff up here?"

"Pack mules. I made several trips."

"I guess you were pretty comfortable then."

"I even had a feather mattress."

"Where'd you get it?"

He was relaxed, his chin on his chest. "I stole it off a clothesline."

I didn't say anything.

"Okay, I bought it off a clothesline."

I used my thumbs down his spine, then my fingertips and the heels of my hands across his shoulders.

He raised his head. "You know, some old trapper probably cut these logs with an ax, split the boards by hand. I used to wonder what happened to him, whether he'd moved or died. I might have frozen to death if he hadn't built this place."

"How's this?" I said.

"Better."

I picked up our plates and the empty C-ration can. I put them in the washbasin with the stew pot and poured water from the kettle over them. I refilled the kettle from a plastic jug and hung it on the trivet. I put more wood on the fire. He sat with his back against the wall, watching me.

I dragged the stool to the edge of the bed and set our coffee on it. I got an apple off the table, and his pants off the floor where he'd dropped them. I was unsnapping the scabbard on his belt.

"Easy," he said. "That's pretty sharp."

I slipped the knife from its sheath. The blade was dark, the same dark metal as the handle. It felt cold and heavy as I turned it in my hand. "Why is the blade dark like this?"

I laid it across his palm, and looked at him.

He kept his eyes on the apple he was quartering. He cut

it into four pieces, cut the seeds out and laid them on the stool. He looked up, offering me a piece. "It doesn't reflect light."

Of course, I thought, realizing what kind of knife it was.

He lined up the other three pieces on the bed.

I sat down, folding one leg under me.

"What's wrong?" he said.

"Nothing."

He watched me.

"It's just . . . Okay, I think it's pretty gruesome to cut your food with the same knife that you cut people's throats with."

"Gooks' throats. It's just a knife," he said. "Maybe I should put it in the trunk with my medals."

"Maybe you should," I said.

He doubled his hands into fists. "Where do I put these then?"

He slipped the knife back in its scabbard. "I did hate you at first, you were right. I hated Joe. Hated you both.

"At night, I'd lie here and think about you, wondering what *your* life was like." He reached for his cup and drank, then set it back on the stool. "When you told me he was dead, I thought of all the times I'd pictured his plane being shot out from under him.

"He'd always get out because I wanted him to get out, so I could imagine his parachute coming down in the middle of a village. He'd be able to see the people under him, reaching up for him. Sometimes they'd give him to the women, the ones who'd lost sons and fathers and husbands. Sometimes the men would interrogate him."

He looked up and saw my face. "Oh, Jesus," he said.

"Maybe that's what happened." I felt myself sinking.

"No. That's not what happened." He reached to touch me. "Guys see a puff of smoke, they say it's a parachute. They think it's kinder to leave room for hope. Sarah, I'm sorry."

"It isn't," I said. "It's not kinder."

He took a breath and let it out. "Joe died in the crash."

"You can't be sure."

"More than likely."

I used the black-gum brush and his toothpaste to clean my teeth. I'd have given anything for a long hot shower. I went ahead and washed the few dishes from our meal and rinsed out my sweater and underwear. I set the stool in front of the fire and draped the clothes over it.

Sonny was outside again. He'd said he was going for wood, which we didn't need. He seemed restless, moody. I thought he must want to be alone.

I wondered if they'd found the canoe today. I wondered if they were dragging the river for our bodies.

The full moon was riding white and huge against the black eastern sky, tree limbs cross-hatching its face. It was bright and somehow comforting through the room's small window. It was past nine o'clock; I wondered what could be keeping him.

He had to be tired. I wasn't sure how much rest he'd gotten the last couple of days, but I knew it wasn't much. He had to be thinking about going back, what we were going to say when they asked us what happened. I wondered again what was taking him so long as I straightened the sleeping bags and crawled between them.

I lay there trying not to think about morning.

Then the door opened, and he pushed it shut with his shoulder. He dropped an armload of wood beside the hearth and brushed bark from his sleeves. He checked the door again, making sure it was tightly closed, and came and sat down on the bed and started unlacing his boots.

"The wind's shifting," he said. "It'll probably rain by morning." He undressed and put the light out, and came to bed.

For a long time, we just held each other. Once I thought he was asleep. "Do you remember John Petrie?" he said finally.

"No." I moved my head on his shoulder. "Should I?"

"He was a senior when Joe and I were freshmen. He was six-four or six-five, and weighed about two hundred fifty. Part Cherokee on his mother's side and looked it, too—the cheekbones and a hooked nose. Jet black hair, remember?"

"Huh-uh," I said.

"His dad was Charles Wilson Petrie III. He was a lawyer. You'd see him around town in a blue vested suit and wingtips. He was on the radio a lot during the Cuban missile scare. You remember that, don't you?"

I hesitated, trying to. "How old was I in . . . when?"

"In 1962. You were twelve."

I tried to remember being twelve during the Cuban missile crisis. I could remember a recent movie with Martin Sheen playing John Kennedy. Or was it Bobby?

"We called him Little John, naturally—his dad wanted him to be a lawyer, too, but the only place John was bright was on the football field. His senior year he was almost flunking out. No way was he going to make college and law school. But he wasn't so dumb he couldn't see his future if we went to war over Cuba. We already had the draft then, and John was eighteen. He'd come to football practice worrying about missiles and being drafted. He had more information than we did, with his dad in civil defense.

"One day at practice he told us the alert had gone from yellow to red. Said his dad wouldn't even let him use their phone to call his girl, because of the emergency hookup. He was so sure we were about to be nuked that he got Joe and me scared, too. We decided it was time to stock our bomb shelter."

I could see his profile in silhouette against the moonlight. And suddenly, in vivid memory, I could see the entrance to Marshall Gymnasium and the sign beside it: three triangles inside a circle and big block letters underneath, FALLOUT SHELTER, and a smaller circle listing the capacity. Stark black and yellow, these signs were everywhere when we were growing up.

In the 50s and 60s, lots of people built fallout shelters, or if they hadn't actually built one themselves, they knew someone who had. We all had a corner of the basement picked out, should the need arise. Some people laid in a supply of bottled water, canned goods and candles. Mr. Humphreys up the street from us built a real bomb shelter, and all the neighbors speculated on who he'd let in if the Soviets attacked. There was a lot of talk about survival of the fittest and the law of the jungle.

I remembered one of my earliest childhood terrors, the sound of a low-flying plane, especially at night. It seems odd to me now that I imagined death carried in the bellies of bombers rather than in the nose cones of missiles. My fears were not technically accurate, but they were accurate enough.

"You and Joe had a bomb shelter?" I said.

"Yeah, we did."

When atomic weapons were relatively new, we'd believed in them so much more. *When did we get to be fatalists,* I wondered. Maybe in the face of such insane plans as the evacuation of New York City. "Why didn't I know about it?"

"We didn't want to worry you. We were going to tell you when the time came.

"You remember the deserted farmhouse a mile or so past my house? There was a storm cellar around back. It was dark and spidery and smelled like moldy potatoes. You had to go down some slimy concrete steps; there were a couple of shelves with mason jars full of dead fruit, and a rusty lantern."

"Sounds lovely."

"We had a couple of water jugs and a few cans of pork and beans, a couple of old quilts. We thought we were ready." He laughed.

"We tried it out one night, pretending the Russians had dropped the bomb. It took maybe three hours for us to get bored stiff."

We'd been raised with the specter of nuclear attack, the cold war. It was as normal a part of our daily lives as television and rock 'n' roll. As children, we were already mutants, living under threat of the mushroom cloud. We'd absorbed it into our bones like radiation; we'd always understood the real legacy our parents' generation left us. We were the war babies, heirs to atomic fission. Why were they surprised at our rebellion?

He tightened his arm around me. "We didn't see any reason to scare you ahead of time."

"Who else were you going to save?"

"There wasn't room for anyone else.

". . . Anyway, John Petrie took it on himself to look out for me on the football team, I don't know why, but he did. Upperclassmen usually had it in for freshmen—they'd paid their dues, and now it was our turn."

"As I remember, you had a pretty razzle-dazzle freshman year."

"I'm glad you remember *something*. John helped me learn the tricks, helped me live through some bad afternoons of grass drill. And the first game I played in, Jerry Atchison was the quarterback, and he called my number in the huddle—dive, forty-four, on two. I'll never forget it. My mouth went as dry as dust.

"John looked at me, just his black eyes and hook nose showing above his face guard, and he said, 'Sonny boy, let's do it.' And we did. He opened a hole in their line a tank could have gone through."

He was quiet for a while. I listened to his breathing, feeling his chest rising, falling, against my cheek. "John Petrie was the first of us, the first in our county, to die in Vietnam. When he was worried sick about Cuba, we'd never heard of Vietnam. But he was right about one thing; he was drafted fresh out of high school. By 1965 he was dead."

"Did you know that when you were drafted?" I said.

"I must have, but I guess it didn't make the same impression on me then, not until I got back. I'm probably boring you with this."

"You're not," I said. "I wish I remembered him."

"I located his name on the Wall. It was all right because I already *knew* he was dead. But the guys in my squad, all the times I'd wondered about them. I stood in front of the book of names, other people were waiting in line behind me. My hands started shaking, I broke out in a sweat." He yawned. "I don't know."

"Don't you want to sleep now?"

"No."

I stroked his chest, twining the dark hair around my fingers. "What about Isaac?"

"The dust-off took us out with him; he was unconscious. They'd given him more morphine before they even tried to get him loose, and they did get him loose. They flew him to a hospital in Japan. We were told he would be all right, but sterile. As Duel put it, 'His weapon would only fire blanks.'

"We'd convinced ourselves whatever Charlie could do, the doctors could undo. They sure did a lot, but maybe they saved some guys it would have been kinder to let die."

"What happened?" I touched his knee. "And your back, and here?" I said, brushing the hair from his forehead.

"Just scratches. The knee got infected, or it wouldn't have left a scar. This one, the impact knocked me out. When I came around, they told me the bullet had pierced my helmet, bounced off my thick skull, and lodged in the top of the liner. I kept that bullet for a long time. Then I lost it one day on patrol."

"You were lucky," I said.

"Yes, I was lucky."

"Tell me more about the Montagnard family. You wrote me that their daughter looked like the girl in *South Pacific*. Do you remember? Was she really that beautiful?"

"The Tonkinese were North Vietnamese. Did you know that when we were kids watching *South Pacific*? The Gulf of Tonkin? Funny how things come around."

I'd noticed a change in the timbre of his voice, but I was

already thinking about the next thing I wanted to say. "I was so jealous," I said. "I kept seeing you as John Kerr to her France Nuyen."

"It wasn't like that." His voice was different now, flat. "She was only a child."

I lifted my head to look at him. His breathing was different, too.

"Her father was Montagnard, her mother was probably middle-class Vietnamese—she was educated. They were refugees from a large search-and-destroy mission, part of our forced urbanization plan. The mother's family had disowned her for marrying beneath her; she was dead to them. The Montagnards were mountain people, very primitive. The plains Vietnamese considered them savages. In this country, it would be like a middle-class southern white woman marrying a black tenant farmer. Even without me, they had enough problems." His voice was a monotone.

"The girl's name was Lon. Her mother was Pyong, she was our hootch maid. Five days a week, she made our beds, swept floors, did our laundry. We each paid her the equivalent of one dollar a week in piasters or military scrip. We had to tell new guys not to pay their hootch maids more. You didn't want a situation where a hootch maid was richer than the mayor of the village." He laughed, a hollow sound. "Lon came with her mother to clean. She could speak French, and a little English. She was so beautiful, so bright. She was like a breath of fresh air in hell."

His skin felt clammy under my hand. "Maybe you shouldn't talk about this," I said.

"She was like any little kid, she loved sweets. I'd give her C-ration chocolate. Then I made it a point to have a couple of Hershey bars on hand. She was eleven years old. Her baby skin was the color of honey. Her eyes were like brown velvet. She was like a fawn that's lost its spots, but isn't quite a doe. She was always smiling, always happy.

"The father started walking Lon and Pyong to and from the village. There'd been some problem with the hootch maids being robbed when they left the base. His name was Bao. He was tall for a Vietnamese, and carried himself well. I liked his looks. I offered him a pack of cigarettes one day, and he bowed to me and took it. The next time we got in from the boonies, there was this crossbow on my bunk." Sonny moved his hand, indicating the wall where it hung now.

His voice sounded tight, he was perspiring. I sat up and threw the cover back.

"The next day Lon made me understand that the bow was from her father. I went with her and her mother to the gate that afternoon, hoping Bao would be waiting to walk them home, and he was. I handed the bow back and told him I couldn't accept it, shaking my head, saying 'No takee, no takee.' What I wanted to do was pay him for it. God, what a mess that was.

"I could tell from the look on his face that he was less than pleased. He looked like he wanted to kill me. I'd insulted him by refusing the bow, and it took Lon a while to get it straightened out. Pyong flapped her hands and jabbered in French, which I didn't understand, and Bao didn't appear to, either.

"Lon spoke to her father first, bowing several times. And then she got around to me, scowling at my wallet, and finally pushing my hand away, indicating I should get it out of sight immediately. Then she held out her hands for the bow, which he gave her, and she offered it to me, and I took it. I felt like a jackass, finally realizing that he'd made me a gift and an offer of friendship which I'd belittled by trying to pay.

"Or maybe he knew what would happen when the other guys saw my bow. Either way, I helped set up his business. He sold crossbows as fast as he could make them, at three dollars apiece. I thought I was so smart. I knew better than to let him make too much."

The tone of his voice, the way he was perspiring—I was starting to be afraid. "Sonny . . ."

He took my hand. "They invited me into their home. I ate with them. My CO would have died if he'd known this, but I went with Bao into the jungle more than once. When he'd take me out, all he wore was a loincloth and his Ho Chi Minh sandals. He showed me how to look for disturbances in the environment, how to listen to the birds and the monkeys. How to judge the terrain. He showed me places for booby traps I would never have thought of. What he taught me saved our lives, more than once.

"I loved Pyong's spicy noodle soup. I couldn't stomach nuoc mom, the rancid fish oil they considered a delicacy. They'd laugh at the face I made just smelling it. I'd bring small gifts from the PX. A single bar of soap was an extravagance to them. It made me feel good to give them things. You betcha, I was really doing my part to win the hearts and minds of the people.

"At the same time, we were going on search-and-destroy missions, burning entire villages. We captured and brought back a couple of NVA cadres and turned them over to the ARVN for interrogation, knowing they wouldn't survive the questioning. I was getting better at my job, I was adjusting. I'd learned to compartmentalize my thinking so that nothing bothered me, at least when I was in the field.

"We had a supply sergeant, Sergeant Dunlop. He could 'find' just about anything for a price. I told him I wanted an Oriental doll. It was a Japanese geisha doll I ended up with, and I was afraid she wouldn't like it.

"That morning I could hear her outside, laughing and cutting up with some of the guys. I sat on my bunk and hid the doll behind me, waiting for her to come see me, like she always did when we were on stand-down. And I yelled, 'Come in here a minute, Lon.' I brought the doll around from behind me and held it out to her, watching her face.

"Her eyes got big and she made this 'Ahhhh' sound deep in her throat. And then she flew across the floor and threw her arms around my neck and hugged me. She said, 'Lon love you,

Sonny.' The way she'd pronounce my name, it sounded like 'Sony.' And after she'd gone to show the doll to her mother, I sat there on my bunk and cried because I'd just come back from a village where we'd accidentally hit two kids."

I didn't try to stop him; I sat still and waited for it to be over. I wasn't sure he was even aware of me being there, though he still had a grip on my hand.

"One morning I woke up, someone was yelling my name. Something in Vietnamese and then my name. I ran outside with my rifle in my hand; it wasn't even daylight. The guard had this old Papa-san collared, dragging him along, almost lifting him off the ground by his pajama top. Papa-san had been yelling for me through the fence. I recognized him from Lon's village.

"I was going to go with him right then, but the others wouldn't let me. After Tet, when we'd all heard the stories about the barber hanging in the barbed wire, the same nice little man who'd shaved you with his straight razor, it made sense to be paranoid. But I had to know what the old man was so upset about. The guys got their gear and came with me."

Sonny wasn't just remembering it. He was watching it happen.

"We took a deuce-and-a-half with a mine sweeper. I thought we'd never get there, dreading when we would, not knowing what I expected to find. I was trying to make some sense of what the old guy was saying. Bannowski spoke a little pidgin and I was asking if he could make out anything. He kept avoiding my eyes, shaking his head. I knew he was lying, his face looked like green cheese. I knew the word for *dead*; I knew it was going to be bad. I kept hoping it was somebody else.

"The sun was just coming up when we got there. I jumped down and took about two steps before Bannowski tackled me and pinned me to the ground. He lay on top of me, holding me down while the others went to see. I was screaming at him, calling him a motherfucking Polack, any filthy thing I could think of. The old guy was taking them straight to Bao's hut. The villagers stood around, watching.

"Isaac finally comes out, with the others following close, looking like they're about to puke. 'Let him up,' he says. 'Don't go in there, Sonny,' he said. 'It ain't gonna do them or you any good.' Bannowski still has a grip on my arms. I'm getting ready to kill him if he doesn't turn me loose. Isaac tells him to let me go."

It was awful listening to him struggle for control.

"They'd tied Bao to the center-pole and made him watch . . . They probably did Lon first, so Pyong and Bao both could watch. They'd raped her, of course, God knows how many times. And then . . . there was . . ." His voice faltered and stopped.

I got up and lit the lantern, turning it low. I poured water from the kettle into the basin and brought it to the side of the bed. I bathed his face, it was beaded with sweat. I sponged his body, not knowing what else to do, needing to do something. I blew the lantern out and came back to bed. I put my arms around him and pressed his head to my chest.

"I don't think it was Cong who did it. I'll always believe it was the ARVN's or the villagers themselves. But I set them up, I made Bao prosperous, a filthy Montagnard, when the others had so little."

"You don't know that," I said.

"It was my name the old guy was calling."

I held him, combing his hair with my fingers.

"I was responsible," he said.

"You were their friend."

"My friendship got them *tortured* and *killed*."

"You did the best you knew how, Sonny. Stop blaming yourself."

I held him, turning my body to his. I rubbed his shoulders, his back, gently raked my nails over his buttocks. I wanted to comfort him. For a few minutes, I could make him forget.

"What happened to your feather mattress?"

"Um?" He sounded almost out.

"Never mind."

"No. What?"

"I just asked what happened to your feather mattress."

He turned, laid one arm across my waist. "Aren't you comfortable?"

"I'm fine."

"Mice got in it."

"Mice."

"Field mice."

"Uh huh."

"I better tell you, if you hear something howl, it's only coyotes."

"Right."

"Something that sounds like a woman screaming, that's a painter."

"A what?"

"Cougar. Mountain lion. Carlton would call them painters."

"What about bears?" I said.

"You're not really worried, are you?"

"No," I said.

"Because there's nothing out here to be afraid of."

"Go to sleep." I stretched my arm across his chest.

Soon his breathing grew deep and even. *Nothing out here to be afraid of*, he'd said. I thought of all the terrors he carried around with him.

26

During the night, something woke me. It's frightening to awake suddenly in total darkness, and not know where you are.

"Sarah," he said. "It's just thunder."

I turned toward the voice and put out my hand, unable to see, expecting the texture of Dick's chest and not finding it. *This isn't my husband* was my first conscious thought.

The room was completely black; the fire was out and clouds covered the moon.

"Your heart's beating like a trip-hammer," he said.

I lay back down.

Sounds and smells seemed magnified in the darkness. There was the sound of rain on dry leaves and earth, the smells of rain and our bodies and sex.

I felt him move, and sensed when he was leaning over me. "What is it?" he said. "What's wrong?" His fingers touched my face.

"I don't know," I said.

He held me, and let me cry. "It's all right," he said.

I was disoriented and frightened. I felt torn in half—it seemed right to be where I was, in his arms, and at the same time, I was irrationally angry at Dick for letting me be here.

I wondered if he was awake and thinking about me.

Pale light spilled through the window; I could hear rain falling softly.

"You're like a little girl when you sleep, you know that?" His eyes looked rested and clear. "Stay put while I get this thing lit."

He swung his feet out and pulled on his pants. I watched him work with the kerosene heater, cursing when he pinched his thumb. I asked him why not build the fire again, since there was plenty of dry wood left. He hesitated, then pivoted on one knee. "Too much smoke," he said, and turned to the heater again.

He set the coffee on one burner of the camp stove, and started a kettle of water heating on the other. He moved around the room, humming and picking up clothes. He went behind the blanket; when he came out, I sat holding the cover to me, my knees drawn to my chin.

I watched as he buckled his belt.

He took a poncho from one of the nails and the empty water jugs from the shelf. "The Vietnamese go out in the mornings in a group, the whole village to one place. Sometimes we'd fly over and see them squatting in a rice paddy, doing their business."

"How exciting," I said.

"I'll be outside." He was smiling as he closed the door.

We had oatmeal with raisins, and Tang for breakfast. Now I was sitting on the bed brushing my hair and watching him shave. He was using a small mirror propped on the top shelf, bending to peer into it. He'd said it was much warmer out, almost balmy for this time of year, and the rain was slacking off.

"When do you think it might stop?" I said. It was past eight already.

He dried his face on the towel, took a camouflage shirt off a nail and put it on, leaving it open. He poured more coffee. "We can't make it all the way back today. We can start today."

He looked at me, searching my face for something. "It's a full day's walk sunup to sundown. No canoe rides.

"Or I can light a big signal fire. Somebody's sure to see it."

He held the coffee cup, staring into it.

I didn't know what to say. A signal fire.

He set the cup on the table and crossed to the window. "I just wanted to see you again. That's all I had in mind when I finagled an invitation from Clifford. When I asked Joanne to pack a picnic lunch, I guess she thought it was a surprise for

Lou. I must have had this in the back of my mind since you told me about Joe, but I didn't really think I'd go through with it."

He turned his head. "*I'd* have found you by now. You do realize that?"

"Maybe you would have," I said. "That's hardly fair, though, is it? Dick doesn't have this kind of experience."

"When I was getting this kind of experience wading through jungles up to my nuts, what was he doing?"

He took a breath, and let it out.

"All right. But has life been fair to you and me, would you say?" He leaned against the window, looking out, his palms flat against the facings.

I remembered thinking how it would be interesting to see him again, a little painful maybe, certainly nostalgic.

"I knew you'd be scared, you'd think I was crazy. Even in the canoe, I was thinking I can't go through with this, it's insane. I thought, I'll take her all the way to the bridge, we'll get a ride back. And then we got to the place where I had to do it if I was going to." He was quiet, staring out the window. "It's stopped raining. Let's go outside for a minute, get some air."

It was a fine morning, especially after having been so cold. I hardly needed my jacket. The rain had passed; gray clouds were parting against chunks of blue sky. The air smelled laundered. I walked with him to the stream and stood in a cathedral of winter timber and silence. There were no street sounds, no factory noises, just miles and miles of mountain wilderness.

"Nobody knows about this place, do they?" I said.

He leaned over and picked up a rock, tossed it into the stream. "Right about there, in the spring, you can find watercress."

"I don't think you should light a signal fire," I said. Dick and Louellen would have to stand it another day. And my parents. After what they went through with Joe, I hoped this didn't kill them. "I think we should just go back, Sonny. Tell the authorities the canoe tipped over—something."

"What will you tell Dick?" he said.

"I'll tell him the truth, what happened."

He nodded. "I can tell him."

"I think *I* should."

"When we were kids, I'd pretend you were my sister. In Vietnam, sometimes I'd think I can't do this anymore, let them kill me—and then I'd remember you. I don't know what I thought would happen up here, Sarah."

He took me by the shoulders and turned me to him. "But I know I didn't expect you'd still love me."

When I realized what he was saying, I put my head on his chest so he couldn't see my face.

"It won't be easy," he said, his arms around me.

Dear God, I thought.

27

I sat on the stool at the table, watching him pack. He seemed to know what he wanted to take, and what to leave. He was leaving the rifle, and taking the crossbow. He was taking a sleeping bag, a ground cloth, the poncho.

I watched him transfer the things in my canvas tote to another rucksack, a smaller version of the one he'd be carrying. It would leave my hands free, he said, make walking easier. He picked up my sketchbook; it wasn't going to fit.

"You still come here," I said. "Pretty often?"

"Every time, I expect to see that somebody else has been here." He folded the canvas tote and put it in the rucksack, along with a few packets of instant and dehydrated food, then closed it.

"I don't see how anyone could find this place."

He looked around the room, then walked behind me to the bed and started rolling one of the sleeping bags. "They'll find it, eventually. Just a matter of time."

"Maybe you shouldn't leave your rifle."

"I'd rather lose it than the bow."

"I'm not being much help," I said.

He tied the cord and turned, surveying the room again.

"What can I do?"

"We're almost ready." He sat on the corner of the table and picked up the sketchbook. "I can put this in my pack."

"You want some coffee before I fill the thermos?" I said.

"Better leave the thermos." He was turning the pages, looking at the drawings. There were several of him that I'd done last night. "If Bob Jones checks my pack, he's going to wonder how these stayed dry. Not to mention when you did them."

"Who's Bob Jones?"

"Sheriff." He put the book aside. "Let's have some coffee, be a waste to throw it all out."

I poured it and set the cups on the table. "Careful, it's hot," I said. He seemed preoccupied, reaching for his cup.

"I hate lying," he said.

"To the authorities, you mean." *Would* the sheriff check his pack? I put the pot back on the stove and sat down.

He sighed. "Sarah, Carlton suspected something before we left. Half the time, Lou knows what I'm going to do before I do. She knows about you. She's always known. Calling the 'authorities' is about the last thing they'd do."

I sat there, staring at him.

"I don't know if she'd say something to Dick," he said. "It would be hard for her, either way. But you know Trudie did."

"You're telling me they wouldn't have reported us missing?" I said.

"Probably not, no."

"What if they found the canoe?"

"Then, yes. Maybe. People around here aren't real quick to call the law."

I'd pictured something like the entire National Guard out looking for us.

"There *is* the canoe. If it hasn't already been found, it probably will be." He set the cup down. "But it could have pulled loose accidentally. There's no law that says two adults, two *consenting* adults, can't be out here camping." He was silent for a moment, as if he were waiting for me to understand something. Then he got up and walked around, his fists in his pockets.

"Dick called the police," I said. He would have called the police, or the park rangers—the proper authorities—immediately, and told them we were lost. I tried to imagine what that scene must have been like: "Your wife, sir? And your husband, ma'am? On a picnic?" What would the police be thinking?

"He'd have called the police," I said again.

Sonny stopped pacing. "Sarah, I *know* he called the police. Don't you think I know that?"

"Then what?"

He came back and sat on the table. "We'll tell them the canoe capsized. You bumped your head or swallowed a lot of water. Something to account for the time." He wouldn't look at me, suddenly. He seemed changed: sad, not quite angry.

"That's reasonable, isn't it?" I said.

"Entirely possible."

"What *is* it?" I said.

He took my hand. "We lost the rifle, so I couldn't fire any shots. But we kept a fire going. Too bad nobody saw it. All right so far?"

"I guess so," I said. "What do you think?"

"They can find the canoe downriver. We'd decided on a hike and canoe ride instead of Medicine Springs. Because it was a pretty day. I managed to snag our packs, but that's all. This other I'll stash before we get there. Anything you're not certain about, just say you don't remember."

"Don't you think the sheriff will believe you?"

He didn't answer, just kept tracing the lines in my palm.

I stood abruptly and walked to the window, finally realizing what he'd been saying: there was no law against going camping; Louellen already knew. So why didn't I want him to tell Dick what had happened between us? That's what was bothering him.

I heard him get up, and cross the room. When he put his arms around me, I leaned my head against his chest, and closed my eyes.

It was a little past eleven when he shut the door to the cabin behind us. We walked down the path to the stream, and I turned to look back. I could hardly see it, the roof covered in vines and leaves, three walls overhung with honeysuckle and blackberry. Sumac. I wouldn't see it at all if I didn't know it was there. The landscape seemed to absorb it.

It felt sad to be leaving, yet I was glad to be starting back. I felt as I had last night, torn in opposite directions.

Surely I'd have a clearer perspective on things once we were back. Sonny would, too. The isolation out here, the quiet—it was like being the only two people in the world.

The sun was warm, a few birds were singing. We were walking at a pace that was fast for me, but was probably a stroll for him. A couple of times he asked if I wanted to rest, or slow down. I told him I'd tell him if I felt tired. I'd already taken my jacket off and tucked it in the straps of my backpack.

I followed behind him, mostly, because I had no idea which way we were going. He called the country we were in "hardwood uplands." There were stands of white oak, hickory, basswood, maple, other trees that he knew the names of. It was pretty; I could see why he loved it.

We stopped to rest at the crest of a hill with a ravine in front of us that looked just like the one at our backs. I didn't see how he had any idea where we were or where we were headed. He slipped out of his pack and helped me with mine, rubbing my shoulders where the straps rode. "You okay?" he said. "Sure I'm not walking too fast for you?"

"I'm fine," I said.

He spread the ground cloth over leaves wet from last night's rain, then took two granola bars out of his pack and lay down, propping himself on one elbow. He glanced up at me, and I sat down.

The crackling of paper as I unwrapped the granola bar seemed very loud. Before I had it open, he was almost finished with his, the muscles in his jaw working as he chewed; he wadded the wrapper and stuffed it in his pocket, then stretched out, hands behind his head, staring at the sky. As far as I knew, we were the only human beings for miles.

Isolation itself was a kind of intimacy. I thought about last night: We'd been alone, completely alone, as we were now. There'd been hours to get through before morning, with nowhere to go, locked in by wilderness, nothing to hear but the sound of our own voices; both of us feeling anger, regret, loss.

—

If I'd thought of Dick at all when I was unfolding the sleeping bags, it was to put him firmly out of mind. *For Sonny to have done this,* I was thinking, *to have brought me here like this, he must want me . . . and we should have been lovers.*

But it hadn't been just some selfless commemoration of times past on my part, not if I was to be honest about it. I'd wanted him, too. But only for a harmless fraction of time? Just to know what it might have been like between us? Is that what I'd been thinking, or had I managed not to think at all? Sonny had risked everything to bring me out here. Had I imagined he'd do that for a one-night stand? It scared me to think where this was going to end.

I didn't avoid his eyes as he turned his head—I looked directly into them—but I made myself see circles, triangles, cones, the variations of light and shadow. It was like drawing live models; I'd see everything except their nakedness.

"What're you thinking?" he said.

"How this sounds like rocks I'm chewing."

He smiled, and closed his eyes.

"So quiet out here," I said. I put the last bite in my mouth. "Could I have some water?" He sat partway up, unclipped the canteen and gave it to me. The water tasted plastic. Then he took a drink and screwed the top on.

I stretched, feeling muscles that were unused to the weight of a backpack. I looked around me, down the hill we were on, across to the next one. It all looked the same—trees and dead leaves and pockets of brambles and underbrush. "How do you know where you're going?" I said.

He had his eyes closed; he might have been asleep. "Direction," he said. "Landmarks."

"Like what?"

"Far off, the shape of different peaks, for instance. Up close you pay attention to where you've been, remember anything unusual, tree formations, an unusual rock face. Just about what you'd do in a strange city."

"It can't be that easy," I said.

"You better rest now," he said. "We have a long walk ahead."

I lay flat on my back, as he was doing, and thought about how I hadn't done this since I was a child, when I'd lie on our lawn and look at the sky until I seemed to be falling into it. I tried closing my eyes, but they wouldn't stay closed. I was very conscious of him next to me, and the quiet all around us. Finally, I sat up.

He turned on his side, resting his head in his hand. His other hand lay on the ground cloth between us, and I found myself remembering last night again.

"Have you read what they're doing in Brazil?" he said.

"In Brazil?"

"They're cutting down the rain forests. Trees that produce a fourth of the earth's oxygen, and they're cutting them down." He glanced at me. "A hundred acres every five minutes, some figure like that."

"What made you think about that?" I said.

He looked away. "I don't know." Then he lay back again, closed his eyes.

I thought I must have missed something.

"You should rest," he said.

"I am resting." I sat still and quiet, looking around me. A hawk, or a buzzard, was flying overhead. I tried to remember how you could tell the difference. I looked at the bow tied to his rucksack, with its sleek stock and the trigger mechanism like a rifle's. It was made of some dark wood with dragons carved on it. I leaned across him and touched it; the wood felt satiny smooth. "Do you hunt with this?" I said.

I thought he wasn't going to answer. "The Montagnards hunted tigers with them."

"There were tigers in Vietnam?"

"Like everything else, not as many as there used to be." He opened his eyes, looking at the sky. "You about ready to walk some more?"

"If you are," I said.

He gave me a hand up and helped me with my backpack. He shook out the ground cloth and folded it.

As we started down the hill, I felt more tired than I had before we stopped to rest. The muscles in my calves and thighs had tightened. I was all right again after we'd walked for a while. Then I began to think how lost I'd be out here if something were to happen to him. I'd die of exposure; even with all these plants and animals around me, I'd probably starve. I wondered if he'd thought about *that* before he brought me out here.

As the afternoon wore on, we didn't talk at all; we walked. My feet were tired; the arches ached. Stepping on a sharp rock or tree root was painful. I'd collected several stinging scratches on my hands and forearms from briars and tree limbs. Once when I wasn't paying attention, I'd almost poked my eye out on a low-hanging branch. My fingernails were dirty; I'd broken two. My jeans were too tight for this. They had started to chafe the insides of my thighs.

He never seemed to take a misstep; *his* boot never hit a slick rock and twisted sideways. His paces were measured, steady.

I was feeling good and sorry for myself by the time we finally stopped again at a little past four.

"How you doing?" he said.

"How much farther?" The muscles in my legs twitched. I tried to find new territory for the straps cutting into my shoulders. The rucksack felt like lead.

"It's up to you. We can stop soon, or keep going," he said.

"I guess you could walk another twenty miles."

"We'll start looking for a campsite."

What's wrong with right here, I thought. I wanted to sit down. Wet leaves, stickers—I didn't care.

"The first good-looking spot, we'll stop," he said.

"What's that supposed to mean, 'good-looking spot'?" I tugged at the shoulder straps; they were cutting my arms off. I heard how my voice sounded and didn't care.

He put his hand out. "Let me take it."

"I'll carry it," I said.

"You're tired, let me take it."

"I said I'll carry it!" I felt my bottom lip start to tremble and clamped my jaws tight.

I looked around me at miles and miles of goddamn trees.

28

We'd hardly spoken since I'd snapped at him about the rucksack. He had spread the ground cloth, and I'd collapsed on it. Then he said he was going for firewood.

My shoulders felt dislocated. The muscles in my legs jumped and twitched; soon they'd be tight and sore. I wanted a bath. And now that I'd stopped moving, I was cold.

We were at the base of a hill. He'd called it *the lee side*. There was a fir tree clinging to the rocks just above us. Shelter from dew, he'd said. The ground was as close to dry as we would get after the rain. I dragged my pack to me and took out the container of wet towelettes I use to clean charcoal off my hands.

I washed my face and loosened my bootlaces. And felt a little better. I could hear him nearby, breaking sticks. By the time he came back, it was dusk; there was a soft rose backlight on the hills.

"Where do you want the fire?" I said. I thought I'd get up and help.

He dropped the armload of wood. "Don't worry about it." He turned and walked off.

Well, fine, I thought.

When he must have decided he'd brought in enough wood, he raked together some dead grass and sticks and reached in his shirt pocket for a match, striking it with his thumbnail.

I watched the tinder catch, watched him add larger sticks. When I could feel the warmth, I took my boots off. He added more wood, then sat back, locking his arms around his knees.

I thought about saying I was sorry, but for what? Sorry I couldn't walk as far as he could without getting tired? I put my jacket under my head and lay down, facing the fire. He sat there, not saying anything, staring into it. *Fine,* I thought. I closed my eyes, listening to the comforting sounds a fire makes.

I woke up; he was shaking my shoulder. The poncho covered me. He'd done that. I sat up, rubbing my eyes and smelling something good.

It was completely dark now outside the circle of firelight. There was a small pan steaming at the edge of the coals.

He poured soup into cups and opened a tin of crackers. I watched him, trying to gauge his mood. While I'd slept he had kept the fire going and fixed us something to eat.

I took the cup and plastic spoon he offered. He sat down with his portion and started eating.

I tasted the soup—vegetable beef—and picked up a piece of cracker. We ate in silence while I waited for him to say something. He ignored me.

"There's this game Dick told me about," I said.

He set his cup aside, picked up a packet of trail mix, and looked at me for a second.

"He played it at a corporate retreat one time. It was called Fallout Shelter." I thought of his story about the fallout shelter he and Joe had.

"Hold out your hand."

I set my cup down and put out my hand, watching him shake trail mix into it.

"What kind of game is this?" His voice sounded as it had when he was talking to Braxton, trying to tell him about the deer.

"I didn't mean to throw a tantrum before. I was just really tired."

"You said you'd tell me when you got tired."

That's true, I had.

"It was a decision-making exercise," I said. "You're supposed to imagine that the missiles are on the way."

I put some of the trail mix in my mouth, talking around it. "There were ten people in Dick's group, and room for only six in the fallout shelter. They had thirty minutes to decide which six would live, or all ten would die. Are you going to stay mad the rest of the night?"

"Maybe *I'm* tired. Ever think about that?"

I chewed the dry cereal and hard dry fruit. Swallowed. "Each person had a role to play. Dick was a black militant second-year medical student."

"You make me feel so damn responsible," he said.

"The others were supposed to be a pregnant woman and her husband, a policeman with a gun, a priest, maybe, and a college girl. I forget what else."

"Didn't I ask you, two or three times, if you needed to rest, was I going too fast?"

"The thing was, each person had to convince the others that he or she should be saved. Then everybody voted, and the six with the most votes lived."

He opened the canteen and offered it to me.

"One woman really came on to all the men. Said she was a fantastic lover, a good mother. She would service them all, have lots of babies."

I drank some water and gave him the canteen.

His face was turned so that the firelight painted one side of it red and deepened the sockets of his eyes. "Go on."

"That's it," I said.

"So who'd they pick?"

"You'd be chosen. Because you can do all *this*." *And I wouldn't,* I was thinking, *because I can't do anything, and I'm barren*. "I didn't want you having to slow down for me, all right?"

He got up and took a bottle out of the rucksack. He held it down to me.

"So you can stop feeling *responsible*."

"Have a drink," he said.

"I don't want it."

He drank and sat down beside me, and rested the bottle on my knee. "I insist."

I took a drink. "There'd be you and that woman, and the medical student."

"So that's what corporate executives do on retreats," he said.

"Don't make fun of him."

"I'm not."

"The hell you're not."

"Where do you live?" he said. He took the bottle and sipped it. "Where in Nashville?"

Where do I live? In a beautiful Tudor house, with a studio added on for north light. On an acre adjoining Percy Warner Park. My MGB in the three-car garage. "Out past Green Hills," I said.

"Pretty nice neighborhood."

I reached for the bottle.

"He makes a lot of money, doesn't he?"

I thought about equivocating as I brought it to my mouth—what was a lot? "Yes," I said and gave the bottle back to him.

"What do you do? Say on a normal day."

I lie in bed while Dick showers, half asleep and planning my day. Then I get up, brush my teeth, my hair, go down and fix his cereal or eggs. When he's left for work, I dress, think about dinner, whether we're going out or eating in, whether there are any special instructions for the housekeeper. Then I work in my studio till noon, and sometimes past, depending on what I'm doing. Two afternoons a week, I teach a children's art class at the museum, two afternoons I help Joshua with his students.

I told him about the art classes and helping Joshua.

"And Dick manages a computer company." He leaned forward and fed more sticks to the fire, laying a large piece on top.

"They manufacture hardware primarily; there's some research. Trudie's father is chairman of the board. I told you that's how we met, through Trudie."

He held the bottle between us, our knees touching. "What has always amazed me about people like Dick, and Braxton, you and Joe, you always knew who you were. Where you wanted to be when you grew up." He took a drink, then offered it to me.

"I've had enough."

"One more," he said. "For the cold."

I drank, and gave the bottle back to him. He capped it and put it aside. "Didn't you always know you were an artist?"

"I suppose so," I said.

"And Joe was a one-man mission to change the world. Civil rights, human rights, he was going to get all that *fixed*." He laughed.

"The times I sat at your dinner table and watched him and your dad go at it over something in the news. Joe taking one side, your dad the other, just for the hell of it."

"I remember," I said.

"Remember the time Joe wanted Governor Faubus hanged on the Little Rock courthouse lawn? Made a good case for it, I thought. And your dad, nodding, before he disagreed. 'Now, son, ahem, violence is just a stopgap solution.' "

I smiled. I'd heard Dad say that in just that tone.

"He must really miss him."

Joe with his quick temper and cutting wit. Dad egging him on. The good-natured yelling back and forth across the dinner table.

But one of their last discussions had been deadly serious. Dad couldn't see Joe volunteering for service. Joe said he'd rather join than be drafted. He was going to join or he was going to Canada. He wasn't going to wait for the decision to be made for him. Dad had begged him to take a student deferment; Joe wouldn't do it. He said it wasn't fair.

Sonny threw another stick on the fire. "Our house. He'd come in off a haul and she'd have country-fried steak because that was his favorite. He'd wait for me to reach for a second helping so he could slap the side of my head. I'd always do it, too, whether I wanted it or not. Just to see if he'd hit me.

"I got back from Vietnam and he said, 'How'd it go?' And I said, 'I did all right.' End of discussion." He coughed and stared into the fire.

"He asked to see your medals."

He reached for the bottle and took a drink, then another. He set it down in front of him. "I never knew who the fuck *I* was."

I put my hand over his on the bottle. "Clifford says you're the best guide in the southeastern United States."

He pushed my hand away. "Since when do you care what Clifford says?"

"I guess he's entitled to be right occasionally."

"Things sure have a way of turning to shit, don't they?" He raised the bottle.

"Sonny, don't."

"He loves you. Makes a good living for you."

I didn't say anything.

He laughed. "Computers." He screwed the cap on the bottle and swung it around, pointing at the darkness. "There's sure no future in this."

He'd put the bottle into the rucksack, taken the soup pan and gone off into the night. He came back with the pan full of water and set it in the coals. Then he untied the sleeping bag and opened it all the way, like a comforter.

I made my trip to the bushes, brushed my hair, rubbed toothpaste over my teeth.

We used our jackets for pillows, the sleeping bag for a blanket. There was the fire between me and the dark on one side, and he was on the other. He was quiet for a long time; I couldn't tell what his mood was.

"That game you were talking about before . . ." He sat up for a minute, rearranging his jacket. "Are you warm enough?"

"I'm comfortable," I said.

He pulled the sleeping bag over us again, lying on his side. "It's a nice night. Shouldn't get very cold."

"It's a dumb game," I said. "If it ever comes to all-out nuclear war, I hope I'm at ground zero."

"When," he said. "*When* it comes. Then who would do the next cave drawings?"

"Someone like you, on a rainy day." I lay on my back. In front of us I could see the corona where the moon would rise soon from behind the mountains. "Can you picture an artist being saved before a farmer, or a machinist? A pharmacist? Anybody?"

"That's what I'm getting to. It wouldn't be who to save. It would be who's going to die."

"I'm afraid I don't see the difference. Six live, and four die."

"You'd see the difference if you were one of the four," he said. "Would you fight to stay alive, or let somebody vote on it?"

"I don't know." I stopped looking at the stars and looked at him. "It's just a game."

"So was Hamburger Hill. Except for the poor fucks who took it."

"Great," I said. "We're back to that. Take whatever I say and twist it all around."

For a minute, I thought I'd made him angry. "I guess I did," he said.

He found my hand, lacing our fingers together. "People don't seem to realize how close we are to anarchy, at any time. About two days after transportation and communications break down, and the lights go off. When fresh and frozen foods start to go over. Supermarket shelves are emptied. You think people would vote then?"

"There'd be martial law," I said.

"What's to keep the soldiers from taking all the food and clean water for themselves and their families?"

"Nothing," I said. "Except human decency."

I heard him sigh.

"Well?" I said.

He didn't answer me.

We were quiet again, thinking our own thoughts.

I was looking at the sky, black with a zillion stars, when I heard something on the ridge above us, about where the fir tree was. It sounded like something was up there. "Are you asleep?" I said.

"No."

"I heard a noise." I held my breath. "I don't hear it now," I said.

"What was it?"

"Something moving. Right up there."

"Walking? Crawling? Going bump in the night?"

"Forget it." I turned my back to him, staring into the fire.

"There!" I said. I sat straight up. "Don't tell me you didn't hear that!" I could hear it still, something skittering through the leaves.

"Oh, that," he said. He was lying on his back, unconcerned, his hands behind his head. "Maybe it's a bear. Or ghosts. Lots of dead Cherokees in these mountains."

He made me so mad I was shaking; I hated him. I sat with my knees drawn up, rubbing the goose bumps on my arms.

"If you listen, you'll hear things all night long. Small nocturnal sounds. What you just heard was probably a possum. Or a raccoon, they're curious as hell. Bears sometimes do come into camp, but that's generally where people are sloppy with their garbage. Or where fresh meat is hanging."

I poked the coals and put more wood on the fire. "You could have just said that. You didn't have to be smart about it. You don't even have a rifle."

"I have the bow. Right here. Right beside me."

"Well, you could have told me that, too." I sat hugging my knees, my back to him. There were other noises out there in the night that I could hear now that I was listening. Little rustling sounds.

"You want to hear a ghost story?"

"Go to hell."

"Remember how scared you used to get listening to Joe and me tell ghost stories?"

What are we doing, I thought, *in the middle of the wilderness, talking about ghosts.* That we had come together finally seemed inevitable, the twined threads of our childhoods—the formative years that made us who we are, events that with Joe dead only we knew about, our first love—all these blended in a tapestry that Dick couldn't share no matter how I might try to weave him in.

"Do you really think I'd let something get you?" he said.

I kept my back to him, a lump in my throat.

"There's nothing out here. If there were, it would be afraid of us."

Not out here, I thought. *But we can't stay out here.* "What's the bow for?" I said.

"You always were a big chicken."

I lay down and put my head on his shoulder. "I still am," I said.

He held me, stroking my arm. "What are you afraid of?"

"Lots of things," I said.

"Like what?"

"The world situation. Dying. Being helpless to do anything about it."

"What would you do different if you were in charge?"

"There isn't anyone in charge. That's just it. We can't even communicate."

"The Tower of Babel," he said.

"Before that. Adam and Eve."

He was quiet for a while. "You still go to church?"

"Sometimes."

"You still believe?"

"I believe God's in charge, if that's what you're getting at." I raised my head to smooth a wrinkle in his shirt that was bothering my cheek, then lay down again. "I don't understand why he gives us so much rope."

"You believe in angels? All that?"

"There's a Christian dogma that demons are the restless spirits of evil men."

"We're in trouble. This bow won't kill demons."

"Cute," I said. "Aren't you ever scared?"

He kissed the crown of my head, his breath warm on my hair. It was an innocent kiss intended to placate and comfort; its very lack of any other intent was what caught us off guard. I could feel Sonny's arousal, him growing hard against me. "Damn," he said, "I didn't mean . . ."

"Sonny . . ."

"Don't move, don't even breathe. Don't talk! He won't listen, he has no conscience. You're in serious danger. But don't worry, I can handle this. Stop laughing, he heard what I said."

We tried to make it funny. Last night had been different; it wasn't even necessary to rationalize. Tonight we were headed back; tonight didn't belong to us. In a few minutes, he asked if I was asleep. "Not yet," I said.

"You should be."

"You're not tired, I guess."

"Still afraid?" he said. "Bigfoot might come and get you."

"Aren't you?" I said. "Ever?"

He didn't answer immediately. "After all that happened over there, most things now seem kind of trivial. It would take a lot to surprise me. Nothing makes me very happy, or very sad." He got up and fed the fire. He sat on his heels, staring into it. "You really think Joe's spirit exists somewhere?"

"Yes, I do." I sat up.

"You truly believe it?"

"Wherever Joe is, Valhalla or heaven, some beautiful place, he's still Joe."

"What I said, about nothing making me very happy, I wasn't talking about the last three days."

29

It was just before sunrise. The horizon was a slender band of silver against a wider band of gray. The trees, the hills—everything looked gray and silver in this light. It was quiet. There was no breeze; nothing was moving but us.

He was watching me open the packets of instant oatmeal and empty them into the cracker tins I was using for bowls.

I'd waked twice during the night and found him sitting by the fire. Each time, when he saw I was awake, he'd laid on more wood, as if that's what he'd gotten up to do, and come back to lie down.

I thought I knew what he'd been thinking about, what he was thinking now; I was thinking the same things.

We'd be at the lodge by this afternoon.

When I'd put instant coffee into the cups, there was nothing left to do but wait for the water to boil. Everything other than the ground cloth we sat on was packed.

"How're you feeling?"

"Pretty good," I said. I wasn't as sore as I'd expected to be. "You didn't sleep much."

"We should reach the road by one, two at the latest, since we're getting an early start. We'll come out near a general store." He was facing me, sitting as I always picture him, with his ankles crossed, arms around his knees, the heavy lashes shading eyes that could change so fast. "Will Dick be at the lodge, or was someone else scheduled to have it?"

"I don't know." I wished I did. I wished I had a better idea of what to expect. I wondered if our names had been in the papers.

"We'll call there first."

I thought about hearing Dick's voice when he picked up the phone. I couldn't wait and I dreaded it.

Sonny was watching me with no expression, or one I couldn't read.

"I'm a little nervous, I guess." I thought how he must feel.

"What will you say?" He rubbed his mouth, and the stubble on his chin. I didn't like the way his eyes looked.

"You mean to Dick? I won't say anything until we get home. Then I'll tell him."

"Tell it to me, like you will to him," he said.

"You mean now?"

"Couldn't hurt. Could it?"

"I just haven't thought about it. Not the actual words."

He didn't say anything.

"All right." My mouth felt dry. "Let me think how to start."

"Take your time."

"We, you and I, we discovered that what we'd believed all these years wasn't true." I wished he'd look away instead of right at me. "I hadn't known what actually happened to you . . . that you'd been in the hospital. You hadn't known Joe was dead or that he hadn't told me what you'd asked him to."

"I would guess Trudie's already told him that much, but maybe he'll want to hear it from you. Go on."

"The water's boiling."

He pulled the pan to the edge of the fire.

"I thought you wanted to get an early start." I laughed; it sounded wrong.

"Just pretend you're telling him."

"You hadn't known Joe was dead, that he hadn't told me what you'd asked him to. I said that, didn't I? Okay . . . it upset you. You wanted us to talk. Wasn't that how you felt? You wanted to be sure we finally had it all straight?"

"Are you asking me?"

"Maybe you were a little angry. You had every right to be. You took us where we could be alone and talk. You took me somewhere in the mountains, I could never find it in a million years . . . to a cabin." I was having a great deal of trouble now.

"If you can't talk to me," he said, "what makes you think you can tell him?

"I know it's confusing. When we were making love, when I was inside you, I didn't think there was anybody else in bed with us."

"Don't make it ugly." My face burned.

"What's he supposed to think?"

"Were *you* thinking ahead this far? Because I wasn't."

"Let me talk to him, Sarah. I got you into this."

"And I guess you're planning to just stand there when Dick tries to kill you?"

Sonny picked up the pan and poured water into our bowls and cups. I watched him stirring the coffee. "Are you sorry?" he said.

"It's possible to love both of you. Is that so difficult to understand?"

Sonny looked at me. "He may wonder if you love either of us enough."

We ate the oatmeal. I didn't want it, but I ate it because I would need the fuel. I couldn't help thinking that I hadn't asked for this to happen. My life a few days ago had been so uncomplicated.

And I couldn't help remembering how good it had been between us. How safe and right I'd felt in his arms. Did I think I could go back now and just forget about him? I thought about Dick and how I'd been positive I could tell him everything and make him understand, because what had happened with Sonny and me didn't have anything to do with our marriage or our life together.

Who did I think I was kidding?

Sonny stood up and snapped his jacket. The sun was gold and vermilion behind the hills.

"There's not a way to fix this," I said. "Not any good way at all."

"That's a start." He looked down at me. "Are you still not sorry, now?"

. . .

We had stopped to rest. The route seemed easier today. Either that, or I was getting used to walking.

We'd stopped in a clearing, sunshine and blue sky overhead—as only an October sky can be. I was sitting on a log; he was standing a few yards away, looking worried. I leaned over and pulled up my socks, turning them over the tops of my boots.

He came and sat down. It was ten o'clock in the morning, the sun was shining, it was warm and the air smelled clean. He studied his hands, rubbing the ball of his thumb over a callus. "We're making good time," he said.

Somewhere a single crow was cawing.

"How much farther?" I said.

"I'd say we're at least an hour ahead of where I thought we'd be." He glanced at me, smiling. "You're getting the hang of this."

Our rucksacks were on the ground at our feet. He pushed at his with the toe of his boot. "Hungry?"

"Not yet," I said.

Then we were quiet for a while. He kept worrying the callus, occasionally looking up and staring into the distance. I had broken a branch off a sassafras sapling behind me and was stripping the bark off. "All right," he said. "When we get there, better let me do the talking. Bob Jones will be there, probably, and he'll be so happy you're safe, that's about all he'll be interested in."

"He won't ask me anything?"

"Try not to blush if he does."

"Do you think he will?"

Sonny rubbed his hands on his knees and stood up. "He'll want to know if you're all right."

"I can't help it," I said. "I've got these butterflies."

"There's no law against two people turning a canoe over. Not that I know of. But I've put some people to a lot of trouble and expense, looking for us."

"And worry," I said.

He glanced at me, then walked a few steps away. "Dick's going to be very pissed, as he should be. The way he'll see it, I didn't tell anyone where we were going. I got you stranded in the boonies, could have gotten you killed.

"He'll no doubt suspect a lot more." He turned and looked at me. "Why postpone it?"

I threw the branch aside without answering.

"Come on," he said. "Let's get going."

30

When he hid the sleeping bag and the bow above eye-level in the fork of a large sycamore, it really began to hit me. Not just our story, but everything—the way we'd have to tell it, how we'd have to look at each other, or not look at each other—all of it would be lies.

We climbed the last hill a few minutes past twelve and stood looking down on asphalt. The narrow paved road seemed to me like some boundary we were getting ready to cross; I wasn't sure I wanted to. He took my hand, and then we started down.

When we opened the door at the general store, a bell jingled, causing the owner and his wife to look up from their noon meal. For a moment, they sat motionless; then they pushed their chairs away from the small square table at the back of the room and hurried to the front. They surrounded Sonny, patting his arms and back, obviously very happy to see him. They stole glances at me from the corners of their eyes.

The man was short and heavyset with a monk's fringe of white hair. His smooth pink face registered concern and relief. "Just about given up on you," he said.

Sonny laid his hand on the rounded shoulder. "Mr. Walters, I need to use your phone."

The woman, gray hair gathered in a soft bun, handled my elbow as if I might break. She dragged a chair away from the table, and I thanked her and sank into it. I could smell cornbread and green beans; they smelled terrific. "We're disturbing your lunch," I said.

"Don't you go worrying about that," she said.

Sonny went behind the counter. I told him the number at the lodge and got up again as he dialed it. He handed me the receiver across the scarred glass top, and I held it tight, counting the rings, my heart beating hard as I waited to hear Dick's voice. "There's no answer," I said. My knees were weak as I sat back down.

He dialed another number, fixing on a spot above my head as it rang, his face tight and strained. "Carlton," he said. He listened for a few seconds, and then, impatient, interrupted. He told Carlton where we were and that he would need to come get us. He would explain later, to everyone at one time. He asked about Dick, watching me as he did so, and drew circles in the air. "Can you get somebody to radio him?" And then his expression changed. He closed his eyes for a second, I saw him swallow, and I knew that Lou had come on the line.

I turned to the woman standing behind me. "May I use your bathroom?" I said.

She showed me through a door at the back that opened on their living quarters. There was a wood furnace in the sitting room, where everything looked well-worn and comfortable. She showed me the bathroom off the kitchen, and told me I would find clean towels in the cabinet. I washed my face and hands and stared at my reflection in the mirror until I was sure he'd had time to be finished on the phone.

At the table, I sipped the hot tea Mrs. Walters brought. She wanted us to eat something, and I told her I couldn't. The food smelled delicious, I said, but I just couldn't eat right now. She seemed to understand.

Sonny stood at the window, staring out.

"They found your car late yesterday," Mr. Walters said. "Till then, we didn't know what might have happened, nothing much to go on, you know." He waited, and when Sonny didn't comment, went on. "Radio said a hunter found it off Signal Point Road."

"We had a canoeing accident," I said when it became clear Sonny wasn't going to volunteer anything. I thought my voice sounded all right. It was an easier lie than I'd thought it would be.

"Oh my," the woman said. "You could of drowned!"

"I'd never been whitewater canoeing before."

She patted my arm. "You poor little thing."

Sonny kept his back to us, staring out the front window.

It hadn't been more than twenty minutes since he'd hung up the phone when I heard the *whup, whup, whup* of helicopter rotors, rapidly getting louder. He turned. I think we'd both assumed that Carlton would be the first to get here in the truck.

I went to the window, standing beside him. It was Fed Cavanaugh's helicopter, PRECISION COMPUTERS in red across the side.

It hovered a few seconds at treetop level, then descended to land where the road shoulder ran into the Walters' front yard. Sunlight on the bubble momentarily blinded me. Then I could see two men; one of them would have to be Dick.

"Here we go," Sonny said softly.

The skids were touching ground as he moved around me and opened the door, holding it open. I was still at the window, watching, when I saw Dick climbing out, crouching beneath the blades, and then I was out the door and down the steps, running.

When he released me, and held me away to look at me, his eyes were wet and red, the lids swollen as if he hadn't slept in days. "I've been so scared," he said. He touched my face, his hand trembling.

"I'm all right," I said.

He held me tighter, pressing his cheek against my hair. "I thought I'd lost you."

Behind me, I heard the bell attached to the door.

When I turned, Sonny was standing on the porch, a rucksack in each hand. The Walters had followed him out, smiling and looking pleased about all the excitement. He said something to them before he started down the steps.

"Don't be angry," I said. Dick's jaws were set as he watched Sonny walking toward us.

Sonny leaned to lay the packs on the ground, then rested

his hands on his hips. For several seconds, they just looked at each other.

"What happened?" Dick said.

Sonny hesitated, glancing behind him at Mr. and Mrs. Walters crossing the yard. "Maybe this ought to wait."

The pilot was getting out of the helicopter.

"It's up to you," Sonny said.

"I think you better have a good explanation," Dick said as the Walters reached us and were waiting to be noticed.

Mr. Walters' glasses had slipped, exposing shiny spots on either side of his nose. "You're a lucky man," he said to Dick when I'd introduced him.

Sonny had walked away, and stood talking to the pilot.

"Yes, I realize." Dick put his arm around me.

Mr. Walters looked at his wife. "About three years ago, wasn't it, those young hikers?"

She was staring at Dick, her hand at her throat. "That's right. Two young boys, they just disappeared."

"Had bloodhounds and everything, searching for them. Never found hide nor hair." Mr. Walters pushed his glasses up. "Yessir, you're lucky."

"I know," Dick said. "I have a lot to be thankful for."

"Your wife'd been canoeing with somebody else, you might not have been so lucky. Sonny knows these mountains like the back of his hand."

Dick's smile now was forced.

"You're staying up at that lodge, I reckon."

"Right," Dick said finally.

"You fellas deer hunting, I guess. Having any luck?"

"Some," Dick said. "I think we better . . ."

"Yessir," Mr. Walters said. "You need to be going." He shook his head. "Don't understand it myself."

"What's that?" Dick said.

"The risks you young folks take. Ain't life risky enough?"

We shook their hands, and I thanked them for their kindness. Dick had his arm around my shoulder, walking me to the helicopter.

"Did you get a deer?" I said.

"Get in." He helped me up, and climbed in back beside me. The pilot had seen us and was taking a last drag on his cigarette. Dick turned in his seat. "Why didn't you tell me?"

"I was going to."

"You were *going* to."

"Yes."

"And you went canoeing with him?"

"I was going to tell you."

The pilot stuck his head in the door. "Mrs. Lannom, I'm real glad you're all right."

"Thank you," I said.

"Sarah, this is Pete Myers."

The man smiled, straight white teeth under a dark mustache. "We all set?" He pulled his head back out and told Sonny we were ready to take off.

"Louellen's at the lodge," Dick said as Sonny was getting in front.

She was waiting, a small figure in the yard, with a forearm held to shield her face from the churned-up dust and leaves. Sonny got out first. I watched as he embraced her.

I stepped down then, wondering how I would manage to get through these next minutes, how I'd be able to face her. Dick might not know yet, but she did. She came across the yard to meet me on almost the exact spot where a few nights ago we'd stood talking.

She spoke to Dick. "Why don't you go ahead in. We'll be along in a minute."

He hesitated.

"I won't take long," she said. "I think the sheriff wants to talk to you."

"Where's Trudie?" I asked him.

"They had to get back to the boys," he said. "I've called her."

"And Mom and Dad?"

"Sarah, I didn't see any reason to tell your parents anything until I had something definite to tell them."

"They don't know?" I said.

"What was I supposed to say?"

"I mean, I'm glad. You were right not to," I said.

Dick had been happy and relieved that I was safe. He could afford to be angry now, too.

He went inside, and Lou and I were left alone, about midway between the helicopter and the house.

"Can you just tell me why?" Lou said.

I told her.

She took my hands and held them with a constant steadying pressure.

"I don't know what happens next," I said.

"Do you love him?"

"Don't be understanding," I said. I was suddenly exhausted. "I don't know how I feel." I looked past her at the lodge. "I can't go in there."

"There's just Clifford and Buster, and Bob Jones—he's the sheriff—and a deputy. That's all. Just a few questions so they can write a report."

"I can't," I said. "He wants to do the talking anyway."

"You have to help him." The sharpness of her tone finally betrayed the stress she'd been under. "You ought to know, he's terrible at lying."

We went in together, her arm around my waist. She presented me to the police officers as her cousin and Sonny's lifelong friend. Her manner defied them to find any fault with that. She made me feel small.

The sheriff looked ordinary, in his mid-forties, starting to go a little soft. His brown hair was thinning, and his brown eyes seemed only normally suspicious. His uniform might have been fresh yesterday. His voice was of medium pitch. Everything about Sheriff Jones, including his name, seemed nonthreatening.

His deputy was Paul Lassic, young and handsome in a storm-trooper kind of way, with blow-dried sandy hair and eyes like a strip search. "Ma'am," he said, drawing it out. I disliked him instantly.

Clifford and a freckled, redheaded man that had to be Buster sat on the hearth on either side of the dead fire. Neither of them looked directly at me when they spoke, saying how happy they were that I was all right. I sat on the couch beside Dick. Lou sat on the arm of Sonny's chair.

When coffee and food had been offered and refused, Bob Jones scooted forward in the wing chair across from Sonny. He turned his hat in his hands, seeming at a loss for the best way to start. "First thing, the most important thing," he said, "both Sonny and Mrs. Lannom are all right."

He laid the hat on the coffee table. "I know we're all glad of that."

Dick's arm lay across the back of the couch. "Sheriff, my wife is tired." He touched my shoulder as he spoke. "We'd like to get this over with as quickly as possible. We'd like to go home."

"Good," the sheriff said. "That's fine. Sonny, if you'd just reconstruct what happened."

"There was a change of plans," Sonny said. "Sarah and I decided to run the river down to Slaughter's Bridge instead of going to Medicine Springs."

The deputy was writing it down.

"We didn't make it."

"Nobody knew you'd changed your plans." It was a statement. The sheriff's tone was encouraging.

"No. It just seemed like a good idea at the time. It was a nice day." Sonny hadn't looked at me once. "We capsized."

"About where did this happen, would you say?" the sheriff asked.

"About midway."

"Midway," Bob Jones said, glancing at his deputy. "Could you tell us how it happened?"

The room was completely still.

Lou put her hand on his back, and I realized I was holding my breath as Sonny looked at the sheriff for what seemed forever.

"Was there a rough stretch of water?" the sheriff asked him.

Sonny didn't answer.

I felt my face getting hot. I focused on Sheriff Jones, trying not to see anyone else. "This is embarrassing," I said.

The sheriff looked embarrassed for me. There was a lewd grin on the deputy's face.

"I don't think we actually capsized."

Lou stared at me, silently offering support.

"He told me I should hold to the sides if I got scared, or slide off the seat to the bottom. I'm afraid that what happened is, I stood up."

"You fell overboard?" the sheriff said.

"The water was so cold," I said. "In my nose and mouth, roaring in my ears."

"So actually what happened, you went in after her," the sheriff said.

"Sarah must have hit her head when she fell. She was nearly unconscious, and I was afraid she'd swallowed a lot of water." He sounded almost convincing. "I had to get a fire started. By the time I could look downriver for the canoe . . ."

"So there you were," the sheriff said.

"That's right."

Deputy Lassic stopped writing and tapped his pencil against his notebook. "You were headed for the bridge?" he said, watching me rather than Sonny.

"Right," Sonny said.

"Had you given any thought to a ride back?"

"No," Sonny said.

"Why's that?"

Bob Jones looked pained. "Have you run this river before, Sonny, for Christ's sake?"

"Yes."

"Any problem with transportation before?"

"Jimmy Spinks is usually available."

"So Jimmy would take you back to your car, is what you'd planned?" the sheriff said. "Are you writing this down?" he said to the deputy.

"I already told you we'd changed our plans."

"Where is this leading?" Dick leaned around me, talking to the deputy. His jaws were tight. "Is there a point to this, or not?"

"Take it easy," the sheriff said.

"I'll take it easy when we stop going around in circles."

Clifford cleared his throat. "Sonny could have called me or Buster, Carlton, hell, any of us, if they needed a ride."

"All right." Bob Jones put his hands on his knees. "Let's wind this up. Sonny, you and Mrs. Lannom had to walk out, a pretty good hike, would you say?"

"You ever been in there, Bob?"

"Hell, no, and I don't plan to be."

"I've got a question," the deputy said.

The sheriff stood up, ignoring him. "That's all, unless you have something."

"No," Dick said.

"For the record, then, you're satisfied with this inquiry?"

"Thanks for your help," Dick said. "Please thank the people who turned out this morning."

The sheriff and his deputy were gone. Our bags were in the helicopter. Clifford was telling Dick that he would bring the bow and rifle, the cooler, some other odds and ends stacked by the front door. He would see to closing the lodge. Buster would package Dick's deer for the freezer. These things settled, we stood in awkward silence around the coffee table.

Sonny said, "I'd like to speak to Sarah alone a minute."

"Me and Buster'll be outside," Clifford said, then didn't move. He rolled a cigarette back and forth between thumb and index finger.

"You've really got some balls, don't you?" Dick's voice was shaking. "I'd like to speak to *you* alone."

Lou came around the coffee table and touched Dick's elbow. "Walk with me?" she said. "Please?"

When the door closed, leaving us together, Sonny's shoulders sagged. I started to him, and he put his hand up, stopping me, and his voice when he spoke sounded thick and dull. "Go home." His olive skin looked sallow. "I got what I wanted. Go home while he'll still have you."

"Don't," I said.

"You think they didn't know you were lying?" He tried to look at me and turned away. "Joe'd be real proud of you, wouldn't he?"

"It won't work, Sonny." But it hurt.

"Have you ever seen a woman with more class? She puts her arms around you, and defends you. Feel good about yourself?" He turned around to face me. There were beads of sweat across his upper lip.

The ashtrays were full; there was a layer of dust on the furniture, mud on the hardwood someone had tracked in. I thought of Dick in here, pacing these floors. "Do you know what Joe would say?" I asked him.

The sound he made was somewhere between a laugh and a groan. His eyes were wet.

"*We're* still alive." I walked to the door. With my hand on the knob, I turned and looked at him.

"Go home," he said. "Forget it ever happened."

31

I couldn't understand why he was doing this, but from now on, no matter what Sonny said, or did, he would never again make me believe he didn't love me. I closed the door and crossed the yard without looking back. I hugged Lou and climbed into the helicopter. Then we lifted off and I watched her grow small below me. *Call me,* she'd said.

I looked out at the scenery for a while, thinking as I always do when flying how neat and artificial the world seems at a distance. Dick was watching out his side, so I laid my head against the seat-back and closed my eyes. After I did that, he moved to the cockpit with the pilot.

When Pete Myers set us down in our driveway, he made it look effortless, like a butterfly alighting. He was our age: there was an extra depth, like some dark sad wisdom, in his eyes.

"You flew in Vietnam, didn't you?" I said.

He smiled at me over his shoulder. "Yes ma'am, I did."

"When were you there?"

Dick took my arm.

"Sixty-nine," Pete Myers said.

"My brother was a pilot in the Air Force."

"Yeah? Well, you know, they sure did a job. I flew dust-offs. I'd wanted gunships."

Dick was urging me to get out, gentle pressure on my arm. "Thanks, Pete," he said.

"Sure glad you're all right, Mrs. Lannom." Pete Myers had a nice smile.

I took a long, long shower, letting the water run over my face and hair and skin. I put on a terry robe, soft and clean, and when I came into our bedroom toweling my hair, Dick had made scrambled eggs, toast, and a pot of hot tea. He didn't ask me any questions while we were eating. We were both hungry.

Now I sat at the dresser, combing my hair.

"More tea?"

"Not right now," I said.

He poured himself some, slowly stirring in cream and sugar. I could see him in the reflection of the mirror, sitting on the side of the bed, and watching me across the rim of the cup. Then he set it down and dropped his head in his hands, running his fingers through his hair.

I got up and went to him.

"I don't even know how I'm supposed to feel," he said. "I'm happy you're all right, but *Christ*."

I sat down beside him.

He kept looking at the floor. "I'd gotten my deer, I couldn't wait to tell you about it." He laughed. "I wanted him to know what a fine shot I'd made. I get there and Trudie tells me you two have gone somewhere. And I think, Okay, sure. Why not?

"Then by the time Carlton brought Lou back, it was nearly dark, and then it kept getting later and later." He turned his head. "Why didn't you tell me who he was?"

"I did. The night I'd had too much to drink. You thought I was talking about Joe."

I could see he was trying to remember. He let me take his hand. "The first night," I said, "you were nervous about hunting the next morning. That didn't seem like a good time to tell you. It didn't seem important then anyway."

He stood up, and paced. "Trudie said you found out some things about him you hadn't known before."

"The first morning," I said. "He told me he'd shown you a good stand, and he was looking for deer sign. Where you trout fished last summer—I'd gotten up early, and gone there to do some drawing . . ."

He stopped, his fists knotted in his pockets. "And he just *happened* by, I suppose."

"I don't know."

"Didn't you wonder, for Christ's sake?"

I looked at him.

"What am I yelling at you for?" He came and sat down and took my face between his hands. "Baby, help me understand. Did you know it was him before we went?"

"I thought it probably was."

"But you didn't tell me." He got up again and moved to the chair across from me.

"I didn't know he'd been in a veterans' hospital and come looking for me and all this other until after we got there."

He looked so tired. "But then he told you, and Trudie told you. And you still went canoeing with him?"

I started at the beginning, when Joe and Sonny and I were children. I told him how that was, and how we fell in love, how little time we'd had before he went to Vietnam, about the letters, and the night in my apartment. Then his getting out of the hospital and learning I was married, what he must have thought. I told Dick what happened to Sonny in Vietnam that Joe was supposed to have told me, and hadn't.

I told him I'd thought Sonny and I had a few things to talk over.

He sat slumped in the chair.

I took a breath, and let it out. "There wasn't any canoeing accident. That part didn't happen. The canoe didn't capsize, I didn't almost drown. We . . ."

"Wait. Just wait a minute." He had sat up, and was leaning toward me. "You're telling me you didn't go canoeing?"

"We did go canoeing, but we didn't capsize. He paddled the canoe to shore. I understood we were walking somewhere to get a ride back, but really, we were going to a cabin where he'd stayed when he got out of the hospital."

"You did *what?*"

"I thought we were walking to our ride. Then it started to get late, and I asked him how much farther we had to walk. He said we weren't going back."

I'd never seen him look like this, pale and with a vein bulging in the center of his forehead; it frightened me.

"Dick, I didn't know *where* we were going; I didn't know where we *were*. I asked him to take me back to the lodge, and he said he couldn't because it was too far."

"He kidnapped you, that's what you're telling me."

"I know it seems that way."

"*Seems* that way!" His face was chalk-white. "Why did you lie?"

I looked down at my hands, clenched in my lap.

He stood up so suddenly he knocked his chair over. For a full minute, at least, neither of us said a word. He paced back and forth across the room. I expected him to break something.

Finally, he picked the chair up and set it directly in front of me. He sat down, one hand locked in the other, the vein throbbing in his forehead. "All right. Now go on."

"I think he was just so angry," I said. "It was late at night or early the next morning when we got there. I hardly remember, I was so tired. I didn't wake up until that afternoon. Sunday afternoon."

He nodded.

"Then it took us two days to walk out."

He didn't say anything, just waited.

I heard the sound at the back of my throat as I swallowed. "He wanted to know how I could have loved him, and married you within four months. That's what it was."

He seemed to be thinking about it, staring off to the side.

"What did you tell him?" He looked at me.

"That I loved you."

"What did you eat?"

For a minute, I wasn't sure I'd heard him.

"Roots? Berries?" he asked me.

"There were some C-rations already there. He'd brought some other food in the rucksack—instant soup and trail mix, things like that. Why?"

"That was what you ate then?"

"He killed a rabbit."

"I didn't think he had a gun."

"He had a rifle, but he caught the rabbit in a snare. Why are you asking me all this?"

"He *did* have a rifle?" Even so tired, his eyes bloodshot, fatigue lines around his mouth, he was so strikingly handsome. "Do you mind telling me about it?"

"No, of course not."

"Tell me more about where he took you. The cabin, what was it like?"

"It was small, just one room with a fireplace. There was a creek down the hill in front of it."

"No indoor plumbing and central heat, I guess." He didn't seem as angry now.

"He said it was probably an old trapper's cabin. He'd made a lot of repairs to it."

"What did he say when you told him you loved me?"

"He . . . I don't . . ." I shook my head. "He said something . . . that he understood, that he could see what kind of man you are."

"I want to be sure I've got this right. He brought food, he made certain nobody knew where you were going, he had a rifle but didn't use it because somebody might hear the shots. He *planned* it. That's right, isn't it?"

Why had I thought he would understand? "You can't imagine what he went through, Dick, the things he saw. I know the war's over, but I don't think he's ever going to be over it. It's just . . . he's always going to be scarred." I swallowed. "Like Joe is always going to be dead."

"Sarah. I know how hard this must be for you. I know you grew up with him, he was your brother's best friend, you even loved him." He put his hand gently on my cheek. "He hurt you, didn't he? Forced you. Isn't that what you're trying to tell me?"

"No."

He held my face, lifting it, making me look at him.

"Dick, *I* made love to *him*."

I'll never forget the look in his eyes. Not for as long as I live.

I was listening for his car to start, for the engine to kick over, for him to back it out of the garage and gun it down the long driveway to the road. I sat where he'd left me on the side of the bed.

He had drawn away from me; he had actually recoiled, and when I'd tried to explain, wanting to make him see *how* it had come to happen, he was walking toward the door. "Please," I'd said. He'd paused, his hand on the doorknob, and without turning around, opened it and closed it behind him.

He needed the anger, I understood that. But I thought I might lose my mind if he left me tonight.

I thought about calling Trudie.

I thought about last night, and made myself stop.

For what seemed a long time, I sat there, praying I wouldn't hear his car start, and trying to think what to do. I saw the tray on the floor at my feet and did the next thing. I picked it up and went downstairs to the kitchen.

He wasn't there. The skillet he'd used to scramble the eggs was soaking in the sink. I set the tray on the counter and walked down the hall to the den. The lights were off. I could sense his presence before my eyes adjusted to the dark, before I could see him, a shadow in the chair. I knew he could see me silhouetted in the doorway.

I started to him.

"Go back upstairs."

I stopped, then went on. I knelt beside his chair.

He got up and crossed to the window. "Go back upstairs," he said.

"Let me talk to you."

"Not tonight."

"I want you to understand how it was."

"All right," he said. "How was it?"

"It didn't have anything to do . . ."

"On a scale of one to ten."

". . . to do with us. Out there, it seemed . . ."

"Go upstairs, Sarah."

"It was like turning the clock back."

He slammed his fist into the wall. "Go . . . upstairs . . . now." He spoke softly, enunciating each word.

I lay on top of the bedspread, curled on my side, holding myself tight. I must have fallen asleep listening for his car.

When I woke the next morning, he was gone. He'd left a note saying he'd be staying in town, for at least the next day or two.

Trudie called around nine. When I heard her voice, I broke down. "He . . . he . . . he . . ." punctuated by sobs, was the best I could do.

"Hang on," she said. "I'm coming."

"I can't help wondering what would have happened if I'd told you years ago, right after he came to my apartment," she said.

I was dressed. We were having orange juice on the sunporch. It was Wednesday, October 30th, a clear bright morning. A week ago tonight, we'd sat at the dining room table listening to Braxton and Dick talk about deer hunting.

"Maybe I should have. I thought I was doing the best thing." Trudie sat beside me on the rattan couch. It was comforting just to have her there. "What are you *thinking* about doing?"

I felt my eyes fill again. I shrugged my shoulders. I'd shown her Dick's note, it was on the table in front of us. I'd told her everything.

"Do you want some advice?"

I laughed and wiped my eyes. "Sure."

"Don't do anything now. Let it alone for a few days. Try

not to even think about it. You're both out of kilter right now."

"I wanted him just as much as I ever did. It was *just* the same. I wasn't thinking about hurting Dick or anyone else. It wasn't an issue." I looked at her. "And I'd do it again. I'd have to do the same thing again."

"I know," she said.

"If Dick asks me, I'll have to tell him that."

"He won't. Not if he's got any sense." She tucked her hair behind her ear, and a ray of sunlight flashed straight off her earring to the back of my skull. "What about this house, the kind of life you're used to?"

I didn't answer her.

"Forget I said that."

It was so quiet I could hear Edna all the way upstairs vacuuming one of the bedrooms. We sat like this for a few moments.

I picked up my glass, took a drink of juice.

"Joe and I tried too hard to protect you, I guess, keep you from getting hurt any worse. I don't think he believed it anyway, about you and Sonny."

My heart started to pound. "Did you talk to him?"

She set her glass on the table. "His date, what was her name?"

"Janet?"

"I talked to her."

I waited. "Trudie, what did she say?"

"I don't remember exactly what she said . . ." She looked at me. "Let me think. It was . . ." She chewed her bottom lip. "Joe told her something like he couldn't believe it about you two, he had a hard time getting used to you two. Something like that. Is this important?"

"I don't know," I said. Joe had said the same thing to Sonny and me, but before Sonny went to Vietnam. "Probably not."

"I tried to warn Dick. She really loves this guy, I told him. He didn't care. Dick really didn't care if you loved him or not when you married him. He told me that. He said he'd be happy if you loved him even a fraction as much as you'd loved 'this other guy.' He was sure you'd *learn* to love him after you were married."

"He was right," I said.

"Don't blame yourself too much. We all had a hand in this."

After she left, I wandered around my studio, taking joy for the thousandth time in the beautiful arrangement of it, the perfect north light. Dick had consulted Joshua about what I would need and like in a studio, then commissioned an architect to design it. He'd surprised me with the plans and a detailed architectural rendering.

I loved this room.

I stopped before the unfinished canvas on the easel. It seemed like some stranger had done this work, not me.

I packed a few brushes and some tubes of paint, hardly noticing or caring what colors I threw in the case, or whether they were polymers or oils.

I told Edna I was going downtown to Joshua's studio. She wanted to know if she should start something for dinner. I told her not to, that Dick would be gone tonight, and maybe for the next few days. Business, I said.

After I'd backed out of the garage and pointed the control to close the door, I paused to look at my house, lovely wood and stone and creamy stucco. I turned the MGB in the paved area where Pete Myers had landed yesterday. This time yesterday, I'd been sitting on a fallen log talking to Sonny.

I wound through the gears going down the drive and took Hillsboro Road into town.

32

Dick came home Friday afternoon.

He'd phoned from work, letting me know to expect him. I was afraid to hope for anything, but I was glad he was coming home; I'd missed him terribly.

He'd called early, before I left for the studio. I called Joshua and told him I wouldn't be able to help with his class today.

I went to the grocery and helped Edna prepare dinner: Dick's favorite roast, and lemon pie, a special salad, knowing the whole time that probably both of us would be too tense to enjoy it. But at least he would know I'd made the effort.

I wore a dress he liked and took extra care with my hair and nails. I was stirring the drinks when I heard his car in the driveway. Then the door from the garage into the kitchen opened, and I turned around, conscious of wanting to look pretty, and trying to smile with the corners of my mouth trembling.

He looked well, he looked rested. He was carrying his jacket slung over one shoulder, his tie was loosened—the way he'd come home on countless evenings. He shut the door and tossed the jacket across the butcher block.

"I've missed you," I said.

For a moment I thought I saw a softening in his expression. "Hello, Sarah."

He let me prattle about dinner and accepted the drink I offered. I watched while he tasted it; I'd been careful to make it dry and thoroughly chilled, with a twist of lemon. "It's good," he said, and set it down.

He leaned against the counter and looked around, seeing things fresh, I thought, as I had for the last three days. Familiar things made strange by the abrupt and massive change in our lives. "Well, I think I'll go upstairs," he said.

"Sure. Dinner won't be ready for a few minutes yet."

He finished the drink and put the glass down, picked up his jacket and left the kitchen.

Okay, I thought, *what did you expect?*

He ate with appetite, commenting on how good everything was. He'd taken a long time upstairs, changing into chinos and a blue V-necked sweater, one I'd given him a couple of years ago, the same color as his eyes.

I had trouble swallowing my food, but I pushed it around on my plate to make it look like I was eating. "So how are things at the office?"

He nodded and took a sip of water before he answered. "Fine. Fed sends his regards."

I weaved a sliver of roast between the tines of my fork and carried it to my mouth. Chewed.

His laugh had a brittle ring. "I told him the official version."

I looked up but he kept his eyes on his plate.

"More roast?" I said.

"I've had enough. It was good."

"There's lemon pie."

He folded his napkin and laid it on the table. "Maybe later."

"Coffee?"

"I don't think so." He glanced at my plate to see if I was finished.

I put my napkin down.

"I'll help you clear, then there's a game I'd like to watch."

"I can do this," I said.

He stood and picked up his plate and the roast platter, backing through the swinging door to the kitchen. The last trip, he set our water glasses and the salad bowl on the countertop. Not once since he'd come home, not during the entire meal, had he really looked at me.

"Who's playing?" I said.

"Kentucky."

"And who?"

"Indiana, I think it is." He had his hand on the door. "Can you handle it now?"

"Sure, I've got it," I said, too quick, too bright.

He almost turned. "It was a good dinner." Then he was gone, the door swinging in-and-back, in-and-back.

I put the food away and loaded the dishwasher. I took my time, doing things carefully and deliberately. When I was finished, I would turn out the light, and go into the den, and sit quietly and watch the game with him. It would take time, that was all.

He wasn't in the den. He wasn't in the bedroom, but his closet door was ajar. I pulled it all the way open, seeing the empty spaces where his clothes had hung, and almost simultaneously, heard the faint TV sounds behind the closed door of the guest room down the hall. I walked like a cripple to the bed and sat down. *All right,* I thought, *what did you expect?*

During the next weeks, we were carefully polite to each other. He would call if he was going to be home in time for dinner. He seldom was. He usually came in late and left early. Weekends were the most difficult, but it was a big house and one of us could always find an errand that needed running, or someplace to go. I spent a lot of time walking in Edwin and Percy Warner Parks. In some places, if I followed the winding roads high enough, it was almost like being in the mountains.

Edna cleaned the guest room without comment, and tiptoed around the house looking worried.

My mother knew things weren't right between us, picking it up more from what wasn't said than what was. In effect, I asked her not to ask. A little problem. Some difficulties to iron out. Don't worry, I told her, and please understand if we can't make it home for Thanksgiving.

I began to realize what Dick was waiting for, why he hadn't left completely, and it was the one thing I couldn't say. If I could have gone to him and said, *I'm sorry. Please forgive me,* I think he would have done so. But I couldn't.

I thought about Sonny, and tried to envision a future for us. I kept remembering Louellen's hands holding mine, her arm around my waist. Obliquely, never able to think it through head-on, I tried to reach a decision. What was the right thing to do? There had to be a best thing, didn't there?

33

November was half gone, and nothing was resolved. I felt exhausted all the time. I went to bed early and woke with dark circles under my eyes. Trudie called, or I called her, each day or two. More and more, I left it up to her to call. *I'm fine,* I'd say, *just riding it out*.

If it hadn't been for my work, I think I'd have gone mad. I couldn't paint at home now, not in that room, so by default, without really asking, I had taken over a corner of Joshua's space, like in the old days. It was the one place where I felt at all comfortable anymore, as if I belonged. He didn't question me, at least, not for a while. He pretended he didn't notice that I had practically moved in.

I continued with the children's classes at the museum until one afternoon he asked if I would mind letting one of his graduate students take over for a few weeks. The student needed experience for his secondary certification. "And how about you stay for dinner," he said. "And how about you cook it."

We were sitting down to salmon croquettes, lima beans and a salad. He was pouring the wine. "You look awful," he said.

"Thanks a lot." I spread the napkin over my lap.

"I'm serious. You look like death riding a white horse eating a cracker."

I picked up my fork. And laid it back down.

"Bad timing. I'm sorry." He took a bite of salmon. "Eat, goddamnit, I said I was sorry."

He reached across the table and covered my hand with his. "Come on, Sarah, you can't face life on an empty stomach." His eyes were so kind. This gentle man. "We'll talk later. After dinner you're going to tell me all about it. But I'll say this much, whatever it is, it certainly hasn't hurt your work any."

I was working with the same intensity, and putting in the

long hours, that I had in California on the beach paintings. Only now, I didn't destroy them.

We'd left the dishes; Joshua said he'd do them later. He set me down on the couch. "Okay," he said. "Let's have it."

Now he was puffing on his pipe, holding a match to the bowl. I laid my head against the back of his overstuffed sofa and wished I could stay right here tonight, not have to drive home.

He sat down beside me. I usually enjoy the smell of his brand, a cherry blend, but tonight it made me slightly nauseated. I turned away from the smoke, and he gave me a funny look and put the pipe in an ashtray at the other end of the couch. "So he took you right out from under Dick's nose and whisked you off to his cabin. You know what's really crazy? I don't blame him." He slipped an arm under my shoulders. He smelled of paint and turpentine, tobacco. Comforting smells. "Then he brings you back, looks Dick in the eye and tells him the goddamn canoe tipped over. And Dick, in front of God and everybody, pretends to believe it. No wonder you look like a gutted snowbird."

"Some days I wish he'd just leave."

"And make the decision for you," he said.

"Then, when it's time for him to be home and he hasn't called, I catch myself . . . maybe I'm reading, and I'll see it's the same page over and over."

"You think about Sonny?"

I stared at the ceiling, my head on Joshua's arm.

"You think Dick doesn't know that? But still he comes home." He laid his cheek against my hair. "I have to tell you," he said. "That night you came to me, I thought Sonny was a fool. Any weekend, I could see fifty like him—swaggering, skin-headed Ft. Campbell soldiers down on Church Street looking to get laid—and there he was, with a girl like you. For Christ's sake, put either him or Dick out of his misery."

"Don't you think I'm trying?" I said.

He kissed my temple; his strong fingers squeezed my arm.

"If Dick would only try," I said. "Sonny and I were together—if he could accept that, and let it go."

"Let you keep it, you mean."

"All right, yes. Three days, Joshua. It's not so much."

"Is it enough?"

By the time I left Joshua's and drove home, it was past ten o'clock. Dick had told me he would be staying in town for a late board meeting, so I was surprised to find him in the kitchen, making a sandwich.

He looked over his shoulder as I came in, then turned back to the open refrigerator, moving things around. "We have any lettuce?"

I found it for him. He tore off a leaf and laid it on top of the ham. "Fed canceled at the last minute," he said, in answer to my unspoken question.

"I've been at Joshua's," I said.

He put the lettuce back in the refrigerator and took out the milk.

"Trying to get the show organized." I moved aside so he could get to the cabinet holding the glasses. "He said to tell you hi."

Dick carried his plate and glass of milk to the breakfast nook and sat down.

I poured a glass for myself, more to have something to do than because I wanted it. "I'm having trouble deciding which are my best pieces. As opposed to my favorites." I leaned against the counter, sipping the milk. "You want some chips with that?"

He shook his head, his mouth full.

"So," I said. "How's your work been going?"

He looked at me while he chewed and swallowed, his gaze level and cold. He dropped the sandwich on his plate and let his breath out in disgust.

I felt my throat and chest constrict. I turned away and set my glass on the counter.

"Look," he said, "it doesn't *have* to go on this way."

I stood with my back to him, struggling not to cry.

"If you want to, we can get past this."

"I want to," I said. When I turned, he had pushed the half-eaten sandwich away and crossed his arms on the table. He sat staring at the Formica. "I love you," I said. "I didn't mean to hurt you."

Seconds passed while the only sound in the room was the hum of the electric clock.

"You didn't agree to go with him, he forced you to go with him. Was that the truth?"

"Dick . . ." My eyes started to fill.

"Is that what happened, or not?"

"Yes."

"He scared you, terrorized you, isn't that right? You must have realized he had to be fucking nuts to pull a stunt like that. After he'd dragged you off to his lair, you knew what the next step was going to be. If you didn't do it, he was going to rape you."

I thought about the cabin, how alone we had been, not another human being for miles. It was true that Sonny could have done anything he wanted; there had been no one around to stop him. Except he hadn't.

"That's sexual coercion, any way you cut it."

I thought about how he had wanted me, when I touched him the very first time. How I'd wanted him.

"You didn't have any choice. Not really." Dick was waiting, all I had to do was agree. I wouldn't even have to speak; I could just nod, or bow my head and not say anything.

I looked at my husband, tears blurring my eyes. "Why would you *prefer* that I'd been raped?"

Dick stared at me for several seconds before he stood up and left the room. I finished my milk and dragged myself to bed.

34

The second Friday night in December was the annual benefit dinner and dance for the Arts Council. It had been on our calendar for months. I got up early that morning to catch Dick before he left for work. I wanted to know if he was still planning on going with me.

He was sitting in the breakfast nook, reading the paper and eating a bowl of cornflakes. He glanced up as I came in, and then he stopped and really looked at me. We'd hardly seen each other the last several days.

I didn't know what was wrong with me. I almost cried at the look of concern that crossed his face, but it was there and gone. He went back to reading his paper.

"Would you like some juice?" I said.

"No thanks."

I poured myself a glass and stood at the sink, drinking it. He had to be wondering what I was doing up, what I wanted. *How amusing,* I thought, *that you don't ask*.

"The fund-raiser for the Arts Council," I said. "It's tonight."

He laid the paper down.

"I was just wondering if you were going."

He sighed. "I forgot about it."

"It's all right," I said.

"No, I just forgot. I have a late-afternoon appointment."

"It's okay."

He stared out the window into the backyard. It was a dismal gray day, threatening rain. "What's wrong with you? Are you sick?"

"Just tired, I guess. I've been working pretty hard."

He stared out the window some more. "If you'll bring my tux so I can change at the office, I should be able to make it."

"It's all right if you don't want to," I said.

"This is the big wingding, isn't it? What time does it start?"

"Cocktails at six."

"So we'll be fashionably late. Okay?"

"Thank you," I said.

He pushed the cereal bowl away and stood up. He adjusted his tie and his belt, his cuffs. He always used to kiss me before he left in the mornings. Not even our hands had touched since the night I told him about Sonny. "The appointment's at five-thirty," he said. "I'll see if I can cut it short."

I took a sip of juice.

He started to pick up his bowl to put it in the sink, but I was in the way, he'd have to come close, so he left the bowl where it was.

He tucked the paper under his arm and opened the door. "Maybe you ought to go back to bed, get a little more sleep or something."

I stared at myself in the vanity mirror. My eyes looked haunted and my dress didn't fit. I'd seen the dress and bought it weeks ago especially for this party. And now it didn't fit right. I did what I could with makeup.

I put Dick's shirt, tux, shoes and socks in a garment bag and left the house a few minutes past five, allowing time for traffic.

I pulled into the slot beside his Skylark a little before six. The parking lot was almost empty, but Clifford's Jeep was still there. I saw him through the window from the back hallway as I was starting to go in. It was the first time I'd seen Clifford since the weekend at the lodge. Dick was just walking away. Evidently, they'd been discussing something. My hands full, I was having some trouble opening the door.

Clifford got there first. "Night on the town, looks like," he said, holding the door for me.

I gave Dick the clothes. We were near the loading docks, Clifford's territory. "I'll wait for you down here," I said.

While Dick took the elevator up to change, Clifford brought me a plastic chair.

"Aren't you going tonight?" I asked him.

"You couldn't get me there with a forklift."

"Why'd you let me sell you the tickets then?"

"Hell, I support the arts. I'm not a barbarian." He laughed, hitching at his pants.

"What about Janice? Wouldn't she like to go?"

He lifted another molded plastic chair from beside the door and sat in it. He cleared his throat in that way he has. "I was just talking to Dick. About bringing him his venison."

"Oh?"

"I'm headed up to the lodge this weekend."

"You are," I said.

"Taking Monday off, be back sometime in the early afternoon." He looked out the windows overseeing the loading docks and the parking lot. "Anyway, I was wondering about bringing the venison by your house Monday afternoon."

"Sure," I said. "If I'm not there, Edna will be."

"All right."

It was quiet for a moment, then both of us spoke at the same time. He let me go first, and I couldn't think what to say. He didn't look at me while I took a Kleenex out of my bag.

"You're going hunting?" I took a breath and held it.

"Yeah, probably. Didn't get one the last time."

I nodded. "I'll be home Monday."

"More likely we'll get drunk. Hell of a thing, isn't it? Those soldiers?" he said.

I looked at him. I didn't know what he was talking about.

"The airplane crash. Killed all those Ft. Campbell soldiers. Jesus, Sarah, don't you read the papers?" He got up and went into his office and came out with the *Tennessean*.

The picture jumped off the page at me, and the cutline: *Two hundred forty-eight Ft. Campbell soldiers were killed yesterday when their chartered Arrow Air DC8 crashed and burned shortly after taking off from a refueling stop in Gander, New-*

foundland. They were coming back from a six-month peacekeeping assignment in the Sinai Desert.

I looked up at Clifford, then quickly scanned the rest of the article. The soldiers who died were all members of the 101st Airborne Division.

"Dear God," I said.

"Yeah, I know. Sonny's old outfit." Clifford coughed and shook his head. "I mean, when we can't even get our boys home for Christmas."

Dick paused at the door, surveying the crowd. The decorations were lovely, the lights and holly, the enormous, beautifully decorated cedar tree, the wreaths and sprays of freshly cut pine. Christmas. I'd hardly given it a thought. All those soldiers. All those families.

"How long do we stay?" he said.

We'd taken his car, leaving mine in the parking lot at the plant. I'd suggested, as we were driving into town, that we didn't have to stay long if he'd rather not. He hadn't answered me then, he'd seemed preoccupied; probably he hadn't heard me.

"Only as long as you want to," I said. I was trying to be agreeable.

He smiled and spoke to a couple I vaguely remembered meeting once, calling them by name. When he turned to me, the smile was gone. "It's your party."

He brought me a drink and left me. I mingled, speaking to people I knew, smiling.

He came back to escort me through the buffet line. I ate something. I don't remember what. I was getting a headache. He had left me again.

The Council's most generous patron cornered me and talked, endlessly. I smiled until my jaws ached.

People were starting to dance. I noticed that Dick was dancing. I made myself stop staring at the woman he was with.

I searched the room for Joshua. He'd told me he would be late. The ballroom was crowded now with people in evening dress—smiling, laughing. I looked around for someone to talk to.

The orchestra finished the soft-rock medley they were playing. The next song was a slow Christmas tune, "Have Yourself a Merry Little Christmas."

Dick and the brunette were still dancing. Apparently they were having a great time. Her dress was a champagne beige color, watered silk, and it *fit*. She was tall and slender; in her high heels, she was nearly as tall as Dick. She could lift her lashes and gaze straight into his eyes. I knew just how it would feel, his arms around her like that.

I went to powder my nose.

When I came back, I finally saw Joshua. He'd brought a date.

The man Dick had spoken to at the door asked me to dance, and I begged off. I felt dizzy, although I'd had almost nothing to drink. The music seemed too loud, the lights too bright. And then Joshua had hold of my elbow and was introducing me to Claire. She was lovely. Everyone was lovely and seemed to be having such a good time. He said something to her, then hooked his arm through mine and walked me out the door.

"You wouldn't happen to have an aspirin?" I said.

"You're going home."

It was cooler in the entrance hall, out of the ballroom, and quieter. "Can't," I said. "Not yet."

"Sarah, you're white as a sheet."

"I need some water is all."

At the water fountain, I did start to feel better, which made me realize how bad I'd felt before, how woozy and strange. "I'm okay now," I said. "Things were closing in. I don't like crowds much."

"Where's Dick?"

"Poor Joshua." I kissed his cheek. "Go back to Claire. I approve, by the way—she seems nice."

"Where's Dick?" Joshua can be insistent. "Let's go find him."

They weren't dancing now, they were standing by the Christmas tree. Her face was turned toward me. I didn't know her. I'd never seen her before tonight. I wondered who she was and how Dick knew her so well.

"See," I said, pointing them out to Joshua. "He's right over there. Now, go. I'm fine." I made shooing motions with my hands.

After Joshua had reclaimed his date and they were dancing, I saw Dick notice me from across the room. Our eyes met. Then, very deliberately, he turned away. I went to the restroom and threw up.

Jealousy? I'd never been jealous before, but he'd never done this before either. I pressed a damp paper towel to my forehead. The attendant asked if I was all right. *Fine,* I said, *I'm fine.*

I sat on the couch in the ladies' lounge, and closed my eyes. Then Claire was standing over me. She left, and came back, helping me stand up. She said Dick was going to get the car.

While we waited on the curb, outside in the fresh air, I began to feel better again. Joshua was on one side, holding my arm; Claire had the other. "I'm so sorry," I said.

Joshua snorted. I saw them glance at each other over my head.

"I'm a party poop," I said.

She patted my arm.

"Was it too hot in there, maybe?" I asked her.

"Yes, maybe that was it," Claire said. Her voice was very nice, Nashville southern.

I saw the Skylark turn the corner.

Joshua held the door open and helped me get in. "I'm real sorry," I told him. He kissed my cheek. His lips felt cool.

Then he leaned around me to Dick and started to say something; he changed his mind. He stared at Dick for a second or two. "I'll call you," he said to me. He backed out, and shut the door.

Going home, I laid my head against the back of the seat. I had to concentrate on not being sick again.

I stared at Dick's profile in the moonlight. *God,* I thought. *You're so beautiful in a tux.*

"You're going to see a doctor," he said.

35

The next morning I called to make the appointment. Dick sat drinking coffee in the breakfast nook.

"How about next Thursday at nine?" the girl said.

"Don't you have an opening sooner?"

"Is this an emergency?"

I stretched across the counter for my cup. "Not really. Sort of."

Dick got up and took the phone out of my hand. "Today," he said. "Preferably this morning." He listened. "Lannom, first name Sarah. Right." And hung up. "It's at ten-thirty. I'll take you," he said to me.

"I'll take me," I said. "It's probably the flu. There'll be a waiting room full of people with the same thing. You might catch it."

"It isn't the goddamned flu."

With complications, I thought.

I read the paper while I waited my turn. There were more articles on the airplane crash. It made my heart ache, and I couldn't help but think how Sonny must feel. Dr. Taylor was the physician on duty. I followed his nurse to one of the consultation rooms.

She laid the folder containing my records in the center of the desk, her clipboard on the corner. She leaned over it, jotting things down as I told her my symptoms. "Lots of that going around," she said. "Would you step on the scales, please?"

I stood up and stepped on the scales. She read my weight in kilograms and consulted a conversion chart on the wall.

I sat down again, and she took my blood pressure. She took my temperature with a digital thermometer.

"Age?" she said.

I told her.

"Date of your last period?" She waited, then looked at me.

I stared at her.

I didn't keep up anymore, not since California and the tedium of temperature charts. I'd been regular as clockwork then, and so what? The last time I'd thought about my period was packing for the lodge, whether I needed to pack tampons or not.

I rested my head against the wall. My last period ended sometime during the first or second week of October. Today was December 14.

I gave her the approximate date.

"Are you using any birth-control device?"

I shook my head.

She turned and opened a drawer on the examination table, and handed me a gown. She looked sympathetic. "Better get undressed."

Dr. Taylor rocked in his desk chair and watched me over tented fingers. "It happens. Years go by and then whammo. How do you feel about it? You want this baby?"

"I'm just . . . I didn't think I could have children."

He nodded. "Well, congratulations. I'm going to refer you to Dr. Bannister unless there's an obstetrician you'd rather see," he said.

"No. I mean Dr. Bannister's fine."

"Okey-doke. Make an appointment at the front desk." He wrote out a prescription and tore it off the pad. "I'd rather you not take this or any medication unless you're feeling *really* nauseated."

"No, I won't," I said.

"Quite a surprise to give your husband."

I sat in the car in the clinic parking lot holding on to the wheel. All these years. So sure that it was me that was infertile, I hadn't once considered it might be because of something wrong with Dick that we'd never had a baby. *Pregnant*. I couldn't believe it.

I stopped at the drugstore to get the prescription filled. When I got back in the car, I stared at my reflection in the rearview mirror. Through the windshield, the sun felt warm on my skin. I cupped my hands over my abdomen, and thought about Sonny making love with me.

I drove slowly, carefully. When I reached the driveway, I drove on past, and climbed the winding roads of Percy Warner Park, finally parking my car beside a small isolated pavilion at the top of the highest hill. I got out and sat on the picnic table, looking down on bare trees and the narrow twisting road that disappeared and reappeared in a steadily diminishing spiral. It was so quiet I could hear my heart beat.

What was going to happen when I told Dick I was pregnant? Would he be thrilled in that instant before he realized that the baby wasn't his? Then would come the realization that we were childless because of him. And then he would look at me—it would finish us.

How would Sonny's face look when I told him I was pregnant—after I had told him I was barren? I remembered the painful scene with Aunt Hester begging for grandchildren, and the look on his face when he had talked about Lon and the other children he had seen maimed and killed in the war. He could never forget the misery of his own childhood. First I would see pain, then sorrow, and then a terrible, desperate resignation. He would leave Lou and marry me, and do his best to be a good father. And I would live the rest of my life trying to make him forget what he'd done to Lou and how *her* face had looked. She would give him up, because that's how much she loved him.

I looked around me at blue sky and brilliant sunlight on the hills. It was a glorious day, as beautiful as yesterday had been dull. Today was like the October days. I remembered something Sonny had asked me that quiet morning in the mountains: *Are you still not sorry, now?*

As I was pulling into the garage, Dick opened the door from the kitchen. I'd been hoping to have some time, that he'd be watching a ballgame or something so that I could compose myself a little better and think how to tell him. What difference did it make? I was going to lose him, no matter how I said it.

He waited in the doorway as I got out of the car. It was hard to see inside the garage after the bright sunlight, with the back light from the kitchen shadowing his face even more. "I was starting to get worried," he said. "You were gone a long time." The concern in his voice was real. The past weeks, he'd been cold to me because he was hurt. Now I would hurt him worse than ever.

I went inside, and walked past him into the living room. He followed me.

After my studio, I loved this room best. It was light and airy, facing the downward slope of lawn to Hillsboro Road. It was serene, rather than formal or stiff. I had enjoyed reading here and listening to music. Dick had bought this house because he'd seen immediately how much I liked it.

"What did the doctor say?" he asked. Time passed while he waited, looking at me. *I'm not going to be able to stand this,* I thought.

"You're pregnant," he said. "That's it, isn't it?" He turned and left the room.

I sat on the couch until I could face climbing the stairs, then went into the bathroom and washed my face in cool water, looking at myself in the mirror. In our bedroom, I paced, trying to think, then went to the closet and laid my suitcase on the bed.

I heard the door click open behind me. He was standing there, taking in the suitcase, the clothes on the bed, bureau drawers pulled out. There was a kind of wild hilarity in his eyes.

He crossed to the window and stood with his back turned, looking out.

"I should have seen this coming," he said. "The minute Trudie told me who he was, and you hadn't. Stupid of me. I couldn't understand why nobody wanted me to call the police. Lou kept begging me to wait. Even Braxton, sitting there cracking his knuckles.

"The sheriff didn't believe you were lost. Not possible—not the *great* Sonny Woods. Then that hunter found the car . . . I was so scared."

I leaned over the suitcase, moving things around.

"And then you come back with that cockamamie story about a canoe accident." He paused. "I don't know how many times I've kicked myself for accepting it, instead of pressing you for the truth."

He had moved away from the window, and was raking his fingers through his hair.

I picked up a blouse and started to fold it.

"See, if you'd just pretended it was rape . . . not that it matters now." He shrugged, trying to laugh. "The sterile cuckold."

The blouse slipped through my fingers.

He stood there for a minute, looking at it crumpled on the floor. He came around the bed and picked it up, and tried to fold it. With the sheerness of the fabric, and his clumsiness, it got away from him, too.

I sat down beside the open suitcase and put my face in my hands. He bent again and picked up the blouse and laid it on the bed. I took a Kleenex from the box on the bedside table and blew my nose. For several moments neither of us said anything.

He pushed the suitcase out of the way and sat beside me. "So is he meeting you, or what?"

"I'm going home," I said. I had to stop until I could get my voice under control. "I'll stay with my parents through Christmas, then find a place of my own." He'd been staring at the floor. Now he was looking at me. "I haven't called him," I said. "I don't think I'm going to."

He was quiet. Then he said, "Seems to me you should."

"He thought I couldn't have children. He doesn't want children."

We sat there, side by side, sunlight streaming across the floor.

He said, "I'm going out for a while." I saw him glance at my arms crossed over my abdomen. He stood up. "Will you do this for me? Will you not leave until I get back?"

It was past nine o'clock when I heard his car pull into the garage, and a few seconds later, his door closed down the hall. I hadn't had the energy to finish packing that afternoon. I'd slipped the suitcase under the bed the way it was.

I was sitting at my dresser brushing my hair, wondering where he'd been, what he'd been doing. I shouldn't have agreed to wait. I should have left in the afternoon, before I'd had time to think what life without him was going to be like. I laid the brush aside and stood up, the sudden movement making my head swim.

I'd eaten nothing since breakfast, which was no way to start. In the hallway, I paused at the top of the stairs just as his bedroom door was opening, and he stepped out, closing it behind him. His hair was damp and combed off his forehead.

He had changed to the sweater I'd given him that brought out the color of his eyes. "Are you all right?" he said. I took a firmer grip on the banister. "I was thinking about some milk. Does that sound good to you at all?"

"I'll get it," I said.

"Better let me." At the landing I noticed he stopped and looked up at me before going the rest of the way down.

He set the tray on the bedside table, handed me my glass and set a plate of cheddar and crackers on the bed between us.

I took a sip of milk.

"I've been driving around." He drank half of his, then rested his forearms across his knees. He swirled the glass, staring into it. "All these years you've thought you couldn't get pregnant. I *had* wondered a few times whether it might be me." He paused, his voice sounding thick. "But you were always so sure it was you. And maybe I didn't want to know it was me." He drained the glass and set it on the table. I reached to put mine beside it; my hand was shaking.

He sat hunched, staring at the floor. "I'm beginning to understand how you must have felt."

"Dick . . ."

"Are you all packed?"

"Just about," I said. *This is how it is,* I thought—*feeling your heart break*.

"These past weeks—I'd appreciate it if you could forgive me for being such a bastard." He was turned so I couldn't see his face.

"Nothing to forgive," I said.

He laughed. "Well. I gave it my best shot."

He was silent for a while. "So you'll stay with your folks till the baby comes?"

"I'll find an apartment."

"Here in Nashville?" He glanced at me when I didn't answer.

"Somewhere . . . near the university," I said.

"Ah yes. To be near Joshua. All that." He was quiet then for a long time. "Why don't you wait until morning?"

"I'd rather go tonight."

He got up, his back to me. "Suit yourself."

Mother answered the phone. "I need to come home," I said. I could picture her in her nightgown, clutching the receiver, Dad just starting to wake. *Who is it?* he'd be saying. "I'm sorry it's so late," I said.

—

"What's wrong?" she said.

"I'd like to sleep in Joe's room, if that's all right."

"Sarah, is Dick there?"

"I shouldn't be much more than an hour."

"Roy'll come and get you," she said.

"No. I can drive."

"I'll make some hot chocolate," she said.

"Good," I said. "That sounds great."

Dick was waiting at the foot of the stairs. He took my bag while I went to the closet for my coat. "I checked the oil," he said. "You've got over half a tank of gas. Give me your keys, I'll start it for you."

I heard the trunk close, the engine kick over.

"There's chicken in the refrigerator," I said, when he came back in. "Tell Edna it ought to be cooked in the next day or two. Her present's in the upstairs closet."

"Drive carefully," he said. He held the door for me.

It was almost one o'clock; they'd been watching for me. Dad took my suitcase. On the front porch, he set it down and hugged me.

In the living room, Mother held my coat, folded over one arm. "Is he seeing someone?"

"I'll get you a drink," Dad said.

"I've made hot chocolate." She laid the coat across the suitcase. "Is he seeing someone?"

"In October, when we went to the mountains," I said. "Sonny was there."

"Our Sonny?" Dad said.

I had to sit down. "He's married to Lou Tolliver."

They looked at each other, at a loss.

"One afternoon she had to . . . she took Aunt Hester to the doctor," I said. "Dick and Braxton were hunting." I opened my hands, my throat closing.

Dad sat beside me. "Sonny's married to Hester and Campbell's girl?"

"He's a guide. They have a place . . . a kind of . . . on the river."

He squeezed my knee, then got up and brought me a glass of Scotch. *I shouldn't drink this,* I thought, and drank. I tried to breathe evenly. "Sonny and I, we . . ."

"I'd no idea what had become of him," Dad said.

Mother sat in the chair across from us. "You're saying that you and Sonny Woods had an affair?"

"Made love," I said.

"That's what you do with your *husband* . . ."

"Not now," he said to her. "Bottoms up, down the hatch."

I swallowed the rest of the drink.

"How *could* you . . . you have *everything,*" she said.

"Not now," he said and helped me to my feet.

The bed was turned down, with pale-green sheets that had been dried on the line, crisp and smelling of fresh air the way Joe liked them. I looked above me at the bulletin board—Joe's high school and college life—thumbtacked in place. There would be a letter jacket hanging in the closet. Dad put the suitcase beside the chest of drawers, then sat close to me on the bed. "How's Sonny doing?" he said.

I told him about the military hospital, watching Dad's face to see if he'd known. He hadn't. "We got our signals crossed," I said.

"Dick's a good man. Give him some time, he'll get over this."

"I'm pregnant," I said. He straightened; I watched the conflicting emotions in his face. "I saw the doctor today."

He put his arm around my shoulders, swallowing hard. He held me while it sank in, patting my arm. Broken toys, hurt feelings—I'd always brought them to my father. *It's all right,* I wanted to tell him. *I know you can't help me fix this one.*

"Daddy, remember when Sonny'd come here? He'd have

bruises or a black eye. I walked in this room once, Joe was putting Mercurochrome on his back." He turned his head away, his eyes full. "He doesn't want children," I said.

He took a breath; it caught in his chest. "Let's get some sleep," he said. "We'll talk in the morning."

36

The house was quiet, two in the morning, with a faint refraction of streetlights through the blinds. I heard the creak of a floorboard overhead in my parents' room, and the grandmother clock in the hall. I lay on my side facing the window. I was remembering.

I could see Joe propped on this bed doing homework, headphones piping in Jose Feliciano, Simon and Garfunkel, Paul Desmond. He'd glance up when I opened his door, coming from my room across the hall. I'd hold up my algebra, chemistry, solid geometry book. He'd ignore me. Finally, yanking the headphones off, he'd ask why didn't I just take home ec.

I'd known where he stashed his contraband, which sweaters I could borrow, the order of his record collection on the bookcase. Number last was a Vaughn Meader—*the* Vaughn Meader album. The day he got it, he and Sonny and I listened to it together; recorded in October, 1962, it was a riot for almost exactly one year. The laughs we'd had here, the fights, sometimes about boys he didn't want me going out with.

"Sonny!" he'd said when I told him, amazement all over his face.

"Before he left," I said. "We drove around and he asked me."

He came and sat beside me on the bed. "Sonny asked you for a date?" he said.

"When he gets another pass." I was tense with him watching me.

"What'd you say?"

"I said I'd go."

Joe was smiling, a funny sad kind of smile. "Did he kiss you?"

"Cut it out," I said, blushing.

We sat there a while.

"I guess you know," he'd said. "Even to ask you, he's not just fooling around."

I don't remember what I answered. I must have been thinking about Sonny and me in his car behind the stadium.

The last of Joe, his voice on the MARS line: "I want you to be happy, Sis."

Mother had poked her head into the room. "It's after eleven," she said. "Did I wake you?"

"No," I said. "I was awake."

"I thought you might be hungry." She came in, her hands clasped at her waist. "I've fixed a tray."

I started to say I'd rather get up. "Wonderful," I said. "Just let me use the bathroom."

There was a poached egg on toast, two strips of bacon, tomato juice, coffee, an enormous glass of milk.

"Roy's at church." She was wearing a yoked apron over her Sunday dress; the probable plan was that tonight she'd go to services and Dad would stay with me. I cut a bite of egg and toast. "Try some bacon with it," she said, and sat on the bed at my feet. "Did you sleep all right?"

"Fine." I concentrated on the breakfast she'd prepared. *Just eat it,* I thought, *don't think about it.*

She sat quiet a few moments, then got up and tidied the clothes I'd had on last night. She rearranged my robe at the foot of the bed.

"I thought it was flu," I said. "Dick made me see a doctor." I drank some milk, trying to wash down the lump that came with saying his name.

She left me to deal with the tray while she unpacked my suitcase and emptied a drawer of Joe's bureau. She took his things away—some books and papers—and came back with hangers. She hung my blouses and skirts and slacks, then sat down next to me. "You're due in July."

"The twenty-ninth," I said.

She smoothed her apron, picking at the hem. "What will he do for Christmas?"

"I don't know."

She took the tray and set it on the floor. I rested my neck against the cool brass rail of the headboard. "You couldn't know this would happen," she said. "If you'd known you'd get pregnant . . ."

"Maybe he'll fly home," I said.

She wiped her eyes on the apron.

Believing I was infertile, and with Joe dead, my parents had long ago given up hoping for a grandchild; they couldn't be sorry I was pregnant. And they worried about Dick. More than once, Mother threatened to call him. *What will you say to him?* Dad asked her. I overheard them Monday night in the living room.

"We can ask if he's all right," she said.

"He's not."

"We can tell him we're thinking about him."

"I'm sure he knows that."

"Then it won't hurt to tell him," she said. "We have to do something."

"We are," he said. "We're staying out of it." I went back to Joe's room and closed the door.

I'd told them my plans; I would get an apartment, I would work, I would teach. That's as far as I'd gotten. *What about the baby?* Mother said. I didn't know, but I would manage. For now, I slept much of the time. She said that was a natural part of early pregnancy—and it was a great escape for me. I read, and ate my mother's cooking. I got through the first few days.

Dad and I went for walks. There were Christmas decorations on the lampposts, the stores stayed open late. I'd mailed Dick's parents' gifts after Thanksgiving. I thought about Mother and Dad's gifts in the upstairs hall closet—kid gloves, a sweater I'd thought just right for her, a set of woodcutting tools for him.

I would buy them something else. I'd walk with my father through town and around the court square, thinking about Christmas presents, and Dick, while everything I saw reminded me of Sonny.

I missed the sound of Dick's voice, and my being there when he came home in the evenings, the funny stories he'd tell about his work, his genuine interest in mine, the whole life we'd built together—until the past several weeks when it started to fall apart. I'd caused the pain in his eyes, the questions—how could I have done it? Hadn't he loved me, hadn't I loved him? What had he done wrong? *Nothing,* I tried to tell him, *you didn't do anything*. Then the growing coldness, and a kind of speculative appraisal sometimes when he'd look at me, as if he were imagining me in bed with Sonny. The increasing distance between us—all this before we knew I was pregnant.

I'd think about Sonny, all the things he'd been in my life—friend, brother-protector, first love, and now the father of our child. Lying awake in my dead brother's room, I'd think about Sonny and me in the cabin, how that had been, and lying in his arms beside a campfire. It seemed despicable and yet I couldn't help it—missing one man and wanting another.

What did Sonny want? *Go home,* he'd said. *Forget it ever happened*. Dick was probably spending Christmas in California; after the holidays, he'd file for divorce. What about the baby I was carrying? What about Lou? What about *me*?

Wednesday morning Mother and Dad went to an estate auction; they'd be gone all day. At nine-forty, I called the operator for Sonny's number and dialed it, dreading Lou's voice, knowing she would answer, and having no idea what I'd say to her.

"Lou, it's Sarah," I said. There was silence at the other end; I could picture her holding tight to the phone. What now: *I'm sorry, but I have to do this? I loved him first?*

"I think he's . . . have you tried the shop?" she said.

"I don't have the number."

She gave it to me, repeated it to be sure I had it.

"Lou . . ."

"No," she said. "Let him tell me."

He carefully described the location of a roadside park almost equidistant between us. "You know the place?" he said.

"I called the house first, Sonny. I'd forgotten the name of the shop."

There was a pause. "Give me thirty minutes," he said. "I'm on my way."

I left a note on the kitchen table: *Back soon, or I'll call.*

I got there and walked the winding paths between picnic tables, shaking with cold and anticipation. *I love you,* I'd say to him. *I've always loved you, even before I knew it. You wanted me to be sure.* In the distance I could hear cars going by on the highway. It was like him to want to meet outdoors. It would be pretty here in summer, but now the trees were skeletal, the sky overcast and ugly. I'd pictured us meeting in a coffee shop—someplace warm.

I heard tires crunching on gravel and saw him park beside the MG and get out, looking for me, then waiting while I walked to him. He opened the door, and I climbed into the Blazer, sliding under the wheel. He restarted the engine and turned on the heater. We sat there silently for a while, our breath fogging the windshield.

He put his back to the door and propped one leg on the seat. "You know Clifford came up last week."

"Yes," I said. "He told me."

"Lou and I manage to stay pretty isolated; we get our paper a day late." It hurt to hear him link himself with Lou like that, a couple. "We hadn't heard about the plane crash either."

He stared out the windshield at the dreary park. "Clifford got there late Friday night. After Lou went to bed, he told me he'd seen you. He said you were on your way to a party."

"A benefit. For the Arts Council."

" 'I thought we were friends,' Clifford said. 'You used me

to set it up.' He said, 'Sarah's not looking so good, asshole. Lou looks like she's been gutshot.' "

I didn't say anything. It was quiet except for the heater and idling motor.

He rested his head against the window. The dark gray eyes, dark hair touched with gray. "What could I tell him? That I hadn't planned it that way? You see, Cliff old buddy—I didn't tell you Sarah and I grew up together, that your boss is her husband, she and Lou are cousins—Why? because I thought it would make a nice surprise. We'd all have so much in common. Why didn't I tell Lou? Well, because I didn't want her to worry, of course." Sonny laughed, more like a groan.

"Let's get some coffee," I said. "There's a truck stop down the road."

"I was intentionally late getting to the lodge; let everybody have time to sort out the relationships. Maybe Clifford had told Dick at work who his guests were. Dick would register my name; I'd sure as hell remembered his. Let's say I was a little tense. And then there you were, meeting me on the porch. You looked so good, and seemed so glad to see me. You and Lou were hitting it off, talking, and bad-mouthing Clifford. I'd been right, we'd have a great weekend.

"I went inside—seeing Trudie was a shock. I hadn't known she would be there. Clifford introduces me, and she pretends we've never met. Other than what Clifford's told him, Dick doesn't know me from Adam; Braxton hates my guts—what's going on here? 'Wonder what's keeping Sarah?' Dick says. Trudie looks at him, glances at me. Then you come in, and suddenly you don't know me either."

He was looking past me, out the side window. I sensed I should be quiet and let him talk.

"Driving to the stands the next morning, I kept waiting for Dick to say something—'Oh by the way, Sarah told me you two know each other.' When he didn't, *I* told him I grew up in Cedar Point, I'd practically lived at your house, wasn't it funny we didn't get around to talking about it last night—probably Sarah had mentioned it later? Actually, no, he said.

"I kept trying to figure it out while he told me Braxton's fine points: he was a good sportsman, a careful hunter, usually a very nice guy. Maybe Dick's the jealous type, I thought. Then why wasn't he asking *me* questions? He should be wondering, too. Hell, I thought, I'll ask Sarah. I got him situated in a stand and was headed back to the lodge when it clicked, it all fell in place. Or so I thought.

"It was nothing unusual in Vietnam: the girl back home gets lonesome and starts seeing someone else. She's scared to tell her boyfriend in country; if he gets killed, it might be her fault. So she keeps writing—'I love you, I'm praying for you.' The minute he's home safe in the states, she plans to drop him like a live grenade. That's it, I thought, you'd met Dick while I was in Vietnam. Now you felt bad about the letters, and he'd rather not talk about it either. All Trudie could remember was what a fool I'd made of myself at her apartment."

"Did you believe that?" I said.

Sonny took his jacket off and laid it behind the seat. "We hadn't had much practice at being lovers before I shipped out. Dick isn't exactly Quasimoto. You wouldn't have written me a 'Dear John,' and I should be thankful you didn't. All right, I thought, but I'd be damned if you'd get away with not admitting it. I saw you crossing the field in back of the lodge. I followed you."

He paused, his knuckles white on the steering wheel. " 'Joe's dead, Sonny.' 'You were in what hospital?' I couldn't believe it. I could not *believe* it. I tried to find someone to blame. Joe? Joe was fucking dead, it wasn't his fault anyway. I couldn't even blame the war." He was perspiring. I turned the heater to low. "*I* should have told you what was going on with me. *You* should have waited to get married."

I moved to him, across the seat.

He caught my shoulders and pushed me away. "Not a good idea."

"This doesn't help," I said.

"I stumbled around out there for hours, trying to get right with myself. I finally decided to get Lou and go home. Make some excuse. Then Dick meets me at the door, takes me aside and tells me that Braxton had wounded a deer. After that . . ." He lifted his hand, and let it drop. "I knew I should get away from you, but where was the harm in talking, just being together for a couple of days? Then I wanted to show you things, places. It couldn't hurt, taking you to Medicine Springs; then the other seemed so much better. Packing the supplies—we wouldn't be needing them, but just in case."

"Sonny, that's all behind us," I said. "We're talking about the rest of our lives."

He was silent, his expression unreadable—always the expert at covering his feelings. What good did it do, assigning guilt for things past undoing? Maybe it *was* our fault, according to his rules—never more rigidly applied than to himself. But we'd been young, we'd had no time to learn how to trust each other. I could blame the war for that; Sonny and I, Lou and Dick—weren't we all victims? I wanted to say that people get divorced every day, and someone gets hurt, it doesn't have to be us this time. And I had to be careful what I said to him about hurting people; he was sick of causing pain, while his whole life had conditioned him to take it.

"Does it matter who was to blame?" I said.

"There isn't any excuse, except the longer I was with you . . . Dick had stolen you when I was in the hospital; he was playing Boy Scout while I was in Vietnam. We'd play hardball this time. I had to know how you could have married him so fast.

"Then at the lodge, all he cared about was getting you home. I owed him an explanation. I felt like scum, lying to him. And Lou, the way she . . ." He stopped, his expression weary.

I remembered Lou seated at his feet the first night, his fingers entwined in her hair; Lou in his arms the night he'd found Braxton's buck; Lou rushing to meet him under the whirling blades of the helicopter.

"Dick makes more in one month that I do in a year. I own this car and some weapons. What have you ever had to do without?" he said, his voice low. "What have you ever wanted that you couldn't afford?"

I couldn't say it didn't matter, because it mattered to *him* that he couldn't afford all the things Dick could. And it wouldn't be just me he'd worry about; there was the baby. "We'll manage," I said, not wanting to think about it. My teaching and paintings didn't bring in much; Dick had bought the house, the cars, everything in both our names. Did I expect him to split it down the middle; did I imagine Sonny would accept Dick's money?

"Manage," he said.

I realized something else. Now, Sonny could afford to pick and choose his clients; with a child to support, he'd let every screwball who came along hire him, even those men who slaughtered deer from four-wheelers. *He doesn't have to work for people like that,* Lou had said. *One of these days, one of them's going to kill him.*

He could get another job then, there are all kinds of other jobs he could do. He could . . . I tried to picture him selling cars or insurance. Counting money at my father's bank. I had to turn away and look out the window. We'd spent half our lives together, but always against *my* background. Now I couldn't picture Sonny anywhere that wasn't surrounded by mountains and wilderness.

"I was planning to use my G.I. benefits when I got back, give you just the life you were born for. *Shoulda, coulda,* Sarah. Don't you see?"

The bare trees, blackened bones against the sky, started to blur in my vision. I didn't want to see. I wanted it the way it should have been.

"You've been happy with Dick. If we'd never seen each other again . . . I wish to God I hadn't . . ."

"Go ahead," I said. "Don't leave us *anything*. I love you," I said, crying. "Doesn't that count?"

It was quiet for a moment. Then a sound, and he pulled me to him. I could have him, or what would be left of him; two more words is all it would take. He'd said the wilderness wouldn't last anyway; they'd cut the trees and pollute the streams, kill off the wildlife. Except right now the cougars were coming back.

I let him hold me as long as I could stand it, his face buried in my neck and shoulder. *Remember this,* I was thinking, *I have to remember this*. I pushed him away and got the door open and got out. I had to, or I would have told him I was pregnant.

Two good men had loved me; if I had to lose them both, at least I could love one of them enough.

If Mother and Dad were home I wanted them to think I'd been shopping; I had to look like I'd been shopping. I stopped on the edge of town at Cedar Point's oldest cemetery and walked through the graves, where it was quiet, not another living soul but me.

Sonny belonged in the mountains where he was valuable and content. He knew who he was now, he'd found his place. Lou had helped him find it.

I found myself standing in front of a marker, bone-white and streaked with moss. At the top were the letters CSA—many Confederate soldiers are buried there. At the bottom was an inscription from Ecclesiastes: *Time and chance happen to us all*.

It was Sunday afternoon, a week had passed. We'd been to church and had lunch. I was in the living room reading one of Mother's family-saga novels, when the phone rang. Dad was in the basement refinishing an old bureau, and Mother, I thought, was in the kitchen, baking a cake. When she hadn't answered by the third ring, I got up and ran to the phone. "Wheatley residence."

"Where'd I get you from? You sound out of breath." It was Dick.

"I thought Mother was in here," I said. She was, now, standing in the doorway at the top of the basement steps.

"When are your folks going to join the twentieth century and get more than one phone?"

"You know Dad would have this one out if he could," I said.

He laughed. She formed his name, a question. I nodded and turned away.

"I was wondering," he said. "If you're not real busy tomorrow, I thought I might drive up there."

"Tomorrow, no, I don't think so," I said. Mother had moved into my line of sight, whispering and waving her hands.

"You don't think so, or you're not too busy?"

"We're not busy, I'm not. I'm sorry, Mother's trying to tell me something."

"Tell him to come for dinner," she said.

"She wants you to come for dinner."

"Ask her what she's having," he said.

"He wants to know what we're having. She says chicken and dumplings."

"Tell her to make a potful," he said. There was a pause. "I thought I'd bring their presents."

"Good," I said.

"Are you well?"

"Okay," I said. "You?"

"Edna and Warren brought me a tree. Edna thinks it's a disgrace to the neighborhood not having a tree in the front window." He waited. "It's a white pine. I can't seem to find the lights."

"In the garage," I said.

"Great."

"Top left cabinet," I said, hearing the click on the other end. I hung the receiver up and sobbed.

"He's coming, isn't he?" Mother said.

. . .

"When are you going to get ready?" she said.

It was after five; I had on jeans and an old flannel shirt.

Dad looked at her from under his brows. He was reading the paper; I was holding a book. She'd fussed with the house all day, probably driven the butcher to distraction selecting the hen I could now smell stewing in the kitchen.

"Put on some lipstick at least."

"Margie," he said. She threw up her hands and went back to the kitchen.

I hadn't expected to sleep well last night and had slept like a stone. Already my body was taking what it needed, separate and apart from my mind. But I had calculated how I wanted to look; Dick knew how I dressed at home.

Dad continued reading as car lights shot up the drive, folding the paper by his chair only when the bell rang. He winked at me and answered the door.

"How's the used-furniture business?" Dick said.

"Beats banking," Dad said. "How's computers?"

"Beats banking." It had been their standard joke since Dad retired and started restoring antiques. "I come bearing gifts," Dick said.

I took the packages from him. He hesitated, then bent to my cheek. Mother hugged him as I laid their gifts under the tree.

"Tell you what I did," Dad said. "I don't suppose you're aware there's a game on tonight?"

"Couple of rinky-dink California teams," Dick said.

The Raiders were playing the Rams, Monday Night Football. Dick was a Raiders fan.

"Thought we might watch it, but I forgot the beer," Dad said, looking at me. There was beer in the refrigerator downstairs.

"My car's warm," Dick said.

Dad reached for his wallet. "I guess you think your man's going to win," he said, meaning Marcus Allen, the Heisman Trophy winner from USC.

Dick laughed. "By about two six-packs." Dick graduated from USC.

Then we all stood there.

"I'll get your coat," Mother said to me.

We drove to the city park. I watched houses go by outside my window, tree lights. He stopped at the tennis courts and left the engine running. "Joshua called," he said. "And Trudie, of course."

"I guess they're doing okay," I said.

"Joshua was leaving town; he's spending the holidays with somebody."

"Claire," I said.

He was quiet for a while. "Supposed to snow tonight."

"I thought you might go to Long Beach."

"They're in Hawaii about now. Dad said to tell you he was taking the putter."

I'd asked Dick if he thought his father would like it; it was a new design. I'd bought his mother two pieces of flow blue crystal for her collection.

He turned on the seat, looked at me. "Know what else he said? He said, 'Well, son, you've always wanted a baby.' "

I had to look away.

"If you'd given me some time . . ." A police car slowed, then went by. "Consider him a sperm donor."

"Just stop," I said. "This isn't some anonymous child I'm carrying."

"I want you to come home." He slammed the gears into reverse and backed into the street. A block from the house, he said, "Shit, I forgot the beer."

"It doesn't matter," I said. "There's a refrigerator full in the basement."

He bought beer at an all-night market. In the driveway, I

asked him not to mention that Sonny had taken me to a cabin, that we'd been missing for three days. "They don't need to know that," I said. "He's too much a part of Joe."

"I wouldn't bring it up," he said. He came around and opened the door for me. It was starting to snow.

Chicken and dumplings was a favorite of Dick's. Before we married, he'd never had it the way Mother prepared it, and now he ate two large servings, which pleased her. An omen. He and Dad talked football and business, then retired to the television and the pregame show.

In the kitchen I could tell Mother wanted to ask questions, but didn't. I helped her clean up and took two beers to the living room. Dick looked at me as I handed him one.

I lay curled on the couch, watching the game and listening to them discuss the players. It was still snowing outside. Mother brought the quilt she was working on and sat at the other end, under the light. Chris Bahr kicked a field goal.

I want you to come home, he'd said. Maybe he meant it, or thought he did. But I wasn't showing yet.

"What'd I tell you?" Dick said.

"Keep your shirt on," Dad said. "It's only the first quarter." Marcus Allen had just rushed for thirty-four yards.

"Your Rams are cooked. No defense."

"Are you warm enough?" Mother said. She pulled the afghan off the back of the couch and laid it over me.

Dick was in the easy chair across from me. *What about when I look like a basketball?*

Somebody fumbled and the Rams recovered. Dad cackled. If there'd been two teams playing that neither of them cared about, they'd have chosen sides anyway, for the fun of it.

The Rams scored but failed to make the extra point. Six to six. "Where's this rout you were talking about?" Dad said. He took the empties and went to the kitchen.

"Who's winning?" Mother said.

"We're tied," Dick said, and stretched. "Dinner was great, did I tell you?"

"One for you, freebie for me." Dad handed him a beer. The crowd cheered and they were back to the game.

Mother and Dad loved him. He was telling them he wanted us to stay a family—whatever pride he had to swallow in the process.

I'd been asleep. The announcers were wrapping up, the Raiders over the Rams, 16–6.

"Looks pretty rough," Dad said. He and Dick were at the window. "Maybe if you had front-wheel drive."

"Don't be silly," Mother said. "He's not leaving in this."

"Do you have to work tomorrow?" I said.

"No." He let the curtain drop.

I stood up and folded the afghan. "You want the bathroom first?"

"Go ahead."

I could hear Mother and Dad moving around upstairs as I undressed. I brushed my hair, then put my robe on and crossed the hall. He glanced over his shoulder when I opened the door to my old room, now the guest room, and went back to watching it snow.

"It wouldn't work," I said. He turned and leaned against the windowsill. "It was bad enough before you knew I was pregnant."

"It can," he said.

"Like the dance." I sat on the bed. "That was sure fun."

"You know what I've been noticing lately?" he said.

"I noticed *you* had a good time."

"Toys. The stores are full of them."

"Who was she, by the way?"

He looked at me—something in his eyes, like a warning. "I want you to come home," he said. "I want this baby."

It hit me. The way they'd been together, so easy with each other—familiar. Joshua and Claire when he was bringing the car around, the glance they'd exchanged over my head. All the nights he hadn't come home. I'd pictured him alone, in some monastic cell at the club. "God, you must have thought I was dumb," I said. *How does it feel?* I thought. *How do you like it?* "Who is she?" I said.

"You don't know her."

"I *know* I don't know her."

"It's done," he said. "She deserved better."

"Don't we all."

He came and stood over me. "We're going to those classes," he said. "Where they teach you how to breathe."

I laughed. "Was she before or after?"

"I'm going to feel it move inside you."

I stood up and started to the door. He caught my arm, spinning me around. "I'm going to be there," he said.

I woke up looking at the clock, his arm across my hip; it was eight-twenty in the morning. I could feel the rise and fall of his chest against my back.

He'd torn my gown off the night before, and taken me with the lights on. He'd known where to touch, what made me respond—seventeen years' worth of knowing. He'd bring me close, then stop, making me wait. I'd try to move, he'd hold me still, pinning me with his weight. *Now,* I'd say. *Please*.

His breathing changed. I turned into his arms, not saying anything. We lay quiet for some time.

"You should see a doctor," I said. "It might be something minor."

"I've been thinking about it."

"A minor blockage in the plumbing."

"Drāno," he said.

"Idiot." I raised myself on one elbow.

"Say I can be fixed, or unfixed, as the case may be. How would you like to make another baby? Maybe three or four."

"Whoa, boy."

His eyes held mine. "It wouldn't change anything. I'd still want this one. But there's something we have to talk about."

He sat up, leaning against the headboard. "Years from now, when we're raising this child who's the image of his father, and he says, 'Mom, Dad, why do I have dark hair when you guys are blond?' Say the baby has blond hair that stays blond. Not likely, if I remember my genetics, but let's suppose." He watched me. "We're never going to tell him who his natural father is? Come on, Sarah. Haven't you learned *anything* from all this?"

"He doesn't want children," I said.

"He's got one."

"No," I said. "I can't."

He threw the covers back and reached for his pants. "I don't want you within a hundred miles of him. *I'll* tell him after the baby's born. When he realizes *you* didn't, I think he'll figure it out."

He turned, zipping up. "I'm kind of looking forward to seeing his face."

"No, you won't," I said. "And if you . . . if you do, so help me God . . ."

He stared at me, his mouth getting white, and left the room.

"I'll tell him," I said. "When it's time."

Mother and I sat in the kitchen, drinking coffee. "They'll have the roads plowed and salted by now," she said. "I can understand his wanting to get home."

Dick had told them he wanted to be in Nashville by dark; he and Dad were outside shoveling the drive. "You need to be alone with each other," she said.

We sat down to eat; Dad offered thanks and carved the

turkey. He was trying to make small talk about how good everything was, about the white Christmas—the first in so many years. Dick wasn't saying much.

"Joe had a VW Bug," Dad said. "When it snowed he and Sarah would take it up in the hills, use it like a toboggan. Remember that?"

Yes, I remembered. Joe and Sarah and Sonny. "But only where there was no traffic," I said.

"Didn't think I knew, did you? Come home with snow packed under the fenders."

"We were always careful," I said.

"More turkey?" Mother asked Dick.

"No thanks."

"We used to cut our own tree." Dad dismissed with a wave of his hand the artificial one standing in the living room. "We'd look for a cedar, shaped just so. And it had to have a bird nest."

"We'd go surfing," Dick said, his voice flat. "One year we decorated a cactus."

"There's boiled custard," Mother said. "Cake."

He shook his head.

Dad pushed his chair back and stood. "Your present's in the basement."

"Dad, it's beautiful," I said. It was an antique platform rocker. Dick had helped him carry it upstairs.

"Your mother did the seat cushion."

"It's beautiful," I said.

Dick was looking at it, his hands in his pockets. "Is it oak?"

"Walnut," Dad said. "It's sturdy, try it out."

Dick sat down. "You know, I was wondering. Joe and Sarah's rooms were downstairs. How could you hear them cry?" He got up. There was a moment's silence.

"They slept in with us," Mother said. "When they were tiny. The bassinet's still in the attic."

"Maybe we shouldn't rock it," he said, looking at my midsection.

"Don't worry, babies do not spoil," Mother said.

Dad put his hand on Dick's shoulder. "When they're old enough to be spoiled, *that's* when you move them downstairs."

He and Dad had packed the cars. By moving the front seats forward, they were able to fit the rocker in the Skylark. I was to go first in the MG; Dick was starting it.

"Anything we can do," Dad said, his arm around me. "You let us know."

Mother came out with a wicker basket. "Just some sliced turkey and cake, a little boiled custard," she said. "You have anything to cook for tomorrow?"

"We'll find something," Dick said, holding the door for me; I hugged her and got in. "We'll call when we get there."

"Good," Dad said. "We'd appreciate it."

Not all the city streets had been plowed. The MG handled well in snow, but I saw Dick's car fishtailing once or twice. When we reached the interstate, I stayed under fifty, keeping an eye on the rearview mirror. At the outskirts of Nashville, I saw him signal. I pulled into the emergency lane and rolled the window down. Dick got out of his car. "Am I going too fast?"

"Let's take the Harding Road exit," he said. "There'll be less traffic."

"What about the driveway?"

"What about it?" A semi roared by, throwing slush.

"Maybe we should just stop at the entrance," I said.

"Leave the cars on Hillsboro Road? I don't think so."

"You're getting drenched," I said.

He brushed at his pants. Another truck blew past, this one too close, the driver sounding a blast on his horn. "Something I didn't tell you," Dick said.

"You're about to get killed."

"I'm real glad you're coming home."

37

Dick took off the entire week between Christmas and New Year's. I think he believed if we could get through these first days, we'd get through the rest. But it was hard, this convalescing.

On Monday morning, Clifford called.

I was hearing Dick's end of the conversation. "Won't it keep?" he said. We'd slept late and were just having breakfast. I got up and moved his coffee where he could reach it. "Oh. Guess I better meet you at the office then." He looked at me, listening. "That sounds good, if you're sure it's no trouble."

He hung the phone up and brought his cup back to the table. "Clifford's coming over. Some invoices he thinks I ought to see."

"That can't wait until Thursday?" I said.

"He won't be there Thursday. He's going to the mountains."

A few minutes later he answered the door and took Clifford to the den. I finished loading the dishwasher before I joined them.

They were sitting on the couch, leaning over some forms scattered on the table in front of them. "See, that's three hundred units off this one," Clifford said, "and here's another mistake." He looked up when I came in.

"How about some coffee?" I said.

"No, thanks, Sarah, I can't stay."

"We're almost finished," Dick said.

I took the chair across from them.

"I'll make some phone calls this afternoon." Dick scanned another page, then shuffled the papers together, tapping the edges neat.

"I thought you might want to catch it early." Clifford paused. "I was in Green Hills anyway, running some errands for Janice. She's going with me this time."

"You haven't gotten a deer *yet?*" I said.

"Let me tell you, they get smarter the more they're shot at. They learn to lay up when you think they'll be feeding, then come out when *you* head in for lunch."

"Good for them," I said.

He grinned at me. "But it's damned embarrassing." He turned to Dick. "You planning to try again?"

"I didn't enjoy it that much the last time." There was a brief, heavy silence. "It was exciting, I'm not saying it wasn't. When I had him in my sights, *knew* I had him . . ."

"Kind of like being God for a minute," Clifford said.

"I was proud I made a clean shot."

Clifford was nodding. "He taste pretty good?"

"We haven't eaten any yet."

"Janice has some good recipes."

"Does she hunt?" I said.

"Janice?" He laughed. "She likes to hear us swap lies, sitting around at night. She thinks the world of Lou and Joanne. 'Course, you didn't get to meet Joanne."

Dick touched the invoices, signaling their business was finished. "Maybe you'll have better luck this time," he said.

"Maybe." Clifford cleared his throat. "This ex-marine Buster knows. He comes up every year, and brings his boy with him. He's taught the kid how to hunt and handle a bow and rifle, how not to get lost.

"It's funny, his boy generally gets one, but this guy has yet to kill a deer. Buster says he'll stay in camp a lot of the time and read a book. I have to think he's not trying."

"Is that your problem, you're not trying?" I said.

"Me? I get skunked, I won't hear the last of it!"

"Get Sonny to help you," Dick said.

Clifford looked at the floor. "That might be worse. I might never live that down." He put his hands on his knees, preparing to stand. "I ever tell you Joanne's doe story?"

"No," I said.

"Happened three, four years ago, I guess." He sat back

again. "Joanne and Buster's littlest one was just a baby then. Yeah, Eric's about four now. You heard this one?"

"I don't remember it," Dick said.

"Joanne has the baby out for some air, see, carrying him down this old logging road behind their place. It was a nice fall day, she's walking along taking her time.

"All of a sudden, Eric starts cooing and gurgling. She smiles, thinking he's talking to Momma, right? But he's looking over her shoulder at something. She turns to see what he's so happy about, and there's a doe about twenty paces behind them. Just standing there." Clifford patted his shirt pocket.

I started to go get him an ashtray.

"No, I've quit." He took his hand down.

"That's great," Dick said.

Clifford made a sour face. "Janice's Christmas present. Sometimes I forget. The first time I hit this pocket and Sonny notices . . . him and Buster will *laugh*. Nobody meaner than a couple of reformed smokers." He examined the toe of one shoe. "Anyway, this doe just stands there while the baby squeals and points, making all kinds of racket.

"Joanne walks a little further and looks back again, expecting it to be gone. The doe's following them. When Joanne stops, the doe stops. This goes on for quite a while. Eric's laughing and carrying on—he thought it was great. Joanne's about half scared. She's never heard of a rabid deer, but this is damned unusual."

"Something happened to its baby," I said.

"Yeah, that's what Joanne thought. Some asshole shot its fawn."

It was quiet for a moment. "Janice is probably wondering what's keeping me."

"Thanks for dropping these by," Dick said.

"Like I told you, I was out this way."

"I'll call her when you get back," I said. "Ask her about those recipes."

"There's one with wine," he said. "It's real good."

"Why don't you show Clifford out, Sarah." Dick tried to look as if he were studying the forms.

We stood by the Jeep. Clifford leaned against the door, looking off down the hill.

"You had a good Christmas?" I said. "Santa found your house all right?"

"Hell, we may have to add on a room."

"We went home. Visited my folks."

"Cedar Point," he said.

I rubbed my arms against the cold. "Tell Lou I hope her mother's doing better. Tell her I said hello."

I was thinking, *In a few hours you'll be with him in the mountains. Maybe you'll be with him someday when he takes his son or daughter hunting.*

"Anything else?" he said.

"Don't shoot any does."

He glanced at me.

"No," I said. "Nothing else."

Acknowledgments

My sincere gratitude to B. J. Robbins and to Marie Arana-Ward for invaluable editorial guidance.

The text type in this book was set via
the Linotron 606 in Caledonia.
The display type was set in Caslon Openface.
Composed by PennSet, a division of the
Maryland Linotype Composition Co., Inc.
Baltimore, Maryland
Printed and bound by R. R. Donnelley & Sons Company,
Harrisonburg, Virginia